THE
WOMAN DRIVER

BY JEAN THOMPSON

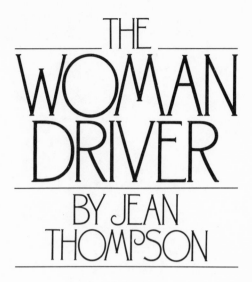

FRANKLIN WATTS
NEW YORK LONDON TORONTO
SYDNEY 1985

Library of Congress Cataloging in Publication Data

Thompson, Jean, 1950–
The woman driver.

I. Title.
PS3570.H625W6   1985   813'.54   84-21021
ISBN 0-531-09789-7

FOR MY GRANDMOTHER
ELIZABETH HENDEL

THE WOMAN DRIVER

JUNE 27, 1984

For Jerry,

many thanks, good
wishes, and happy
motoring. best,

Jean Thoryson

CHAPTER 1

Who knows how things begin. Consequences are what we have to live with anyway.

On the day her husband left for good, if that was how you were to think of it, Flora Reynolds put her car in a shallow ditch ten miles outside of town. She wasn't hurt, though it took her some time to realize it. She'd landed in the back seat with her chin wedged into the crack of the cushions, so that her first sensations were the stale taste and smell of vinyl. Her tongue uncurled, exploring. The seat was cold. She breathed in its grittiness and wondered if she were dying, and this was to be her last earthly vision, that which would launch her into the hereafter or the whatever, this tame stink of rubber skin. But she seemed alive, or at least, undead. She found herself staring into a rectangle of scarred mud, neatly framed by glass, a few inches from her face. The car had come to rest on one side, the driver's side, and she was head down in the ditch, supported only by the tilt of the seat and perhaps her own ignorance of gravity.

The window pressed into the earth reminded Flora of the ant farms of her childhood. Except there were no minute tunnelling organized lives here, only the brown and rose dirt pressed into weals and ridges, and uprooted strings of grass. By supporting her weight on one forearm she managed to crane in the other direction. The mild sky seemed to pierce the metal everywhere, like lace. A turn signal ticked, very slowly, in the dashboard; the green arrowhead fluttered on the edge of her sight in a little mechanical coma. The inside of the car seemed smaller than it ought to be. She should not have been able to see the hood from where she was, but it had reared up, snouty and compressed, until it filled the windshield. The space in which she lay was narrow and precisely enclosing. The car might have been constructed for this purpose alone, as some ingenious cage that would suspend her, weakly paddling, between earth and air. She could not remember the accident, the sequence of mistakes and violence, how she came to be here, so neatly planted, a pale unsprouted root.

Her stomach loosened and she retched thinly, and with some difficulty, into the narrow space below her head. She was aware of many small and probably painful sensations: neck, knees, teeth. It was as if her body had been waiting some polite interval before it presented its rightful claims. Shock, Flora told herself reasonably. I'm in shock. She crumpled over until she was kneeling in a space she would not have thought it possible to kneel in, but then, there was so much she would not have thought possible before this day: the casual flight of wingless vehicles, the treachery of gravity and of human connections in general, and most of all, her own survival.

Her husband often remarked that she had no sense of proportion whatsoever.

A man's face was peering in through the back window, tapping at the glass to get her attention. An old man with a wattled neck and a brimmed cap. Flora felt embarrassed, untidy. Then, seeing the flat terror on his face, she found herself wanting to reassure him. She smiled and nodded, even raised a hand, as if to convince him that she was whole and unbloody, demonstrating her working parts. The face disappeared and a moment later the back door opened above her. She climbed out, surprisingly brisk and nimble. She might have been some newly hatched creature, emerging from its broken shell. "Just shaken up, I think," Flora heard herself answering in response to whatever the old man was saying, something querulous and piping. "I think," she went on, frowning a little, "that it all happened too fast to hurt me. I mean, dying would have been too *easy.*"

She was trying not to look at the car. It was a ten-year-old

Chevy Impala, turquoise and cream. It looked like some exotic tropical insect, gaudy and very dead. She turned and gazed instead at the unplanted field behind her, scattered with the remains of winter-bleached cornstalks. The earth was scored and tracked and stamped with heavy tire marks, beaten into a grid from last season's harvest. Even the smell of it was oiled, mechanical, or maybe that was just the accident, the seeping juices of her car. It seemed to her only fair, since machines had trampled and exhausted the fields, that now one of them should reach out and snare her car in revenge. Maybe she ought to be worrying about the gas tank exploding. Instead she dropped to her knees in the heavy brown clods and began vomiting once more.

This seemed to be the sort of thing that was expected of her, more satisfactory to the old man and the other eventual onlookers than any bravery or control on her part. They did not want to see actual death, perhaps, but they wanted all the trappings of it, the hysteria and sirens and gratifying drama. The sheriff had not arrived, but any number of other cars and pickups were stopped along both sides of the road. She wondered if there were some kind of rural network that transmitted such news, like birds perched on a wire. People leaned against their vehicles, chatting. Flora didn't resent their presence or their curiosity, which seemed only natural; indeed, she was a little sorry for them that there was not more to see. A few of the men examined the wreck, importantly, but as there was nothing that could be done with it, besides hauling it off, they soon lost interest. Somewhat by default, they turned their attention to Flora. Her head ached sharply. She was having trouble fixing things before her, the sunshine and the casual crowd. She could not decide why she was here.

Someone suggested that she be taken to the nearest house to wait for the wrecker and the sheriff. "Oh no," she heard herself saying, out of pure polite reflex, "no, I couldn't possibly impose." She was very kindly ignored. After all, what else could be done with her? She imagined how she must look, wild-haired and fouled. She was wearing an ancient flannel shirt her husband had hated, jeans and moccasins. She had dressed this badly out of spite, out of lovelessness, as if to punish herself for being un-loved. She was a woman who had to exert herself to prettiness even at the best of times, and now she felt quite unsexed.

It had been a very ordinary marriage, but its undoing was making her behave in extraordinary ways. She stood by the side of the road, placid, obedient, short-circuited. Later she remem-bered producing her driver's license from her wallet and showing it to someone, a man who was asking a question about the tires, as if identifying herself would explain and resolve everything. The man took it politely enough. It contained various unhelpful sta-tistics, and the usual outlandish photograph. He stood there studying it, as if comparing Flora's official image with the actual-ity. It was one of the few occasions when the photograph came off better. "You ought to hang on to that," he said, handing it back. He was a young, fattish man, and the hand which held the license bore a class ring, an egg of bright blue glass. Flora fol-lowed it with her eyes, imagining all his gestures as regal and ab-solving.

And so eventually she found herself borne away, watching the same fields, in motion again, this time from behind the spar-kling windshield of a stranger's car. She abandoned herself to the luxury of helplessness, of being a helpless woman. It was a man and his half-grown son who drove her, or so she guessed from their identical pale thick unsurprised faces. She imagined they were farmers, living out where they did, substantial Midwestern agri-cultural magnates who busied themselves largely with machinery and financing. She knew nothing of farming, but she was aware there was little that was pastoral about it these days. It was large-scale enterprise, with crops measured in tons and money in dizzy thousands, everything vast, efficient, and even hygenic.

The two men seemed both embarrassed and pleased to have Flora in their charge. The father, who drove, said there had been an accident along that very same stretch of road this winter.

"What happened?" Flora asked idly. She felt comfortable, unwilling to be curious. The man shook his head, sorrowing. "That road ices up, it gets as slick as snot. That curve now, the one you missed, it's a pistol." He coughed, as if he'd thought better of

—4—

going on. He fiddled with the radio and asked Flora if she liked country music. "Oh yes," she lied. "Sure." Though by rights, by virtue of her exalted if temporary status as victim, she should have been able to request anything she wanted. She obviously needed more practice at this sort of thing. Some pasteurized yodeling came from the radio. In the back seat the son made a muttering sound. He was slouched against one window, his heavy, scraped-looking jaw set in perfect boredom. Flora felt she knew everything about him, at least, everything that mattered, his youth and his impatience, his lurking fantasies. It was an odd sensation, being shoved into such intimacy with strangers, as if her car in its flight had hurled her out of her own life entirely.

That sensation was even stronger once they reached the farmhouse, which was as white and trim and clean as Flora could have wished it. She was escorted into the kitchen and stood there, grinning weakly, while she was explained. (Nobody introduced themselves. A friendly tribe, Midwesterners are, but not necessarily a gracious one.) Everything in the room delighted her: the ceramic rooster that served as a cookie jar, the African violets on the windowsill, the sense of tidy clutter. Everything was homely and real. The mistress of the house, a pale plump red-haired woman who matched her kitchen exactly, overcame her first alarm at events and asked Flora if she wouldn't like a glass of water, or coffee, or to lie down.

Flora asked for the bathroom. She was beginning to remember the details of the accident now, and she was afraid of being sick again. She sat on the edge of the bathtub, amid the strident perfumes and pink soap, and let herself think about it. She hadn't planned the accident, but in a way she'd done it on purpose. She had been going too fast, being deliberately careless, when she felt the gravel shoulder under the tires. Even then she might have prevented more from happening, but the same murderous impulse made her yank the wheel too hard, and then she saw all over again the hood spinning up to meet her and the sun crashing through everywhere. She didn't get sick, but she ran cold water over her face for a long time. She looked every bit as bad as she had imagined.

When she returned to the kitchen, the woman and a small girl Flora hadn't seen before were coloring Easter eggs. The men had disappeared, either gone out again or retreated to some den or shop that was their own preserve. Flora accepted a glass of water and sat in a corner out of their way, and after a little time they relaxed enough to ignore her. There was a vinegar smell in the air that Flora remembered from childhood. The tints of the eggs were the same also, lemon and sky blue and lavender, and the flimsy wire egg holders, and the little girl's frustration at not getting the colors deep enough. No matter how long she soaked the eggs, the dye ran off; the shells were too porous to hold it. "Try some decals, Linda," the mother suggested, but the little girl would not be consoled. Decals, Flora recalled, had always been a poor second best. Flora sat quietly in her corner, loving it all, the buttery sunlight, the fussy kitchen, the child's ritual, the mother's patience, her own place in this unremarkable and perfect family circle.

Of course it couldn't last. The sheriff arrived, and Flora's car was consigned to a wrecker, and she was clearly expected to call someone who would carry her away also. She thought of calling home, just to prove to herself that no one was there. But she didn't want to do it, not really, didn't want to set the phone's silvery ringing loose in the empty, darkening rooms. She wasn't at all sure where her husband had gone, and even if she could have found him, even though she must have wanted to inflict some violence on herself for his sake, she didn't want to talk to him now. She was disgusted with herself. Would women ever learn that making themselves pathetic accomplished nothing, as far as men were concerned? She should have aimed her car at her husband. He was the one she'd wanted to hurt, that much seemed clear, and instead she'd done the cowardly, the weak, the female thing, and turned it on herself.

She called a friend, who asked, reasonably, if she were all right. "Oh yes," she told him. "Yes, perfectly." She sounded like a guest at a party, she thought, effortlessly insincere. The one apparently indestructible part of her personality was manners. Her friend was not convinced. "Flora? Listen, I'll be there soon as I can. Have yourself a great walloping drink of something, OK?" And she agreed, since she was being so strenuously agreeable. Though she wouldn't for the world have sent her hostess rummaging through the shelves of oatmeal and cocoa for the bottle of whatever they might keep on hand, if such a household drank at all. She wouldn't have imposed. But also, she could hardly bear more such private knowledge of them, much more gratified curiosity.

When Flora got off the phone she did ask the woman if she could lie down for a little now, that is, if she wouldn't muss anything. The woman told her of course not, not to worry about a thing, and showed Flora into a small bedroom. She seemed glad to have some request to grant. Flora supposed if she were to stay there long enough, she'd have to invent any number of acceptable needs (she would, in fact, have enjoyed a drink), just to keep things moving along. The room had a white chenille bedspread and white net curtains and a blue glass swan on the dresser. Flora fell asleep thinking of blue water, glass air.

By the time her friend arrived it was late afternoon. He shook his head at Flora when she emerged, and she could tell by his wryness that he was trying not to show alarm, that she was, as she remembered her mother saying, a sight. Her friend, whose name was Paul, looked as out of place in the acute domesticity of the kitchen as Flora did, but then Paul managed to look out of place almost everywhere. He thumped Flora on the back and her ribs rattled. "Well, old girl." He peered down at her through his rimless glasses, warily. He was trying to gauge what tone to take with her, some combination of cheeriness and sympathy he couldn't quite carry off. "You seem intact, I'm glad to say. Let's get you on home."

He was embarrassed, she knew, by her bedraggled state, and maybe also at the prospect of having to console her. The woman too was looking at them cautiously, as if she found their joint presence alarming, some geometrical progression of inconvenience. Flora was sorry for both of them. She had succeeded at making herself into a burden, which was perhaps what she'd wanted all along, but now she felt too scrupulous to enjoy any of it.

Later Flora would wonder why everyone kept taking her word for it that she was fine.

They said their good-byes. Flora watched the farmhouse recede. The sky, the air itself, was pink and gold from the setting sun. The light was nearly liquid, the shadows of the fields and ditches heavy, soft-looking. The world was bathed in pink and gold, in kindliness and order. The sun itself might have grown one of those beaming storybook faces, smiling down on the tidy world. The farmhouse windows blazed gold. The driveway was edged with a row of whitewashed stones. A square of garden to one side had been freshly turned; the new loam showed very black in the heavy light. Flora wanted to stay there forever. She wanted the sun to balance right where it was, in that moment before it flooded the world with pink and gold. But it was already behind her. Again she was reminded of ants, those simple industrious lives displayed between sheets of glass. The simplicity, she was aware, was only a matter of perspective. Even ants had their own quite adequate ant-sized problems. But she had to wonder just what angle or distance could have made her own life seem either well organized or picturesque. She turned around in the seat. Paul was driving with unnecessary concentration, bearing down on the wheel as if it might fly loose. "Gordon moved out today," she told him. "Did you know?"

"No, I didn't." He wasn't looking at Flora, but at the steadily unreeling road. Usually he drove way too fast. Perhaps Flora's accident had made him feel more mortal. Though statistically and superstitiously, it was unlikely that she'd see the inside of a ditch twice in one day. She was, she reflected, a sort of temporary good luck charm. After a moment Paul added, "Poor Florrie. Just today? That's shit."

"Shit indeed."

"Where did he go? Or is it indelicate to ask?"

"You mean does he have another woman? I don't think so.

I don't know where he went. It's hard to imagine Gordon with some sort of guilty passion going, isn't it? Anyway, if he had a woman, I'm sure he would have thrown it up to me by now."

Paul said nothing, and Flora had at that point, a qualm: it had to do with her new status as one half of a sundered couple, and whether Paul would feel she was merely informing him, or enlisting his support, asking him to choose sides. Maybe she was doing just that, without being aware of it. Paul was one of the few friends she and Gordon had equal claim to. Most people began aligned to one or the other of them: Flora's old roommate, Gordon's co-worker or hometown buddy, until Flora imagined they'd established proprietorship over everyone. Paul's credentials, so far at least, were impeccably neutral, and here Flora was summoning him to her side, stealing a march on Gordon. It depressed her to think how unconsciously devious she seemed to be. Then she dismissed her guilt as over-subtle, because after all somebody had to come fetch her. Still, she felt sorry for Paul. Such shifting sands, such deep waters to negotiate. He'd sounded so cautious. Maybe he *had* known about Gordon. But all she said was, "You don't sound too surprised about it all."

"Of course I'm not surprised. How could I be? I don't know what to say. I never do when things like this happen. You know I'm sorry. But isn't it almost a relief?"

"I suppose so." In fact, she was thinking, it no doubt came as a relief to Paul and to all their friends. How bored they must be by now with the spectacle of Gordon and herself dissolving as a couple. It had gone on so long, and it must have been perfectly predictable, perfectly obvious to everyone but her and Gordon that they would come to such an end. Yes, of course everyone would feel relief.

"But you know," she said, "it doesn't really feel over. Maybe you wouldn't even want it to be. It would make you seem less than human. Lobotomized."

"Of course you wouldn't," said Paul, too promptly, and Flora looked away, frowning. He was being too willing to say whatever he thought she wanted to hear, too obliging. It wasn't his style, and besides, he was mistaken. She hadn't really been talking about any residual affection she still felt for her husband. What she meant was, there was no way to disengage yourself from such stunning misery; it was too much a part of you by now. And it had been misery, no matter how tedious or familiar its course had been, for who these days did not come to grief with marriage. Maybe it was all she had left to call her own, this unhappiness, and she embraced it too readily. Because there was not yet any sense of relief in Gordon's leaving, nothing remotely pleasurable or compensating.

She looked over at Paul, who was probably aware of being watched. Ah Lord, how self-involved unhappiness made you, what an effort it took to remember other people at all. What an unpleasant creature I am turning into, she thought, surrounding myself with layers of tears and gloom, like so many ugly veils. How much longer will anyone put up with me. Poor Paul, with his abruptness and panicky limbs and his own problems, she was sure. How unlucky for him that she knew his phone number by heart. Here he was, manfully attempting to cope with her, an unlikely rescuer, hardly the heroic type. But then, neither was she looking very impressive herself, very much worth rescuing. Flora sneaked a glance at her hands. As usual, the fingernails had ragged edges and faint, suspect rims of indelible gray, like volcanic ash. She would get a manicure, and then a divorce.

"You haven't told me," Paul said, bravely breaking silence. "What the hell were you doing, all the way out here. Were you running away from home?"

"Sort of. I had to go somewhere. Anywhere." She supposed eventually she'd have to admit that the accident was in many ways not accidental at all, that she'd really been having a large, mechanically assisted tantrum. "I was letting off steam." She waved her hand, dismissing it. She was beginning to sense just how much of an embarrassment the whole incident was going to be. She gazed at the wide brown monotonous fields, rapidly darkening in the spring twilight. She tried to see again the kindly aspect she had imagined in them, but now they were only flat and tedious, without landmarks, without either history or promise. "Do you remember," she asked Paul, attempting to shake her mood, "the time we drove out to that Mexican restaurant in the country? It was miles and miles away from anything. We thought since it was inconvenient it had to be fabulous. How stupid of us. What back-assward snobbery."

"Warm guacamole and cold beans. The waitress looked like she had tuberculosis. It served us right." Paul too seemed happier talking about the safe, already-accomplished past. "The depressing thing is, people still go to that place in droves. They must think it's some quaint country inn. The nastier it is, the more delighted they are. Jesus. It makes you wonder what they expect out of life in general. Oh well. That's just another kind of snobbery, telling people they're enjoying something for the wrong reasons."

"They had sangría in pitchers. You told the waitress it tasted like cologne. You started dabbing it behind your ears and calling for another round of Evening in Paris."

"I did no such thing."

"You did. How could I make something like that up?" Though Flora wasn't entirely certain, at that point, if she had made it up. That is, her memory was clear enough, sharply visual, right down to the sticky-shiny texture of the green plastic tablecloths. But she mistrusted memory, or, more accurately, nostalgia. The incident seemed too perfectly anecdotal, too perfectly in character for Paul, too much like something you would have expected him to do. Anyway, what weariness, what waste to keep dredging up long-forgotten meals in useless detail, who ate what and how it tasted, to enshrine them, to insist on a past happiness when the treacherous unshaped present lurked all around you. Now that she thought again about that evening, Flora recalled Gordon being irritated with it all, and not in any companionable fashion. Just sour ill-humor, as if he had been conspired against, as if she, Flora, had expressly and with great forethought arranged a bad dinner for him. She never understood the logic by which she became responsible for such situations, but it seemed clear enough to him.

She wondered if in some opaque future she would look back on today and remember it fondly too.

"Lucy. Lucy was with us that night."

"Was she? I'd forgotten." And of course Paul was right, Lucy was there. Lucy had been one of the more disastrous of Paul's occasional girls, a sullen blonde with big horsey collarbones, who cultivated her moods to the point of aberration. You'd all be talking or laughing pleasantly enough when you'd become aware of Lucy smoldering away at your elbow. And always you felt obliged to try and accommodate her, to let the conversation limp and stagger down to her pace. Don't you think so, Lucy? How about it, Lucy, another drink? And of course none of the solicitude did any good, there was no way Lucy would allow herself to become part of the social contract. She'd only toss more hair into her eyes (she had, Flora thought, a great deal of unnecessary hair), and continue shredding paper napkins or bending straws or whatever mess she always made at tables. No, she wasn't thirsty, wasn't hungry, wasn't anything at all. Smiling sourly, to indicate just how inappropriate your good humor was, and just what crass buffoons you all were. She was good at it, was Lucy. Flora had never known anyone to be quite so intimidating with such a minimum expenditure of energy. Somehow, no one ever had enough sense to take Lucy at her word and ignore her. Flora remembered Lucy wandering into her kitchen at a dinner party (Lord, another meal), and glowering at the spice rack. "What's *this?*" she demanded, indicating a jar. Flora was trying to keep the chicken in the broiler from detonating, but nevertheless answered helpfully. It was cardamom seed, you crushed it up for baking. Coffee cakes, things like that. Lucy sniffed. "They look like teeth, don't they? Little dead, petrified teeth. That's what I'd keep thinking about, if I had to smash them up."

After she and Paul had parted ways, Lucy did things like write him poisonous letters and badger him on the phone. Once she'd actually shown up at his apartment flourishing a knife. On one level Flora had to admire her, for Lucy, unlike herself, at least appeared to be directing her hostility towards its source. But then, the knife had been an ordinary kitchen knife, dulled from years of honorable service on vegetables, and the whole episode had come to nothing. Then too, perhaps Lucy had only meant to puncture herself and make a gratifying mess all over Paul's floor. Paul was rather sentimental about Lucy. Men always seemed to feel that way about the really difficult and crazy ones, at least, they did once things were safely over. Flora had to be careful on the subject of Lucy, so as not to hurt his feelings.

"And what did Lucy think of the restaurant?" Flora asked, though she thought she remembered all too well.

"The food made her sick and she spent most of the night in the Ladies'. She wanted me to take her to an emergency room. I think she did break out in hives later."

"Hives? Poor Lucy. I'm sure she would have preferred having her stomach pumped, and being in mortal danger and all." This was more truthful than tactful, so Flora went on, quickly. "What a crew we must have been. You know, I was remembering it as a lark, a high old time, but each of us was stewing in our own juices all along. Little nasty undercurrents."

"How's that?" They'd reached the unimpressive outskirts of town, and Paul slowed the car. Like most Midwestern cities, the line between town and country was an untidy one. A venerable barn with trailer courts sprung up around it. Straggling commercial buildings: a franchise hot-dog restaurant, a health club, a drycleaner's. Overextended enterprise, very new and gleaming and already doomed.

"Just that we were all probably pissed off at one thing or another, besides the food, I mean. You were worrying about Lucy. Lucy was busy hatching hives and plots. And Gordon. I remember Gordon being absolutely hateful, now that I think about it."

"Really? How so?"

"Oh, just your common, garden-variety hatefulness. Don't look at me like that. You don't have to believe me. But that's how it was. He was rude and hateful and wouldn't even try and unbend about any of it, you know, see it as a comedy of errors."

"Gordon isn't a rude person. Whatever else he is."

"Oh, you probably wouldn't recognize it as such. I mean, he doesn't slurp his soup or pick his nose. He's very controlled about it. Very deliberate. He can aim it at will. In fact, he's probably only rude to me. I'm sorry. I'm beginning to rant. Poor Paul. You'll probably have to hear the same sort of thing from Gordon."

"I doubt it. Believe it or not, Flora dear, men spend very little of their time together talking about women."

"I believe it. They usually go to women to complain about other women."

They were silent then. The sun had set, and the sky had been washed clear of its brilliance. It was blue on blue now, layer on layer of tender half-light. The rolling shadow of the car was black and chill, as were the shadows of curbs, the shadows beneath the half-leafed trees. It had been a late spring, and any warmth was still fragile, dependent on light. Flora watched her own street approaching and tried to feel something other than dread.

"At least you haven't said what a lovely couple we were, or some such muck," she told Paul. They were at the doorstep and she was trying to lay hands on her key ring. Paul was coming in for a drink, and Flora was too grateful to worry much about whether or not he felt obliged to.

"I never say that about anyone. I never make pronouncements about couples. It always sounds obituary, even if they're still together."

"Cynic."

"Not at all. A constantly disappointed romantic."

"The same thing. Tell me something."

"Anything." He made one of his self-mocking gestures, a half-bow.

"I'm serious. Are people meant to be happy? Together, I mean. Is it reasonable to expect? Is it, like they say in Gordon's labs, subject to verification?"

"Not for too long," said Paul, politely holding the screen open, and if she had expected him to say more she was disappointed.

Flora pushed the door open and Paul followed her inside. I'll have to get a pet, she thought vaguely. Something to mew or bleat at me when I walk in. She made a little fuss of turning on lamps and shutting curtains, reestablishing ownership, while Paul wandered off in search of Scotch and ice. The house was a small

—14—

eccentric stucco, built during some craze for inappropriate architecture. Who now would be amused by imagining themselves a pueblo dweller or a Spanish grandee, surrounded by shade trees or snow? You might as well live in Disneyland. Still, Flora liked the arched doorways and coarse plaster walls, the useless window shutters, the frill of wrought iron at the front door. It was all so consistent, so faithful to its mad, out-of-context specifications, it almost qualified as a separate style, something like Chinese Chippendale.

She could hear Paul in the kitchen, complaining about the state of the glassware. And he was probably right; they never had enough decent glasses or coasters or anything else a proper house ought to have. Everything was make-do and pieced together, not so much from thrift as from laziness. Now, looking about the rooms, she felt sad at their drabness and lack of gloss. It seemed a kind of comment on her marriage in general. She almost wished they had vaster property to fight over, jewelry or antiques or something. Not that she wanted a fight, not really, just that it might have invested the marriage and its dissolution with more dignity. As it was, she imagined all their innocent household goods ripped from their moorings and set adrift, piles of humble flowerpots and lamps and ashtrays, looking like not-very-precious salvage.

Paul emerged carrying two drinks in tall glasses with cartoons stenciled on the sides. "The Flintstones or Ronald McDonald?" he inquired, and Flora made a face. "You'd think," Paul said, handing her the Flintstones, "that this was a household of children. Plastic mugs and jelly glasses and these things. Don't you have any real glasses? I always thought married people had real glasses."

"Everything broke, I guess."

"Sorry. God, how stupid. It's like making eye jokes to blind people. I'm really sorry, Flora."

"That's OK. Honest. Can't be helped." Still holding her glass, she began to cry. It burst out of her all at once, hard and furious. She couldn't have said what set it off; not Paul, not even the forsaken, shabby house. Once again she was at the mercy of her body's illogic and timing. She cried and cried. Her face grew wet and red. The longer it lasted the more strength it gathered, until she seemed to be nothing but a hollow bell of ribs, ringing and ringing with the sound of grief. She couldn't stop it, she didn't want to stop it. She wanted only to empty herself entirely, to be done with everything human and failed. With her free hand she clutched at the arm of her chair and screamed. She wanted the scream to come out of her like a long scarf of flame, a magician's trick, burning her throat clean. Her nails dug into the upholstery. It might have been a living thing, that chair, something she wanted to feel pain. She could hear Paul shouting at her, telling her to stop, but she couldn't yet. There was still something left in her. She couldn't reach the end of it. Even when she ceased, as abruptly as she'd begun, and sat staring up at Paul, it wasn't the end. It exhausted her to think of the indestructible root of herself, that part which she could hardly even bruise, it seemed. Eventually she would sleep, and eat, and move about, because this indestructible creature, her body, would insist on it. Then, so refreshed and nourished, it would be ready for more pain. She was shackled to it, this unreliable partner, this source of dismays and mutinies, and whether or not you found it comfortable, you had to admire the creature's stubbornness. She grinned, her lips cracking and rolling back to show her gums.

"Don't," Paul said. "Don't smile like that, Flora, please." It was the only thing so far that seemed to really alarm him.

There are some couples who serve as matrimonial monuments, granite landmarks in the desert wastes. People envy them. People wonder if they are quite real. People take comfort in such marriages, and use them to gauge their own progress. They seem to prove that the thing can still be done, that in the face of all obstacles and temptations, the old forms endure. If such a marriage then ends, the effect is rather like "Ozymandias"; there is a great crashing-down process, and only the vast and trunkless legs of stone remain. Sad. Everyone's surprised. No one's surprised.

Gordon and Flora had been married six years, not long enough to achieve true monument status. Still, their final parting dismayed and alarmed their friends. Everyone liked them. There was little not to like. They were so bright, so amiable, such pleasant company all around. They were so much like everyone else. Their virtues were only the expected ones, but nobody minded. People were too genuinely fond of them. A young couple just starting out, not yet prosperous but with every reasonable expectation of being so soon. Gordon was, still is, a research chemist. An energetic, dry, humorous man. The sort of man who seems effortlessly successful at whatever he does. He read a great deal and could talk amusingly about nearly anything. For those of their friends in other fields Gordon served as an authority and an example. The humane scientist. The responsible technician. For he was responsible; he believed in pollution controls and environmental safeguards and all such right-thinking. Not just believed in them, as a non-scientist might, out of instinctive mistrust of technology, but understood the mechanics, could furnish the economic justifications. It was useful on so many occasions, like having a doctor or plumber on hand. It was agreeable to listen to him, to feel yourself so painlessly informed on the World Health Organization, or the brain chemistry of alcoholics. As long as there were people like Gordon, so clear-headed, so dry and humorous, you felt the species might survive its own inventions. Listening to him, one had a vision of human knowledge, human intelligence. Intelligence as it was meant to be, a living net which connected all things. Intelligence is paramount, enduring; there is nothing that cannot be perceived, nothing that cannot be understood. One came away feeling larger and more hopeful.

Flora worked at the time as a counselor in a job training program. For an impractical person (and she was hugely impractical, in fact she gloried in being so), she did rather well. She fought battles on all fronts, exhorting clients, wheedling and prodding other functionaries in other offices, courting employers. She too could tell stories, either amusing or indignant, about illiteracy, the problems of working mothers, epileptics, immigrants, about hunger, folly, accidents, injustice, good luck and bad, the trampled and the hopeful who passed through her hands. They exhausted her, they energized her. She was grateful for them. She needed their lives and their problems, their richness and disorder. Even the sulkiest teenagers, with their T-shirts advertising various beverages, various rock groups, with their suspect gratifications and near-total unemployability, even toward them she felt a certain tenderness. They were unlikely lilies of the field, toiling and spinning not, but even as she worked to convert them into something more utilitarian, she was amused by them, she almost envied them. "What's going to happen to you in ten years' time?" Flora demanded of such youths, in her best professional stern manner. They only looked at her with mild disbelief. They would surely not live that long, and if they did, it would not be their fault. The Lord would provide. The Division of Employment Services would provide. "I simply can't understand people like that," Flora would complain later at home. Gordon would shake his head and point out that she understood them all too well. The problem was that her job tried to make them into different people altogether, but if they became merely conscientious, dutiful, productive, she'd be bored with them. Flora was forced to admit he was right, as he was right about most things.

(Not monuments. But a familiar presence. More like the battered, old-fashioned statues in certain parks, weatherstained to a slippery green, decorated by birds, scratched over with initials, and representing — What? Minor civic or military heroes. No one remembers anymore.) Gordon and Flora, so well balanced, both within themselves, their own natures — Gordon's humane intelligence, Flora's capable empathy — and as a pair. A working partnership. They knew what to expect of each other, and perhaps more important, what not to expect. If they had bad spells together, or even spells that were less than entirely good, they had only to remind themselves of the reserve of trust and companionship they had accumulated. Comfort, affection, good humor, tolerance: these were things you had a right to, things you had earned. Whatever else there could have been — whatever was not able to be accumulated, measured out, whatever threatened to become too brisk, too dry from time to time — wasn't that inevitable? Couldn't you expect that too? They never talked of such things. It wasn't necessary. It would have done more harm than good. But each of them would have said, if forced to judge, that even if one wanted everything out of life, out of marriage, and in great heaping gluttonous portions, well, if one could not have everything, then what they had been allotted was more than fair.

One wishes to do the marriage justice. One wishes to do Gordon justice, but in fact this is not a story about Gordon at all. We shall do him justice and then we shall dismiss him, as Flora dismissed him by the end of things. One night she came to bed late and stood watching him sleep. He looked feverish, and his mouth was open as if about to cry out something lost, as if sleep had surprised him like death, with some last sadness left unsaid. She felt tender, and grieved that they had let things go so wrong for them, and then almost immediately it all turned around, ah Christ, she thought, who doesn't look vulnerable asleep, who doesn't look more winning, it's only sentiment, a lure, a false light, and nothing has really changed between us.

What first changed, what they really did not expect, was Gordon losing his job. It began, at least as far as the two of them were concerned, one evening when Flora had been reading cozily in bed. She heard Gordon's key in the door, and then he was peering down at her, making the room seem smaller and hotter just by standing there. He always came home trailing whiffs of his busy day, either excited or preoccupied. Little restless noises came from him, coins sifting through his pockets or paper rustling, as if he'd stopped moving too suddenly and things around him were still settling to earth. Now he smiled at her. Floorboards creaked and popped beneath him. "Hey there."

"Hey yourself." Flora closed the book on her hand to mark her place.

"What are you reading?" She held the cover up for him to see. "Ah. Literature. Serious. Any good?"

"So far pretty good." Reading had made her feel dreamy and remote. It annoyed her to be interrupted, though she told herself severely that she was being unfair. It was hardly Gordon's fault that he came home full of energy and ideas and talk, even if it sometimes felt she was only dragging and bumping along behind him. Gordon sat down on the bed beside her. Her tea sloshed in its cup. "Gordon, *watch* it," she complained, then, attempting to sound more wifely, "Hard day?" He seemed particularly edgy and bright, a mood she always found difficult.

"So so."

"Spaghetti for dinner."

"That's fine. You look comfortable. You look like somebody should be peeling grapes for you and popping them in your mouth."

"Feel free."

She was waiting, politely, for Gordon to leave, and after a moment he realized it. "All right," he said, nodding, smiling as if he were carrying on a separate, ironic conversation with himself. "All right, I'll leave you be." He stood up and the bedsprings lurched.

"It's this one chapter I want to finish, then I'll come out and play. I'll lavish attention on you."

"No rush."

"Dinner won't take long to fix, I promise." But he was already out the door. Flora turned back greedily to her book.

The crash was a series of noises, a long waterfall of breaking glass. She didn't jump; without really moving, she sank deeper into her body.

"Gordon?"

Her foot had gone to sleep and she hobbled. "Gordon?" She found him in the study. He was staring down at the wreckage of a little glass-shaded desk lamp. "What happened?" she demanded, and he stared up at her, annoyed. He was a large, ruddy-skinned man, with a big stiff blond fierce beard. Now he looked only petulant.

"Jacobsen lost the grant."

It took her another minute to realize what had happened: that Gordon had broken the lamp deliberately, and that he was being dropped from the research project he'd been working on for the last three years. She seemed unable to separate the two things. "What a mess," she said automatically, bending over the shards of green and ruby glass on the carpet. The bright needles pointed in all directions, like jackstraws. It was pretty, in a way. She even found herself admiring it for a moment. Then she began picking up the pieces, careful not to get cut.

"Bastards," Gordon said. She didn't know who he meant, but then, it hardly mattered. She didn't look at him or answer, just squatted over the ruined lamp, piling up glass in one hand. It was as if she could fool them both into thinking nothing had happened.

Gordon nudged some of the shards into a pile with his toe. He stooped to pick up the lamp base, unplugging it and gathering the cord. He wound it carefully into a smooth loop and tucked the plug underneath. Then he threw it at the aquarium in the corner of the room. The tank didn't break, but blue-green bubbles frothed and boiled from the hoses, and the panicked fish exploded, swimming madly.

"For God's sake." Flora was still squatting, staring up at him.

"Bastards."

"Go away, Gordon."

He looked, for a moment, as if he would have liked to throw something else. Then he turned plaintive. "They're cutting staff in September. Three lousy *months.*"

"Just go away."

"Do you realize what that means? They're shutting down. Kiss your ass good-bye."

"Go sit down or something. Just get out of my way."

Flora turned her back on him and bent over the wreckage once more. She felt him behind her, shifting his weight. The glass made bright tinkly sounds, piece on piece. After a moment he left the room. The house was full of windows, china, mirrors, picture frames. Heaps of things to smash. What a dangerous place they lived in, really. She waited, studying the glass needles. Nothing happened, at least, nothing she could hear. She supposed she should go look for him. Instead she found the broom and finished cleaning up. There was always some you didn't get. Always some little nugget you found weeks or months later embedded in your toe, invisible except for its surrounding bead of bright blood.

Of course they talked it all out later, and of course Gordon apologized about the lamp. Flora said she understood. She apologized too, though she wasn't quite sure for what. For reading a book? For his job? (And why, she kept thinking, couldn't he have just *told* her?) They sat at the kitchen table, eating and eating. Odd how hungry they were. You'd think they'd be sitting around looking stricken, instead of heaping their plates with tomato sauce and making rich red messes all over the table linen. Gordon still wore the clothes he'd come home in, even his tie, though he usually yanked it off the moment he walked in the door. Flora wondered if he were staying in uniform, so to speak, because it consoled him a little. She found the idea pathetic. She looked at his big, blond-furred hands resting idle on the tabletop. "I was acting like a child," he said, and smiled ruefully. There was nothing in his face now that was not familiar to her. There was nothing she had to be ashamed of seeing. Flora told him she understood everything.

Losing the grant was entirely unexpected; they agreed that was the worst part. The research project had been going on for years and years. Everyone attested to its importance, its productivity, its already impressive results, its unlimited potential. Oh, the staff had known times were changing. How could you help but know? Money was disappearing, no one knew where. You'd think it would all have to go someplace, wouldn't you? But apparently it ascended bodily into heaven. Still, none of them had seen the real disaster coming. They had believed too much in their own reports, in how indispensible they were.

"Think about people with kids," Gordon said. "And laid-off factory workers. The poor slobs you see every day at your office."

Flora agreed. She had, in fact, thought of them, but she wasn't sure just what point one might make about them.

"For people like that, it's the end of the line. It's nowhere to go but down." He lifted another forkful of spaghetti, piloting it with care past his beard and into his mouth.

"It can be," Flora said, wondering just what the false note in all this was. There was something unattractive about Gordon consoling himself by pitying the wage slaves. About Gordon pretending not to feel sorry for himself. About her own dutifulness. Clearly, she was expected to indulge him; clearly, she was prepared to do so. Well, wasn't that the way it was supposed to work?

"Of course, if we need the money, I'll take anything I can get. Sell shoes. Load trucks."

"I don't think it'll come to that," Flora said, scrubbing away with her napkin at a particularly impressive spaghetti-mess. She doubted it he'd ever had such jobs in his life, or that he ever would. She cleared her throat. "I guess we won't be going to Mexico now."

"I guess not."

They sat silently, thinking of the vacation they'd planned. Mexico, where they'd never been. They saw white beaches and white sunlight and blazing flowers, saw themselves buying embroidered shirts and painted tin toys, or eating strange pale green and tawny-dappled fruits on a balcony. The colors shimmered and wavered and then broke. They looked in each other's faces and saw something pinched come into them, something diminished and meager, as if this lost vision of richness and pleasure was the new climate of their life together.

How little it took, finally, to drain away the good between them. Much time, but little incident. It was as if that tangle of smashed glass became a compass gone berserk, pointing in all directions and no way was true. They had depended more than they knew on their visible successes, their public and verifiable selves. Eventually Gordon found another position, though it wasn't nearly as good as the one he'd had. He took less and less pleasure in his work, although he was too skilled to be anything other than competent. Maybe losing a job, even through no fault of his own, did something to a man, shrunk him somehow. Flora had seen it often enough in her office, men who moved as if apologizing for their own flesh, wanting there to be less of it. Gordon turned sharper, more ironic, more inclined to moods. He talked about larger and larger discontents: politics, economics, the poisoning of the oceans. "Mercury. Does anyone think they can just ignore mercury? They've got another thing coming." It was as if he kept pushing his unhappiness farther away from himself, into wider circles. He might very well be right about ecological catastrophe or capitalism, Flora thought, but that wasn't the important thing.

At about the same time, Flora's agency nearly went under too, and had to be patched together with less reliable, temporary funding. The agency survived, but it was ominous, an intimation of mortality. Their jobs, both Gordon's and Flora's, had relied on fatness and prosperity, the sunny excess of good times. Now they were finding out how little use the world really had for them, or for anything else that didn't add up to the right numbers. "Imagine," Flora said indignantly to friends. "No one has jobs, so we do away with job training. Hopeless. Imbeciles." The friends agreed, of course, but that changed nothing.

Money had to be tugged and stretched. They fell behind in a loan payment, which shocked them a great deal. They were simply not that kind of people. Or were they? It was no one's fault that events had turned out the way they had (no matter what Gordon said about the government), and that seemed to make it all the harder to cope with.

Flora soon tired of being patient and forbearing with Gordon's gloom, and then she even tired of feeling guilty about being tired. She felt he was being petty, he was behaving unworthily. A little mocking refrain began to accompany even her best attempts at kindness and good will: I am only humoring you. I am only accommodating you. It frightened her to feel that way. She thought if anything they should be pulling harder together, that now, in adversity, they should take more comfort in each other. But that was only romanticism, some echo of old jingly songs. Sometimes she even found herself wishing that some larger, more dramatic catastrophe had overtaken them, something that would have justified all the sourness and worry. Weren't there other people far worse off (she knew there were), weren't they both healthy, did they ever go hungry? It distressed her that such less than mortal wounds showed such large flaws in their natures. Given a greater crisis, she thought, they might have risen more splendidly to the occasion.

Eventually it all broke loose, and they were arguing about each other, not just the world. They had a number of such fights, but one in particular seemed to announce the end. They'd come home from a disappointing party. It was a party at which no one had drunk too much, or even enough. No one had danced. People stood and stood, talking earnestly. There was a decorous air to them, as if they'd been instructed not to have too good a time. Flora sat holding a plastic glass of anonymous wine. It tasted chemical and unclean, but she kept drinking it. Maybe it would rearrange her brain, galvanize it into some new, more cheerful pattern of thought. Next to Flora a thin man in a turtleneck was talking about music. He was talking about jazz piano. Jazz piano, it seemed, was the true religion, but it was threatened by heretics, splinter sects and false prophets. "Peterson and Tatum," the man kept saying plaintively. "They're the ticket. If only people would *listen*. They've got their thumbs jammed in their ears."

Flora brooded. The mild noise of the party irritated her. It was too much like the way she had been living lately: cautiously, and without celebration. She saw Gordon across the room, grazing among the carrot sticks, celery rinds, knobs of cauliflower, and other fodder the hostess had provided. He looked bored too. What was wrong with people when this subdued twittering, this sense of small grievance against the world was the best they could do? She didn't know. She wasn't even sure what she would have wanted of them instead.

Later, in the car, she yawned extravagantly. Blasts of dull heat from the vents blew over her bare knees. The car trundled through the empty streets, through patches of blue, faintly hissing street light, and she felt as if she'd been here forever, jolting between sleep and boredom. "Why was that so depressing?" she asked Gordon. "Everyone reminded me of a herd of — I don't know. Rabbits or something. Big furry sad polite rabbits. Maybe it was just the food."

"The food was OK."

"Suit yourself. The place was lousy with celery."

"What's wrong with celery?"

"I guess it's more that there's nothing *right* with it."

The wheels rolled and rolled. She was tired. She was asleep. Gordon spoke and she jerked awake: "You're always saying things like that, you know?"

"What? Things like what?" Flora blinked. Her neck had gone stiff.

"Rabbits. Christ."

"What do you mean, things like that. No, tell me."

"I mean the little sarcastic digs. The little amusing put-downs. Being witty and critical at someone else's expense."

Although she was getting angry, another yawn squeezed itself out, a big teary one. Gordon was slouched behind the wheel, not looking at her. There was something irritating and Jehovah-like about his pronouncements, emerging so abruptly out of nothingness. "All right," Flora said, awake by now. "It was a fabulous party. I especially liked it when they threw the diamonds in the swimming pool and we all dove in after them."

"There you go again. That's exactly the sort of thing I'm talking about. You presume superiority. Do you ever stop to think about all the things you disapprove of? Game shows on TV and horoscopes and microwave ovens. People who buy fancy toilet paper. People who name their kids Kyle or Sandi."

"Meaning?" Flora was only being calm because she could hardly believe he was antagonizing her so baldly.

"Meaning that you only seem comfortable when you criticize people. I'm just pointing it out." They were home by now. Gordon shut the engine off and walked up the drive and Flora trailed behind. She was angry not just at what he'd said, but at this attempt to get away with the last word. She found him inside, in the hallway, engrossed in a newspaper. His big bulky shoulders were drawn up around his neck, turtle-like. "And you," she said, "by virtue of your sterling character, are well within your rights to criticize me."

He pretended, furiously, to be reading for another moment before he put the paper down. "I didn't say that."

"Of course you didn't. It's presumed."

"I'm just saying nobody likes cattiness."

"You're making another raid on me, Gordon. It seems to be the only thing that cheers you up about yourself lately."

"What the hell is that supposed to mean?"

Flora was amazed at how well and how fluently they were arguing about nothing, nothing at all. So they had argued, these past weeks, about shower curtains, postage stamps, and other minutiae. Gordon's face was heavy with peevishness and ill temper, but Flora no longer felt anger, tears, or anything else she might have expected. Only boredom. It hardly seemed worth the effort of gearing up for it all, building ever more elaborate structures of sarcasm, treading out the same old ground. Boring, God yes it was boring. And the worst part was, there was nothing genuine about it. They would never talk about anything they really felt. Gordon would never admit that he despised her for having witnessed his weakness. Flora would never tell him that she was beginning to feel a mild contempt for him, and nothing much more vital than that. Always there would be false trails and decoys, emotion deflected into mere irritation. She wondered how things had ever grown so small between them. "Oh, never mind," she said. "Never mind." She shook her head and went into the bathroom to brush her teeth.

Gordon followed her, looking through the doorway uncertainly. The bathroom was apparently the one room he was inhibited about arguing in. "Now what."

"Nothing. Really. I'm tired." The toothbrush was an electric one, an old Christmas gift they'd kept as something of a joke. In fact, Flora had come to enjoy its cranky shimmying motion, and even the mild theoretical possibility of electrocuting herself. She squeezed out, with care, a portion of toothpaste. Blue fluorescent-looking jelly. "What's in this stuff?" she asked with sudden interest. "Do you know? Is it anything bad for you?"

"Of course not. Look, are you going to answer me?"

She shook her head, her mouth full of blue foam. The toothbrush whirred and whirred.

"I don't think you can brush your teeth all night, Flora. I think we need to sit down and talk rationally about what's wrong."

Rationally? Flora thought. Rationally there is nothing wrong. Rationally we should still be in love. She rinsed, spat neatly, rinsed again. Reached for the dental floss. "A conscientiously applied program of oral hygiene," she said, nodding at the mirror.

Gordon swung away from the door. She heard his footsteps, a heavy, scattered sound, as if a whole bag full of feet had broken loose in the house. She heard the front door slam, and a minute later the whoom and roar of the car engine. She prodded at her gums, massaging them.

Of course there were other fights, ones worth finishing. There was much more. The machinery of their lives, their marriage, had simply ceased to function. It had been designed according to specifications that no longer existed, some presumption of success and well-being now denied. There was nothing really wrong with them. There was nothing really right with them. The night of the accident, after Paul had gone, Flora lay in bed waiting for sleep. She could feel any number of separate pains surfacing in her flesh, soft spots like bruises on an apple. The shadows in the room were familiar. Gordon had not taken much with him, not much at all. Nothing visible had changed. Through the window she could see a portion of the scrolled ironwork that marked, overgrandly, their front door. You could not, reasonably, verifiably, expect to be happy together. Not for very long. But so completely had all such happiness vanished, she was forced to wonder if it had ever existed, if it had ever been real. Like her mad little stucco castle, it had all been some elaborate structure of illusion, a sorcerer's trick, and once you realized it never again would it serve as shelter.

CHAPTER
2

"Bloody men," Flora is saying. "A fellow in a bar once kept telling me they suffer more than women when relationships end. 'Men's hearts break more deeply,' he said. In fact he insisted on it. He made it sound like an arm-wrestling contest."

She is sitting at a table in a restaurant with the wreckage of a meal pushed to one side, the plates full of exhausted lemon wedges and crumpled napkins. She is talking to her Professional Best Friend. It is the sort of conversation she had hoped not to have. Bloody men, bloody love, bloody life.

"Competitive training," murmurs her Professional Best Friend. She is poking at the cold french fries. "The divorces of an entire generation won on the playing fields of Eton."

"The problem is I even get tired of complaining. The ranting and raving. It doesn't change them and it only wears you out."

"No, the problem is that everything depends on sex. And then you get too old for it."

Which makes them both laugh like hags. They've been here for hours. For years. They always talk like this. And Flora, though she certainly enjoys such conversations, is also tired of them. The ranting and raving. There is such a thing as talking too much. You put too much of yourself into words, and then you can't get the words back.

Perhaps long friendships are as exhausting as long talks. Flora has had this thought too. She's known her friend, whose name is Suzanne, for all her adult life and more. They know everything about each other. Suzanne has heard all about Gordon and the afflictions of the past months. Suzanne is sympathetic in a jolly, astringent sort of way. She reminds Flora that she hates the word relationship anyway. Suzanne is a woman able to take care of herself as well as others. Suzanne likes to talk. She is undeniably clever, ferociously verbal, so much so that even Flora is often a little intimidated by her.

"Well my dear," says Suzanne, when they've finally stopped laughing. "I think we should change the course of things entirely. I think we should make people complain about *us*."

Some things that have already happened:

Flora got a new car, a nifty little Japanese-built soup can, just like everybody else was buying. It was an effort to make herself drive at first. She wasn't afraid of the car itself, which was an obedient machine, stopping, starting, and turning as she instructed it. It wasn't even the memory of staring into all that gouged mud and splintered metal that frightened her. Rather, she wondered if she'd find herself taking another such wild leap into the air, as if she too were a creature of gears and circuits, subject to unexplained commands. She could have killed herself, in fact it seemed she'd tried damned hard to, and without being at all aware of what she was doing. She might do something just as unpredictable again. She might be capable of far worse. Sometimes, on her better days, she convinced herself that the possibility was exhilarating.

Gordon had worried about the insurance.

Things with Gordon were not going well, but then you would hardly expect them to. They had never divorced each other before and simply did not know at all how to go about it. The lawyers and the attendant terrifying legal processes were bad enough, something that made them feel shamed, criminal, and the rest was emotional clumsiness. There was, for instance, the night Gordon called about the eggs. It was well after midnight when the phone rang, and Flora swam up to the surface through some muzzy, panicked dream about sirens and bombs. "Thank God you're home, Flora," the phone said in her ear.

"Where else would I be? Gordon?" She was awake now, thinking of emergency rooms and gaudy death. "Gordon, what's wrong?"

"It's these goddamned eggs. I'm going crazy."

"It's what?" She surely hadn't heard right.

"Eggs."

"You're kidding."

"How in the hell are you supposed to get the shells off after you boil them? The whites keep falling off in big chunks. I've gone through a whole dozen. They all look like golf balls. Worse than that. Like they have leprosy."

"Gordon? Do you know what time it is?" She didn't exactly know herself, but the red dial of the digital clock across the room looked sparse, mostly ones and twos.

"OK, look, I'm sorry."

"He's sorry."

"I didn't know who else to call. Can't you have a nervous breakdown over something stupid? I really was going crazy. I started thinking the little bastards were doing it on purpose, you know, like a suicide squad or something. You should see this kitchen. Full of little egg corpses."

Flora had not, in fact, been invited to view Gordon's rented apartment. There were a number of things she could have said just then, but she chose to tell him about eggs. How he shouldn't boil them too hard, should rinse them well in cold water, crack the shells all over, peel the inner membrane, and so on. "What are you doing cooking eggs in the middle of the night anyway?"

"I had a taste for a hard-boiled egg. It seemed like a harmless enough thing to want."

"Gordon? Is this how you think of me now? As some Betty Crocker hotline?"

"Shit."

"Come on. I'm awake now. You might as well talk to me."

"I don't know, Flora. I guess I thought you wouldn't make me feel any stupider than I already did. Can't we do that for each other? I mean, if you got your hand stuck in a mayonnaise jar or something you could call me."

He sounded plaintive, and Flora felt, simultaneously, rage —
how had he walked the earth this long without learning to boil
his own eggs, was he calling about cooking so he could lead up
to some intimacy, or pretending intimacy just to get his damned
eggs shelled — and sadness. How unlike Gordon to whine and
panic, to let himself be defeated by something as humble as an
egg. At least it was unlike the old bluff Gordon she remembered;
what had they done to each other? And he was right, who else
would you call? Couldn't they still do that for each other?

"Gordon," she said, "it's OK. Go to bed now. Eat an egg
and go to bed."

"You're a pal, Flora."

"That's what I am, am I."

"A prince."

"I'm going back to sleep now, Gordon." It was all either very
funny, she decided, or else just ordinarily depressing.

The weather had turned to true spring at last, with clouds
like white lambs in an enormous sky, with heaps of blossom and
limber tree-wands. Spring is the old fraud of hopefulness, the bad
poetry of desire. Flora made a habit of steering her way cautiously through the anonymous urban grit. She was distracted by
flecks of imprisoned light sparkling in the sidewalks, the white slick
rectangles of gleam on the hoods of passing cars, the brave and
burnished look of everything around her, even among these slabs
of pale cement pudding. Whatever could one do with the heart
in spring, with so much green and gold and pink and white, with
fragrant air and sugar moons? One obeyed all rules of the road
and traffic signals. No excessive speeds. No sharp turns.

Although, on the day she was to meet Suzanne for lunch,
she was thinking, vaguely, that it might be nice to at least get out
of town for a spell, see something other than pigeons and tame
trees. Frolic in the greenwood. Flora, the vernal goddess. The
blooming idiot. She was dressing to go out, facing the mirror with
her usual combination of hopefulness and distress. She was of
that species of near-blondes that seem to just miss out on being
another type entirely. It wasn't even so much a matter of hair

color. If so, she would have given herself over to Miss Clairol long before. No, it had more to do with confidence, or glamour, or — teeth. Yes, she decided, maybe it was teeth. She leaned into the mirror, examining her small, bluish, and far from symmetrical teeth. That was it. She just didn't have the lioness grin of True Blonde-hood. Nothing she wanted to wear looked right either. She tried tying a print scarf around her waist in an attempt to give her outfit a bit of dash or funkiness. The success was still marginal. That was her in a word: a marginal, fitfully visible beauty. Marginal, soon-to-be unwife. She made a face in the mirror and left the house.

The restaurant was one of those large dark battered places known generically as a grill. It was called, in typical ersatz tradition, The Rathskeller, a motif faintly reinforced by a number of ceramic beer steins and a single, elderly stuffed bear. Although it was a little dreary for such fine weather, Suzanne and Flora liked it because you could sit there all day nursing a drink and nobody cared. The interior was full of heavy wooden tables and drowned yellow half-light. The windows were thick paned, violently tinted glass, divided into sham diamond panes and nailed shut. Processed air rattled and hummed from the vents, whether heating or cooling it was impossible to say. Cooking odors, french fries and broiling meat and coffee, circled tiredly. Although it wasn't crowded, Flora stood blinking in the doorway for a long minute before she recognized Suzanne's smooth dark head and realized she was not alone.

The man with Suzanne had his back to Flora; she saw only a rather angular pair of shoulders, slumped over a table. Suzanne was saying something to him, something earnest, it seemed, then she caught sight of Flora, lifted her chin and waved. The man straightened himself also, peering about him through the dim air. Flora advanced, feeling a little self-conscious, but by the time she reached the table, Suzanne was greeting her, typically: "Flora Dora. Come here and make your curtseys."

The man had risen. Flora, who was always rather embarrassed to have people going out of their way for her, even this slightly, poked out her hand to him almost before Suzanne introduced them. "Michael Maggio. My identical twin sister, Flora Reynolds."

"How's it going," said Michael Maggio, not so much shaking Flora's hand as letting his fingers glide over hers, then sinking back into his chair.

"Charmed," Flora said, deciding to be just as rude. When she tried to recall this meeting, first impressions, omens, portents and the like, her clearest memory was of Michael Maggio's perfunctory hand. He had a lot of soft-looking brown hair and eyes a shade lighter than the hair. There was nothing particularly Italian about him, despite his name. She found out later that he was one of those improbable American hybrids, Polish-Italian, further diluted by doses of Irish. A sort of lumpen, Catholic stew. He was a tall man, but rather worn and insubstantial, as if from some prolonged fatigue or perhaps simple joylessness. His face was stony with — suppressed anger? Overt boredom? Flora couldn't tell, and she had no further chance to judge, for as soon as he'd resumed his seat, Michael Maggio stood up again. "I have to take off. Nice meeting you," he said, looking not at Flora, but at Suzanne, who nodded.

"Run along then," she said, and they watched him impatiently navigating through the chairs, then vanishing in the sudden photographic white light of the opened door. Flora sat down, waiting for Suzanne to tell her who he was.

"Unhappy marriage," said Suzanne telegraphically, as if that explained everything about him, and in a sense it did. "I give him aid and counsel. Do you think he's good looking?"

"I don't know," Flora said, and it was the truth. She hadn't been able to see him for very long or very well in all the gloom. "Where do you know him from?"

"Work." Suzanne was the assistant director of a small publishing house, a job she was gradually taming and shaping to her own requirements. She was the only truly ambitious woman Flora knew. "He's one of the authors," she continued. "Some kind of horrible psychologist. Isn't everyone? Lord, I'm tired of psychologists. All they can really do with any accuracy is measure rat saliva and things like that. The rest they only pretend they know. Oh well. Michael's not a bad sort. But so dour. If you gave him a cape, he'd be Rochester in *Jane Eyre*. A professional sufferer. Maybe you should get something going with him."

"Really, Suzanne." Flora disliked sounding prim, disliked letting Suzanne catch her off guard like this. "That's all I need. A married man to tell me his troubles. A melancholy therapist."

"Oh, he isn't a clinical psychologist. He's an industrial person. You know, tells companies what color to paint the walls in the lunchroom for maximum productivity, that sort of thing. I tell you, the two of you'd get along famously. You could arrange the workers' paradise." Suzanne opened the menu just as Flora was about to howl at her. "Let's order. I want something expensive and very bloody. I feel carnivorous today."

Indeed she seemed to, and Flora was going to ask her what sort of advice, aid or counsel she gave poor Michael Maggio, if she thought him such a figure of fun, but instead Suzanne asked her how things were going, and Flora began to tell her. Later, when they'd finished, bloody steak, bloody men and all, Suzanne said, "You ought to get away for a while, you know."

"I'd been thinking of it. But there's work."

"Couldn't you get off if you wanted?"

"I don't know. Maybe I don't want to, not really. Work keeps me from feeling sorry for myself, at least as much as anything can. A vacation could be awful. I'd sit around in some stale motel room drinking, and calling up everyone back home to complain and hiccup."

"For God's sake, Flora, it wouldn't have to be like that. I meant, have some *fun*. Paint your nails silver. Go on a cruise. Take charge."

"I'm not as efficient as you are. I don't make lists of useful short-term emotional goals and then check them off. I can't will myself out of a slump. I wish I could. I wish I could bully myself like you bully me."

Suzanne, as always when confronted with such judgments of herself, looked surprised for the space of a few seconds, then grinned, acknowledging it. The surprise was always genuine. She really didn't think of herself as especially formidable, as impatient with the rest of humanity, who were made of weaker clay. She assumed they were all like her, and only temporary lapses, curable by exhortations, prevented them from splendid achievements. Long ago Flora admitted to herself that she imitated Suzanne, or tried to. They were both aware of it, it was by now an accepted part of their folklore. Suzanne was the standard Flora measured herself against whenever she found herself limp, fainting, bruised and brooding, lacking in spirit. She would have liked to think there was some part of her that Suzanne envied, or at least admired. Once Suzanne said, "You know, Flora, we're perfectly typed, perfect opposites. Snow White and Rose Red, like the fairy tale. You get to hog all the sweetness and light and angelic qualities. I'm stuck with the coarser stuff." But Flora doubted if she was really complaining.

Now Suzanne sighed and rested her little brown paw on Flora's elbow. "I do bully you. I'll stop, if you want. I'll stop directly."

"After all this time? What would we ever find to talk about instead?"

So she returned immediately to the bullying: "Really, Flora, have you thought about a vacation? Getting out of the rut. At least the next time you saw Gordon you could sound all casual and dazzling and thoroughly uninterested in him."

"I don't want to dazzle Gordon. I do want to be thoroughly uninterested. But I have to talk to him a dozen times a week about the mail or his books or the dentist's bill. He's like lint in my pockets I can't get rid of. Sometimes I think it'll go on forever, the two of us trying to get all the pettiness untangled."

"At least you don't have children. They do go on forever."

"I suppose I should be glad. But a child at least is worth fighting about. A child would make me feel — this is going to sound rotten, but it's true — that I'd gotten something out of it, the marriage, I mean."

"So why didn't you? Six years, Flora. You could have had a whole raft of cherubs if you wanted."

"I guess I didn't want. Not badly enough." She didn't want

to keep talking about it either, it was beginning to depress her. She and Gordon had not decided they wouldn't have children. They had simply failed to decide, and not having was the path of least resistance. Now Flora was rather disliking herself for acting as if she'd wanted a child all along. It was weak and hypocritical of her not to know her own mind. And also, though she knew she could still have a child if she wanted one, could at least make the attempt as well as anyone else, events with Gordon had filled her with a sense of exhausted possibilities. It was this more than any simple loneliness that had brought her low these past weeks. She had been through love, marriage, and the sundering of both. She should have grown from it, as they say, should have some sense of the richness and abundance of life, both good and bad, should feel she had served honorably in the thick of it. Instead there was only this fatigue, smallness and defeat. She didn't think she could explain it, not even to Suzanne. She didn't want to explain it. She was tired of taking her emotional temperature.

"Children," said Suzanne, and shook her head. "Nature's way. Reproduce and die."

Suzanne leaned back in her chair and shut her eyes, and for a moment Flora saw her as she was when she did not make the effort to shine, to take charge. A woman like herself, no longer quite young, going dry around the edges. For how many more years would they sit around tables like this, talking, as youth receded and life took smaller and smaller shapes. Quickly, to make herself forget this vision, which she knew was the absolute truth, Flora asked, "How's Carl? Still around?" Carl was Suzanne's fellow. Her beau. Her gentleman friend. All Suzanne's words, meant to assign him his proper status. Speaking of him restored Suzanne's familiar irony, and that shadow self, that aging woman disappeared.

"Oh yes, still around. He comes and goes. It suits us both. It may not be exciting, but it's comfortable. We'll probably go on forever like this, rubbing along."

"Comfort. Maybe that's all you ought to want from men. From life. Trumpets and fanfare and all the other hoopla take too much out of you."

"Yes, well. Given a chance at some really first-rate hoopla, I'm sure you'll change your mind. Shall we go?"

They said good-bye in the parking lot, rather abruptly. There was never a great deal left to say after such encounters. Flora was just about to start her car when she saw, framed in the rearview mirror, Suzanne and Michael Maggio. She could only imagine he'd been waiting out there for all this time, or else he'd come back specifically to find Suzanne. They were some distance away, across the arid expanse of cement. In the mirror they were very small. It was like watching pictures of astronauts on the moon; some very remote drama, played out in slow motion.

Suzanne stood by her car, one hand on the door, as if interrupted in the act of leaving, or perhaps she was still trying to leave. Her back was to Flora. It was windy; the ribbons she wore at her neck and the strands of her hair streamed together, dark and bright. From time to time she raised her free hand impatiently to her head, then let it drop, as if annoyed with the uselessness of it. Michael Maggio was doing all the talking. Even from this distance Flora could tell it was an argument. She had full view of him. Was he good-looking? Flora decided he was, in a gaunt, pale, severe fashion. A professional sufferer. But the next instant he was bending down with his face very near Suzanne's, and lifting one corner of his mouth so his upper teeth showed. It was a gesture so ugly and so wolfish that Flora was immediately alarmed. Who was he anyway, what was going on, should she do something? Of course she did nothing. She wanted to see what would happen next.

Besides, it wasn't necessary to worry about Suzanne. She stood and stood, and whatever words she was saying translated into No. You could tell from the impatient tilt of her body, if nothing else, and finally she shook her head, No, and opened the car door. Michael Maggio reached over to the mirror on the side of the car and broke it off. He seemed surprised at how easy it was to do so, even a little annoyed that the thing hadn't put up more of a fight. He kicked at the radiator grill and the hood bounced. Then he slammed the car door again, so hard that Suzanne, who still held the handle, staggered. Her precarious little high-heeled shoes skidded on the pavement and she reached for a fistful of air. But she didn't fall. She staggered, righted herself, and faced him once again. She said something, and though Flora could see only a hint of chin emerging beyond her hair, she knew exactly what she was saying. If you are going to be childish, if you are going to slam doors and break things, Suzanne told him, there is no point in trying to discuss anything. Michael Maggio lifted his face to the perfect sky, and Flora saw that Suzanne had the best of him. She had the best of him because she had re- fused to fall. He had wanted to push her off her exasperating balance, but she hadn't fallen.

Flora left them. She'd only sat watching them for a minute or two; she doubted if they'd even seen her. She felt agitated, uncomfortably curious, and more than anything else, excited. Suzanne had a lover, a married man who waited for her in park- ing lots and pursued her with arguments. Suzanne had kept it from her, and that itself was enough to invest it all with mystery. She had even offered him up to Flora, frivolously, just to throw her off the track. It puzzled Flora, it had nothing to do with her, really, but still she drove home feeling light and energetic. She had recaptured some sense of the possibilities of life, even if they were other people's possibilities. She felt, vaguely, that the world was a more interesting place if people kept secrets, if they did unexpected, unexplainable, even outlandish things, in fact the more outlandish the better. She felt a little as she had after the accident, when she'd been granted such odd glimpses of other lives. She might again be watching it all from behind glass, she might remain a perpetual voyeur, but at least there were things worth watching. When she got home she cleaned the house in- side out, filling the air with bleach and polish smells, unfurling bedsheets like sails.

She didn't see Suzanne again for more than a week, when she dropped by Flora's house after work. Flora was glad to see her. She was just about to tackle dinner, and her meals alone were turning into something of a defeat. Suzanne found her contemplating a package of gray hamburger, a single carrot, and a puddle of leftover creamed corn.

"I know, I know," Flora said, because Suzanne was looking sadly at this assemblage. "But I keep thinking I can do something clever with it. Dump it all into a casserole and melt cheese over it."

"Why don't you dump it all in the garbage and we'll order pizza," Suzanne suggested, and they did. They sat in the living room companionably drinking beer and digging into the cardboard box. It was pleasant to have company in the house; it was pleasant to be doing something this normal and harmless. Outside the windows the trees were coming into full leaf. The lengthening sun made the beer in their glasses look exactly like beer commercials always make it look: golden, floating, and personable.

"So how's work?" Flora asked after a time, just to have something to say. She knew she couldn't just come flat out and ask about the scene in the parking lot. If there was anything to it Suzanne might not tell her, and if there wasn't, Flora supposed she didn't want to be disappointed by any merely innocent explanation. She wanted Suzanne, everyone, to have secrets worth keeping. Suzanne's car in the driveway still bore the little amputated stump of the mirror. Flora watched Suzanne frown at the crust of pizza in her hand. She wondered why she was depending on Suzanne to give shape and color to her own life.

"Work's busy. All the billing goes out this month. And there's some new shit fit Morris is throwing about production schedules. I have to promise him three times a week I'll have everyone fired and beheaded. I almost forgot. One reason I came by was to invite you to the open house."

"Oh dear. Must you?"

"It'll be different this year, I promise. I'm in charge. No Cheez-Whiz."

"No Hawaiian Punch?"

"Real liquor and hors d'oeuvres. Come on, Flora, be a sport. I want some bodies there. I want Morris to think I'm making him famous."

The last time Flora had gone to Suzanne's open house, she spent the evening talking with various alarmed-looking women, all eyeglasses and earrings. These women conversed nicely enough about what they did, and about what Flora did, and then everyone smiled fondly into their glasses of punch until one or the other backed away. Flora heard herself saying, "I'll stop by. Just for a drink, OK?" She realized how slow life must be getting for her lately.

"You won't be sorry. I'm inviting the world. Friday at five. How's your office, by the way?"

Flora told her it was fine, and she supposed it was. It was no different from what it had always been, but she was coming to realize how little work meant to her. Not just her job, but the entire world of work, which was strange since work was doubly her province.

It didn't interest her, work, if she was honest about it. It was such a large and bulky, legitimate part of life, and everyone assumed it mattered, but it didn't to her, not really. It wasn't just the profit and loss, getting and spending, money-grubbing part of it that wearied her, but all the striving and achieving and busyness, the effort that went into making and using and making again, like a snake biting its tail. It was not what she lived for, it had nothing to do with her real life or its hungers. Flora sat at her desk all day, dutifully attempting to plug people into the right productive slots. And sometimes she could almost believe in what she was doing; she could convince herself it was all necessary and desirable. After all, it made people unhappy to be without work, it seemed to make them happy to find it. She might spend a whole day thus, doling out work without really thinking about it. Then, driving home, she would stop at a railroad crossing and wait for a freight to pass. She'd watch the cars roll by on their slow enormous shrieking wheels, the flats and tanks and boxcars the color of dried blood, the no-color of hot metal, all of them marked with letters and numbers, codes that meant something to someone but nothing to her. And she would rest her head on the steering wheel, suddenly tired, knowing she was about to betray her official self, or maybe the official self was a betrayal of her. What did they mean, these enormous pieces of rusting metal, how did they fit together, why did anyone bother with them? None of it meant anything at all.

On Friday afternoon Flora went straight to Suzanne's office from her own. Suzanne was right; she had invited the world. The office staff, those obscurely agitated women Flora remembered from last year, were present but outnumbered. The room was large and pleasantly crowded, and Flora could tell from the pitch and volume of the voices that Suzanne hadn't lied about getting liquor. She saw Flora right away and waved her over.

"Scotch? Wine? We had some shrimp critters but they might be gone already. Carl's here. I sent him around with a tray of cauliflower. Oh, here he is. Peel me a cauliflower, sweetie."

Something was wrong. It's a sense you get at parties sometimes, even through all the noise and hectic cheer. Flora said hello to Carl (whom she rather liked, and who liked her, but who was probably the sort of man one dispatched with trays of cauliflower), and tried to get her bearings. Suzanne was poking at the vegetables, complaining overbrightly about the drowned look of the parsley garnish. She was what was wrong, but Flora still didn't know why.

"Here, taste this," she told Flora, presenting her with a triangle of toast. "Our famous dog food canapé. Oh don't be silly. It's paté. But I think it lacks a certain, how you say, zest. Like they made it with margarine. Stupid caterers. Eat, eat. It's all for the greater glory of me. Besides, there's a whole tub of this stuff in the back."

Flora thought at first she was drunk, but she wasn't at all. Obediently she ate the paté, which did look a little like dog food. "It's OK," Flora assured her. "Really, it's good. Everything looks good. It's a regular bash."

"Too much secret sauce on the meatballs. And the secretaries are all getting loaded. They're only used to drinks with umbrellas in them. The hell with them. We'll stack them like folding chairs if we have to. Did you know the secretaries are all virgins? I hear them talking in the john. They talk about 'going all the way.' They're being stalked by the young professionals. See?

They're the fellows with ties on. Imagine, Flora, a whole herd of young professionals. It's like observing wildebeest or something. Wildebeest gathering at dusk by the communal watering hole."

Slow down, Flora wanted to tell her, but Carl was with them now, smiling. He was always smiling. "Would you hit her with a baseball bat?" he said to Flora. "She keeps worrying. I tell her the party's launched by now. She should relax and enjoy it."

"Yes, really, relax," Flora said, putting a lot of eyebrows into it, and Suzanne got the message. She looked, for a moment, annoyed, both at herself for being noticeably out of control, and at Flora for noticing. Then she shrugged it off.

"I invited Paul," she said. "Do you think he'll come? I want him to be rude to a few people for me. He promised. Oh well. It's early yet. Is it more crowded, or is everyone just getting noisier?"

They looked out over the room, which was both crowded and noisy, and rapidly shedding its workday personality. The young secretaries were indeed beginning to leap and trill, though they weren't yet to the stage of having lipstick on their teeth, and certainly not yet ready to go all the way. Their bright, cracked little laughter seemed a kind of choral accompaniment to Suzanne's center-stage nerves. Though she'd reined herself in and was standing calmly enough, even managing to look a little bored.

"Here comes a horrid man who wants to meet you, Flora," said Suzanne conversationally. One of the wildebeest-men was edging towards them through the crowd. He had a cap of very blonde hair and a smile which he tried to keep balanced as he jostled and nudged.

Eventually he reached them, and made a little pantomime of exhausted relief. "God, it's thick in here," he said. "Hell of a party. It'll take a fire hose to clear it out, I'm telling you. Hi there."

This last to Flora. Suzanne introduced them. "Flora Reynolds, this is John Denver."

"I doubt it," Flora said. Though he did look a little like John Denver.

"You're right. I'm really Bob Dylan."

"Aren't both of them phony names?" asked Carl, who was always good for turning conversations instructive. "That is, I know about Dylan. I bet Denver is too."

"I'm thinking of changing my name," said Suzanne. "To George Sand."

"Do you work here?" Flora asked John Denver, to spare them more of this.

"He's the payroll person," Suzanne said. "And we all think the world of him."

"My name really is John," he said patiently.

"And mine's really Flora."

"I don't think I've ever met a Flora before."

"If I was a boy, I was going to be Avery. Mother reads."

"It's a pretty name," said John Denver. "It sounds like garlands of flowers, lambs with bells around their necks, things like that." He stuck his nose into his drink, as if appalled by this little surge of gallantry. Flora liked him. He might even be capable of blushing.

"Just don't call her Flo," said Suzanne. "Would you excuse me? I have to go look like I'm in charge."

And so she did, leaving the other three to build the conversation all over again. Both men were looking at Flora expectantly, and she did want to say something bright and helpful, something other than the usual wildebeest-noise of who did what for a living. She didn't find John Denver horrid at all, though she could see already that he was the sort of man who women do not take very seriously. He was young, probably not quite as young as he looked, and full of honest blond enthusiasms and yearnings. She felt a little sorry for him; she thought it was brave and hopeful of him to struggle through a crowded room toward a strange woman, on the meager chance that they might have something to offer each other. So she said, trying to keep her end of things up, "This is much nicer than last year's open house," and both men agreed. Carl asked John Denver if this sort of thing really accomplished much, for business that is.

"Social grease, mainly. I couldn't tell you. I just do the books. The place could be a dairy or a garage, as far as I'm concerned."

They chatted, that was certainly the word, for a time about the press. But John Denver didn't seem too interested in talking shop, and after a spell Carl drifted away to get another drink. Flora was wondering if they'd have to start in on her job now, out of sheer conversational defeat, when John Denver asked how she knew Suzanne.

"Oh, we've known each other since the year one. Since high school, though we weren't really friends then. She was a cheerleader, and I was one of those sad cases who don't shave their legs often enough."

John Denver laughed at this, as he was meant to, and Flora wondered if she was being a little too eager, offering herself up too readily for amusement. It was a pose that, once you began, was too easy to continue. She could see herself sketching in her drooping socks, her battles with hair curlers, and so on, as if none of it had ever pained her, as if she'd foreseen the future value of being gawky and miserable, something she could trade on at parties. The truth was she liked to talk about herself as much as anyone else did, but she usually had to do it in this backhanded, grimacing way, making herself out to be a sort of walking anecdote, a lovable failure. She was all set for it, just gearing up, when John Denver said, "She's funny. Suzanne, I mean."

"Funny?" Flora wasn't going to help him out on that one at all. She supposed she really had wanted to talk about herself.

"You can never tell when she's kidding or not. At least I can't."

"Well," Flora said judiciously, "I don't think she varies much. So either she's never kidding or she's always kidding."

John Denver frowned at this Delphic answer. "Was she really a cheerleader?"

"Oh yes. If you sneak up behind her and start a cheer, she'll probably go into her high kicks."

"I wouldn't dare," said John Denver, though he looked as if he would have liked to. It was beginning to dawn on Flora that he hadn't really crossed the room in order to meet her at all. "So what was she like in high school?" he persisted.

"A champ. A regular golden girl."

"Homecoming queen, I bet."

"No, she wasn't daffy enough for queen."

"Student Council Secretary. Pep Club President."

"Something like that," Flora said, thinking of her own high school credits. French Club, Girls' Chorus, Hall Monitor. Sometimes it really did seem odd to her that the two of them had ended up as friends. "The amazing thing is, she didn't peak back then. So many of the winners do, you know. That's their high water mark. Teenage wonders."

They both turned around then, looking for Suzanne. She was perched on a window ledge across the room, drink in hand, talking. One leg swung beneath her, back and forth. Flora watched that negligently swinging leg, steady as a metronome, though what odd inner music it was set to tonight she couldn't tell. She was going to have to detach herself from this worshipful young man and go see about her. Flora had a feeling of rather complicated, if minor, wounded vanity. For while she wasn't particularly interested in John Denver, she seemed to be competing with Suzanne for the right to reject him. It was annoying to have misjudged things so, as if she couldn't keep up with the pace of normal intrigues any more. Beside her, John gave a little snort.

"He brought his wife tonight. What fun."

"Pardon?" Things really were moving too fast for her.

"Mike. I can't imagine why. It'll only mean trouble."

Flora followed his gaze. Michael Maggio was standing near the door, with the hesitating look of someone just come in. But it was his wife Flora noticed. She was beautiful. Flora was to come to wish she hadn't been, but she was. She was an inch or more taller than Flora, that is, quite tall, but slight. An elegant figure, an elegant woman. Her hair was cut short, copper-brown and curly. She had a wide mouth, deeply colored, and a soft, rather sloping profile. Not one of your contemporary boyish beauties, all cheekbones and angles and sleekness. The two of them together looked oddly isolated and very like each other in their height and unsmiling solemnness, like some new alien species off of Noah's Ark.

John Denver was trying to be wry and amused, but it was a

struggle for him. He seemed to know whatever there was to know about Michael Maggio and Suzanne, and he seemed to think Flora did also. Crafty, Flora asked, "Is she a troublemaker, then?"

"She's certainly got all the skills for it."

"Skills?"

"A more cussedly jealous female you'll never find. Mike must be trying to brazen things out. After all this time, maybe he's just run out of cover stories."

All this time? "His wife is beautiful," Flora said. The two of them were standing together looking irresolute, the way couples do when they can't agree on what they want to drink or where to sit or anything else.

"Oh yes. Who can say. Maybe he brought her along just to keep Suzanne on her toes."

Flora was beginning to feel uncomfortable. Gossip is one thing, but there had been other such occasions when she'd heard more than she ever wanted to about people she knew, or even about total strangers. John Denver was so agitated, he probably would have said much the same things to whoever was standing next to him. Unless he'd already designated Flora as a confidante, a kind of Suzanne-substitute, and she was meant to go drink coffee with him and commiserate and maybe even have him fall in love with her after all, by default. This is how rattled and giddy Flora's thoughts were getting. But as it turned out there was so much emotion going wrong in that room, like water trapped in bad plumbing, squeezed through knots of pipes and valves, spurting out in all the worst places, that maybe she shouldn't have been surprised to find stray peculiar notions floating through her head. It was, as John Denver himself had said, a hell of a party. She tried to think of something tame to say. She asked what sort of book Michael Maggio had written.

"It isn't a book. It's a series of pamphlets, the psychology of the workplace. Nice moneymakers for all concerned. I should know. I write the checks."

Flora was afraid she might have to hear just how much money he and everyone else in the room made, if they kept on, but John Denver was watching Suzanne again. She was still sitting on the window ledge and Carl, dispatched on another supply run, was taking her glass from her. Flora wondered why no one seemed to bother being jealous of Carl. Maybe because his place in the scheme of things was already fixed. He was the prince consort, she thought, and immediately reproached herself for unkindness.

She'd lost track of Michael Maggio, and of Mrs. Michael, and it seemed as good a time as any to move along. "If you'll excuse me," she said to John Denver, but he was so absorbed in his own brooding that he was startled when she spoke. "Later," he said, nodding. So much for anyone falling in love with me, Flora thought.

Suzanne was talking to a middle-aged couple about something businesslike and impenetrable. Flora stood to one side, trying to look like she belonged there. "Acquisitions," Suzanne was saying, and "Retrenchments." Flora watched Suzanne's trim little legs dangling beneath her. She was wearing rather outrageous lemon-yellow stockings, and sandals of light-colored suede. Idly, Flora was trying to recall who it was in what novel she'd read in college who wore outrageous stockings. Gudrun, in *Women in Love*. She was just congratulating herself when she realized she didn't remember anything else about the book. Nor did she remember anything about: *Middlemarch. The Red and the Black. Sister Carrie.* Suzanne's yellow leg made a sudden, seismographic kick. Looking up, Flora saw that Michael Maggio and his wife had joined the group.

Everyone seemed to know everyone else. "You're looking gorgeous as usual, Elizabeth," the middle-aged man was saying gallantly. There was a little space in which everyone smiled, acknowledging this. Elizabeth Maggio smiled too, nicely, the way women who hear such things often enough can. "Michael," said Suzanne. "You remember my friend Flora?"

Well maybe he didn't, but he had to now, and Flora was presented round to the others. The middle-aged couple's name was Kershaw. Flora couldn't take her eyes off Elizabeth. Up close there were new ways to look at her. Maybe it isn't so odd that she made a greater first impression than Michael had, that Flora was to know she was jealous long before she knew she was in love. Elizabeth was standing placidly enough now, holding her drink as if she wasn't very much interested in it, or in anyone else. It was one of those silly drinks with a skewer of fruit in it. Somehow that cheered Flora, perhaps because it seemed a lapse of taste.

If Flora had expected everyone to behave operatically, to launch into hair-pulling and accusations, she was disappointed. Michael Maggio immediately began a professional conversation with the Kershaw man, who was also, as Suzanne might put it, some sort of horrible psychologist. Flora watched Michael Maggio covertly, thinking he must be more interesting than he appeared to be. He was frowning a little over the business of what he was saying. He was saying, "The correlations were insignificant. Useless." He looked only stiff-faced and humorless, Flora decided, and not a bit like anything from *Jane Eyre*. Of course, maybe she didn't remember *Jane Eyre* very well either.

The professional conversation went on and on. Even though the women outnumbered the two men, Flora felt they had been effectively excluded.

Suzanne listened to them for a few moments, then smiled approvingly. If she was nervous, it wasn't showing now. "It's all right," she said. "As long as they play quietly."

"They're impossible," declared the Kershaw woman. "You'd expect a sixty-hour week would be enough for them." She was the sort of jolly professional wife who seemed entirely comfortable making such complaints, having made them for years now. She smiled at Elizabeth. "Does Mike drag journals all over the house like Walt? I think he reads them under the covers at night with a flashlight."

"I don't know," said Elizabeth. "I usually go to sleep early."

It was a curious sort of non-answer, and she said it flatly, without any humor in it. It brought things up short for a moment, then the helpful Mrs. Kershaw said, "I used to try and take an interest. I used to try and understand statistics, and be informed about the research and all that. Not any more. I'd rather do my needlework."

Suzanne said, "It's like those girls' magazines you used to

read growing up. The ones that told you to learn about cars and football.''

''I wonder if magazines are still like that,'' Flora said. ''I wonder how far consciousness has been raised.'' Not that she really cared. She was getting tired of talking about men, or around them, or because of them, when it was all too apparent that men could talk blissfully on and on, without, despite, and heedless of women.

''Goddamn you,'' said Elizabeth Maggio. ''Snake in the grass. Vulture.''

For one frozen moment Flora thought Elizabeth was talking to her, answering her somehow. Suzanne thought it was meant for her; her face went small and rigid and she looked almost ugly. But Elizabeth wasn't talking to either of them. It was for her husband. He didn't quite hear her at first. He half turned away from his conversation, frowning, as if she'd only interrupted him to ask some annoying domestic question. ''What?'' he said, and then he must have seen the faces.

''Goddamn you,'' Elizabeth said again. She was swaying a little as she stood. Her drink dangled at the end of her hand and everyone seemed to be watching it, waiting for her to throw or spill it. ''I don't have to put up with this. I don't.''

''All right,'' said Michael Maggio. ''All right. Whatever it is, you can stop it. Right now.''

''So you can carry on with her. I'm supposed to stand here and watch you carry on with her.''

''Shut up, Elizabeth.''

''I won't. I'm supposed to stand here and watch it? There's such a thing as decency. There is a limit.''

At that moment, this is what was happening: Suzanne was looking icy. Who knows how she managed it, but she'd recovered enough to stand there freezing it all out. The Kershaws were looking distressed but also rather avid, and one couldn't really blame them. Then Flora realized they were giving her sideways glances, they were trying to puzzle out if she was the one Elizabeth was talking about. It annoyed her that she couldn't explain. She imagined she did look guilty, she always did for no good reason. And Michael hadn't provided any clues, hadn't exactly been carrying on with anyone. Flora didn't know if he deserved sympathy, but he looked awful just then. Elizabeth was crying by now. They watched her cry the way you might watch a building burn. She cried with little shiverings and eruptions of breath. Carl walked up carrying a paper plate of meatballs on plastic skewers shaped like swords. "En garde," he said, presenting them.

"I'm sorry," said Michael Maggio. He reached out as if to steer his wife away.

"Don't touch me. I can't stand to have you touch me."

"Elizabeth."

"Don't worry. I'm leaving now."

"Just —"

"Don't worry about it. You'll never see me again."

"All right," said Michael Maggio. "All right now."

"Snake. Slimy snake."

"Christ."

Around them, people were just now beginning to listen.

"Never again. I hope you can live with what you've done. I hope you can sleep nights. It's all on your head."

"Silly boring cow," said Suzanne distinctly. "Why don't you go somewhere and do whatever it is, then, instead of making boring speeches?"

Everything fell apart after that, though not in the way you might imagine. People just left. Elizabeth gave all of them the same wet and uncomprehending stare, her eyes too white. You didn't want to look at her now. She was still beautiful, even with the crying, but she was just on the brink of going awry, you half expected her to start shedding earrings and fingernails. Then she was heading doorward, taking short, trotting steps on her high heels, and Michael was hurrying after her. Suzanne stalked off in another direction and Carl said "I think I'd better . . ." and Flora was left holding the plate of impaled meatballs.

"Well," began Mrs. Kershaw, but even her splendid social gifts weren't equal to the moment. Just to be doing something, Flora offered the meatballs round, and everyone chewed thoughtfully. They all wanted to talk about it, but there didn't seem any decent way to begin. "Well," Mrs. Kershaw began again, depositing her plastic sword on the edge of the plate. "Poor Elizabeth."

"Yes," Flora said, since sympathy was the safe, high road. "I hope things calm down."

"She's so high strung. She's —"

"Nuts," said Mr. Kershaw, pleased with himself for being this blunt, and for being a psychologist and saying Nuts so sportively. "A case."

"Walt," said his wife. "You shouldn't even joke about things like that."

"Have you known them long?" Nasty Flora, so seemingly neutral and concerned, all the while hoping for the dirt.

"Oh, Mike was one of Walt's grad students, years and years ago. One of his best students."

Flora nodded, encouraging her, and Mrs. Kershaw, after a hesitation, meant to imply her sorrowfulness and regret at having to discuss anything unseemly, continued. She was a thoroughgoing gossip after all, Flora decided, one who justified it by telling herself she was just smoothing things over. "We've known Elizabeth since they married. Three years? Three years ago. It's all so sad, when I remember the wedding and how lovely it was, how lovely she looked, like a cloud, all pink and white and floating —"

Mr. Kershaw gave Flora a look that said, Poetry. "She leads him a life of merry hell. This marriage business. People don't seem to want to admit when they've made a bad job of it."

"It's been my experience," Flora said, "that people sometimes do stick with the really bad jobs. Maybe they have more going for them, more vitality at least, than the ones that are just fair to middling."

Nobody said anything to that, then Kershaw spoke. "Maybe. But the two of them are about to vital each other to death. This isn't the first time —"

"I think," said Mrs. Kershaw, "that we need not dwell on this." She was remembering, Flora supposed, that they hardly knew her. Flora was thinking, psychologist, heal thyself, and she was thinking what good camouflage it would be for an actual affair to have a wife who was pathologically jealous, when someone clapped her on the shoulder.

"Hullo hullo. Flora Flora." It was Paul, very drunk, very owlish looking. He was bending from the waist so he could peer into her face, making himself a parody of awkwardness in the way awkward people learn to do. Flora excused herself from the Kershaws, who must have been wondering what sort of sideshow was playing now, and handed Paul the meatballs. "Eat something," she instructed him. "You look like you could use some ballast." She watched him cross two meatball swords in the air before him with great ceremony, then fumble them to the floor. "Terrific. Did you just get here?"

"I think so. I think I'm here. I've been elsewhere. Absolute Elsewhere, like in physics. Who are all these silly people?"

"You're stewed."

"Shall we promenade? I need a drink."

"You don't need a drink," Flora said, but he was pulling her along already. She looked around for Suzanne or Carl or any of the other combatants, but they weren't in the room. Through the long windows you could see the perfect spring twilight, a sky of violet and pearl, and the sparse city trees gathering green-black shadows beneath them, and suddenly she wished she were outside, alone in the harmless night. Paul got them both enormous, poisonous Scotches. "To the revolution," he said.

"What revolution?"

"The revolution of your choice. Dare to struggle, dare to win. To our glorious deaths."

"Come on, Paul, I won't even pretend to drink to any such thing."

"To bloodless coups, then. To constitutional monarchies. Orderly democratic processes."

"You're taking all the fun out of it now," Flora complained, but she lifted her glass anyway.

"Now that you're getting divorced, will you marry me?"

"You're drunk."

"Will you at least sleep with me then? Come on. Be a sport. I have admired you from afar, you know? And now you're anear. Sort of."

"You're drunk."

"Of course I'm drunk. I had to get drunk to say it. I knew you wouldn't want to hear it. Nobody ever wants anyone who wants them, do they?"

"Sometimes it seems that way," Flora said carefully.

"I should be doing this differently. I should be saying something endearing. I wanted to, the day you wrecked your car. That was my big chance and I blew it. This is my little chance. Now I'm blowing it too."

With his shaggy hair and thin, uneven shoulders he looked like some derelict bird, a starling caught in the rain, perhaps. He was gazing at her sadly now, with a drunk's cracked melancholy. Flora was wondering, with dismay, if maybe he'd meant what he said. She didn't want anyone to be in love with her, she decided. At least not this sad failed wisecracking sort of love, which was really only an excuse to feel sorry for yourself. She wondered if this was all people meant by love now, this trick of turning their own sadness into someone else's shape.

"Oh well," he said after a minute. "Dare to struggle, dare to lose."

"I'm sorry," Flora said.

"If people didn't have to talk, you know? If they could just rub and smell each other."

Flora thought he was right. She thought talking was probably most of the trouble. She thought of how badly she, and everyone else she knew, managed their love, trapping it in words and the words all wrong. She was very tired. The evening had been a series of small and large catastrophes, of social explosions going off all around her. She felt as if she were in the middle of one of those large old-fashioned battle paintings, with panoramic views of cavalry charges, tottering flags and dying generals. But it wasn't over yet.

"By the way," said Paul. "I saw Gordon yesterday. At the grocery."

"So how is Gordon?" Flora was trying to show the right sort of strained polite interest, the appropriate note for inquiring about one's ex-spouse, but she was too tired to care very much.

"Fine, I guess. He was buying the oddest groceries. Holland rusks, cocktail onions, frozen pie-crust, chutney. Things like that. I can't imagine what kind of meals he's putting together."

"Oh, he's cooking for a woman," Flora said, feeling suddenly lighthearted. "That's all it is. He's going to make a huge mess flambéeing and saucing things and using every dish in the house. It's OK." She didn't know why she felt cheered at the notion of Gordon with another woman, but she did. Maybe it was a sign that life was progressing on to the next stage. And what stage was that? She didn't know. Paul was acting quite normally now, that is, normal for someone who'd been drinking all night. He didn't seem to be regarding Flora with any special yearning or disappointment or even interest. It was as if nothing had happened between them and maybe nothing had, nothing very serious. Only one more spell of failed feeling between talking animals.

"There you are." It was Suzanne. "I need to talk to you. Hello Paul. You look shit-faced."

"M'lady." He bowed and hiccuped.

"Excuse us." Flora followed her through the crowd, which was getting a little sparser now, but making just as much noise, down a hallway to her office. "A favor," she said, once they were standing in the narrow territory by the desk, the only free space among the stacked papers and bookshelves.

"What's that?"

"Give Mike a ride home. He's in the parking lot."

Flora just looked at her. When she didn't answer Suzanne said, "I can't stand to have anything more to do with him. With either of them. You have no idea what it's like, they thrive on messes and scenes and fits, I can't stand another minute of it. Please, Flora, I'll scream if he isn't out of here."

"Call him a cab, then."

Suzanne leaned against the desk, her hands behind her. A little figure with upswept hair and jaunty yellow legs, leaning back in a mannequin's pose. Flora wondered if she ever did anything, made one move or gesture that was not calculated to charm, or sway, or get something from someone. She wondered if they were really friends at all, if perhaps they balanced always on the edge of some fatal, unforgiveable argument.

"Why me," Flora said. "What am I supposed to do with your discarded lover?"

Suzanne stopped looking guilty for long enough to look annoyed. "You make him sound like a piece of Kleenex."

Flora said, "You like messes and scenes just fine, as long as you're the one setting them up. What am I supposed to do with the poor man?"

"Whatever you want. Nothing. I don't care."

"But I have your permission. You're telling me I have your permission."

"I suppose so. In my tactless way."

"It's your way of showing him off. You're through with him, but you still want to show him off." Her heart was beating all through her skin. She didn't want to understand what Suzanne was saying. She kept trying not to understand. She wanted Flora to sleep with a man she'd slept with. And Suzanne kept talking as she always did, bright, amused, skeptical, as if there was nothing that could not be put into words.

"Am I really that awful, Flora? Do you disapprove of me that much?" She sounded sad now, though she still leaned back against the desk, her hands behind her.

"Sometimes," Flora said. "When you don't even bother to hide your own indecency. And I wish you didn't get away with so much. That's the annoying part."

Suzanne couldn't help grinning a little then, though she tried not to. "I do," she said. "I get away with far too much. Nobody stops me." For a moment longer she stood there, smiling, as if watching herself in a mirror. Then her mood changed and she clapped her hands together. "Oh well. One muddles on. Oh God. There's still Mike. I wonder if he could drive Paul's car. Somebody ought to, besides Paul, I mean. We could pack them both off that way."

"No," Flora said. Her heart was still beating too hard, as if it would burst through her fingertips, and she thought, This is it. What she was afraid of doing all along, another wrench of the steering wheel into perilous air. "No, you can drive Paul, if you want to. I'll take Mike."

CHAPTER
3

"You're beautiful," he told me. I think that's when the trouble started. In another sense, of course, we'd already been in trouble for a long time. "You're beautiful." He looked sadder than anyone had a right to. I didn't want anyone looking at me like that.

"Don't be silly."

"What's silly about it."

"Look at me. On a good day I can be, I don't know. Maybe 'well groomed.' But not beautiful."

"And I think you are."

"Men always want to think that about the women they're in bed with."

I shouldn't have said it. He went very quiet all at once, the way a clock stops ticking. I shouldn't have said it, but I didn't want him looking at me like that, making me into something I wasn't, something he would worship with sadness.

"I'm sorry," I said. He was already sitting up. The room was cold, and the skin of his back looked white and opaque. Like marble, I remember thinking. Like something not real. I touched him and he flinched from it.

"You and your goddamned gleeful witty cynicism," he said.

Talking in bed isn't always what it's made out to be. Sex is the wrong thing to filter words through. Everything comes out meaning too much. Everything is a promise or a threat.

"I suppose you're right," I said. There didn't seem to be any very good way to apologize.

"I'm not some amusing sociological phenomenon. I'm the man who's here with you, right now."

"And I'm just a woman who talks too much. Come on. It's nothing. What are you doing now?" He was up and stalking about the room.

"Tap dancing my way out."

"Oh come on."

"I'm going to leave 'em while they're laughing."

"There really isn't anything wrong, you know. You're just picking a fight."

He didn't answer. He was yanking on his clothes, and I wanted to tell him not to be so careless about the way he dressed, his wife would notice anything wrong. But he'd only think I was being cynical again. Well, hadn't we known what we were getting into, right from the start?

We had and we hadn't. I believe people always know it when they set out to do intentional damage. They just don't admit it to themselves. I don't want to hurt my wife, he said. Of course I agreed. I wanted her husband to find me altogether more desirable, more engaging, more worthy, and every time he looked at her or touched her I wanted him to find her lacking, but I wanted none of this to hurt her, oh no. The things you can say and even believe. We talked it all out beforehand. Imagine. Consenting adults. We were deadly pompous about it all, we did everything but shake hands on it.

I'm trying to explain how it all turned out so badly, how feeling between two people can become so thoroughly poisoned, despite everyone's best intentions, despite one's many gifts, one's intelligence, insight, sensibility, good will. I'd like to think it could be explained, but maybe that's the same mistake as imagining you can agree to terms beforehand. Maybe I just want the luxury of wallowing in self-blame, now that it's too late to change anything. I have this trick of admitting to my own worst motives, you see, which somehow allows me to carry on just as I please. Mike was right, I am thoroughly cynical, fatally clever, a lost soul.

The problem was, I wouldn't be in love with him. That's how he saw it. He only meant I wouldn't be unhappy for him, because I did love him in every normal sense of things. But that wasn't what he wanted, or else it wasn't enough. He was so fundamentally unhappy himself, so mired in hopelessness, he couldn't believe that anything but unhappiness was genuine. He kept looking for it in me, he mistrusted whatever I had of lightheartedness or ease. As if there were something I was holding back from him, and I was an unnatural woman, a cold woman, flawed, incomplete, emotionally dishonest, and on and on. Look, I said to him once, after this sort of talk had gone beyond the point of weariness, Look, don't you think you've got it backwards? You're not miserable because of me, it has nothing to do with me, not really. You begin by feeling guilty, and you want to be in love to justify it all. You want to be in love because then you can feel tragic about it, you like the notion of tragedy better than dishonesty and furtiveness. You want to look at me and see yourself, I am your excuse to feel sorry for yourself. I said that to him. That was how bad it got, eventually.

He wanted me to be someone he could love tragically and I wasn't that. I wasn't that at all. And maybe there's where it started, on that day when I would not be beautiful for him. I want to remember just how it went, and it's easier than you might imagine. I can lay it all out like one of those documented chess matches, minus any strategy, of course, but with every fatal move recorded. I watched Michael dressing in the cold room, watched him feeling injured and angry and sad, and that's when I thought what a bad job we were starting to make of things, or how perhaps it had been a bad job right from the start.

He was tying his tie, peering into the too-small mirror at my dressing table. The glass wasn't good; it had a wavering, underwater quality to it, as if you were watching yourself being drowned. He always wore ties. I thought it was a way he kept himself stern and properly manlike, because he was, usually. That knot around his throat seemed to hold everything in place.

"Ah Mike," I said. "I do worry about you, you know?"

"Don't bother." He was dressed by now, but he wasn't leaving. He was frowning and fishing things out of his pocket, and I knew he was looking for an excuse to stay.

"Come here." He made an impatient move with his head. "Come here." I pushed the snarled sheets aside and knelt on the edge of the bed. I was still naked and it felt strange trying to reach him through those layers of cloth. His cotton shirt had its own clean smell, and beneath it was the richer smell of his skin. Ribbons of muscle, secret bones. I felt him all the way through, as if that might tell me where his sadness came from, what part of him would not let anything be easy.

"You see," I said. "It's OK, really. There's nothing wrong." And I wanted to believe it. I wanted things to go on as they had been.

He did smile a little then. "I like it when you try. When you think I'm worth taking trouble over."

"I always think that."

He sat down on the edge of the bed, looking tired. Not angry anymore, just tired, as he so often did. Like something gray and powdery had been sifted over him. "I do have to go. In just a little."

"I know."

"Stupid, isn't it."

"What is?"

"You know. The tangled web we weave when first we practice to deceive, and all that."

I turned my face away so he wouldn't see how impatient talk like that made me. I didn't see any point in it. You make your choices and you live with them. Talking about the guilt, the ironies, the ambiguities and so on, examining their own sensitivity, is the way people try and convince themselves they haven't really made a choice after all. Like there's some fine print in the moral contract that lets them off the hook.

When I didn't say anything he looked over at me, waiting. "All right," he said finally. "We'll do it your way. I really do have to go now. No, I don't want you to get up. I want you to loll around in the sheets like a sulky harem beauty."

"Have you ever looked at these sheets? They have little pandas all over them. Pandas eating bamboo shoots."

"See, I can make you laugh. When I try, I can make you laugh. I'm leaving now."

And he did. I listened to him wrestling with the front door lock, which he still hadn't learned to manage. When I was certain he was gone, I got up to start the shower running. I thought of him pointing himself homeward now, driving too fast through the muttering traffic, trying to change his shape so he'd fit back into his life the way he was supposed to. I knew he would be thinking of me. I knew he was thinking of me just then, that instant, and I bent all my mind towards him. I wanted him to be thinking of me. I wanted him to keep the shape I'd made him into. That's exactly how I was thinking. Then I stepped into the shower and let the water pour over me.

I didn't see him again for more than a week. It went like that for us sometimes. In fact when I saw him it was an accident, I didn't see him so much as see his car. Someone should really do a study on the importance of the automobile in modern adultery. I don't mean we had sex in cars, though certainly other people must. We weren't that young anymore, we didn't need to. Besides, it was too cold most of the time. Doesn't everyone remember the famous apocryphal high school couple who either froze to death in a parked car or gassed themselves with carbon monoxide, and whose poor stiff bodies had to be pried loose from some fantastic indelicacy? "They're folk heroes," Michael said once, when we were comparing versions of it. "They never existed, but that doesn't mean they aren't real. Like Paul Bunyan or something."

Mike's car was a light blue Toyota with a spray of rust across the hood and a Y-shaped crack in the rear window. He's one of those people who drives cars to death, and never notices them aging. I got so I could recognize that car from several blocks away. I spent a lot of time looking out of windows for it when he was supposed to meet me, or driving past his office to see if he was still working, or, as on this particular day, finding it tethered outside some store. We left notes under windshield wipers. On occasion we rode uneasily in each other's passenger seats, like scouts riding shotgun. Later, when things got really bad between us, I took to parking my own car on a side street so he couldn't drive by and tell I was at home. I'm sure it's possible to have a liaison while relying strictly on public transportation, but it wouldn't be quite the same thing. I used to wonder if this was what people meant when they talked about the American love affair with the automobile.

Anyway, on this day, a mild winter Saturday, I was out doing errands. It was one of those melting days, when the sun comes out and everything drips and puddles, every surface seems to be either water or new-washed glass. Even the few heaps of dwindling snow looked clean. I was driving along thinking about things like buttons and instant coffee and sandpaper. I had the radio on and it was contributing its own commercial debris: fried chicken, carpeting, savings accounts. The streets were busy with people making similar rounds. All-American morning, landscape with consumers. I wasn't thinking about Mike at all. Then I saw his car parked outside a supermarket.

Automatically, I pulled in the lot. You get into habits like that. I parked a little distance away, another habit. After all, his wife might be with him. Although she had her own car, and for all I knew, her own affairs going. I sat there for a little while in the puddle-bright and crowded lot, wondering what to do. I hadn't been thinking about him at all, but now I wanted to see him. I suppose you're curious about the life a man has when he's away from you, even if it's something as humble as buying groceries. You imagine everything is a secret you ought to know.

Once I got out of the car, I felt a little silly pushing my way through all the people trundling their bags of dog food and their screaming toddlers back and forth. What was I doing, trailing him like this? Love among the canned goods. Love in parking lots, love this store only, $1.49. Furtiveness was one thing, I was used to that, but I disliked things being small and comical. I wondered what sort of conversation I'd be able to invent if his wife really was there, wondered if maybe I should have a sheaf of coupons at the ready for an alibi.

But he was alone. I saw him right away, at the butcher's counter, flipping through the plastic trays of packaged meat. He was looking impossibly stern about it, as if the right cut of meat were the object of a quest. As soon as I saw him I felt light and happy, it seemed a very fine thing that we could find each other like this, on a bright morning, in the middle of all these harmless normal people gathering food. It made us seem harmless and normal also, it made me feel we belonged there as much as anyone else did.

"Protein," I said. "Big indigestible hunks of it."

There's always that moment when you wonder if you're about to make a total fool of yourself, catching somebody by surprise. Maybe they're going to blanch at the sight of you, or grit their teeth, or some other reflex before politeness sets in. But he didn't do anything of the sort. "Suzanne," he said, and he really did seem glad. "Look at this stuff," he went on, as if we'd been in the middle of a conversation, or perhaps it was the conversation he'd been having with himself. He showed me two anemic pork chops huddled beneath plastic sheeting. "It's all pallid and processed-looking. Like they grow pigs in tubes these days, and then slice them up. Like Wonder Bread."

"Wonder Pigs," I suggested, and we stood there grinning for no reason at all, except we were happy to see each other and happy we had something to make jokes about. People with carts pushed around us impatiently, as if they could tell just by looking at us that we were up to something illicit and ungrocery-like.

"So what are you doing here?"

"Saw your car," I said, immediately discarding all the excuses I had ready. It seemed silly now to pretend it had been a coincidence. "I'm stalking you."

"Well let's stalk on. You can help me have a nervous breakdown or something. I hate supermarkets. I hate deciding between Blasto and Vroomo."

"Be brave," I murmured. I liked hearing him talk like this.

"I've got to get a whole week's worth of stuff. And I'm not even hungry."

We continued our promenade down the meat counter. We were being slow about it, me because I wanted it to last as long as possible, Mike because he probably couldn't imagine doing anything less than thoroughly. He pulled a list from his pocket and frowned at it. I glanced at it once, then looked away. It was his wife's tidy, small-scale writing. I wasn't going to let it spoil things for me. I wasn't going to think anymore than I had to about the life he lived away from me, this food he would eat there, the shape of the lies he had to tell. I would not do intentional damage to myself.

"Chicken," Mike said. "That sounds easy enough." He tossed a package into his cart. "Except it's sort of blue. Why is it blue?"

"No fat on it," I said knowledgeably. "No taste. Here, look, here's a nice greasy yellow one. Take it."

"I'm not one bit hungry, you know."

It was a large store, one of those airy and brightly lit food palaces, odorless, whispering with Muzak. Even as crowded as it was now, it still managed to look spacious and gleaming. I wasn't like Mike, I enjoyed shopping, whether it was someone else's or my own. I enjoy weighing out onions and picking through lettuces, I like the feeling of abundance and variety. That's what the stores count on, of course, the illusion people get of wallowing in more food than they'll ever need. I like peering into other people's baskets and marveling at what they buy: six cans of generic pork and beans, frozen waffles, bales of potato chips. I like rummaging around in bins of oranges and opening egg cartons to check for cracks, the way I've always been taught to. I don't really understand people who turn up their noses at supermarkets and go around from one little store to another, looking for the runniest cheese or the brownest eggs and so on. I like everything in one place, I like great heaping greedy wasteful vistas.

So all in all I was having a fine time, berating Mike for his taste in packaged baloney and bland yellow mustard, being playful and jolly about it all. So was Mike. "How can anyone who drinks instant coffee pretend to know anything about food?" he complained, and I made a face at him. I remember catching a glimpse of us in the long angled mirrors above the fruits and vegetables — they do that so it seems like more food, you know — and thinking how nice we looked together. We were a handsome young couple out for a jaunt in the land of plenty, we were giggling and carrying on as if it were our heart's desire to be here, pushing a balky cart through acres of food. They could have put us in a commercial. Which goes to show you that anyone enjoying themselves too enormously is probably up to no good. And if you looked at us closely enough, there must have been something strained and self-conscious about us, something a little too edgy and bright, a little aspect of performance to it all. There must have been something for the Sugar Plum Fairy to notice. I don't believe in God or Fate, but I do believe in the uncanny targeting instincts of crazy people.

I saw her first, but not, I guess, before she saw me. She was an unlikely looking crazy lady at first glance. She was well-dressed enough, in a big knobby white wool coat with leather buttons. It was a thoroughly ugly coat, but expensive, the kind you see in clothing stores and marvel at, wondering who in the world would spend that much money to look that ugly. She had a crocheted white hat pulled all the way down over her skull so not one hair showed, and the hat was lumpy too, like the coat. She looked as if she'd been thoroughly beaten and had broken out all over in big fuzzy bumps. There was the hat, and the coat, and the eyeglasses. Oversized no-color frames, with thick lenses that magnified her eyes enormously. Still, you wouldn't have looked twice at her, wouldn't have thought she was anything more than another middle-aged lady gone to seed and tricked out in expensive bad taste. You wouldn't have looked twice at her if she hadn't been eating the bag of sugar.

You've seen people in the grocery nibbling on a grape, or maybe a mother opens a pack of cookies to keep her child from whining. It wasn't like that. Once I even saw a woman drinking little bottles of anise extract off the shelves for the alcohol, and that's sad and dotty enough, but at least she tried to be sneaky about it. The Sugar Plum Fairy was just standing in front of — cereals, I think it was — with a five-pound bag of sugar in the crook of her arm, dipping into it as if it were popcorn. It was no easy thing. She was pinching it between her thumb and forefinger, and ducking her head down to meet it halfway, and of course she was spraying and dribbling sugar all over the place. Her lips were big and colorless, and nuzzling their way through the sugar as avidly as a horse's. That's the way she looked, if you can picture it all.

As I say, she spotted me first. Me, not Mike. I must have been saying something, something that got her attention, because by the time we were rolling her way she was already staring straight at me. She wasn't blocking my path, not technically, because there was plenty of room in the aisle, but her looming, lumpy white bulk made me veer the cart away instinctively. She fell in step with me, shuffling alongside.

"See," she said. "I'm all in white," and it took both of us, Michael and me, a minute to realize she was talking to us.

"What?" said Mike. Your ear isn't listening for things like that, strangers piping up out of nowhere, and besides it was hard to understand her. She mumbled, and the sugar sprayed in all directions.

"It's because I'm getting married."

She was looking straight at me, though Mike was the one who was bending towards her attentively, still trying to understand her. I'd already caught on, *Crazy lady,* and I was yanking the cart to one side, trying to lose her.

"White is purity. Everybody knows that." She was speaking more clearly now. It was as if she were remembering how it was done. Her big colorless lips were only inches from my face.

I pushed the cart on past her, around the corner. Maybe it wasn't very fair of me, bolting on Mike like that, but such people always unnerve me. The street crazies. Usually they want to warn you about something. The poison in your food, the space ships, the FBI microphones in your teeth, the television leaking X rays, the wrath of God. This one was only getting married, but I didn't want to hear any more about it.

After a minute Mike caught up with me, looking amused. "There's sugar all over my coat," he said. And there was, little trails of it caught in the creases and sifting into the pockets. He flicked at it, but that only served to redistribute it more evenly.

"What did she do, throw it at you?"

"No, just spilled it. Maybe we should get her some rice instead. What's the matter?"

"I'm sorry. I just can't handle things like that. I never can."

"They're harmless. There ought to be room in the world for people who want to get married in grocery stores. The mildly loony."

"I know." It didn't seem worthwhile trying to debate him on his own turf, him knowing all the data, the literature, the theory and practice of community mental health. "What happens to people like that?"

He shrugged. "These days, mostly medication."

"She looks like she must have a home somewhere. And she's — well, *adequately* dressed. Still, you wonder."

"Here, you can ask her yourself."

The Sugar Plum Fairy appeared at the end of our aisle, shuffling towards us. It's hard to say if she was in active pursuit of us or not. She was moving sideways, crab fashion, and she didn't appear to be looking at anything in particular. I wondered why the store workers didn't kick her out. She was making a fair-sized mess with the sugar. She wasn't eating it by now, she seemed to have lost interest in it, and one open corner spilled sugar whenever she stooped or swung around. We were in the frozen foods aisle. The Sugar Plum Fairy stopped in front of one of the big glass-fronted cages and was peering into it.

"Orange juice," Mike said, consulting his list, and we navigated slowly upstream. Behind us the woman was still transfixed by the display of packaged ice cream bricks.

Then, just as we were rolling away, she was in our path again. There was a crust of sugar on her upper lip. "I'm getting married."

I think I smiled. Nod, uh huh, smile, keep moving. She wasn't smiling at all.

"It's a secret," the Sugar Plum Fairy said. It was then I noticed how enormously the glasses magnified her watery and insignificant eyes.

"We won't tell anybody," said Mike pleasantly. Then, to me, "I forgot spaghetti. You can go get in line if you want."

And then he was gone, pushing his way up the crowded aisle. The Sugar Plum Fairy and I headed for the checkout. She'd firmly adopted me by now. There didn't seem to be much I could do about it. I should be a good sport. She gave me the creeps but I would be a good sport. Mike was right, she was harmless. Maybe she was even happy. She didn't seem to care if I answered her or not, in fact, answers might interrupt the intricacies of her discourse. I saw right then how people might end up talking to mirrors, trees, park benches, and so on; it would be a sort of natural progression. "White food," she was saying in my ear, "is always best for you."

Everybody in the store seemed to have migrated to the checkouts all at once, the way it always seems to happen when you're in a hurry. I found a slot manned by one of those reliable, wizened middle-aged clerks, the kind who can hurl groceries with the speed of light. The Sugar Plum Fairy was right behind me. I wasn't looking at her, I was busy with the groceries, or at least trying to look as if I were busy. I could hear her murmuring: ". . . oatmeal. milk. cream cheese. bread, if you take the crusts off." She touched my arm just above the elbow. Like everything else about her, her grip was vague and somehow wooly. "I'm getting married," she said, "but it will be a marriage of purity."

I moved my arm free. It was exasperating, like being harassed by a child, perhaps, someone who didn't know his or her own weakness. Where was Mike? I craned my neck around, searching through the crowds and the blur of merchandise. Behind me the Sugar Plum Fairy was saying, now in an almost conversational, chatty tone, "I was married once before. It wasn't pure, though. I caught a disease."

I wondered if anyone else had noticed the unusual flavor of our conversation. But people only stood, or looked into *National Enquirers,* or rummaged through the chewing gum. I was almost done unloading the groceries and I squeezed through to the front of the cart, putting it between us. The Sugar Plum Fairy didn't move, just stayed square in the middle of the checkout lane, as if she'd forgotten all about me and everything else. Her mouth pouted in and out; she might have been tasting her lower lip. Behind her a woman was trying to maneuver into line. "Excuse me," she was saying to the Sugar Plum Fairy's broad fuzzy motionless back. "Excuse me."

Then Mike was beside me, brandishing his box of spaghetti, looking cheerful and mussed. He'd detoured around the blockade in the aisle and was trying to insert the spaghetti into the rolling parade of groceries. "You'd think," he said, "that none of these hordes had eaten in weeks."

"I'm going to wait outside for you," I told him.

I didn't look behind me on my way out but I heard the noise of a cart rattling in the chute. "Excuse me."

Outside the sun bounced from roof to roof of the parked cars, heavily, as if the reflections had weight. I shielded my eyes. Mike's car was unlocked and I got in the passenger side. What happened to people like that? They stood and stood until somebody told them to move. They sent poetry in secret code to the President. They discovered new planets, visible only in the sky seen through the crook of their elbows. They made symphonies out of the music of stick against gravel.

Mike's windshield was dirty. Big dusty freckles turned the sunlight hazy. Once Mike got back there wouldn't be much time to talk, not with the groceries melting and dripping all over the place. There was never enough time to do anything right.

The Sugar Plum Fairy's broad white hesitant shape was moving through the parking lot. At first I thought she was coming after me, I have to admit I even lowered myself a little in my seat, but no, she was only traveling in a series of half circles and detours around the parked cars. I watched her stumbling up against hoods and fenders. She looked like some barely animate snow figure melting in the brightness. She was still a little distance away, a couple of aisles, when I saw that her mouth was covered with blood.

Bright red, though some of it already seemed smeared and

drying. It outlined and enlarged her lips like a clown's. Every so often she touched a fist to her mouth, as if she were coughing. She was past me now on the far side of the lot. The sun caught her eyeglasses as she swung her head from side to side, turning the lenses opaque.

I got out of the car. I looked around for Mike, no sign of him. It was a perfectly normal featureless middle-class street, zoned for office and residential, streaming with efficient traffic, and there weren't any police, let alone mental health workers loitering around. The Sugar Plum Fairy was making her elliptical way toward the curb. "Ma'am?" I called after her. "Ma'am?"

Then Mike was wrestling his cart awkwardly toward the car. "What happened in there?" I said before he was close enough to quite understand me. "What happened with that woman?"

"The sugar lady? Nothing happened."

"Did somebody hit her or something? She's all bloody."

"Where?"

I pointed over my shoulder. The Sugar Plum Fairy had reached the perimeter of the parking lot.

"No, I mean where was she bleeding?"

"Her mouth. All over her mouth. Shouldn't somebody do something?" I wasn't entirely sure if I meant us.

"Well, let's go have a look." He began shoveling his grocery sacks into the back seat. He seemed to enjoy my dithering about something like this. He seemed to enjoy the chance to be competent in an emergency. I imagined him, the good husband, being splendid when the water pipes froze or the car caught on fire.

It was difficult to maneuver through traffic but she had a head start on us, she'd already crossed one street. "What are we supposed to do?" I said. "If she's hurt, I mean. We can't just stuff her in the car and take her to a hospital, can we? Not if she doesn't want to go." This was a mistake, I was sure of it. It always is, trying to save people from themselves.

"First things first," said Mike, meaning, I suppose, that I should shut up and let him handle it. We were stopped at a light. I could no longer see her white lumpy shape ahead.

"I expect she went home or something, I expect she lives around here," I said, trying not to sound too hopeful.

Mike said nothing, only inched the car forward, and when the intersection finally unclogged, swung round the corner where we'd last seen her. The sidewalks were empty. "Hell and death."

"Look," I said, pointing.

The Sugar Plum Fairy was in a kind of alley space between two buildings, stooping over something on the ground. The alley was half pavement and half beat-down dirt edging an apartment building. She was looking through a basement window, bending over or attempting to. The layers of coat bunched around her hips and waist and she had her feet straddled wide apart to keep her balance.

Mike pulled into the alley but stopped the car near the street. "See," I said. "Her mouth."

"OK, let's just try it," he said, and I could tell when it came right down to it that he was as uncertain as I was, for all his professional credentials, or perhaps because of them. His work was with charts and statistics, graphs and reports, nothing that prepared you to go out and drag even harmless crazies in off the street. I wanted to tell him it was all right, he didn't have to be in charge, didn't have to be responsible, but he looked damned well determined to be responsible. I knew him well enough to see that.

We got out of the car and trudged along the pavement, and the woman saw us right away. She turned her oversized, hairless head towards us, so you could see the blank glass framing her eyes, and the red smeared mouth, and then, quicker than I would have imagined, she regained her balance and scuttled away.

"What," I said, and Mike looked confused also. I suppose we both imagined she'd recognize us and come bounding towards us, her confidantes of just a few minutes ago. Instead she was stumping along as fast as she could, disappearing behind the apartment building. We followed after her. Having come this far, there didn't seem to be any choice, though I was heartily wishing one of us had enough sense to retreat.

A few parked cars, a dumpster spilling trash, some over-grown weed-trees and scrub hedge at the back of the lot. No crazy lady. Had she gone inside? Maybe she did live here, this was her burrow. "Enough," I said. "Enough. Let's . . ."

Mike touched my arm and I followed his gaze. She was squatting down between two parked cars, you could see the drooping hem of her ugly coat behind a wheel. "Oh Christ," I said. "Let's leave."

"Why?" he said, looking irritated, as if I'd interrupted him to ask about the weather.

"Because it won't do any good."

"If she's hurt . . ."

"Then let's just go back to the car and wait. This is like when I was a kid, and used to bring in baby birds that fell out of trees. Well not exactly alike, but anyway the birds all died."

I'm trying to show how it was the next Wrong Move be-tween us, what happened then, how we wound up turning it all against each other. I couldn't really explain to Mike why it all seemed such a mistake to me, so grotesque, why we shouldn't be terrifying her with our good intentions. And I was growing an-noyed with Mike's professional-psychologist manner, as if he really knew what the hell he was doing, as if any of them ever do. I was scared, I'll even own up to being cowardly, but I knew we didn't have any business here. We were emissaries from some world of only normal pretense, normal suffering, we were out of our depth. I tried again.

"Come on," I said. "We'll only make things worse. She's scared, this is awful, let's go."

Again he gave me that irritated look; he didn't even bother to answer. That aggravated me more than anything he could have said. I hate it when men refuse to argue with you. Mike was ad-vancing cautiously towards her, picking his way around the un-clean-looking puddles on the cement. The water had a scurf of oil, old soapsuds, and other less identifiable filth. I wondered if the woman would get her coat dirty.

I was trailing along behind Mike, reluctantly, not wanting to admit to being there at all, I suppose. I couldn't see her from my new position, only the snouts of the parked cars. It was still bright noon, still sunshine and dazzle. I must have looked away for a moment, I always do, I'm the one who never sees the shooting star, the rare warbler, the trick play. By the time I looked again, three things were happening: The Sugar Plum Fairy was charging through the waste of sticks and trash behind the cars like some big, broken-winged bird, tangling herself hopelessly. Mike was hobbling on one foot and shouting after her uselessly, things like Wait, and Stop. And a loud, oversized old green Chevy pulled into the lot, rock 'n' roll music roaring from its open windows.

The Chevy contained a young — very young — sullen and uncurious-looking couple, who nevertheless drifted over and converged with the rest of us on the Sugar Plum Fairy. She had tripped herself up in the knotty, winter-naked brush and was down on her hands and knees. She was still trying to scrabble away from us, but she'd gotten so hopelessly mired, all she could do was shift her weight from knee to knee. Her coat was hiked up in back and gray loose flesh swayed over the tops of her stockings.

What happened, everyone seemed to be saying all at once, or maybe it was just me saying it over and over. Mike clutched at his ankle, grimacing. He'd turned it, he said, for no reason at all, it just went out, she must have thought he was trying to fling himself on her. I was attempting to hoist the Sugar Plum Fairy up from her knees. No easy matter; she was so large, so swathed in layers of cloth, and the ground so cluttered I couldn't get any purchase on her. I got the boy from the car to help me. He and his girl had been watching us all this time like we were something on television, but once enlisted he tugged at one arm and I the other and we hauled her more or less upright.

"What's that on her mouth?" the girl asked with sudden interest. She and the boy looked almost exactly alike. It must have been their hair.

"Kool-Aid," I said. "Cherry, I think." Several of the little crumpled paper packets had fallen from her coat pocket. The fingers of one hand were stained the same gorgeous red.

"We thought she was hurt," Mike said to the boy and girl,

as if we owed them an explanation. They had retreated back into their original remote spectatorship, as if none of us were that interesting but there was nothing better to watch. I don't remember if they were chewing gum or not. It certainly seems like they should have been chewing gum.

I was making little brushing gestures, trying to set the woman to rights. Her knit hat was pushed over one ear and you could see her fine, almost colorless hair. It looked exactly like grass that's been growing under a mat. "Don't worry," I said to her. "It'll wash off." I was talking about the Kool-Aid.

All this time she seemed to be trying not to breathe. Her eyes were open but she wasn't seeing anything, it was all reflections going back in. "Lady?" Mike said. "Are you all right?"

"Of course she's not all right. Look at her." She looked as if she were trying to make herself invisible.

"Just shut up, Suzanne. It's OK. Nobody's going to hurt you."

The Sugar Plum Fairy made a noise in her throat — something liquid and ominous — and we all stepped back. She bent over from the waist, vomiting. I tried not to watch.

"For God's sake, get her a Kleenex or something," Mike said after a while.

She smelled syrupy. I scrubbed at her face with the only Kleenex I had, a big shredding wad of it. Her face felt loose and pouchy, like it might slide off if I rubbed too hard. She stood with her arms at her side, as passive and unwieldy as an oversized doll. "There," I said, feeling useless, once the Kleenex had been exhausted. "There now."

She recognized me then. I don't think she had before. "Impurities," she said in a distinct voice, and shook her head sadly.

We watched her walk out to the street. At least she could still walk. Behind me I could hear Mike audibly nursing his ankle. I ignored him. At the sidewalk the woman stumped off in the direction she'd been heading, away from the grocery. I was glad for that. I was glad she was able to keep to her appointed rounds.

"So why are you angry?" Mike said once we were seated in his car again.

"I'm not. I don't know. Oh hell."

"Is it because I wound up looking like a jerk? I'm sorry. I'd really like to know. I'd like to know what I was supposed to do instead."

"Maybe you could be the one to clean up the mess instead of just giving the orders."

"Maybe," he said. "But that's not it. That's not it at all."

"I'm just upset that things like that happen. It's nobody's fault."

"Bullshit. I truly find this interesting. I'm not even sure I can convey the extent of my interest. Sure it's my fault."

"You don't have to start shouting."

"Since when did your ears get so delicate. I just want to know why it's my fault."

"Look, Mike, sometimes there just isn't a right thing to do. Sometimes your good intentions just blow up in your face."

"She scared you," he said, quietly now. We were back in the grocery store lot and he pulled up next to my car, left his engine running. "She scared you and I couldn't make her go away or be well for you."

I didn't say anything. I felt tired, more then tired. My head ached from the glare. I didn't want to think about anything anymore. I closed my eyes and squeezed out all the light. I opened them and said, "Starting over. Right now. Nice to see you."

He looked at me cautiously for a moment. "Nice to see you too."

"I'm going home now. I'm going to put a good record on, have a drink, take a long bath. Maybe paint my nails or make a soufflé. Something entirely useless."

"I'll call you. I'll call you tomorrow." And we squeezed hands instead of kissing, because you could never know who might be watching.

I did just what I told him. I went home and put on my favorite Vivaldi record. I lit a scented candle and poured a glass of sherry. I washed my hair and coiled it up turban-style in a towel while I gave myself a facial. When I was through, although I wasn't going anywhere, I put makeup back on. I drew big smoky eyes, I used all the little trays and tubes of powders and creams with their ridiculous, opulent names: plum, raisin, heather, velvet brown. I drew cheekbones and lips. Honey, frosted peach, burgundy.

It didn't work at all. My skin kept leaching through, an indifferent, patchy surface. My eyes were puffy at the hinges and raw in the corners. They seemed positively anatomical to me, like an illustration in a medical text. I took a step back from the mirror and tried without success to find some angle or trick of light that might change things. I tried smiling; more anatomy. It was a purely muscular effort.

I was not beautiful. Over time, and through sheer force of will, I had made myself any number of other things: vivacious, arresting, modish, prepossessing. I was not beautiful, and maybe I was not in love either. Maybe all this time I had only been trying to strike the right pose.

And finally I thought of my crazy lady, wandering the streets with her blank eyes and her white wool armor and her litany of fuzzy prayers. I thought that maybe she was meant to warn me of something after all, but that it hadn't really been necessary. I knew that I would never be like her, it was one thing I would never have to worry about. I would never lose myself like that. I would not let myself be pitiable or ridiculous, or even embarrassed. There was something in me that would not allow it, something that stayed intact through everything. I wondered if that was all people really meant by love, that willingness to lose yourself. The craziness, the bleeding and jibbering and mess. It would never happen to me that way. It was no one's fault. It was simply the way things were. I picked up one of my lipsticks, Totally Red I think it was called. Watching the mirror closely, I began to draw a bright thick circle around my mouth.

CHAPTER
4

Flora saw him as soon as she walked outside. He was standing at the edge of the brick courtyard, smoking. And since she knew of no other way to begin, she said, "Suzanne sent me to ask if you needed a ride."

He stared at her. The light from the front entrance seemed to dissolve at some point just beyond him. His face looked grainy and remote, like something in an old photograph, somebody already dead. In a passion of cowardice and embarrassment, she saw that he had been expecting Suzanne, maybe had even mistaken her for Suzanne until she spoke. Now he was trying not to look visibly humiliated in front of her. "Thanks," he said finally. He mashed his cigarette underfoot, as if he'd become conscious of using it as a prop or distraction. "If you're sure it won't be out of your way."

"Oh no. No trouble at all." Thank God for manners. Flora knew she would have gladly driven him into the next county, if that would keep things rolling along painlessly. He gave her an address in one of the newer, glossier parts of town. Flora knew it only as a district where all the streets were laid out in curves and circles, and named after things like larks and bluebells. She told him again that it would be no trouble. She was sounding positively joyous about it, she thought. He arranged himself, with some difficulty, in the cramped front seat of her car. It made her nervous, having this large and gloomy man sitting so close. She felt twitchy, all fluttering skin. It wasn't even sex, she decided. Just proximity. She wasn't used to it, she'd been living in a physical vacuum. Now it was sex. That certainly hadn't taken long. Ah Lord she was vulnerable, she was at risk, next she'd probably start riding crowded buses just to rub up against strangers' bodies, she was a sitting duck. Goose, she told herself sternly. Drive.

"Have you lived here long?" she heard herself saying. Pieces of meaningless politeness kept falling out of her mouth, like the girl in the fairy tale who spit out snakes and toads.

"What?"

"Have you lived around here very long?"

"It's a new house."

"No, I meant in town. Have you lived in town long? Me, I've been here all my life. A couple of lifetimes, it seems like."

"Nine years. Ten."

Flora waited for him to say, I'm originally from Little Rock, Arkansas, or, I'm from out East. He didn't. She said, "Actually, I was born in St. Louis, but my family moved here when I was just two."

If she kept on, she'd start talking about her allergies or her favorite colors. He was still sitting there looking massively uncomfortable, looking like he might at any moment put a foot through the windshield. She decided to give up on talk entirely, even if that meant there would be nothing to distract her from her alarmingly sportive body. This was all a mistake, she was wrong to be here, a witness to his embarrassment, the least she could do for him was pretend to be inanimate. But then he said, "I'm sorry. I'm about three beats off the pace."

"Pardon?"

"Making conversation. You'd think I was learning a new language."

"Oh that's all right. I understand, I mean, I probably talk too much anyway. I'm like one of those dogs that licks people to death, I'm a social pest."

"I'm sure you're not," he said, and though she didn't dare look in his direction, he was at least attempting to be pleasant. He was not a person cursed with manners, she had observed. Oh but you're wrong, she wanted to say, I'm dreadful, I'm entirely devious, I only pretend to be a nice person. I am here, or rather, you are here with me, under false pretenses. I am not a helpful bystander, I am doing this because your ex-lover, my (ex?) friend, dared me to. I am doing this out of boredom and wounded pride, I am seeing if you have anything to offer me.

Monster, Flora told herself, but it wouldn't stick, she didn't believe it for a minute. Whatever part of her she relied on to feel guilty or judgmental wasn't functioning. Should, ought, do, don't, what was all that except a way of denying what she really wanted, what she really was? What she really wanted was him. She wanted some natural disaster to intervene and trap them together, an earthquake maybe, or a voice from the sky ordering everyone on the planet's surface to make instantaneous and violent love. She wanted something to happen that wouldn't be her fault. Chicken. Sissy. She should make something happen. Pretend to run out of gas? Suzanne, she thought, would go about this differently. Had no doubt gone about it differently.

"Turn left here," Michael Maggio said, and Flora realized that they'd reached his neighborhood. While she'd been having this interesting subterranean wrangle with herself, she'd apparently still been driving toward their destination, steer, stop, go, look, aim, a whole series of complicated tasks. Fascinating, how the brain managed these things, kept you from thinking you were doing something else entirely, baking a cake or playing baseball. Flora thought that was probably what happened to schizophrenics. Their brain told them they were doing something else entirely.

"Whoa," said Michael, and Flora apologized. She'd taken the turn rather too fast.

The streets weren't streets. They were something else entirely. They were Drives, Lanes, Courts, Circles, or Ways. The roads curved and looped. The houses were large and somehow overassertive. They jutted and loomed and projected, they were all angles and overhangs and enormous blank fields of glass. It was how modern architecture made things look expensive, she realized. Left here, right here, Michael Maggio directed her, and Flora obediently orbited. Bonnie Brook, Laurel, Heather. All very botanical and inappropriate.

"I'm afraid I don't really know my way around here," she

said, backing out of a dead end. She'd righted when she should have lefted.

"Oh that's OK. Nobody does. I see people circling for hours. Days. The Lost Patrol."

They were silent then, and Flora thought they'd probably gotten all possible mileage out of the topic. But he said, "It's a little like Disneyland."

"It is?"

"I meant, it's all such an artifact, this landscape. The developer even brought in extra dirt to make hills."

"It is sort of new and shiny, isn't it?" It was the closest they'd come so far to having a normal conversation, and she hurried to keep it going. "But where should people live instead, what's — you know — indigenous or genuine."

"Around here? Barns."

"Root cellars, maybe. No, trailer parks. Which way do I go?"

"Bear right. It's just —"

He stopped abruptly. Flora followed his gaze. The house on the corner had every light burning, cellar to attic, you would have said in another type of architecture. None of the curtains were drawn. It looked rowdy and unnatural, all those bare windows with the light escaping. Flora caught glimpses of picture frames, wallpaper, bookshelves. Doll-house rooms. Nobody moving inside. The front door stood open, a slice of light.

Mike was getting out of the car, even as she pulled up to the curb. He hadn't told her to follow him. He hadn't told her not to. She tracked across the lawn, wobbling on the soft ground. He was already inside when she reached the open door. She could hear his voice in a room beyond her, then he passed through the hallway again, glancing at Flora but not stopping, maybe not even seeing her, disappearing again.

Flora took a few paces, found herself looking into the kitchen, Nothing. Lights blazing, everything clean and bare. Nothing that reminded you of food. She heard feet, voices overhead, but when had he gone upstairs? Flora tried to retreat to the hallway, found herself, inexplicably, in a blank corridor with a closed door at the end. Come on, she told herself sternly. It isn't that big a house, and in fact she wasn't lost at all. Two steps and she was back at the front door. A staircase led up, but she could only see as far as the first turning. It was a new house all right. You could tell from the way it still smelled of plaster and bareness.

There was a heavy indistinct noise from upstairs, like furniture being moved. She should leave, he was dragging his wife around by the hair, it was burglars, murder. Flora moved toward the door again, not really deciding anything. Things were decided for her. Feet drummed in the hallway above her, then on the stairs. It was Elizabeth. Flora had expected her to be in some sort of undress or disarray, a torn nightgown perhaps, but she was wearing jeans and a sweater, even shoes. She looked at Flora with perfect blankness. Flora thought she probably didn't remember her.

Then Mike was downstairs also, looking at her as if he too had forgotten who she was, and Flora said "I'm sorry. If you don't need me I'll leave now."

"Is this another one?" said Elizabeth. "Is this the new one?"

"I'm sorry," said Flora again.

"Is she spending the night?" said Elizabeth.

"You can apologize for that," said Mike.

"For what. I asked a question. I'd like to go about things differently this time, that's all. So I'm asking. What's the good word?"

"I gave him a ride home," said Flora. All at once she was wet everywhere, she could smell her own sweat.

"There's nothing she has to explain," said Mike.

"Well that's one way to go about it," said Elizabeth. "That's really very thoughtful of you." Then, to Mike, "I can't find my purse. Did you see it upstairs?"

"Oh stuff it."

"I'm perfectly calm, see? I'm leaving. You're bringing them into the house now."

She did look calm. She looked entirely calm and entirely hazardous, all at once. Calmly, she widened her perfect crimson mouth into a grin and showed Flora her teeth biting against each other.

"Do we have to keep doing this?" asked Mike. "Don't you

get tired of embarrassing yourself, Elizabeth? Do we have to go through this every time?"

"If you keep finding new ones we do."

"Screw you. I met her tonight. I only met her tonight." Mike looked at Flora, and she could see he was remembering their earlier meeting. It was an inadvertent lie, but a lie just the same.

"Oh, you're just getting started. Excuse me. How thought- less of me. Always blundering in." Then she wasn't paying atten- tion to them any more, she was looking toward the stairs. The next instant she was climbing them, and Flora heard a child crying. It was a thin, bleating sound, without much air behind it.

"I didn't know you had children," Flora said to Michael Maggio once they were alone. It came out sounding as if she were accusing him of it.

"Only one." He might have been apologizing. For not hav- ing more? For having any in the first place? No, she was imag- ining things, they were both so shell shocked, nothing made sense. They stared at each other for a moment more, then Flora said, "Well . . ."

"No. Don't go yet."

She stared at him. What did he want her to do?

"Not yet. I'm sorry." He was whispering, and bending to- wards her, elaborately careful not to change position. He looked like a very clumsy ventriloquist. "If you'll just stay a minute. It'll be OK now. Just . . ." Elizabeth was coming downstairs again. Her feet made clopping noises.

"Guess who's hungry?" she said liltingly. The child in her arms bleated again. Its sex was indistinguishable. It had a red fat face and wet blue eyes. It didn't look at all like either of them.

"Hello," said Flora to the baby, since it seemed she was ex- pected to say something. She was one of those adults who find themselves making the most appalling grimaces and noises around babies, for lack of anything else to do with them. "Hello there, what's your name?"

"Robin," said Elizabeth. No help at all, as far as sexing it. Even the child's nightgown and blanket were a neutral yellow. It looked overlarge somehow. It was nearly bursting with redness and fatness. Elizabeth juggled the baby on her hip, cooing to it. Everything had changed, gone instantly civilized. All of them now seemed to be beaming at the baby, clucking and making faces. "Who's got a chin?" said Elizabeth. "Who's got a chinny chin chin?"

Flora caught Michael Maggio's eye. He crooked his mouth at her, the bad ventriloquist again, as if he were trying to shrug invisibly. He was standing next to his wife and child, a noncommittal but necessary component of this domestic scene. "Why don't we make some coffee?" said Elizabeth. "It only takes a second."

"All right," said Flora, and they all trooped obediently into the kitchen. She felt a little dazed, something was wrong, changing too fast. They were smoothing things over, she told herself. Surely if they could drink coffee and talk baby-talk together, then they could pretend none of the rest of it had happened.

It was a perfect kitchen. Flora could see that now. "A fresh pot," Elizabeth directed. As the two of them, Mike and Elizabeth, moved back and forth, hauling out mugs, sugar, jars of green and yellow mash for the baby, Flora found a stool to perch on, trying to look inobtrusive. Why did she always end up in strangers' kitchens, spying on their lives? Counter space. There was lots of counter space. There were islands and peninsulas of beige Formica. There were ranks of wood-grain cupboards. A set of stoneware canisters. Did anyone, Flora wondered, really keep tea in the one marked Tea? There were any number of other things on display: wooden spoons, potholders in the shape of animals, calico place-mats on the table, copper kettle on the stove. It all reminded Flora of a Crate and Barrel store. She was being a reverse snob. Just because she cooked out of a tatty kitchen with a homemade rope of garlic on the wall and a bloodstain over the sink didn't mean the rest of the world had to, there was nothing inherently virtuous in shabbiness or inherently sinful in coordinated dishcloths. So Flora told herself, but she didn't really believe it. She believed it was, if not exactly sinful, at least silly, she mistrusted display, mistrusted anything that bristled with newness and ornament, mistrusted microwaves, food processors, electric can openers, toaster ovens, even the Mr. Coffee that Mike was now activating. She romanticized inconvenience, she decided, but only as much inconvenience as she was willing to tolerate. She did not cook over an open fire or pump her water from a well. She was a hypocrite, a hopeless case, she was probably only jealous of people with nice things. She was trying very hard to keep herself thinking about kitchens, nothing else.

"Coffee in a jiff," said Mike, and Flora, taking her tone from him, said, "Great. I could use some." She tried not to sound too hearty and animated.

"I probably shouldn't be drinking any this late in the evening," he went on, "but I really can't resist. It's worse than alcohol."

"At least it smells better," said Flora. They seemed doomed to beat harmless subjects into the ground.

"I didn't drink coffee the whole time I was pregnant," said Elizabeth. "Just fruit juices."

"We bought a juicer," explained Mike. "It has two dozen attachments. You could probably make juice out of tennis balls with it."

Elizabeth was bundling the baby into the high chair. Its legs were rolls of red fat, it seemed to be smothering in its own flesh. It was really a most distressing-looking child, but then, what did she know about children, maybe they were supposed to look like this. Elizabeth fussed with bibs and spoons, and the baby smiled at her through veils of spittle.

"How old is Robin?" asked Flora.

"Eight months now. Eight months this week. Bananas. You like bananas, don't you, pumpkin pie?"

"Cream? Sugar?" asked Mike, who was making a great deal of clatter with the mugs. Flora told him she took it black. He still looked haggard, edgy, but for all Flora knew it was his natural state. For all she knew, this was how they always spent their evenings, berating each other in front of witnesses, then settling down for a nightcap. Mike put the coffee in front of Flora and she thanked him, swallowing it straight off. It was terrible coffee, it tasted both oily and burnt.

"Big bite," said Elizabeth. "One more." The baby was making a face of acute affliction. Strained bananas leaked out of its mouth. It was not unlike the face Flora would have liked to make at the coffee.

"Do you have children?"

It was Elizabeth asking. She was smiling. Flora wondered what the right answer was.

"No," she said. "No, I don't."

It seemed to be the right thing to say. "Well," said Elizabeth consolingly. "I wouldn't worry. There's plenty of time yet for you."

Bitch. Why should people assume you wanted children at all, or that you were envious of theirs? Flora smiled and ducked into her coffee mug. Apparently that was why she was here. She was meant to bear witness to them as a family unit, to observe all the cooing and clucking and doting and the new floor tile and the pottery-handled spoons and matching mugs. She was brought in here to be envious, that was the whole point of things. Bitch. I don't want your overstuffed child or your unfaithful husband or your juice machine. I don't want your bad coffee or your bad marriage. It's all pathetic.

Flora looked up at Mike then. Yes, he seemed to be saying with his eyes. It's pathetic. I'm sorry.

She managed to get the rest of the coffee down. "I really have to be going. Thanks again." When you began thanking people for their hostility, and thanking them profusely, it was surely time to go.

Elizabeth looked at Flora. You could almost forget how beautiful she was until she made you remember. She was making Flora remember now. "I always wanted children. Lots of them. Even when I was little. I wanted a family like in *The Sound of Music*. I used to make up lists of names for them."

Flora, who had already stood up, nodded. "I used to do that too." In fact she had, she'd done all such girls' rituals, though she couldn't remember any of the names. Do re me fa so la ti.

"Would you like to see Robin's room?" Elizabeth stood up also. "Here," she told her husband. "You finish with this. Make him eat some peas."

So it was a boy. That was good. Flora decided it made a better boy than girl. Elizabeth was already leading the way. Would she ever get out of here? Another room, well, she could manage that, couldn't she? Flora didn't even look at Mike, she was tired of furtive glances. She followed Elizabeth. Her jeans were new, the kind with elaborate embroidery across the behind. The embroidery was in the shape of thunderbirds. The jeans were tight, and the thunderbirds stretched and crumpled as Elizabeth climbed the stairs. They were really a quite unmatronly thing to wear. The carpet was pale blue and springy underfoot. The stairs were killing her. Elizabeth was at the top, waiting.

"Out of shape," said Flora, by way of apology. Elizabeth looked uncomprehending, or perhaps only uninterested. Flora was beginning to realize that the woman didn't hold conversations in the normal sense. There was no response, no exchange or give-and-take. As if she never really heard what anyone else said.

"It's this way," directed Elizabeth, sounding impatient.

"How sweet," said Flora once they reached the nursery. She probably would have said it anyway, it was expected of her, but it happened to be true. It was another perfect room, it was Babyland. Here the light was soft, the curtains drawn. There were pink lamps and white wallpaper with an old-fashioned ribbon pattern of ivy and flowers, and gingham, and swimming ducks, and clowns, and prancing circus elephants, and much more. The room smelled, very faintly, of rubber.

"It's lovely," said Flora, and since that didn't seem quite enough to say, "It's the one room that ought to be like this. I mean, be perfect."

"The wallpaper isn't really right. For a boy, I mean. I guess we'll have to change it when he gets older." Elizabeth was looking fixedly at the walls, her beautiful soft profile now melancholy. It was a gift, thought Flora, being able to look that soulful over the prospect of changing wallpaper, that photogenic and melting. "What is it boys ought to have on their walls. All I can think of is cars or soldiers. How stupid. Machines and violence. I don't want him to grow up with that."

"There's sports. Or animals. But I know what you mean."

"Stupid," repeated Elizabeth. "I don't want him to grow up into one of those little macho creeps. You know, the cowboy who loves the horse more than the girl."

"Or the cowboy who talks more to the horse than the girl."

"The cowboy who says he's going to call you next week and never does."

"The cowboy who doesn't know how to do his own laundry. Oh mercy." Flora was giggling by now, part amusement, part nervous release. It was an actual conversation. It was almost an exchange of ideas, maybe the woman wasn't even stupid. Flora realized she'd been comforted by the notion Elizabeth was stupid. It meant you had to take her less seriously. It meant that she somehow deserved to have her husband lusted over.

"Oh well." Elizabeth smiled, a little sourly, and pushed a hand into her hair. It was very fashionable hair, Flora decided, very artful, well suited for things like head tossing. Beside Elizabeth Flora felt faded, even a little seedy, entirely too limp and semi-blonde, an outmoded creature whose skirt was too long and definitely too flowered. "Oh well," Elizabeth went on, "there's only so much you can do, isn't there? I mean, the world takes over. Boys will be boys. Men will be boys."

"Yes," agreed Flora, cautiously now. If they began talking about men and their transgressions, things might get unpleasant again.

But Elizabeth seemed to have forgotten all that. She was looking around the room again, examining it. Was she wondering if it was perfect enough? How quiet everything was. The whole house was quiet. Flora, listening, heard no sound anywhere, no traffic from the street, no humming air or running water or other household machinery, no child's cry or father's voice. "Listen," said Elizabeth. "I can trust you, can't I?"

What Flora managed to say was that she hoped so.

"You're a nice person. I can tell you are."

Flora thought, I really must get my hair styled. And begin dressing better.

"What I mean is, you won't get Mike in trouble. You won't be bad for him."

There was a moment while they stared at each other, Elizabeth looking tired now, Flora — she couldn't imagine how her own face looked. Angry, she hoped. "I don't know what you mean," she said, as flatly as she could manage.

"Oh . . ." and Elizabeth seemed embarrassed. She turned and looked round the room again, as if for reassurance. "I just thought . . . it wouldn't be such a bad thing, someone I liked . . ." She shrugged and turned back to Flora, waiting.

"I don't think that was what you were saying before. When I got here." She would be polite, Flora decided, politeness was her only refuge. She was determined to force the woman into admitting her own contradictions. She was determined to make her *behave,* the way you would an aggravating child. Why should she be allowed to get away with saying such things, with manipulating people, with her calculated hysterias and calculated outrageousness?

"Oh. Well." Elizabeth laughed, a little breezy, almost affectionate laugh. "But I didn't know you then."

The house was so quiet. So bright, with all those lights there should have been noise and motion, it wasn't right at all . . . Elizabeth was still smiling. And what if it wasn't calculated, Flora thought, what if she believes what she says, this is all real to her, what she imagines has already happened, she knows me, we're great pals. There were people like that, weren't there? It happened. Electrical failures in the brain. Information not sorted or coded properly, wrong cue, wrong response. It happened, and maybe this was how it happened. Nuts. Mr. ———. What was his name, at the party, saying Nuts, so pleased with himself. She couldn't remember now, she was not sorting or coding well herself. And the hell of it was, Elizabeth wasn't entirely wrong about things, was she, not about adultery actual or adultery committed in the heart, she saw things right but said them wrong . . .

"Look," said Elizabeth. "Look, isn't this just precious?" She held up a pincushion, a calico doll with a big red yarn smile and a body skewered with pins.

"It is," said Flora, with more sincerity than she would have thought possible. She felt rather like the doll herself.

"I got it at a craft fair." Elizabeth made a vague gesture that included the room, and beyond. "I went a little crazy buying crafts. You should see the bathroom."

Mike was coming up the stairs with the baby. They heard his voice advancing, warning them. "Hop, hop, hoppity, hoppity."

Then he was peering in at the door. "So how's the tour going?"

Oh, swimmingly, your wife has been kind enough to agree to rental terms for you, poor bastard, you couldn't stand it down there alone, could you, you had to come check on us, you had to let us know you were coming so we could get our fists out of each other's hair if we had to. "It's a lovely room," said Flora.

Elizabeth held out her arms for the baby. It squirmed and kicked as it was being handed over, like a fish they were trying to land. (Flora still thought of it as *it*.) Once more they were all civilized by its presence, as if they had been transported into church. Mike and Elizabeth bent over the child in her arms and it crowed at them. Maybe it wasn't so ugly after all, just sort of old-fashioned and round, like the Campbell's Soup Kids. Pink light streamed from the lamp by the crib, and for a moment Flora saw the three of them blessed by light, by tranquility, a perfect silhouette. It was only a trick of light, she told herself. Only an approximation, a sentimental illusion. In another five minutes they could be screeching and clawing at each other all over again. Still she felt weary, watching that which excluded her. "I'll be going now," she said.

"I'll see you out." Mike looked over at Elizabeth. Once more she might have forgotten both of them. She was busy with the crib blankets, she only nodded.

Flora went down the stairs first. She could feel him behind her, an indistinct warmth. At the bottom of the steps she paused, she expected that to be it, but he opened the door for her and waited. He was coming out to the car with her. She didn't want him to. She didn't want anything else to happen. The night was very dark, almost blind. Their feet sounded clumsy and furtive, even on the soft lawn. He was a clumsy shadow beside her, a heavy shape that breathed too loudly. She tried to remember how she'd felt earlier, that prickle of sex. It all seemed like an accident now. It seemed like something that must have happened to someone else. She was stumbling with fatigue.

When they reached the car she turned and faced him. "Don't say it."

"What."

"Don't say you're sorry. Do you know how many times you've apologized to me since you've met me?"

"Well. But you didn't ask to find yourself in the middle of all this."

By all this, Flora supposed he meant his messes with women. He was rummaging around for a cigarette, lighting it, and the motion made him a little less shadowy and indistinct. Once again he had identifiable limbs, and a red ember mouth.

"In a way maybe I did," Flora said. "Ask for it, I mean. Maybe I'm one of those innocuous people who watches other people live. I've thought that before."

"That's not true. You're just better behaved than some of us."

"Why do you say that. It's just another way of apologizing. You don't even know me. You don't know me at all. I doubt if you ever will, either."

She was shaking, the night was colder than it had been. I am so tired, Flora thought, but it wasn't just that. It was some deeper bitterness. When he didn't speak — she had embarrassed him, she imagined — she said, "Although we were given permission, you know. Everyone's given us permission." She was behaving foolishly, she didn't care.

"What? What permission?"

She couldn't entirely retreat. She decided she would tell him half of it. "Oh, your wife just now told me she didn't much mind if the two of us . . ." Flora had been about to say, if the two of us got it on, or something else jaunty and crude, but she stopped short. Still, it seemed less awful somehow to tell him that his wife, rather than his mistress, had been the one offering him up.

"What did she say?"

"I'm sorry. I shouldn't even have mentioned it."

"Tell me what she said."

At least he sounded as if he believed her. At least he didn't seem to think she was making it all up. He seemed angry, but not at her. Flora said, "She told me I wouldn't be bad for you."

He turned and looked back at the house. It was still blazing away in the night. It looked rather like a ship under full sail, or perhaps a riverboat, gliding along a current of darkness. When he still didn't turn or speak, Flora asked, "Why did she say that?"

He only shook his head. Flora waited, one hand on the car door. She remembered Suzanne standing in just the same pose, that day in the parking lot. Well, but this was different, night instead of day, silence instead of speech, strangers not lovers, everything she did was a bad imitation of someone else. Then Mike spoke. "I don't know why she said it. I mean, I don't know what she really expects to happen. It's like she's playing out some scene in her head that no one else sees. I don't know why. I don't know anything about anything anymore."

"Maybe she wants to see how people react," suggested Flora, but she felt less wise and cynical than she sounded. It was all too sad, too grotesque, the blazing house floating toward catastrophe, or maybe steaming full speed ahead.

"She's a good mother. You can see that."

"Yes."

"She really is. No matter what else happens. She's always good with Robin, he makes all the difference."

They were silent. The silence was like a pool of liquid rising about them. Flora thought, he can't say more without saying too much. He can't go on and say, she's a good mother but a bad wife, you can see what I'm up against. I don't want to make excuses but you see what I'm up against. He can't say any of that. Flora couldn't decide if it was admirable of him or not, such restraint, such splendid verbal tact. What did tact matter when you blundered around behaving as unwisely as he had? She couldn't decide if she even liked him.

After a while he said, "So I suppose you've seen me at my absolute worst."

He spoke quietly. It wasn't asking for sympathy, it wasn't an attempt to display himself attractively. She could like that about him at least. He didn't use his unhappiness as bait.

He was still talking: "Funny way to get to know somebody. Sometimes it takes years, doesn't it, getting to see someone's absolute worst. Oh well. Lucky you. The short course."

Flora's eyes were adjusting to the darkness, she could see him quite well. He was gazing away from her, out over the lawn, his head lowered. That soft-looking hair. The eyes soft too. He was beautiful, she saw that now, why hadn't she done so right from the start? He was another woman's man. He was every woman's man, it seemed, except her own.

"Absolute worst," Flora said. "How does anyone ever know the worst they could be?"

"You're right. You could certainly keep working on it, couldn't you?" He held out his hand to her. Confused, Flora half shook, half grasped it, her fingers curling inside his. "Good night."

"Good night," she told him, and Drive, she told herself for the second time that night. Just drive.

When she thought about that evening — and she thought of very little else for some time afterwards — she couldn't decide how accidental her own part in it had been. Would anyone else have done just as well for them, she wondered, would they have heard the same arguments, been offered the same bad coffee, the same intimacy, even the same sporting chance at the man of the house? Of course they would, she told herself. She was only new meat, a fresh audience. They thrived on scenes and messiness, Suzanne said. Anyone would have done just as well.

But she didn't want to believe it. She wanted to believe instead that they had chosen her and her alone to hear their secrets, to be accused and appealed to, to become some part of their improbable and discordant lives. She wanted to be a part of it, of them. What did it mean that she thought of *them,* not *him.* Perhaps she didn't even want Michael purely for himself, as a man, but only as a component of some glorious emotional violence. And just what was the answer to them, how could two people make each other so thoroughly miserable? Among other things, she wondered why he tolerated his wife's outbursts.

Something that she had not wanted to admit was that he seemed faintly afraid of her.

Flora supposed she believed that other people were always more interesting than herself. She was a statistical median. Once you knew her age, sex, race and educational level, it seemed to Flora, you could deduce everything else about her from her marital status to her shoe size. She was the perfect marketing research profile. It was a kind of protective coloration, blending in so well with one's background. But perhaps she was bored with that self, just as her marriage too had expired of boredom. Perhaps she was ready to become some new and unrecognizable creature, if not an Elizabeth, if not a Suzanne, at least a kind of gaudy moth trailing the wreckage of her old life behind her, old habits, old marriage, even the old car she'd so thoroughly and ritually destroyed.

One summer several years back she and Gordon had lived in a frowzy rented house in a neighborhood of college students and even younger, less identifiable types who had a fondness for loud cars and louder music and hanging about on porches in nice weather. A transient, sloppy, good-humored sort of neighborhood where she and Gordon, though not much older, had been entirely too married to ever fit in. The house next to theirs was separated only by a narrow driveway. The windows lined up with exasperating neatness; nothing else in the architecture of either house had the slightest regularity to it. Three young women lived there. They were students, Flora was certain, although they seemed slightly older. That, and a certain collective faded, unpretty quality about them made Flora think they were graduate students. Probably because of the embarrassing closeness, she and Gordon never went beyond simple greetings with them. It was bad enough to keep catching each other in nightgowns whenever you raised the windowshades. It was best to pretend you were simply invisible.

She remembered a particular incident from that time with something close to shame, though she imagined no one else would ever understand why. She had been home alone on a hot afternoon, napping, when the noise of violent crying woke her. It was coming from next door and for a moment, startled out of sleep, she mistook it for a radio or television. It was just as loud, and nearly songlike in a peculiar way. Flora moved quietly to the window. The afternoon sun blazed in on her, she knew she could not be seen. Across the drive, in the barely visible second-floor bedroom, the girl Flora had come to think of as youngest sister, because of her smallness and relative bloom, walked back and forth, crying and crying. Flora watched her for a time. The girl's face was out of sight but Flora didn't need to see it. She knew what sort of face went along with that open-throated grief and that blind walking. She watched and listened, knowing she would only do that. She would never in a hundred years go next door to ask what was the matter, could she help, exchange life histories, administer sympathy; she had not introduced herself before when it would have been simple civility, she would not do it now. At most, if the noise became too alarming, she might call the police.

After a moment Flora became aware that the girl was not alone, nor was she the only watcher. Downstairs another of the roommates sat cross-legged on a cushion. She sat as still as Flora herself, listening. This girl was the middle sister, if Flora wanted to extend her conceit, a bulging, sullen, moon-faced creature who yanked curtains fiercely across windows at dusk. Now her head was lowered and her long hair drooped over her shoulders. She might have been meditating, with the crying as a kind of background chant. Suddenly the downstairs girl straightened, raised her head and threw one arm into the air in a fist. Once again the face was indistinct to Flora, a blurred moon, but the pantomime was clear, a pale arm raised in the dimness, an almost theatrical gesture of malevolence.

Flora, frightened, had turned away from the window and watched no more. It would have seemed theatrical if she'd tried to tell anyone about it, and so she never did. It was no great mystery to hear a girl crying, God knows that happened everywhere and all the time, God knows girls had reason enough to cry. There were also arguments to be made for not intruding, reasons of privacy and tact. But finally it seemed shameful to Flora, a secret she should not know, as if she'd seen too much and understood too little. She knew in that abrupt instant that the girl downstairs hated, absolutely hated the girl upstairs, and was glad she cried. She, Flora, was too casual a witness to other people's emotions.

After a time the crying had stopped. And after a time she and Gordon had found another house. Nothing ever came of any of it.

Now she wondered if she was a little crazed with solitude and manlessness, and she decided that she was, probably, but that wasn't the most important thing. The most important thing was having something come of it.

He called her up at home a week or so later. It was that simple. She hadn't dared pretend he would, she had told herself severely that he wouldn't call. His voice on the phone surprised her, like voices do when you hear them the first time, disembodied, laced with current, coming out of nowhere. "This is Mike Maggio." It was odd, having this rolling, ceremonial voice, which she could not connect with him, coming out of the thing in her hand.

"How have you been?" She imagined him listening to her too. She was conscious of trying to sound melodious, like something other than a burst of wind and electricity.

"I've been OK. I mean that, there's nothing wrong, no crisis or anything. Listen, I'd like to talk to you. The phone's awful, though."

"It is awful," she said happily, glad he'd admitted to it. "Purely awful. It's an infernal machine."

"I could do something like ask you out to lunch."

"That's too innocuous, isn't it?"

"Yeah. And dinner's —"

"Too intimate?" Where was she getting the nerve to say these things?

"Something. Too much of a production. How about drinks? That's assuming you drink, I suppose you shouldn't assume things like that."

"No, that's all right, I mean, assume away, I certainly do take a drop now and then." Too coy, too hugely enthusiastic. She probably sounded like some derelict, delighted at the prospect of a free drink. "Listen," she heard herself saying, "why don't you just come over here?"

There was a small silence, the space of a double heartbeat, which meant he was alarmed. *Now you've done it,* Flora told herself, you're yanking him along too fast, and then *Oh hell.* It was the way she wanted things to be, and if he didn't, it was best she found out now.

A double heartbeat, that was all it was, before he asked if tonight would be good for her. It would be fine, she told him. She gave him directions and they settled on a time. She wished she were fey or desperate enough to say now, come over right now. She simply didn't want to spend the next few hours in a state of goofy anticipation, climbing into her best underwear, spraying cologne on the lightbulbs, or any of the thousand hideous preparations you made on such occasions. Nine o'clock, then, she told him.

Once she was off the phone, the reaction set in. Whatever have I done? she asked herself, then answered, Nothing yet. She strolled through her rooms for a time, thinking of nothing. Nothing yet. I have not committed myself, I am not obliged to sleep with him or even flirt, though that's certainly what's behind all this isn't it. Who knows what he wants or expects, or you either, a married man, jerk, idiot, dunderhead, what are you doing? She knew perfectly well she was going to sleep with him, though how they would maneuver toward it she had no idea.

She was ready well before nine, of course. She kept herself severely away from mirrors, and when he got there she was able to smile nicely, very nearly spontaneously. He seemed determined to do a good job of it too. "Maple Street," he said, "and you even have maples."

"But look at the house. Casa Peculiar."

"Oh I don't know. It's sort of pleasant. It's like an old Hollywood movie set." Obligingly, he was eyeing the stucco. "You know, Zorro. Douglas Fairbanks."

"What can I get you to drink? I have Scotch. And beer. And some off-brand wine. I think it's from Bulgaria. It has pictures of Alexander the Great or somebody on the label."

"How about a beer." He was lowering himself into a chair, she was glad to see. Standing, he took up too much space. He was an object that seemed to demand attention, rather as if someone had deposited a grand piano in the center of her small room.

It wasn't until Flora came back with the beer that she felt her first serious attack of nerves. He was sitting in the scruffiest chair in the house, a humpbacked, unsprung relic which she knew must smell of ancient damps and distressed cats. The lamp behind him threw down its bloom of light. His knit shirt was open at the throat and the skin was tinted with clear gold. He smiled, accepting the glass she gave him. Once again Flora saw that his greatest charm might be that he did not attempt to be charming, he did not strike poses. Only sat there, looking grave and courteous. How long has it been, she thought. Weeks and weeks. Through the open windows she heard the thousand small lives of the spring night, threading the air with sound. She smelled the curious raw perfume of the new growth, a scent not too far removed yet from mud. Something was wrong, out of place. She decided it was the chair, with its flabby, sin-speckled green flesh. It gave her away, it reminded her too plainly of her unchaste and devious motives, he didn't belong in her chair, her bed, her house, not at all. She sat down on the couch opposite and Mike asked her if she wasn't drinking anything. She'd forgotten all about it, she was too busy making speeches to the furniture. *Get a hold of yourself.*

She jumped up again, immediately, brightly. "I'll try some wine," she called from the kitchen, and a minute later, returning, unable to stop talking, "It isn't bad. It's what you call 'drinkable.' I was wrong, it's from Romania. Look here. Vin Romanesc. The Wine of Romance. It says so right on the label. Oh heavens." She was on the couch again, her face hot. "What a thing to serve. I'm sorry, I won't try to foist any on you, stick to beer by all means."

She felt so massively foolish, she had so needlessly embarrassed herself, that her eyes teared a bit. She saw his gold-edged shape as through a prism. "Hey," he said. "It's all right. It's only funny."

"I suppose it is. Maybe I'm only funny."

"Well, we can both be funny," he said kindly.

She nodded over her glass. "A couple of sports."

"Right."

She smiled, still not seeing him too clearly. She felt once more as if, against all odds, they had reestablished connections. The telephone rang in the kitchen.

"I'll get it," she announced, as if anyone else was likely to instead. She carried her glass with her. "Hello."

"Hey kiddo. So what's the good word."

It was Gordon. "Hey yourself." She glanced towards Mike. He was doing what good manners required, that is, pretending he could hear nothing.

"So what's the good word, huh?"

"What's that supposed to mean?" He was sounding breezy, almost slurred. Whenever he began using archaic slang, she wondered about him. Maybe he'd been drinking the Wine of Romance himself.

"It means I'm a cool guy, dummy. I just called to say hi, how are ya, that sort of thing. I just called to be sociable."

"Well that's nice. I've been fine. Nothing new, really."

"Well I've been nice, fine, and not new too. How about that. I'll see your nice and raise you a terrific. So what're you up to tonight?"

"Not much. Just some things I have to get done." Mealymouth, she scolded herself. Why didn't she just say she had company, she couldn't stay on the phone? She thought perhaps she couldn't decide who to feel more guilty about, Gordon or Mike.

"So would you like to go out and be nice together? My treat."

"When, tonight? I can't really, thanks." I have a pie in the oven. I have to wash the chickens. Flora hoped he'd just cease and desist, she knew she wouldn't be able to come up with any convincing excuse, at least not with Mike there listening to her lie. And although she didn't particularly want to see Gordon at all, out of pure weakness she added, "We could try some other time if you like."

"Why not tonight? Why not throw caution to the winds and go out on a Tuesday, huh? We can rent a convertible. Drive around with the top down."

"I really can't, OK? We'd have to make it some other time." Her voice was getting thin. She'd been standing with her back to the living room to give at least the illusion of privacy, and now she glanced over her shoulder at Mike. He had recrossed his legs, taken a pull at his drink, examined the two-month-old copy of *Newsweek* on the table, in short, distracted himself to the best of his abilities with the meager props on hand. The *Newsweek* was Gordon's subscription, Flora remembered. She'd let it lapse.

"C'mon, The moon is shining bright as day, hey nonny nonny. Don't be a drip."

"I'm trying to tell you, I'm busy tonight."

"Oh I see. You've got something going." Living with someone for six years gave them unfair advantages when it came to such insights. Gordon had dropped the breeziness, all the air gone out of it. Now he sounded dignified, which she mistrusted even more. "Why didn't you just say so? The least we can do is be adult about things, Flora. The least we can do is try and communicate. I can handle it, really."

"No one's asking you to handle anything. I have to get off the phone now. Thanks for calling."

"Yeah, thanks."

"There's no need to sulk, Gordon."

"I'm not sulking. I'm disappointed in you. You never did learn to verbalize desires, did you?"

"I don't believe this."

"I just wish you felt we had some basis for trust and openness. I wish you could be straight with me about these things."

"I'm not obliged to be anything with you, Gordon, remember? Especially on demand. Especially since I'm sure I wasn't even the first woman you called tonight." The small, flat silence that followed told her she was right about this. Encouraged, she went on. "You want straight? OK. I don't want to get into any more contests with you to see who can be the most *adult*, the most *open*, the most goddamned *intelligent* about the situation. Those are all just your code words for manipulation. Good night."

"I hope he knows what he's in for," she heard the receiver say on its way down.

All the while Flora had been gripping her wineglass, until now she'd completely smudged and fouled it. She drank the wine straight off, poured another clean glass, and marched back into the living room. "Well," she said. "There's some absolute worst for you. A species of absolute worst."

"Sorry."

"Oh it's nothing. An ex-husband species. Harmless, really. I mean, he won't show up at the door or anything. None of this Woman Shot by Estranged Spouse business."

Flora could tell as soon as she said it that he hadn't even considered such a possibility. He raised his eyebrows mildly. People like them didn't shoot each other. He probably couldn't decide if she was being melodramatic or just unfunny. Flora sat back down on the couch, determined not to say another wrong word. Neither of them said anything at all for a time. Whatever small social ease they'd begun with had quite gone. Then Flora, feeling rather like a hostess in a Jane Austen novel, launched a new topic. "You're a writer, I hear."

"A species of writer. I write what are basically manuals. They're like How to Train Your Puppy, except it's for industry."

"How to Train Your Wage Slave?"

"More or less."

She was boring him, more or less. She could tell from the way he sank back in his chair, resigned to a spell of polite conversation. Well damnit, what did he want, why couldn't he take some of it on himself, damn and blast men and their silences. No one ever said it was *easy*, why couldn't he help? She supposed she expected preliminaries and courtship. Well then she'd given herself away too cheaply, she was entirely too available and he knew it. She had made a horrible mistake, look at him sitting there already bored with her. This was how rapidly and blackly her thoughts were escalating, when the phone rang again.

"I can never resist answering a phone," said Flora.

"Me neither."

She trudged into the kitchen once more. But it wasn't Gordon, it was Suzanne. "Flora? You won't believe this. Go turn on the TV."

"Why, what's on?"

"Just do it. *Now.*"

Flora crossed the living room, waving a hand at Mike in what she hoped was an eloquent, I'll-explain-later gesture. The TV screen brightened. Figures on motorcycles were chasing each other through what appeared to be the sewers of Paris. Flora retrieved the phone. "Which —"

"The news, hurry."

Finally she found the channel. A young boy, his face unnaturally whitened by floodlights, was saying ". . . he told me not to go near him, just stay where I was, and there was this popping noise, and I guess that's when they threw the gas. I ran to the back door and hollered, and the two policemen came and got me out."

There was an inaudible question from someone off camera, and a sweep of red light in the night street behind him, then the boy said, "No sir. Not towards the end. Towards the end I was pretty sure he wasn't going to hurt anyone."

There was something familiar about the boy's narrow, serious face, even thus magnified and weirdly illuminated. "My God," said Flora into the phone. "Isn't that Caleb?"

"It is. I'm shaking. I'm actually shaking, Flora."

Caleb was Carl's eleven-year-old son from his defunct marriage, a child who had grown prematurely polite and adult, it seemed to Flora, from the burdens of divorce and a peculiar name. Carl brought him along to barbecues and other such excursions, where he was always the lone child, a small bored polite figure dangling his feet in oversized tennis shoes. But how had he gotten on TV?

"What happened? I didn't see it all."

"Oh God. It's really awful, Flora. He had nothing to do with any of it except he happened to be in the house. See, there's this family down the street that he hangs around with — real trash, I'm sure, but you know Darlene, the kid could enlist and she wouldn't notice for a week — anyway, this trashy household with a kid about Caleb's age, and a greasy mother, and an unemployed semi-criminal father on the premises, and who knows what else. I suppose you can see the attraction for a kid like Caleb. It's exotic and different, and it's some sort of family life, no matter how low-rent, and maybe that's different too. Well, Caleb's over there today watching them tune engines, or whatever it is people like that do all day, when a guy comes charging in, saying the father cheated him on a drug deal. He's got three or four guns strapped to him, and he's probably high already. A crazy. He keeps everyone there all day, maybe he wants to talk to the Pope or the president of Coca-Cola, who knows, anyway, about nightfall he lets everybody go but Caleb. They talked about *baseball,* Caleb says. Can you imagine? Waving guns around and taking breaks to talk baseball with an eleven-year-old. I ask you, isn't that perfect male regressive behavior?"

"But is Caleb all right? What happened?"

"Oh, he's fine, Carl says he's fine. He didn't get hurt, neither did the crazy guy for that matter. Carl's over there now. He called me this afternoon. I've been sitting by the phone all day, you can't imagine how strange it's been."

"I can imagine." Flora had left her wine glass in the other room this time. She wished she hadn't.

"He's not my child, you know, Caleb, but I almost feel responsible for him. I know you ought to feel responsible for all children, but your sweetheart's, you can't help it, it's *ex officio.* Poor Caleb. When I think of him trapped in the house with this loony, having to calm him down, talk sense to him, talk baseball, whatever, He's so *reliable.* He has to be around Darlene, I guess. Did you hear him on TV? He was actually reassuring people."

Poor kid, Flora was about to say, but Suzanne said it first. "Poor kid. Everything in his life is so screwed up anyway. Sometimes I feel like support personnel. Or a role model. That's it. Like I ought to try and be a good example of something for him. Like we're all responsible for everyone and everything . . ."

There was a pause, and Flora imagined Suzanne shrugging, collecting herself, becoming aware that Flora was not really answering. Mike was watching the sports on TV.

"Well anyway," said Suzanne in a different voice. "Thanks for listening. I just had to call someone. It's so bizarre."

"Sure. That's OK."

"Listen, about the other night. I'm sorry. I wasn't behaving very well, was I."

"That's OK. Really. Don't even think about it."

"Well, I wanted to apologize. What a bloody mess. I think I was a little bonkers. It was crummy of me to try and dump everything in your lap. Don't worry about me and Mike. We'll work things out, we always do. Good night now."

"Good night." Flora hung up and joined Mike at the television. Why, she wondered without curiosity, were they playing ice hockey in May?

"That was Suzanne, wasn't it?"

She stared at him.

"I've met Caleb," he went on. "Strange kid. He seems about a hundred years old, doesn't he? I suppose that's what happens these days. Kids growing up too fast. I suppose he's had to."

"People make such messes, don't they?" she said wildly. "I mean everybody. What's wrong with the world, that nobody can stay with anybody, and all the children are little sad dwarfs, and all we make are mistakes?"

She could hear the tears in her voice, and once again her vision blurred. He was a gold-edged shadow moving toward her. "Oh no," she said. "This is another mistake. You don't want me, really, I'm dreadful, I'm no good to anyone."

He wasn't kissing her, not yet, only clasping her hard round the shoulders. His voice was somewhere above and all around her. Like God's, she thought hazily. Except God was saying, "And look at me. Shopworn. A proven bad deal."

"Oh let's not mind any of that. Let's not mind any of that just now."

It was not really a promise. It was no way to start things, she thought. She watched him drawing her light hair out in his hands, examining its length and fineness as if he thought it beautiful, she watched her arms rise up around him and then she ceased watching. She was inside herself, her body, and there was no need to. For once, for a little while at least, she would be inside everything.

CHAPTER
5

Flora talked to herself, an invisible current of bright indistinct emotion that ran just below the surface of her daily routine. At any moment she could reach into it, even as she went about the business of her normal, unenchanted life. *I am in love,* she informed herself, deploying her car into its slot at work. She still wasn't comfortable with the manual transmission, and there were times she had to wrestle and grind the thing into motion. *Love,* as she lurched forward, the gear whining and straining. She commanded the mechanical demons under the hood, she bade them, in the name of love, to still themselves and let her find reverse, and they did. *Love,* she said to old women in laundromats, sorrowing over their dish towels, or to the indifferent teenagers who pushed boxed hamburgers over the counters at cheap restaurants, or to anyone else who did not know her and never would. *Oh I am in love.*

There was no one else she could tell. Not about any of it. Flora supposed if she wanted to she could rent a therapist, or maybe a priest. She could dig a hole in the ground and talk into it, like Midas's barber. But what would she say? "I am in love with a man I hardly know, by any reasonable standards, a man with a failed marriage and a history of dishonesty, a man who has made me no promises. By any reasonable standards, I suppose, this is a Bad Idea." That was how she would feel obliged to begin. "But in spite of everything," she would then say (to the therapist, or God, or the police, or whoever it was that she imagined ultimately disapproving of her), "in spite of everything, I'm perfectly happy. Silly, isn't it?" How lame it would have sounded, how daft, and finally, how thin and spiritless. Telling anyone meant she would apologize and qualify her joy to death.

It was all too new, there was too much to learn. When it is not so new, Flora told herself, then I will stop and make sense of it all. The mechanics of adultery, she imagined, were familiar to any number of people but not to her. Was this the way one went about it? They didn't discuss terms; they simply let things become habit. Mike would call her at home or at work, and she would invite him over. "You're not in the middle of something?" he'd ask, overpolitely. His voice on the phone still startled her, a majestic, detached thing. "You're sure I'm not interrupting?" No, he wasn't. Did he think she did anything besides wait for him to call, or that she had anything better to do? She didn't. He probably knew it; she had no talent for coyness or pretense, no useful female stratagems. She supposed it would have been nice to be able to call him too. She didn't dare ask about it. It seemed perilous to discuss anything, to make demands, to do anything other than let things lurch along of their own momentum. They had come together so haphazardly, so accidentally, one breath of sober planning might destroy the whole implausible structure. They seemed to have regressed to some stage of embarrassed courtship, to decorousness and tact, as if, having begun things much too quickly, they could not quite keep up the pace.

He had a scar on his stomach. She learned that. It was a faint ridge of white welting that ran north and south for several inches. Flora discovered it one summery afternoon as they lay in the fine wreck of her bed. "We're like lions after a meal," Flora had said some time ago, expecting no answer. Her voice dropped away into the drowsy heat and silence. The sheets were white with a pattern of green sprigs. Green sunlight filtered through the leaves outside, through the drifting curtains. Even the spiderwebs in the bushes glittered and raced with hot light. In years to come she would always be able to picture exactly that room, its heat and dappled sun and moving veils of cloth, that afternoon, its peace and perfect bodily contentment. It was as if some part of her had declared, this is where I will make my home, always.

Now she studied the odd little pucker of flesh, once more awake and curious. "Appendectomy," Flora pronounced, tracing it lightly with a fingertip. She herself detested being tickled.

Mike had been lying back with his arms folded behind his head. He raised himself up and peered down at her. "Nope. It was some other kind of operation. When I was a kid."

"What was it?"

"I'm not sure. Not appendix, but something intestinal."

"Well, how old were you?" persisted Flora. She disliked his being vague about any part of his history; there was so much she didn't know about him. Although she had a presentiment that there would be things she did not want to learn at all, or more accurately, things she would not be able to resist learning just for the sake of wounding herself. "Were you old enough to be scared?"

"Probably not. I think I was only five. I remember feeling sick, mostly."

"What else?"

"I remember my mother sitting up in a chair all night watching me, and me pretending to be asleep. In the hospital."

"And what else?"

"Oh, they gave me a big chocolate thing when I got well. A bear, I think. With edible eyes." Once more he lifted his head to regard the pale expanse of himself, then he fell back and closed his eyes again, as if it was all too much effort, as if his long body was too distant to entirely concern him.

She waited for him to say something else, and when he didn't she said, "You should make sure you know the details. Just for your medical history." She was disappointed that he couldn't tell her more, some anecdote or confidence she could regard as a gift. "I wish everything that ever happened to you had left a scar. I mean —" Flora hurried to explain, for his eyes were open now, he was somewhere between amusement and alarm, "I wish there was an easy way to learn everything about you. I could point at different parts and say, tell me about this, and this, and this. Tell me this story."

"What a funny thought. You wouldn't like me. I'd be all warts and sin."

"No you wouldn't. I can't imagine . . ." Flora was about to say, I can't imagine not loving your body, but shyness stopped her. She did love it, with all the worried pride of a new owner, loved its length and strength and its wealth of fine, pale gold skin. "I can't imagine you ugly," she finished flatly.

"Can you imagine me bald? Look." He sat up straighter in the nest of sheets and pushed his hair back from his forehead. On each temple was a V-shaped inroad of scalp, dimly shining.

"You're not bald," Flora protested, reaching up to free his hand. In fact she didn't like that odd, skinned image of him, the face gone suddenly anatomical and unfamiliar.

"Getting there."

"You're too young."

"Thirty-three."

"Oh, ancient."

"Older than you are. And more mortal. I could prove it to you with the demographic charts."

"Statistics," said Flora, which was her way of pronouncing dismissal.

"All the same. There are times I feel so — not old. Damaged, maybe. You wonder how you'll ever limp through the next half of your life. Like your idea about the scars. Maybe that really does happen to people, once you accumulate enough bad history. You just can't see them."

They were quiet then. Flora thought, this is the wrong conversation for us to be having. It's out of scale, what business do we have talking about time, old age, the future?

"Not that it's ever anyone's fault but your own, the mistakes you make," Mike said quickly, as if she might suspect him of only feeling sorry for himself. "Not that we shouldn't take responsibility."

"You're always saying things like that," said Flora dangerously. "What do you mean? You mean you go ahead and do whatever you want to, and then you make it all right by feeling guilty."

Flora felt the room shrinking, growing too hot. Even her own comfortable nakedness — for she had been admiring the ease with which she fit inside her own skin — seemed quite gone. She felt ugly, angular, raw. It was the Garden of Eden, and she had mentioned the serpent, guilt.

But when he spoke he only sounded thoughtful: "I suppose I should stop making pitiful little guilty noises. Whining. That's what you're talking about."

Flora nodded, not wanting to look at him. She had meant she didn't like him feeling guilty about *her.* But why should I be afraid to talk to him, she was thinking, why should I be afraid to say anything? We can't go on much longer tiptoeing around the edges, the worst he can do is leave.

The worst he could do was leave. She did look up at him then: this man she'd somehow trapped in her bed, this pale forked shape, this beautiful stranger. "I don't want you to get tired of me," she said, and while he was making the appropriate protests, she hurried on: "I don't want to assume anything, I don't want to sound like I'm contracting you to anything, God knows."

He was waiting for her to say *But.* Well, there was no way around it. "But if it keeps on, I have to find some way of living with things. I have to make sense of things somehow."

"Most human arrangements don't make a great deal of sense, do they?"

"No rules in a knife fight," Flora agreed. She felt him reaching out to grasp her by the hips — she was curled over his knees, with her back to him — reaching out to persuade her with his body, since words were so tricky, since he was only using words to evade her, she felt. Maybe he was so often silent out of policy, out of prudence. Maybe he only wanted her obligingly silent presence, nothing more than that, nothing more of her. She said, "Does Elizabeth know?"

And that stopped him, as she knew it would. He left his hands on her, casually. But they felt slack, withdrawn, he was alarmed, she thought, and wondering what to say. "I don't know. We don't discuss it. We don't discuss much of anything."

Flora wanted to ask, well, then who do you talk to, if not me, if not her, but then she remembered that she herself was isolated in silence. She couldn't very well accuse him of the usual male diseases: emotional reticence, lack of intimacy, and so on, when she herself had all the same symptoms. "She probably knows," said Flora. "She's like a shotgun blast. She covers too wide an angle, but she usually hits something, doesn't she."

"I suppose."

"Oh, I know you don't want to talk about her. It's just that I don't understand any of it. I don't know what you want from me."

She was waiting for any number of words to come out of his mouth. Child, duty, home, complicated, responsibility, even money, any of those familiar words that were entirely appropriate, even obligatory, and any of which would be excuses, would have made her decide never to see him again. She felt almost peaceful, perched there on the edge of ruin, waiting for it all to end. She wondered how she had come here so fast, willing to end it all, when only a little time ago she'd been content to walk so carefully around the edges.

What he said was, "I want to start my life over. I don't know if you can. I don't know if anyone has that luxury. But that's what I want. And I want you to be around while I try."

Flora contemplated this. "What do you mean, start over?" she said finally. She had wanted to ask what wanting her around meant. She couldn't imagine any vaguer way of putting things.

"I mean I'm tired of making myself unhappy. Of making the people around me unhappy. I keep thinking, it doesn't have to be that way. I keep thinking you ought to be able to —" he hesitated. "This is going to sound like the worst kind of hypocrisy, under the circumstances. You ought to find some ethic to live by. Some standards of judgment."

"I see," said Flora, as if she quite understood. Or rather, she understood the words themselves, ethic, standard, hypocrisy, and so on, but what did they signify, should she be afraid of them? She supposed the only words women *ever* really wanted to hear from a lover were *you* and *me*. Still, he was trying to explain something serious, it was important that she listen. "I see," she said, like an intelligent student not wanting to disappoint a teacher.

"You think I'm full of shit. I am a pompous son of a bitch, aren't I?"

"You're lovely. You're perfect. Keep talking."

"No, I'm through. You talk. Do you have any idea how happy you make me?"

Outside, flies looped and buzzed, the green breezes blew, the spiderwebs glittered and raced with light. "Why me?" said Flora. *Words,* she was thinking, *we kill each other with words, ah love, shall we be worthy of love?* "There's nothing special about me. I'm just convenient, I'm harmless, I'm something you stumbled across —"

He put his hand, very gently, over her mouth to stop her. "Just to get a few things straight. You're spectacularly inconvenient for me. And not at all harmless."

"But why me? Why me instead of anyone else?"

"You need a reason?"

"Yes, I dare you to come up with one, quick."

"I like watching things come to the surface in you. I like watching you act on impulse, you even surprise yourself sometimes."

"That's a nice way of saying I don't ever know what I'm doing."

"I'm flattering you. I'm saying you're not afraid to leap before you look. You're braver than I am."

"Bull."

"It's true. And you aren't angry, I can tell. I can tell when you're only pretending to be angry."

"Mr. Sexy Psychologist," she said, because he was right, she wasn't a bit angry, she was pleased at this odd reflection of herself in him. The last thing she would have *ever* called herself was brave. "You know everything about everyone, don't you?"

"I'm infallible. Come here."

"Can I say one thing serious first? Just one?"

He was wrestling with her now, trying to trap her between his legs. He stopped, obligingly, and gazed down at her. His eyes were a shade lighter than his hair. The sun turned them to caramel. Something edible. But he was waiting for her to speak.

"It's just this. Whatever we do, I don't want what happens to — other people like us. All the lying and sneaking around. I don't want it to be the way it always happens, there's too much of that. It's poison, it's never any good."

"No," he said, and she watched his eyes turn even lighter, caramel to gold. It was curious, as if he had suddenly absented himself and the light shone through him. "No, it's never any good." And Flora knew they were both thinking of Suzanne.

Later she would realize how little he'd told her, or promised her. He had agreed, in principle, that they must not be like other people, that they were better than that, finer than that, but what did that mean, what did he propose to do about it? She supposed she was doing what women always did, asking for pledges, setting up rules, it was too soon, she should back off. Five times, she told herself, for that was the simplest, crudest, most accurate way of gauging how well she knew him. Five times we've been in bed. How much did that entitle you to? She understood nothing of his marriage, its history, its rationale, its future, and that meant in many ways she understood nothing about him. He had not wanted to discuss it. Well, perhaps it was one of those things she really did not want to know. Perhaps he was only being discreet, even loyal to Elizabeth, in some obscure, overrefined fashion, perhaps that was something she should applaud. All very well and good, but what was she, Flora, left with? She could make no rules, but he had his own. She could ask nothing of him. She was the simplest kind of fool. And yet . . .

And yet. She loved him, or thought she did. She loved sleeping with him. That was one place to start. That was one time he was not silent, nor cautious. Sometimes Flora thought if she could define what she liked about sex with him, she could better justify loving him. He was neither silent nor cautious. He told her what he wanted, he made her do what he wanted. No, that wasn't all of it, though she had to admit she liked that. No matter what it said about her, she liked that. She balanced absurdly on her hands and knees, hair falling over her wrists, her eyelashes damp. Be still, he had told her. Be quite still, and she was, even the ragged breath in her throat was still, waiting. In that stillness her very skin seemed to rise up toward him. Who could have thought that could happen, this extraordinary sensation of being all skin, entirely sensitive. Oh, that's just sex, she'd heard people say, dismissing everything, explaining it all away, turning it into mere cleverness, a diagnosis. Oh, that's just the flu, you might as well say, and maybe they were right, it was temporary, it would subside in time.

And yet. He was good-hearted, she felt, he could be genuinely kind. Didn't a man's small kindnesses count for something, no matter what else happened? Once he showed up at her house without phoning first — which pleased her, she rather wanted him to do things like that — as she was wrestling with the lawnmower. She had never mowed a lawn in her life, and by now, with Gordon's absence, the grass was nearly tropical. Flora imagined elderly neighbors glowering at her dandelions, small children entirely disappearing in the snarl of brush, policemen descending on her with summonses about the weed ordinance. And so she put on her stoutest shoes, since the only wisdom she had about mowing lawns was a store of cautionary tales about mangled feet, rocks spitting out of the blades and so on, and marched into the garage to do battle. The garage smelled of oil and exhaust and insecticide and other darkly staining fluids. It was Gordon's preserve, not her own, and Flora entered it with the grim sense of doing battle.

Whether it was her own expectations of failure, or the fact that the machine had languished unattended for so long, the thing wouldn't start. When Mike arrived, he found her shying pieces of gravel at the mower. She was pitching them with a fine, deliberate air, paying close attention to the trajectory, resonance, and interval of her shots, savoring the tart sting of the metal. For nearly an hour she'd labored over the greasy innards of the machine, expecting it at any moment to roar into life and sprinkle her with severed fingers. She'd given up on that and was now at least having the satisfaction of stoning it.

"That won't hurt it," said Mike, coming up behind her in the driveway. "If you really want to do it in, you should feed it something like bricks."

"It won't *start*," she announced wrathfully. He was already removing his suit coat and squatting down in the dust in his elegant beige shoes. Flora knew she was not at her best in such situations; she was likely to be petulant and unloveable. "I was one of those female children who weren't allowed near wrenches and things," she said, attempting lightness. In fact she was about to cry, she felt all too childish. It was too typical of her to be dithering and whining like this, defeated by machinery. Why didn't she do something like take a home repair course at the Y, it wasn't as if she'd been fated at birth to a house held together with string and contact paper. She supposed her problem was that she didn't really believe machines were governed by mechanical principles or physical laws. She believed in superstition, good and bad magic, a complicated voodoo in which motors were animate and usually malign.

But then, she wasn't doing too well contending with the natural world either. Flora looked around her yard at the undernourished tulips that had scarcely bloomed this year, their foliage as lank and trailing as something growing underwater. Thistles and trees-of-heaven had established themselves in the flowerbeds, wild morning glories strangled the porch. The grass itself was uneven, with defeated brown spots. "I think I'll have everything paved over," she said in the same testy, I-ought-to-be-amused-but-I'm-not voice.

"Well, this isn't really a state of the art machine," Mike said, indicating the mower. It was a tinny, rusting contraption, bought secondhand and allowed to deteriorate. And although he was trying to console her, Flora had a vision of what his own lawnmower must be like: a splendid sleek roaring apparatus to match his house. He probably had all sorts of electric clippers and power rakes and snazzy tools hung neatly on pegboards. She felt shabbier than ever, shamed, sweaty, as if he had found her out somehow.

"The yard doesn't really deserve any better, does it," she said gloomily. "It's not exactly a state of the art yard."

"It'll look just fine. Wait and see. Hey. It's OK. You've just been watching too many grass-seed commercials."

Flora knew he was going to get the mower started, and it would be something simple and idiotic she'd neglected, but that he would not berate her for. (In fact it was out of gas.) She knew he would proceed to mow the entire yard, in his elegant shoes and unsuitable pants. There was nothing left for her to do except stand by and let herself be calmed by the emerging orderliness of her lawn. She watched Mike from the front porch, pulling the mower in neat geometrical paths, much neater than she would have done herself even if she'd managed to get the machine launched. He was frowning a little in concentration, not looking up at her even when he passed her. And Flora loved him, not just for getting the bloody lawn done or even for not making her feel more incompetent than she already did. She loved watching him frown and sweat and show off for her. She loved him for being out there in her yard in front of God and everyone, as if he didn't much care who might drive by and see him. Not that there was anything licentious about mowing a lawn, but she felt absurdly pleased by the public character of the act. Another sort of woman might feel the same if a man tattooed her name on his arm. She sat on the porch ready to administer beer and lemonade when he was done, and she thought, If only we can keep doing things for each other. If only we can keep thinking well of each other.

If only it didn't all blow up in her face. It became a matter of policy for her not to think about the rest of his life, that is, the life he spent away from her. If she could have arranged it, she would have preferred he not exist at all except when he was in her presence, like the genie of the lamp. She herself had so little life that seemed to matter aside from him. It hardly seemed fair that he walked out her door and did any number of absorbing, important, or even trivial things, that he might forget her for hours at a time, most of a day, for days. She made him take her up to his office one night so she could better imagine him there. She was jealous of his most ordinary routines, since she could not share them. At different times of the day she tried to envision him drinking coffee or reading newspapers, tried to see him right *now,* what he was doing that instant, but this sort of magic usually failed her. It hardly seemed fair that she had so little to conjure with. It hardly seemed fair that he might go home and make love to his wife.

There, it was out, her one true poisoned thought. You might make it your policy not to think about such things, but it was useless, really useless, to hold yourself to it, to pretend you wouldn't scratch the itch. Whenever she found herself indulging in such thoughts, she scolded herself, as if simple exhortation ever accomplished anything. This was indeed how people drove themselves mad. Bile. Snakes. Corrosiveness. Bad mental hygiene, negative energy, the all too familiar course of the disease.

O my dear, people would say. You're just Having An Affair With A Married Man. Another diagnosis. And of course they would be right. Everything she felt was entirely to be expected, these exquisite pangs and sensibilities, these nearly enjoyable twinges of guilt and jealousy. It was almost the worst part, realizing how predictable it was. Whatever made her feel she would be more gifted, more blessed, more expert than anyone else? I don't want what happens to other people, she had told him, and he had agreed, but you could say that all you want. They must not be like other people. Flora kept turning it over in her mind, looking for a way to solve it. You might as well try and convince mathematical proofs to come out differently. They must not be like other people, but the only way to prevent that, the only real control she had was to end it.

In fact things did begin happening differently, but it was through no decision or action of their own. It was Elizabeth who caused it, and then too it was not in any of the ways Flora might have expected. Elizabeth did not seek Flora out to make scenes and cause damage, as Flora had pictured in some of her more highly developed fantasies. Time after time she had mentally armed Elizabeth with guns (always elegant, silver plated, purse-sized), or sometimes vials of disfiguring acid, like the old-time *vitrioleuses*. Quaint fantasy weapons, unlike the utilitarian guns and bludgeons people used in the newspapers. She had imagined Elizabeth thrusting her rosy and inflated child at Flora, imploring Flora, in its name, not to destroy a family's happiness. She had visualized, in acute detail, Elizabeth confronting her and Mike in a restaurant, or sometimes it was Flora who encountered the two of them together and had to sit at the next table drinking daiquiris with a broken heart and a smile. All of these theatricals were agreeable, to some extent, all of them could be rehearsed. What Flora had never imagined was some encounter with Elizabeth that did not involve enmity.

This is how it began. It was the end of June, the first true heat of summer. The sky had a powdery look to it, and people moved continually, delicately within their clothes, as if attempting to shed them. Flora had gone to a shopping mall, an aimless after-dinner excursion. She was drifting along in the current of chilly air-conditioning like a fish in water. There was something fishlike, or at least aquariumlike, about gazing into the glass storefronts. Although Flora exhausted the conceit at that point, she couldn't decide if she was a fish looking out, or if the strange headless mannequins they seemed to use these days were the inmates.

She knew she wasn't going to buy anything. She didn't have the energy to burrow into the racks and emerge triumphant with the ideal garment. The styles all seemed suspect to her anyway. They were either ruffled where one least expected ruffles, or short where one expected long, or violently colored, in general too whimsical for her taste. Flora realized, without amusement, that they were all too young for her. Surely there were clothes for people like herself, clothes that transformed you, came with built-in style and confidence the way swimsuits used to come with bras. She doubted it, but out of boredom she picked a dress to try on. The salesgirls too were bored, the store nearly empty. "I told him,

I might be crazy but I'm not dumb," one was saying to the other. "I told him, you go to hell, and you can call me if you need a ride there."

The dressing room was large and unpartitioned, with a mirrored wall at one end. Elizabeth Maggio was standing in front of the mirror in a bra and a pair of pink cotton trousers.

There was no one else in the room. Flora saw herself in the mirror, goggling stupidly. I look as guilty as sin, she thought, and this was what got her moving again, propelled her forward to hang the dress on a peg. Maybe Elizabeth wouldn't recognize her. What a feeble thought, feeble hope, why should she flatter herself that she alone was invisible, all-observant, blessed with anonymity? Elizabeth was already looking over her shoulder, nodding at the real Flora. "Oh, hi."

"Hi, how are you?" Nodding back, even smiling. "Do you know that I sleep with your husband?" No, she hadn't said that, what she actually said, thrashing around for scraps of words, was, "A nice night for shopping. Gets you out of the heat."

Elizabeth had turned back to the mirror and was contemplating her image. The light in the dressing room was yellow and unflattering, the universal atmosphere of such rooms, it seemed. They felt stuffy even as they raised goose bumps on you. How thin Elizabeth looked without her clothes, pared down to the minimum of flesh. There were shadows in the hollows of her collar bone and ribs. They made her look gaunt, even menacing, no, that was Flora imagining things. She looked like a perfectly ordinary woman absorbed in clothes buying. "I don't know about these pants," Elizabeth said.

"What don't you like?" Flora was happy to be consulted on this, if they had to talk at all.

"The waist. The waist is too high."

"Oh I don't know. They look all right."

"They cut you up the middle if they don't fit right," said Elizabeth with finality. She unzipped them and stepped out, hopping briefly on one foot. Elizabeth's underwear (there was no way you couldn't notice such things), was new and satiny-looking and she smelled of lemon cologne. Her fingernails were lacquered, candy pink. She reached for her clothes. "What are you trying on?"

It was one thing to say to herself, or even to Mike, Oh, of course Eizabeth knows, how could she not know. How easy, how airy, how painless. Coward, liar; she was afraid even to take off her clothes in front of the woman. Flora considered pretending she'd gotten the wrong size and bolting, or otherwise stalling until Elizabeth left. "Oh, just this dress," she said, automatically disparaging it.

"Let's see how it looks."

Elizabeth had finished dressing, but she seemed determined on staying. She must have a consuming interest in clothes, like so many professional beauties. She must know nothing, nothing at all. The dress, now that Flora looked at it again, was an unexciting article, a shirtwaist in a muddy blue color with a halfhearted frill at the neck.

"I'm not really planning on buying anything today," said Flora, since it was easier to talk than stay silent. She was attempting to strike the right note of blasé locker-room semi-nudity as she peeled off her clothes. At least she'd bathed, she didn't have her period, her straps weren't held together by safety pins.

She caught sight of herself almost by accident over her shoulder, without her usual stiff, mirror-facing grimace. Her body surprised her. It had its own store of simple beauty, familiar grace. There was no reason to be ashamed of it. After all, it was the body her lover loved and took pleasure in. Elizabeth was combing her hair. The copper curls obediently smoothed themselves. She was tawny colored, Flora milky; long where Flora was rounded. Flora shivered, someone walking over your grave, people said. But she felt another sort of ghostliness, imaginary hands and mouth, the man who was not there. Maybe he'd enjoy seeing the two of us side by side, she thought, comparing us, choosing, maybe he'd like that.

Get hold of yourself. She shimmied into the dress and tried to stand up straight, even preen a little in the mirror, as you were supposed to do at such times. In the corner of her vision she caught Elizabeth looking at her, not at the image in the mirror but at her, Flora. Elizabeth's eyes were narrowed, her face motionless and intent. Flora felt her armpits going liquid. Elizabeth knew everything.

"The color doesn't do much for you, does it?" pronounced Elizabeth, and Flora could only agree. "Why don't I go out and see what else there is, what do you take, a nine?"

And a minute later she was back. "Here," she directed. "Try this one."

Flora did as she was told. Perhaps this was her punishment, she'd wandered into some Twilight Zone or private hell where she would be endlessly scrutinized by Elizabeth in a state of undress. Elizabeth was helping her tug the dress over her head, fussing with the tags and belt. Flora could feel Elizabeth's deft, businesslike hands moving over her.

The odd thing was that the dress worked. It worked perfectly. Flora wouldn't have tried it in a million years, a combination of red, green, and turquoise stripes. Theoretically ugly, but here she was, peering at herself in the mirror with gratified vanity. She looked different, jazzier. She looked, for once, as if she were not at war with what she was wearing.

"There now," said Elizabeth.

"It's really nice. Funny. Usually red makes me look bleached out."

"Oh, the blue reds are good on blondes." Elizabeth was standing next to Flora, looking into the mirror also, adjusting the belt on her own pale green, rather abbreviated shorts. She knew nothing. She couldn't stand there fussing over clothes if she knew anything at all. But maybe she, Flora, was the one who didn't know anything, maybe Elizabeth was playing some elaborate game for her own reasons, let's see who can act more normal, neutral, friendly even. Maybe the real trick would come later. Aha, she'd say, stepping out of her friendly mirror image, now I have you. Why didn't there seem to be anyone else in this store?

"So are you going to buy it?"

"Oh, like I said, I hadn't really . . ."

"I think you ought to. It looks good."

"It does," agreed Flora. She was thinking of some echo of a story, a myth or fairy tale about a beautiful dress given to a woman by her enemy. When the woman put it on, the dress burst into flames. Was the story Greek? Japanese? Hopi Indian? What did it matter where it came from, bits of quaintness you didn't believe in anyway, no help to anyone now. Almost as an afterthought, Flora looked at the price tag. Thirty-five dollars, neither extravagant nor entirely cheap. She supposed women like Elizabeth looked at mirrors, not price tags. In fact she knew she was going to buy the dress. She was going to buy it because Elizabeth told her to.

Flora stood at the cash register waiting for the dress to be encased in tissue paper. Elizabeth was browsing through the silk scarves. Elizabeth was not going away. The scarves were beautiful narrow lengths of yellow, jade, iris, black, poppy. Butterfly colors, jellybean colors, stripes, stars, dots, fleur de lis. They were the sort of thing that attracted Flora, although she knew perfectly well that what she wanted was to drape herself in the whole glorious display, not settle for one lone item. She watched Elizabeth examining the silks, shaking them out, visibly considering. She could wear this with the pink blouse, or the turquoise sweater, this red wouldn't do at all . . . Such a lot of work it must be, all the choosing and rejecting. What a stupid business it finally was, vanity, Flora thought, handing over money she had not meant to spend. Ashes to ashes, and all that. Who was she buying this dress for anyway? Herself, or Mike, or Elizabeth? It seemed almost a group project.

Shopping bag in hand, she rejoined Elizabeth. "Well . . ." she began, as a preface to detaching herself.

"Do you have more shopping to do?"

"No, there's nothing I need. I really hadn't intended to get anything at all."

"The dress looks great on you. You'll see. You'll wear it a lot." Elizabeth said this with what seemed to Flora an uncomfortable air of prophecy. They were drifting out of the store now, Elizabeth seeming to have no destination of her own. The mall was nearly empty, the few shoppers looking idle, wasting time like themselves. Long beams of sunset light inched across the floor. Their feet echoed on the tiles. They were walking slowly, matching steps.

"You're not married, are you?"

"Divorced," said Flora automatically. It did not seem like the sort of question you could be less than forthcoming in answering.

"So what happened?"

"You mean, why did we get divorced?"

Elizabeth nodded. Flora considered the possibility that Elizabeth merely said whatever she thought, without regard to tact or consequences. The more she saw of Elizabeth, the less she seemed to be a creature of fantastic guile, weaving subtle traps, trying to trick Flora into some guilty confessional outburst, like an old Perry Mason show. Then she considered how to answer the question, if indeed she should answer it at all. "We irritated each other, I guess. You can get to the point where there's nothing left between two people but irritation."

"Yes," said Elizabeth, sounding tentative.

"Maybe there's a shelf life on relationships, like breakfast cereals or something. An expiration date you aren't aware of until one morning there's this stale taste in your mouth . . ."

"You have to keep working at a marriage," pronounced Elizabeth. "You have to expect difficulties, you know, you have to be willing to give and take."

And Flora was able to agree with this, although whether Elizabeth meant it as a judgment on Flora, or a comment on her own marriage, or simply a repetition of the wisdom of women's magazines, Flora couldn't tell. Elizabeth had strayed over to another shop window and was regarding the clothes. Perhaps she, Flora, was being too sensitive. There was too much divorce in the air for her to flinch every time the subject was mentioned. There was too much sexual misbehavior, for that matter, she should toughen up. She joined Elizabeth at the window. The mannequins here were silver and they had heads but no hair or features. Just the slightest hint of planes and hollows, cheekbones and eye sockets. They were wearing pleated trousers in gay, impractical colors, lavender and rose, and shirts with patterns of airplanes.

"Cute," murmured Elizabeth.

"Summery," offered Flora. She wondered what she'd look like in pleated pants. Too sporty for the rest of her wardrobe, indeed, nearly schizophrenic. Cut her up the middle, they would. "Aren't the mannequins odd?" Flora said. "I can't get used to big silver blobs where the faces ought to be. They look too unearthly."

"Like all you are is clothes," said Elizabeth unexpectedly. "Like the women themselves are interchangeable."

"Just different sizes and color choices," said Flora. She wondered if she and Elizabeth were interchangeable. Just different styles. If Mike really preferred one of them to the other, or if it was simply a matter of proximity for him, a matter of convenience. If the blue shirt was in the wash, you would wear the white. And she hated him then, just for that moment, for having his choice of them, making use of them. It came out of nowhere, the hate, and disappeared as suddenly, but it was real enough to shake her. Maybe it was because of Elizabeth. Maybe it was a bad idea to let yourself confuse who it was you were meant to hate, or love either, it was not good policy to allow yourself even this small agreement, this female rapport.

They were walking again. "I didn't buy anything," said Elizabeth. "I didn't see one thing I really liked, you know how there are days like that?"

"Oh, I have whole weeks like that. Months. There are times I hardly even notice what I'm wearing."

Elizabeth received this information in silence. The silence had a polite, shocked quality to it, Flora felt, as if she'd announced that she'd eaten cat food for dinner. "Well, they'll be coming out with the fall clothes soon," said Elizabeth after a moment, as if Flora would then have an opportunity to regain lost ground.

They had reached the parking lot. Flora opened the glass doors and the heat rushed over them. The sun was smeared and angry looking, filmed over with heat haze. The air was dead, sluggish; it made you feel as if you'd awakened ill from sleep.

Elizabeth was still accompanying her, drifting over the arid cement. Would she want to get in the car and go home with Flora, like a stray dog one had unwisely been kind to? Just to be saying something, Flora remarked, "It's nice you're able to get out by yourself, away from the baby, I mean."

Elizabeth nodded. "There's a neighbor girl who sits for us. I have to get back soon." She added, as explanation, "Mike had a meeting tonight."

All this time Flora had assumed him to be at home. She'd even taken a sort of pleasure in the notion of him safely confined to an evening of television and bottle warming, and now he wasn't there at all. Once more he'd managed to elude even her imagination. He had a meeting. Well maybe he did, there was no real reason to doubt it. Except that it seemed so much like the kind of thing men told their wives when they were up to something else. It was probably what he said whenever he came to see Flora.

But here was her car. Flora unlocked it and let the first wave of furnacelike heat escape. "Hey, thanks for helping me shop."

"Oh sure. It was fun."

They smiled expectantly for a moment, but there was really nothing else to say. Even after Flora started her car and backed out (the vinyl seat scorched her; if Elizabeth hadn't been watching, Flora would have sat on the shopping bag), even after she waved once more and chugged off, she could see Elizabeth in the mirror. Elizabeth was still standing, as if she had simply been deposited there in the shallow cement plain, waiting for some reason to move. She might have been — odd thought, but then you couldn't help what you thought, could you? — one of the discarded mannequins, an elegant wax doll melting in the heat.

Flora drove home with a headache beginning to bloom just beneath one ear. Hardly surprising. Nervous tension. Stress. All those fashionable words for good old-fashioned worry. As she was walking up to her own door, a sudden wave of pain and nausea stopped her in her tracks. Pain pushed its way up from the root of her brain, it pressed against her eyes and down her throat like a growing thing seeking room. Bits of sky, sidewalk, and shorn grass revolved very slowly in her vision, fragmenting, drifting away, as if everything had lost its meaning. Her stomach shuddered. *Inside,* she told herself. *Quickly.*

The house was darker than the air outside, or perhaps it was her eyes' failure. Streaks of dull light reflected from the bare wood floors; she raised her feet over them carefully, as though they might trip her. She felt dizzy, stumbling; she couldn't recall ever being so suddenly and completely ill. Food poisoning? She crouched over the toilet. She was wet, clammy wet, and the porcelain too was sweating under her hands. She'd eaten another of her frugal non-meals for supper, an apple and a piece of buttered bread. No unrefrigerated mayonnaise, dented cans or rancid meat. She stared down into the watery eye of the bowl, waiting for the thing within her to loosen, but nothing came. Black liquid tides rumbled through her. What had poisoned her? Love, perhaps, this fantastic growth that was battering her skin from the inside now, or maybe there were other, less attractive names for it. Jealousy. Guilt. Cruelty. Whatever it was, she'd swallowed it down greedily.

After a time, when nothing happened, she felt it was safe to lie down; she was at least not afraid of fainting outright. She dragged a quilt over herself and lay there waiting to sleep, or die, or heal, whatever might happen. It didn't occur to her to call for help. There could be no help, she felt, from anything outside herself. There was a bitter taste in the back of her throat which she could neither expel nor swallow, even if she'd had the strength to raise her head.

She couldn't judge if her body's misery was giving her extraordinary insight, or if she was only being delirious, spectacularly unreliable. She'd never been delirious before, it didn't seem the sort of thing you could practice for. She wondered if she had made herself ill, if she was punishing herself for — she wasn't entirely sure for what. For the knowledge that Elizabeth was a human being, was the closest she could come to it. For being unable now to regard her as a mere obstacle, or some monstrous inexplicable figure of jealousy and ill will that you would not have to take seriously. Up close, Elizabeth seemed only lonesome, and perhaps a little less than bright, but more pathetic than anything else. Not someone Flora might automatically befriend, but at least someone to be treated with charity. And what Flora felt was not at all charity. She had to admit that to herself, even as her stomach lurched and shifted, even as small sanctimonious voices, like the good angels of her childhood, told her all she had to do to feel better was renounce her wicked thoughts. She felt pity for Elizabeth, but that did not keep her from wanting to win out over her. In a sense, it had only made her more determined to win out, to hurt her if she had to, as she must. That was the truth. Realizing someone's humanity did not necessarily make you want to treat them humanely. She felt she now understood something about murderers, executioners and terrorists, she felt she was one of them in a sense. How seeing weakness could make you want to smash down harder. The closest she'd ever come to such a feeling before—and the idea was so ridiculous it made her smile even in the middle of her griping pain — was cooking live lobsters. She remembered standing by the stove holding a lobster over the pot of furious water, holding it by the tail while its small ugly mottled brown snout wriggled stupidly, helplessly back and forth. She remembered thinking with satisfaction, I'm bigger than you, and I am going to eat you. Silly thought; you couldn't help what you thought, could you? Ah, but you could help what you did. That you could help.

Was she delirious, or was she seeing more clearly than she ever had? A spasm of pain made her break out in new sweat. It was deep down in her guts now, this burrowing thing, this unhealthy love she'd taken into herself. And she knew it was within her power to vomit or shit it out, it was trying to leak out through her very pores, and she knew she would not let it. She would not heal herself. She would keep it and tend it, this love, this sickness, this extravagance of feeling, even of pain, because her body wanted it, wanted the wrong food the way some people crave the taste of chalk or dirt.

CHAPTER
6

It is one of those Midwest summer days when the sky is a layer of gray paste, spread with perfect evenness from horizon to horizon. Everything is hot and bright, with light and heat so diffused that you don't notice the absence of sun. It is mirage weather, this heat and haze and indistinct brightness. Objects float and waver; only the air seems to have weight. The line of softening tar on the sidewalk at noonday is a black snake. Invisible insects tickle your ears. The exhausted grass is on fire, buildings sweat, the white air tastes metallic. The world becomes untrustworthy at such times. Nothing stays in its rightful place, nothing gives pleasure.

A man and a woman are walking together along the edge of a small city park. They walk slowly, although the glossy, angled reflection from a parked car shows them skimming effortlessly several feet above the ground. Their faces have a remote, inward look. They might be quarreling, or maybe it's just the sullen afternoon. The man gazes into the park, as if there were something to see besides the nearly colorless grass and dusty trees. On a day like this the park too is a kind of mirage; shadeless, and what green there is is hot to the touch. The man is encased in proper shoes and socks and even a tie and dark jacket, as if he has decided to ignore climate altogether. He is uncomfortable, he could hardly be otherwise, and his expression is one of precarious concentration. It is the face of martyrs in certain religious paintings, attempting sublime indifference to the arrows or flames.

The woman wears a light summer dress, red with bright green-blue stripes. In spite of her jaunty, seasonable clothing, her mouth hangs open a little and her feet drag. It's plain the heat exhausts her. From time to time she glances over at the man. She wants to say something and is visibly hesitating. In such weather everyone is trapped in their own miserable skins, separate as planets. It's hard to force words and meaning through the dead air without having them take queer turns, flatten or stall entirely.

Then, just as visibly, the woman decides to speak. She lags behind for half a pace and turns towards the man, forcing him to slow. She is speaking earnestly, she is saying, Don't you like my dress, or Don't you love me anymore? She is saying, What have I done, why do you look so unhappy, what's wrong, I don't make you happy anymore, nothing is the same, love love me you me you, why are you doing this to me?

The man frowns, listening. You can imagine him frowning at a lot of things. The two of them have stopped walking. He begins to explain and his explanation is like everything else about him, serious and reassuring. Of course he loves her dress, didn't he already say so? Of course he loves her, she is so lovely, she means so much, no other, nothing, there is nothing to worry about. She is only imagining things, she is too sensitive. It's only the weather. He will always take care of her. She will see. Everything will work out for them, nothing has changed. Everything will work out forever and ever.

He puts an arm around her shoulders and they begin walking again, even more slowly than before. He is so tall that walking together, joined like this, hobbles them. It is surely some proof of love to embrace in such weather. At the corner where the park ends, they get into a car; the man opens the passenger door for her and the woman makes a little protesting, fanning motion with her hand. It's so hot in here, she says, oh I just hate this. You know what would taste good is ice cream, what do you think, do you feel like ice cream, honey?

Across the street a woman sitting in a parked car has been watching them. She stays there even after the couple drive away, even though her car too is intolerably hot. Her light, oak-colored hair is pulled back into a braid. Wet strands lie across her fore-head. Her clothing has the peculiar defeated texture of fabric that has been soaked through with sweat, wrinkled and rewrinkled. She wears a bright, pretty dress, red with green-blue stripes, like the sail of a racing boat. There is some trick to the colors, they are exact opposites. The eye cancels them out, so they alter-nately leap and recede. The woman leans over the steering wheel, which is slippery from her hands' hard grip. She is waiting to cry but nothing comes. There is no water left in her, it has sweated quite away. She stays like that, bent over, not moving, for a long time. Someone passing by might look twice at her, wondering if she is really ill, even dead, if it's something they'll read about in the newspaper tomorrow. There was a story like that not too long ago, the passerby remembers, peering into the car as he ap-proaches from behind. The woman's shoulder blades jut up through the cloth of her dress. There was this guy died in his car, heart attack or something. Broad daylight, busy street, and he was even half hanging out of the door. And nobody helps him or seems to notice him for hours, which doesn't surprise you, people these days, but the crazy thing is he gets two parking tick-ets. Crazy. The passerby is considering all this, idly, judiciously, wondering if anything as interesting will ever happen to him, not die of course but maybe find somebody dead. Wouldn't that be something. Just then the woman lifts her head and stares out in front of her. She is not at all dead, although this heat is enough to murder you, not dead at all, pretty face, too hot, not dead, just pale, drenched, dazed, no worse off than anybody else out in this weather. She's coming more and more to life now, fum-bling around on the seat for something, keys probably. Not dead at all. He didn't want her to be dead, not really. What a thing to think. Screwy day, when you even have thoughts like that.

Flora started her car and drove home. She still could not think clearly, she supposed she might never think clearly again, but she had a sense of prearranged, appropriately ludicrous punishment; she felt singled out. Or as her mother would have said, it served her right. It served you right, for your dishonesty and vanity, to end up in the middle of an old joke, a bad cartoon. And it was the sort of thing you could never tell anyone. You couldn't say, I went to meet my lover but his wife showed up first, wearing the same dress I was. At least, you couldn't say it and not expect people to think it was funny.

It served her right. She wondered what else would serve her right, what else she was entitled to. She wondered when you stopped making bad decisions. She'd taken a day off from work and wanted to see Mike, maybe talk him into leaving work too. She was too timid to call him at his office, even though he'd never told her not to. All those secretaries and switchboard operators who'd wonder who she was. Flora knew what offices were like. She knew that any attractive man generated, like a magnetic field, currents of interest and fantasies. That Mr. Maggio, what a hunk, well he was, who could blame them for noticing, for wanting to have somebody to dress up for at work. Flora imagined the sweet eager telephone voices. May I say who's calling? No, you can't. Or maybe you hung up, which was even worse.

Flora decided it would be a better plan to wait outside his office and present herself when he appeared. She was even rather pleased with herself, it seemed a suitably bold thing to do, something out of a well-produced perfume ad, perhaps. It went along with the dress. She sat in her car outside the big blond factory-like building. What exactly was it they did or made or sold in there, she couldn't remember. Something about surveys. The building's windows were nearly opaque, some hideous trick of modern architecture. On bright days they glittered. Today they were somewhere between smeared and smoky. She wasn't even sure she remembered which window was Mike's. She'd ask him again, although you couldn't really imagine anyone behind those identical glazed squares, they hardly seemed worth getting sentimental about.

At a few minutes before noon people began to emerge. The big blond-and-smoke building was animate after all. The clerks and secretaries came first, hurrying to run errands or eat diet plates or just get the hell out. Then a herd of neat young men, young men on the way up, walking more slowly, conscious of their future dignity. People seemed to be leaving in roughly the same order as the salary scale, and Flora watched the doors more attentively. I'm middle management, Mike had told her. The midlife middleman. I have a job of middling importance. He always talked like that, disparagingly, though Flora sensed he wouldn't want anyone else talking that way about his work. She was beginning to wonder if there was more than one door.

The dress came out the front entrance slowly and lingered on the sidewalk for a moment, as if testing the air outside. Flora stared at it; the colors were trying to tell her something, like a stoplight, but she didn't yet know what. The dress was on Elizabeth, Elizabeth was with Mike, and the two of them were crossing the street less than a block in front of her. For a long freezing minute she couldn't move, she couldn't drive off anyway without them seeing her. At that moment Flora would rather have been caught naked than to have them see her there in that dress, how could she explain any of it, what was Elizabeth doing wearing it anyway? She couldn't decide if it was cruel or merely grotesque, sinister or coincidence, she couldn't think about any of it now. Mike and Elizabeth had reached Flora's side of the street. Flora could see them through the cloudy windshields of the cars ahead of her, talking, probably trying to decide on lunch. There was nowhere to hide, unless she buried her head in the upholstery like an ostrich.

Then she lost sight of them. She whirled, but they weren't at her elbow, they'd gone the other way. She saw them, a dark shape and a red-green-blue shape, receding into the heat haze.

She waited until they'd turned a corner, then she started her car and followed them. That was the real craziness, the part she wouldn't have admitted to anyone, even if she told them everything else. She followed them for more than half an hour, Flora the Phantom, sweat-maddened, sick with jealousy, risking everything. Her little car lurched and hiccuped, it shimmied into parking spaces and idled at intersections. She watched them buy sandwiches and cartons of orange juice from a street vendor with a blue umbrella. Elizabeth patted at the neck of the dress, yes, the facing did tend to ride up, Flora felt it at her own throat. Mike gave Elizabeth the change from the sandwiches, money for dry cleaning or gas, unfolding the bills so she could put them in her wallet. They'd done things like that a hundred times. That was what made up the texture of a life together, things you'd done a hundred hundred times. Elizabeth looked good in the dress, leggy and elegant. If the two of them, Flora and Elizabeth, stood side by side, wouldn't labels appear beneath them, WRONG and RIGHT?

They never once looked behind them or they surely would have seen her following. She was not very good at this sort of thing, but something told Flora she was doomed to get better at it. She would become an urban tracker, a creature of stealth and cunning, a menace on the streets, a dialer of anonymous phone calls. She followed them until she saw what she supposed she'd been waiting for all along, some irresistible humiliation or pain, a proof of the affection she pretended did not exist between them. Then she let them go.

It was taking her forever to get home, now that she really wanted to go somewhere, she had been driving forever. A horn sounded behind her. In the rearview mirror she saw arms waving from both sides of a car. *God.* But it wasn't them at all, she saw in the next instant, squinting through the windshield glare. It was Suzanne and Paul, in Paul's car. They honked again cheerily, they wanted her to stop. Flora supposed it was better to do so than to have them keep pursuing her. She pulled into a drugstore parking lot and they followed. She didn't want to see anyone, she wasn't sure she could manage normal conversation. If she opened her mouth she might bark or growl. Even getting out of the car felt odd; she'd been crouched and cramped and hidden within it for so long. What would they think of her dress, no, it wouldn't mean anything at all to them. That part was all right.

"Flora Dora."

"Adorable Flora."

"Hello you horrible drunks," she said, trying to sound light and amused. They weren't drunk but they did seem overenthusiastic about something, too hectic and jolly for the weather. Stoned, she decided, watching them grin and blink. At least it seemed to keep them from noticing anything wrong with her. "What are you doing loose on the streets?"

"Fishing," said Suzanne promptly. "We've gone fishing. Want to come with us?"

Flora regarded them soberly. "No, really," said Paul. "We're going to drive out to a lake. I have some little rafts and a cooler and we're going to drink beer and get all red and buggy. Doesn't that sound like fun? Come with us. We spotted you and now you have to come with us."

"Isn't anyone working today?" Flora inquired.

"I'm working at home," said Suzanne. "Can't you tell?"

"And I'm sick. I've been sick for days. I think it's leprosy."

"Hence, his infectious mood."

"Come with us, we'll infect you."

"Yes, do, Flora. What else can you do on a day like today except spend it underwater?"

I can't, she started to say, but really, why couldn't she? Because she was unhappy and humiliated, and wanted to wallow in it for a while longer. It was almost like a chore she had to complete. Was there a point in every affair, she wondered, when it became work to keep yourself properly fired up, stirred up, whatever? I can't do anything, I have to go home and be in love. Yes, Flora told them, I'll come with you, and they whooped and pounded her on the back. She would have a life of her own. She already *had* one. She would adopt an upbeat, grabby, confident attitude, like all the magazines told you to do, she would be an independent and self-actualizing person. That was always a relief to men anyway, at least, they didn't want to see you moaning and stewing over them. It would be therapeutic to spend time with her friends, it was nearly her duty to enjoy herself. Paul and Suzanne followed her home and rummaged through her refrigerator, looking for things of interest to commandeer. It felt good to have friends who would go through your refrigerator. ("This stuff gives you unholy munchies, here Flora, smoke some. Munchy pig-out. Why don't you have any ice cream?") Flora changed into a swimsuit, T-shirt and cut-offs, and left the red dress in a wet ball on the floor.

They floated on the green surface of the lake, each on their own sagging, underinflated raft. They'd considered swimming, but everyone agreed even that was too much effort. The lake was man made and mud bottomed, tucked under the shoulder of a highway and surrounded by bean fields. It was no more than a good-sized pond, hardly worth anyone's attention, and so they had it all to themselves. Red-winged blackbirds sang in the half-submerged grass at the edges. Metallic dragonflies skimmed the water's surface. Every so often one of the three on the rafts would rise up and fog the air with insect repellent, then sink back. The sun was bleeding through the clouds now, a white and shifting light. Flora paddled her feet in the green water. It was cold and it moved slowly through her toes. She tried to feel nothing but the cold sluggish water. On my day off I went with friends to the lake. That was a reasonable, normal thing to do, you could tell people that.

Suzanne's raft nudged against her own. Suzanne's bare arm was thrown across her eyes and her thin brown legs were stretched out straight. She looked like a little brown stick, straight, spare, motionless, her sharp clever face hidden. Once you took away the part of her that moved or spoke, she became something different altogether. Flora felt dazed from smoking dope, but not unpleasantly so. She was drowsy, floating. Suzanne was a brown stick, Flora was a white-and-strawberry one. Paul — she had to lift her head to see him — managed to look like a whole bundle of sticks flung out in all directions. They were all harmless wood, floating above everything human and complicated. Prick. In spite of herself she was thinking of Mike again, she was getting angry. What excuse did he have for loving two women when he couldn't do right by either of them, why shouldn't she be angry. Flora wondered if he'd even think in terms of love, if he wouldn't use some other, more technical terminology. He was involved with. He was committed to. She imagined him trying to explain it to someone, frowning, picking his words with care.

For some reason she saw him in an office, he was talking with another man. This man was a psychologist too, a clinical psychologist. Mike had gone to him because he needed to establish a perspective, that is, he needed to have a sensible conversation about the whole mess. The clinical psychologist was enough like Mike to be his twin: thoughtful, articulate, professional, and he had to fight the women off with both hands. Together he and Mike attempted to articulate the right terminology. The right ethic to live by, the standards of judgment. They agreed that one had to balance one's needs for individual freedom and growth against the responsibilities of one's social persona. Prick. She shouldn't let herself think like this, it was interfering with her achievement of Stickhood. But she had to admit the part of him she most mistrusted was his ability to turn things into abstractions. The main value of people and events to him, she suspected, was that they furnished data for principles and theories, codes and guidelines. Not exactly the statistics he made his living from, but some set of grand, immovable truths. She was afraid he would some day come up with a mathematically irrefutable reason for abandoning her.

Flora let one arm trail in the water. She would anesthetize herself, think no more about him. She was off duty. Out of uniform. Suzanne was looking at her. One green-brown eye showed from underneath her brown stick arm. It was like swimming alongside what you took to be a floating log, until it winked at you and turned into an alligator.

"What are you thinking about, Flora?"

"I was thinking you look like an alligator," said Flora. "It was something about your eye looking out at me. Well, you asked."

"So I did. Silly me."

"You are an alligator, Suzanne," said Paul, splashing water at her. "Aren't you. Aren't you a sort of alligator."

"Piss off," Suzanne told him idly.

"I meant it as a compliment. You're a predator, but you're so cute."

"What *are* you talking about?"

"About you. You and your competitive instincts. Wouldn't you say you had a highly developed competitive instinct?"

"I suppose so, but alligators?"

"The alligator," said Paul happily, warming up now, "is a fearless creature superbly adapted to its environment. No natural enemies. Nothing it can't swallow."

"Prized for its hide, don't forget that," Suzanne couldn't resist adding, although she was starting to get annoyed.

"No, really, the rest of us would like to be alligators if we could. We'd love to be the eater instead of the eatee for a change. Isn't that right, Flora, wouldn't you like to be an alligator?"

"I was thinking of being a floating log, actually. It sounds more restful."

"Most of us," continued Paul, just as if Flora had agreed with him, "are mere harmless goggling fishes. Alligator bait. We don't have Suzanne's talent for ruthlessness. We flounder, if you will, through the swamps of life. We perch precariously — "

"Why am I an alligator, Paul? Where did all this crap come from?"

"Flora started it."

"Oh she did not."

"I can't tell you. You'll eat me. Chomp chomp."

"Paul."

Suzanne looked over at Flora, and Flora lowered her eyes to the green water. Suzanne was genuinely angry, she could see, and was trying to decide just how far to rein it in or let it out. It wasn't Flora's fight, she wasn't even sure it was a fight yet, but why did such things so often spring up around her? Did she have unsuspected talents as an audience or provocateur?

Paul grinned at them. It was a grin that reminded you somehow of a dog wagging its tail. He said, "I'm sorry. Really. It's my way of saying I envy your self-confidence. My indirect and annoying way. My deft, ironic touch. I'm sorry, Suzy."

"Let's just drop it, OK?"

"You're still mad."

"Of course I am. It's an attack disguised as a compliment. Harmless fish, my ass."

"Vile, nasty, despicable fish," agreed Paul, but Suzanne was not appeased.

"You have no idea how tired you can get of hearing things like that. If people perceive you as a successful woman — I'm not sure what that means, except you must be wearing the right clothes — anyway, people just find new and different ways of calling you a bitch."

"But I'd love to be a bitch," protested Paul. "I guess that's the whole point. Oh boy, would I love to be a thoroughgoing bitch. I'd love to inspire fear and loathing."

"Is that me, Paul? Do people fear and loathe me?" Suzanne was beginning to smile in spite of herself at Paul's passionate yearning for bitchhood.

"Only the ones you want to."

"You can turn it on and off at will," said Flora. "That's the admirable part."

Paul said, "You're our very favorite pet alligator."

"My self-concept," said Suzanne, "is that I'm a sensitive fawnlike creature, tragically misunderstood. Oh all right." She managed to shrug while lying flat on her back. "Let's drop it, please."

"You're still mad. Isn't there anything I can do to make it up to you? Drown or something?"

"No, hey — " began Flora, but he was already up on one foot with the raft bucking and wobbling beneath him. He hit the water stomach first, splashing everyone. The two women peered into the sullen water. "I really don't think he can swim," observed Suzanne.

Paul stayed down as long as he could for maximum effect (the water was deep enough to drown in, but barely), then he surfaced, complaining it tasted poisoned. Agricultural runoff, God, why hadn't they thought of that before, he was probably soaking in pure Treflan or PCB, or whatever toxic gunk they dosed beans with. Suzanne said that since he was trying to drown anyway, what difference did it make?

Then they all tried to remember which Kafka story ended with, I sentence you to death by drowning, and then they decided it didn't matter, and then Paul started in again. They would rather he hadn't, they preferred his clowning, which was easier for everyone, but he seemed determined to explain himself. "You don't apologize for yourself," he told Suzanne. "That's what I envy. Most people apologize, one way or the other. I do it by wisecracking. Flora, now — "

"May I be excused?" asked Flora, without much hope of stopping him.

"Flora apologizes for herself by behaving well. Don't you, Flora? You're afraid if you throw a tantrum or let yourself snarl, people won't love you any more."

"I suppose you're right," said Flora.

"Of course I'm right. I mean, not that I'm always right about everything, but I'm usually right about you, aren't I?"

She wondered if it showed. If people could tell there was a part of her that wanted to wreck cars and marriages, wanted to rage and exult and — in general, not behave.

"Alligators," Paul was saying, "or bitches, or whatever, don't apologize for taking what they want. They know they have a perfect right to be angry or greedy or yawn in people's faces at dull parties."

"Do I pick my nose or belch in public?" inquired Suzanne. "Or are you saying if I do, I do so with great verve and charm?"

"You do everything with verve and charm. Flora does everything with modesty and charm. I do everything with self-denigrating humor."

"You really can be funny, at least," said Suzanne. "You're an asshole, but at least you're funny."

"Thank you. Drugs always help."

"People have such strange ideas about themselves," said Suzanne after a moment.

Flora was wondering what Paul would have been like if he'd been born with a different face. If he'd been born a handsome man, would he have felt the need for a sense of humor at all, or would he have turned out serious? A serious gloomy handsome man who couldn't help it if women chose to go apeshit over him. Prick. Don't think about it now. She thought instead of the curious conversation they'd just had, the three of them. Was everyone a little crazed these days, or was she, Flora, carrying around some contagion that made for raw feelings and drama? Paul shouldn't have started in on Suzanne, but that was Paul.

Being friends was not a static condition, Flora decided. You tugged and snapped at each other from time to time, like — well, like the alligators or crocs (whatever was the difference between the two anyway?) that you saw in zoos. She remembered heaps of them piled on top of each other on the rocks in their cement pool, motionless, hardly alive, it seemed. Then one of them would flop and wriggle and heave, and the whole pile would have to rearrange itself before dozing off again in scaly contentment. Oh she loved them, Paul and Suzanne both, loved them precisely because they knew her weaknesses and she theirs. What would they think if she sat up on her rubber pillow and declared, I love you, fellow alligators, I'm so glad we can share the same pool, even fight over the same food, there's no one else I'd rather be an alligator with. They'd say something like, Flora, old girl, we should really give you drugs more often. But they'd know how she felt. They knew how she felt without her even saying it. She loved them.

Nobody spoke for a time. The heat and the drifting green water seemed to have prevailed over conversation. If only you could float always above the surface. If only no one ever had to talk. Mike was saying to the clinical psychologist, "I feel that my involvements with women other than my wife are, ultimately, conflict producing and stressful. They represent my negative aspects: irresponsibility, narcissism, and a tendency to sacrifice long-term goals for short-term gratification." The clinical psychologist agreed with him.

Paul said, "I wonder if there are fish here. I don't know a thing about fish, I'm fish-dumb. When I was a kid we used to go on vacation up in Wisconsin somewhere. It was one of those tired old resort towns, you know, the kind that has a giant fiberglass muskie in front of City Hall, and the restrooms in the bars are marked Pointers and Setters. A sort of lower-middle-class playground. But when I was a kid I thought the place was the Enchanted Forest. We stayed in a cabin, one of those places that's decorated in Total Knotty Pine. I'm waxing rhapsodic. I'm supplying atmosphere."

"I'm with you so far," said Flora, since Suzanne might have been asleep, face down in her raft.

"You should have seen me when I was a kid. The All-American squirt. A baseball cap and no front teeth. A Lone Ranger T-shirt and a permanent wad of bubble gum. I was nearly cute. I was at least authentic."

"An idyllic boyhood," said Suzanne from somewhere within her folded arms. She had been listening after all.

"My father tried to teach me how to fish once. That's what I was thinking about. You've met my father, haven't you?"

Flora had. A huge old man whom she'd rather disliked. Beside him even Paul had seemed small, diminished, a sort of capering antic shadow. Fathers and sons; what did she know about them, except that most of them reminded her of a one-celled animal, imperfectly dividing.

"He likes to tell people how to do things, you know. So do the rest of us. I don't knock it. It's just that he's not very good at it. He lectures. He roars and roars. He took me out at four a.m. to learn me the mystic art of fish stalking, and I cast a hook into his lip. Do you suppose that's Freudian somehow? I haven't been fishing since."

"The female counterpart," said Suzanne, "is Mother Teaching Daughter to Cook. Except I remember my mother letting me make a green, raspberry-flavored cake. That was pretty cool."

"You were an odd little bitch even back then."

"Don't push your luck."

"It's your turn, Flora. Tell us about your childhood. Tell us an amusing story."

Flora considered. She supposed she could do so. She could take her rather terrifying childhood and turn it into amusing anecdotes. Everybody did that. "Well," she began. "Once when I was very small my brother and I saw something on TV about mud baths. I went up to my mother and said, 'Mommy, can we run the hose on the sandbox and turn it into a mudbath?' I swear she said yes."

"So what happened?"

"Oh, we made the thing into a real wallow, and we slopped ourselves from head to foot. It was grand. And when my mother came flying out screeching at us, we said, 'But you *told* us we could.' We felt perfectly innocent."

"Your mother didn't see it that way."

"Hardly," said Flora, and she stopped there, since it made a good stopping point. Besides, what had happened after that didn't fit into the story. Her mother hadn't screeched at all, in fact. Her mother was not a woman who screeched. Her mother had cleaned them up in the basement laundry tub, scoured and shampooed them. Her face was Flora's own thin startled shallow-planed face: Flora was just now the age her mother must have been. Her mother's fingers dug into their scalps but they didn't dare complain. By this time Flora and her brother knew their innocence was a technicality; they were even beginning to think the true hideous sin had been claiming innocence in the first place. They sensed from their mother's unnatural silence that they'd done something too bad for words, something nearly *adult.* Their mother's face was slack and sweated and staring by the time she finished with them. It was cold in the basement, or at least it was cold to stand on the cement floor after they'd been so thoroughly wetted. Their mother knelt down and regarded them as they dripped and shivered. They were still naked, and it was unpleasant to feel her breath so close, its heat and odor. "Filth," she said. "I will never be done with your filth."

She dried them and dressed them in clean clothes and then she went upstairs into her bedroom and locked the door behind her. "Go away," was all she said when the two of them tried to get her to open it. "Go away." There had been nowhere for them to go, and so they huddled outside the closed door for the rest of the day until their father came home.

And then what had happened? She wasn't entirely sure. She could remember remembering it, that was the best she could do. They had stayed by the closed door for — it probably had not been long, how long does it take to frighten a child? The phone ringing and no one answering, and the TV chuckling to itself downstairs. Their father had come home and it had been all right somehow. He had turned on the lights and spoken kindly to them and gotten their mother to unlock the door. He went in the bedroom and after a little while she had come out and it was all right. She was their mother again. She had told them to wash their hands and then she'd gone in and fixed dinner, meat loaf, baked potatoes and green beans.

She was remembering remembering now. But she knew the important parts. Not that much had happened, maybe it wasn't a good story at all. Her mother was not a woman who screeched or punished with words. She was a woman whose fingers dug into your scalp and who locked doors. She was no different from anyone else's mother except for those times when she turned herself into something blank and heavy, when she chose to absent herself, behind silence, behind doors, and then behind the pretense that nothing at all had happened. She simply told everyone to go away. Flora learned to come home from school and test the quality of silence in the house. What had her mother done behind that closed door for all those hours and years? It wasn't even drinking, Flora realized with some surprise when she was old enough to wonder about such things. It wasn't anything unladylike or obtrusive. Her mother was the princess in the tower in a fairytale, who made herself most felt when she did nothing, nothing at all. Flora imagined that many people had at least one parent they blamed for things, at least one family villain, but could you be a villain by default, by your non-presence? She thought of her mother now, a thin pleasant woman who kept a garden and a cocker spaniel and was always glad to see her children these days. A pleasant, mild woman. Maybe it hadn't been so bad, her childhood, maybe all parents had their mad spells, maybe all her mother had ever needed was for her children to grow up. But sometimes Flora wondered how it had affected her, those blank spots, those times they all had to pretend nothing had happened. Perhaps they were what had made her so unwilling to charge into the fray.

It was getting late, they were all of them gritty and fatigued. "Burn-out time," announced Paul. They collected the damp towels and empty beer cans and trudged back to the car. Suzanne lagged behind with Flora. "I'm worried about you," she said abruptly.

Flora laughed. A mistake. Suzanne catching her off guard again. "You always worry about me."

"It's not a pretty job, but somebody has to do it."

"No they don't. They don't have to at all."

"I'm serious. You're so quiet. It's like you're hearing voices."

Flora tried to think of something that would sound neither guilty nor nervous. Why should she feel guilty around Suzanne anyway, except that she hadn't confided in her. Suzanne knew it somehow, she was tackling it head-on, like she did most things. Talk to me. Talk to me. And Flora couldn't. If she had only said something straightforward about Mike in the beginning, it would have been — if not all right, at least more honest. Now it was too late to say anything that really mattered. "Maybe it's post-divorce syndrome," Flora said, pleased to hit on something that was very nearly the truth. "It's like a low-grade infection. You aren't ever really unhappy, but you're not happy either."

"Fun," Suzanne diagnosed. "You need to go out and have heaps of fun."

"This was fun today. I'm glad you ran into me."

"I am too. You looked purely awful, you know. You looked like a murder victim."

"What do you mean?"

"You looked — I don't know. Like you were dead and still walking around. I don't really know what I mean."

Suzanne looked ahead to the car, measuring distance. She was still waiting for Flora to say something and Flora couldn't. Was there ever any end to the damage you did to people with your secrets? She was hurting Suzanne's feelings, though Suzanne was too proud to let it show. Proud, and brave too. Whatever else you thought about her you had to give her that. She was brave with people, she wasn't afraid to risk the damage. She certainly deserved better than to be left measuring the distance between friends.

The sun had broken through the clouds at last, a red sun that softened the edges of everything, that colored the air and the powdery soil at their feet. Even the highway noise seemed far away, a vague, diffused whine. Swallows wheeled and staggered as if the red air had made them drunk. Except for the homely rows of soybeans, they might have imagined themselves on some new and lurid planet.

"I think," said Flora, trying once more to say something that mattered, "if I had to choose, I'd rather be the murderer than the victim. I'd rather be guilty than innocent, if it means surviving."

"So would I," Suzanne agreed, and that was the end of their talk for that day.

"Can I see you?" the phone was saying. "Can I come over? Please. I know it's late, but I need to talk to you. Am I being irresponsibly assertive? I'm sorry. I don't mean to. It's entirely up to you. Tell me what you want to do."

Flora wondered where he was calling from. Was he at home, crouched over the basement extension phone, or in a pay booth? Where did he materialize, this genie of the phone wires, and why did he sound so rattled. Irresponsibly assertive? That was psychologist talk, he never said things like that to her. She told him of course he could come, and he said he'd be right over. It wasn't of course at all, Flora thought after she'd hung up. She'd been reading comfortably in bed, feeling cheerful and nontragic. She hadn't been thinking about Mike at all, she realized. Maybe that was how these things worked; she'd found the right charm or formula. Once you emptied your mind completely of a man, once you became light-hearted and truly contented, that was when he called up begging to see you. The trouble with that — she looked around regretfully at her clean sheets, her serious book, her glass of pale wine — the trouble with that was, by then you genuinely didn't care if he called or not.

Almost grudgingly, she brushed her hair and put on lipstick. He had to talk with her. That was the sort of thing you said to people after you found out you'd given them a disease. Or when women discovered they were pregnant. That was it. Elizabeth was pregnant, Mike was coming over to tell her it was all over for them now, but they would name the child Flora if it was a girl. Why was she thinking this way, where did such outlandish bitchiness come from? She supposed she'd been feeling this unfriendly ever since the Day of the Dress. She'd sulked, a pissed-off, nearly satisfying sulk, except for the fact that she couldn't really blame anyone for it. Maybe she should have told him she couldn't see him.

But once he arrived she wanted him there. You could only sulk for so long, after all. He went straight back to the bedroom and lay down, his legs dangling over the edge of the mattress. "You look terrible," said Flora judiciously, because he did: there were pouches of yellow skin beneath his eyes, and his hair had a frayed, matted texture that reminded Flora of the fur of an unwell animal.

"I know. I'm sorry. I should have looked nice for you. You always try and look nice for me, don't you. That's not a very smooth thing to say is it, I mean, you're not supposed to notice when women do things to themselves. I think I don't know what I'm saying."

"Don't talk, then." In fact she wanted him to keep talking this extravagantly, but whatever was wrong with him?

"I have to. I have to keep babbling. Flora, do you think I'm a real shit? It's all right. You can tell me."

"Of course I don't. Why would I think that."

"Oh, you're being kind now. You don't have to be. I'm a shit because I cheat on my wife, because I hurt her and hurt you, lovely Flora, I'm sorry, I do most everything wrong, don't I?"

"Hey. Hey now."

He was holding her and rocking back and forth with his untidy hair pressed up hard against her mouth, and she was terribly afraid he was crying. But he drew back and said rapidly, "It's OK. I'm OK, really."

"Then let's talk, if it'll make you feel better."

He looked up at her with his tired, cracked eyes. He was exhausted, frayed, but he was not really out of control. There was a measuring quality in the look he gave Flora, and she thought, He's not sure. He's not sure he can explain things, because after all, how could he rationalize or justify the way he lived? He said, "Elizabeth brought your name up tonight."

Flora looked at him, stricken, and he went on. "It's not quite what you think. We were having a fight. I know. What else is new? It was a stupid fight. We have grand-opera fights and we have stupid fights. This one was about not refilling the ice cube trays, at least, that's how it started. You can start a fight anywhere and have it end up in the same place, you know? I will admit, I was the one who didn't fill the ice cube trays. I neglect to do so in order to persecute and humiliate her, you get the idea. Anyway, things were rolling along splendidly, and as the grand finale she threatened to leave. Which she's always threatening and never does. I was tired of hearing it, so this time I asked her where the hell she thought she could go. I'll go to Flora's, she said. And I said, Oh, Flora's, like that was a wonderful idea, like I was really slow for not thinking of it myself. And she said, Yes, why not, she's too nice not to let me. Isn't she a nice woman, wouldn't you like it if all women were that nice."

"Oh my," said Flora, inadequately, and her eyes darted to the windows as if Elizabeth might be there, demanding entry. "What did she, what . . ."

"That's all she said. I didn't care to pursue it. She's jealous of you, she's jealous of all women, she almost can't help that, but she rather likes you too. There was another time when she said she thought the two of you were getting to be friends."

"Friends? But she doesn't know me. We're not even proper enemies, I mean, she doesn't even know me enough for that." Flora found it just as distressing, being the object of an unreasoning friendship, as it was to be unreasonably hated. Maybe worse; it was more patronizing.

After a moment Mike said, "My wife is not the sort of woman who has friends."

"She knows about us," said Flora. "Maybe it's better that way." And at that moment she meant it, she wanted it all unmasked and purged.

"No," said Mike. "She doesn't know. Dear Flora, you underestimate people's capacity for refusing to believe what they don't really want to know."

"Tell me about her," said Flora. She supposed what she meant was, Tell me why you stay with her.

He sat up and rubbed the back of his neck. "She's a very

ordinary woman, in a lot of ways. She wants ordinary things. House, clothes, kids. Attention, affection. Most people want that, there's nothing wrong with it. She's just more afraid than most people. She's terrified that everything she has will be taken away from her."

"She's terrified of losing you," said Flora, and again he gave her the measuring look.

"She's manipulative. I realize that. I realize that sometimes she loses control of herself for effect. I realize she thinks the best way to keep me with her is to make me feel responsible for her, to act unstable and self-destructive. It's a sort of game she plays, I know that."

She was waiting for him to say *But.*

"But she's played it so long and so hard. Sometimes I'm afraid of what she might do, just so it can be my fault. I'm afraid . . ."

He shook his head and went on in a new voice, hard and brittle. "This is the worst thing I can admit about myself. Sometimes I've wondered if she'd hurt our son. Just because she loves him more than anything else in the world, because it's the most horrible thing possible. Can you understand that? And it's crazy, it's monstrous for me to even think that. How bad can things get between two people, when you think things like that."

"You can't help that. Nobody can ever help what they think."

He shrugged and turned silent, as if he felt he had said too much, but then he said, "I don't think we were ever really happy together. You don't realize that at first. That you aren't happy, you're just in love. I don't know. You don't just wake up one morning and smite your forehead and say, Omigod, I've made a mistake. It takes a long time to make mistakes, actually. You have to keep working at them."

"So am I a mistake?" she asked him sadly. "Or are you still working on me?"

"You're not a mistake for me. But I am for you."

"I don't mind," said Flora. "I don't mind any of it."

He pulled her over so she was straddling him. "Do you want to?" she asked.

"Can't you tell?"

"Is it really that easy with men? Is that all you ever have to do, take a reading?"

He tugged her nightgown over her head and kept her that way for a minute, her raised arms held high, tangled in the cloth. With his free hand he pinched the nipples of both breasts until they hardened. "It's that easy," he said. "See, it's easy for you too."

They made love hurriedly, not concerned with taking pleasure in it. Sometimes it was like that. It became important to have the sex as a nearly contractual undertaking. They both knew it and Flora did not feel particularly insulted when, after it was over, Mike said, "Next time we'll do it better. I promise."

"Why don't you come over Friday. I'll grill you a steak. I'll peel you a grape."

"Oh hell." He was still on top of her, propped on his elbows. Flora could see only the underside of his chin, indistinct and shadowy, like the ceiling of a cathedral. "I didn't tell you this."

She could feel herself preparing to be polite, small, hurt. "So tell me now."

"I have to go to New York for a week or so."

"He has to go to New York."

"I'm sorry. It's been arranged for a long time. There's a conference, and we're supposed to meet up with some people in the city."

"Don't be sorry. You need a vacation, I'm sure."

"I don't need this trip. I don't want to be away from you."

"Aren't we behaving well," said Flora. "I'm being good-humored and understanding. You're being properly regretful."

"We're behaving awfully well."

"I hate it like poison. I don't want you to go anywhere."

"And I was afraid to tell you. I was afraid you'd pout."

"I will later. When are you leaving?"

"Thursday after work. We'll fly back the weekend after next."

Flora imagined the days marked out on a calendar, a black-bordered space. The Feast of St. Michael On Vacation. That wasn't right, she was sure, she wasn't Catholic but she was sure that feasts didn't go on for days and days. Maybe things like penances and atonements did. What was she going to do with herself while he was gone? The answer came promptly: very much the same sort of thing she did when he was in town. She'd wait until she could see him again. She'd try to imagine where he was, what he was doing, was he thinking of her at all. It would just be more difficult to imagine him in New York, on streets she'd never seen, with friends she'd never met, in sleek expensive restaurants and glassy hotels, lost among a million million people, any one of whom might at any moment decide to up and murder you, lost in so much noise and money and danger. She would get him to tell her everything before he left, she decided. Flight times, schedules, the names of his friends. She would make him tell her so she would not lose him entirely.

"What are you thinking?" he asked her.

"Of you being gone. Of how I won't be able to reach you. But then, that's not too different from the way it is now, is it. I can't call you here either."

"Sure you can. You can call me at work."

She made a face at him.

"What's that for? What did I say?"

"I can't imagine you want people wondering who I am."

"What people?"

"You know. Secretaries and people like that who answer your phone."

"Flora, I answer my own phone. What do you think I am, a captain of industry? That's where I call you from most of the time. That's where I called you from tonight, dummy."

"I can call you there, really?"

"Good Lord girl, yes. Call me twenty times a day."

"I wanted to last week," Flora said, "but I chickened out. I thought you probably had a secretary who's secretly in love with you." She decided that was as close as she'd come to telling him about the Day of the Dress.

"You're an odd one," he said. "Bloody odd. Come here. You're beautiful."

And she was beautiful, she knew it, she might never again be as beautiful as she was at that moment. She was like a glass filled with clear water, she was the simplest creature in the world, but some lights, some reflections, turned her glorious.

CHAPTER
7

I hate flying. I know people say it's thirty times safer than driving a car, like that's supposed to be a big relief, but I still hate it. I mean all of it: the canned air, the landing gear groaning underneath you, the seat belt sign chiming on in the middle of the flight so you wonder what the pilot knows that you don't. Most of all I hate the notion that you're supposed to be enjoying it all. Does anybody believe those commercials where they show you all those people on planes having the time of their lives, with the stewardesses pouring them coffee and plumping up pillows? I don't. I don't understand people who make their living flying either. You couldn't pay me enough to work on an airplane. Whenever I see them in airports, the stewardesses towing their suitcases on little wheels, the snazzy blue-and-gold pilots, all of them talking so brisk and jolly to each other, I think they must be faking it, just showing off. Nobody ever has that much fun going to work anyway.

I was watching them now, the pilots and the little flirting girls. I was sitting on one of those plastic airport chairs they bolt to the floor, with the baby on my lap and Mike off somewhere looking for cigarettes or whatever it is he pretends to do when he doesn't want to sit still. The gate was crowded and the whole place smelled stale, like too much sweat and breath sealed in a bag. I guessed that one was our pilot. At least he looked older, not too old but like he hadn't just gotten his license. Not that it matters how good the pilot is if a wing decides to fall off. They all seemed to be the greatest buddies in the world, the pilots and the stewardesses, as they filed through the door to the plane. Or maybe they were just telling dirty jokes.

Then I watched the other people waiting, because there was nothing else to do. You can tell by looking who's afraid of flying, at least I can. They look the same as me. We sneak glances at each other and wonder if these are the people we're going to be dead with.

The baby was asleep. He was sleeping as sound as he ever does, I could tell by how heavy he felt in my lap. It wouldn't last, it doesn't on planes. The pressure change hurts their ears and you can't tell them to swallow. That's why babies cry so often at takeoffs and landings. A lot of people don't know that. But he was asleep now, all heavy and open-mouthed. I had our carry-on luggage and baby bags piled up around my feet. I felt like some kind of statue, sitting in the middle of it all. I felt like they'd call the plane and people would get up and take the luggage away and file on board and I'd still be sitting here, not able to move. I was already so tired from the packing and the million things you have to do for a trip. I couldn't really believe I was going anywhere. I didn't want to go anywhere at all.

You know how sometimes the harder you try not to think of something, the more you think of it? I was trying not to think of how people look when they burn. That's how I thought it would happen, the plane crash. We might drop out of the sky like a rock, but it was fire that would kill us. Whoever had to clean up afterwards would find rows of black stick people still strapped in their seats. Black crusts like what comes off the inside of an oven when you clean it. How we'd smell, like scorched hair and plastic and even worse, how they'd try to unbuckle us and hands and feet would drop off like boots and gloves.

It was the wrong way to think, I knew that. I tried to think of New York instead, but that didn't help much. I'd really wanted to go at first. All the stores and people and excitement, and getting dressed up to go places. That's how I'd imagined it. But Mike would be off at his conference the first few days, and the baby and I would have to manage as best we could, killing time in parks and hotel lobbies. I wouldn't know where anything was at all, I wouldn't know anyone. If I complained, Mike would say why don't you go to a gallery or a museum, or some such place I wouldn't know the first thing about. He'd tell me it was my idea to bring the baby, more about that later. I tried to remember how I'd thought it would be, New York. Women with jewelry and men ordering them fancy drinks, people laughing and talking and music somewhere, a nightclub maybe. That's how I'd pictured it, but who were the people, and what did they find to talk about, and how did I fit in? I didn't know, I guess I hadn't ever really known. Oh New York, people kept saying to me when they found out we were going. Oh, you'll love New York. It was beginning to feel like people telling you how you ought to enjoy flying.

Then Mike was back, looking irritated about something. Who could tell what. I knew better than to ask. There wasn't a place to sit next to us so he just stood, trying to smoke three cigarettes at once and frowning. He says he doesn't mind flying. What he means is, he doesn't think he ought to mind it. He patted at his jacket pockets double-checking: tickets, keys, wallet. "How's he doing," he asked, meaning Robin.

"Fine so far. See?"

He didn't really look, just nodded. I don't care how many things you read about fathers taking new, active roles, men don't know what to do around their children. They really don't. Even Mike, who reads all the articles and tries to be good about diapers, and still he's never sure he's doing anything right.

He hadn't wanted the baby to come along. We had a fight about it. What do men think, you can drop children off like the dry cleaning, it's one of those household things you're supposed to manage? I told him he was being selfish, I told him I wouldn't enjoy myself for a minute, worrying, even if we found someone to keep him. "Mommy the Martyr," he said, when he was trying to make me really mad. "I know just what's going to happen. You won't enjoy yourself anyway. It'll be one long trail of tears."

So who wants to go on vacation and worry about strollers and plastic pants and bibs, of course it's easier without a baby. But what did he expect? Even in the middle of the fight I didn't say the worst part: that sometimes he's ashamed of having a child.

He, Mike, gets this look on his face. You can see it. He's embarrassed. Like, Oh God, this thing leaking spit and piss and going off like a siren isn't mine, maybe if I just stand here and do nothing people won't know it's mine, why did I ever think this was a good idea? Then he feels guilty about it, you can see that too, and he tries to make up for it and it never turns out right. Are all men like that? Not just about children, but always telling themselves how they ought to feel? If I told him about it, if I said, The way you feel is all part of having children, it's OK, who hasn't wished them back to where they came from? It's just love, what you're feeling, finally you love them because you have no choice. He honestly wouldn't know what I was saying. He wouldn't let himself know it.

So here we were waiting, and it was getting worse and worse for me, thinking about flying and being in a strange place. Why did we have to do any of it? Nobody was making us go, after all. Mike didn't even have to go to the conference if he didn't want to, nobody ever really *has* to go to things like that. Behaviorist Applications in Industry, or Applied Industrial Behavior, some kind of name that didn't mean anything any way you said it. I thought of our house, all clean and quiet, because I'd left it clean, no garbage or things that would die in the refrigerator, clean sheets and towels, everything waiting for us. What a shame to waste it, all that cleanness, all those perfectly good rooms, just so we could crash on an airplane.

"Michael," I said. "This is such a mistake. Let's just go home."

"What?" he said, though he'd heard me perfectly well.

"Let's not go. Nobody's making us go, are they? I don't want to go. What are we going to do there anyway, there's nothing to do."

"I don't believe this. Even from you."

"I just want to go home. What's so wrong about that? I lived all my life without going to New York, I don't need to go now."

"And tell me again why we have to not go," he said, with this phony patient tone he uses when he's trying to make me mad.

"It's just this feeling I have. Some people get feelings about things before they happen, about plane crashes and things, don't they?"

"Ah Christ," he said, and I could tell I'd gone about it all wrong. He never takes anything I say seriously. "Forget the psychic garbage you read about in the last *National Enquirer*. What if I said fine, we won't go. By tomorrow morning you'd have changed your mind."

"That's not true. That's an unfair thing to say, you don't know that at all."

"A child. I married a child."

"I'm starting to feel sick, I mean it. I'm afraid I'll get sick on the plane, Michael, can't we just talk about this?"

"Listen," he said, and he put his face down close to mine so no one else could hear how ugly he talked. "I. don't. care. I don't care what kind of scene you pull, cry or faint or break a leg. You're going. Spoil things for yourself, if you want, but I won't let you spoil them for me."

Just then the airline people started scurrying around unhooking the velvet ropes, and people stood up the way they do, nervous, too soon. They said for passengers with young children to get on first, that was us, and I could see Mike just daring me to do something, his face all tight and hateful, and instead I got up. I was really doing it. I was walking down that long accordion tunnel into the belly of the airplane in my white summer dress, and the stewardesses were clucking at the baby, and I was going to New York with my husband who hated me.

So we didn't crash. For a while I almost wished we would, just to show him. But we didn't. The three of us sat there looking like a normal family, looking like the people in the commercials in fact. Daddy with his briefcase open, doing Daddy-work. Mommy tending Baby. Just like it was supposed to be. Except Daddy wishes Mommy would drop dead, and Mommy's wondering if she's going to throw up. If she does, she's going to aim it at Daddy. The baby woke up like I knew he would. We were roaring down the runway, everything whistling and popping, and he woke up with his eyes as big as cookies. He took one look at me and started screaming bloody murder. That's the truth. It wasn't the plane that scared him, it was me. I can imagine how I looked, just crazy. Hating Mike and waiting to be dead, even hoping we'd die in the biggest stinking smoking crash you could imagine. How you can fit all that into your face I don't know, but I did and it showed.

Then I felt terrible about what I'd done to him. I gave him his pacifier and rocked him and sang, but he was red and furious by now, and probably soaked clear through. The ground was falling away, I could see the last little square of it over the wing, brown dirt and gray pavement, ugly, the last I'd see in this life and it was ugly. I held the baby as tight as I could. It wouldn't keep me alive, it wouldn't even stop him from screaming, but he was all I had. This wet red squirming thing that knew just how scared I was.

The plane leveled out and Robin stopped crying, finally. I had to change everything he had on, but finally he stopped. That was a relief, if only because the stewardesses left us alone then. While he was carrying on, each one that passed felt she had to stop and bend over with her butt in the air, and talk baby-talk. Which didn't help one bit, of course, only scared him more. All those sticky made-up faces shoved at you. It was all for Mike's benefit, I could tell. He brings out the worst in women. That's the truth. He's what they call an attractive nuisance, like having a swimming pool with no fence.

Somewhere over Pennsylvania, I think, we quit fighting. I don't mean he apologized. Oh no. Just that he'd gotten his way and he didn't have to fight any more. "See," he said, pointing out the window. He likes showing me things. "I bet that's Philadelphia. We're not flying all that high."

He likes explaining things he doesn't really know, too. If I'd asked how high we were, he would have made something up, thirty thousand feet or something. But I didn't ask, and I only pretended to look out the window. Philadelphia, big deal, I didn't care.

"Come on. What will it hurt you to look."

"There's nothing to see," I said, and I was right. A smear of clouds and some dots of light showing through the bare patches. It could have been Winnipeg, for all you could tell.

"Oh, driver. My wife doesn't care for Philadelphia. Could you take us somewhere more satisfactory?"

"Very funny."

"Like my grandmother used to say, you could ride home on that lower lip."

He was trying then at least, he was teasing me. I like him doing that. I said, "Oh, so I'm not as much fun as your girl-friend."

He just gave me a Look.

"You know, Red. The one with the big bottom. Here she comes again. She walks up and down this aisle like she just got picked Miss America, and you're Bert Parks or somebody."

"You want her to hear you? Besides, Bert Parks doesn't do Miss America any more."

But he thought it was funny, I could tell, and when she gave him a big lipstick smile, we both cracked up. She did have a big bottom. Too much baggage stowed beneath the seat.

When we started to come down over New York, that's when I really did start to get excited. Excited, not scared. Landings don't scare me as much as takeoffs, maybe because you're heading in the right direction. I know that's silly but that's how I feel. I did look out the window then at all the lights, what is it about lights that seem so magical? Yellow blue and white, those were the colors turning underneath us, lights and dark water, the city opening wider and wider, and Mike squeezed my hand, and I thought, maybe it will work out. It'll be all right, it won't be a mistake.

That night I couldn't sleep. Can anyone really sleep soundly in a hotel? Mike can, I guess. He was breathing in big windy gusts, flat on his back. He was exhausted, we all were from the plane and wrestling with luggage and taxis and such. Still I couldn't sleep. Everything was strange: the stiff hotel sheets, the rattling air in the vents, most of all the city outside us. You could hear it even fourteen floors up and sealed behind a double layer of glass, locked and chain-locked inside our expensive room. I was going to say, it was like hearing the ocean from a distance, but it was an angrier sound. It was the sound of more people than you could ever comprehend, and all of them too alive. That sounds strange, but that's what it was. Everything was too alive, and there was too much of it, and it didn't matter how well you locked yourself away.

You know how it is when you try too hard to sleep. It never works. You think about everything in the world. You start *here*, your body, you try to find its center like it's a knot you can untie, then you travel out to your skin. There's always an itch or a rub. These sheets smell exactly like skin themselves, dampish and perfumed, how can you sleep in a stranger's skin? This room you don't know. The room you always sleep in. Who's in it now, nobody. Everything's empty, your rooms, the hollows worn in the mattress, clothes hanging in closets, how quickly things lose their shape without you inside. And what are you anyway that so much depends on you to give it shape. A cage of bones and soft parts, how easy it was to tear open, break, burn, horrible, why is hell always fire not water?

After a while I gave up. I got out of bed and stood by Robin's crib. He was asleep too, although he slept more fretfully than Mike. He was on his stomach with both fists doubled up underneath him. When I tried to move him, just so his circulation wouldn't get cut off, he stirred and drew his fists in tighter. Did he get that from me, I wondered, that making himself into a fist? Had I taught him to be afraid while he slept, had I already done that to him?

I went into the bathroom then. I closed the door before I turned on the light so I wouldn't wake the others. Two a.m. It was one of those hotel bathrooms with all this equipment: heat lamp, shower cap sealed in a little plastic sack, shoeshine rag, even a heater for instant coffee. It's supposed to make the place homey. I looked in the mirror. I looked like a crazy woman. All blotched and puffy from not sleeping, and my hair in lumps. Usually a mirror makes you straighten yourself up. But the longer I stared, the stranger I felt. Maybe you've had that happen, you play a sort of game with the mirror and the longer you play, the more you forget what you're playing. Who was this crazy woman in the wrinkled white nightgown? She was too ugly to be me. I let her stand there. Her mouth was heavy and her eyes creased. Even the way she stood was ugly, slumped, like every bone in her was broken. Then I understood why it wasn't me, not really: it was what I would look like dead. Not all cleaned up and painted and laid out at a funeral, but dead from something terrible, an accident or a war. I wasn't even scared then, thinking about it. That's the funny part. Maybe I'd spent so much time scaring myself it didn't work anymore, like a child outgrowing a bedtime story. I opened my mouth and made my teeth bite against each other. Teeth were supposed to last a long time after the rest of you. Crazy woman, dead woman, ghost.

And here's the really funny part. After that I could sleep. I turned off the light and got back into bed. I remember thinking, well, if that's the worst that can happen to us, being dead, that's really not so bad. Once you're already dead, at least nothing more bad can ever happen. I was careful not to wake Mike, but I did draw myself up close to him so we touched along our whole lengths, bone to bone. How silly he would have told me I was being. He's always telling me that, how I make up things to worry about when there's nothing wrong at all.

The next day I learned a lot of things about New York:

Hotel maids are all from Puerto Rico.

You wouldn't believe what some people do to their hair.

A Boston coffee is one with extra cream.

The cab drivers are no help at all.

It was strange all right. But only strange in the ways I expected. The people that make you wonder where they're going at nine o'clock in the morning, because they surely can't be going to work dressed like that. And pigeons. Go to New York and you'll see why they call them flying rats. But mostly it's people, all of them talking funny and walking around with Drop Dead expressions on their faces, like they're daring you to take up room on the sidewalks. At least if you're a lady with a baby most people will be nice to you, most not all. Anyway, when Mike came back at dinnertime I was really proud of myself for managing so well. I showed him the postcards I'd bought, and a fancy picture book for Robin, and a map of the city with everything you were supposed to see on it.

"The Statue of Liberty. We probably ought to see the Statue of Liberty."

"Why?" He was lying on the bed with a gin-and-tonic on his stomach. The TV news was on. It was funny to realize that Dan Rather and Tom Brokaw and the rest of them were right *here*, in the same town, maybe in some building you could see from our hotel window.

"Doesn't everybody go see the Statue of Liberty? I just thought that was something everybody did in New York."

"Sure. That and the Rockettes show."

I asked him what that was, but he wouldn't tell me. He was in a bad mood from the conference. That didn't surprise me, if I had to sit around all day listening to people read papers about fruit flies or whatever I'd be grouchy too. But the thing is, I know he'd spent all day being perfectly polite, even pretending to be *interested*. When he talked to a bunch of old poops with name tags, he'd act serious and agreeable and interested. Then he comes back with the bad mood he's saved up just for me.

What I did then, I put the baby on the bed next to Mike. He, the baby, was fed and bathed already, and he'd had a nap, and you could figure he wasn't going to act up seriously for at least a couple of hours. This was how Mike liked to see him, clean and happy, the way somebody must have convinced him babies came when you ordered them from the factory.

"Hi there, Porky." That's what Mike calls him. I wish he wouldn't, you know how nicknames can stick.

"Mike."

"I know, I know. He's just growing. Hey, hotshot. What are you going to do with that?" Because Robin was yanking at Mike's tie clasp, trying to get it into his mouth. He's a strong baby, isn't it funny how hard they can pull things? He can really hurt you if he gets hold of your hair.

"Maybe he wants you to take your tie off. Come on, Big Daddy. Loosen up."

And he did take it off then. "Shoes too," I told him. "Keep going. Get all comfortable."

I helped him start the laces. He has the funniest feet for somebody tall. They're short, almost chubby, and the toes curl in. He's ticklish there too. "Now. Don't you feel better. Don't I always know what makes you feel better."

"Sure. I'm a new man."

But he did feel better, I could tell. The baby was kicking and crowing and trying to say something that sounded like "lutefisk," Mike said, whatever that was, but Mike got a real charge out of it. "So, sexy lady," said Mike. "What are you going to take off to get comfortable?"

"*Mike*. Honestly. In front of the baby."

"I wouldn't worry about it for another eighteen months at least. Trust me. I've read studies."

"That's not very funny. He'll grow up to be some kind of sex criminal, then let's see how funny it is."

So he took his hand away. But I wasn't angry, not at all. It was what I'd wanted to happen. I knew that this way all through dinner he'd be thinking about it, what we were going to do later. It would all be the way I wanted it.

Is that dishonest, fixing things so they turn out your way? Using the baby, that was the only really bad thing I'd done. I'd used my baby to get my husband to want to make love to me. There. I came out and said it. There are things women will admit to, like trying to look pretty or telling lies, and things they don't even admit to themselves. How you can use a baby like an ornament. It's true. Think about it. All those old madonna pictures, oh, they're holy and all that, but it's the same thing. They knew what they were painting. What *doesn't* make people think of sex, you might wonder that. And then I'd had to pretend to be shocked. It is dishonest, but I guess that's just the way things are set up between men and women.

I'm going to skip a lot here. Not that some of it wasn't interesting. I saw Barbra Streisand in a drugstore and I got to go to Tiffany's. But what's important is the night two nights before we were supposed to leave. August 23.

There are these people, the Roseboros. Mike knows him from going to college together and they live in New York, not the city but someplace outside it. So we were going to have to see them. I'd only met them once before, in Chicago, when they were on a vacation. It's one of those things where Mike thinks he still ought to be friends with the man, his name is Bruce, but it was all so long ago. They sit around and remember when they used to be friends and tell all the old stories and end up feeling bad about it because they aren't twenty-one anymore. Meanwhile she and I, the wife, just sort of sniffed each other over. At least we didn't have to pretend we were great pals.

And now we were going to go to dinner at their house. It was a very big deal, with renting a car and getting a sitter, and everybody trying to out-polite each other. You know, did we want them to come and pick us up, did we want to bring the baby along, did we want to stay overnight? No, we didn't want any of it, and neither did they I'm sure, but we had to act like we did and thank them seventy-five times over the phone before we even got started.

"What are we going to talk about all night?" I asked Mike. "Besides what great guys you and Bruce were about a thousand years ago."

"Just make an effort, OK? Just try and be pleasant. God forbid I should expect you to enjoy yourself."

"You don't have to be so sarcastic."

"And you don't have to be so negative. It's a dinner, Elizabeth, not surgery."

I didn't say anything after that, there wasn't any point in it. I felt jumpy and queer, I had all day. I have a bad attitude. I only make things hard on myself. That's what Mike says. Doesn't he ever get tired of being right? I looked out the car window. It was called the Taconic Parkway, this road we were on. There was nothing to see. Banks of dusty-looking trees and the green highway signs. One of those roads where they make it look like nobody lives within a hundred miles. You could tell it was taking you someplace where rich people lived.

And the Roseboros were rich. Or at least, everything they had was expensive. The house, the shrimp on little frilled toothpicks, even her blonde hair. Her name is Natalie. She asked me if I'd ever seen *The French Lieutenant's Woman,* and I said no. That was the last thing anyone said to me for about two hours.

We sat at the dinner table eating. It was chicken with, I'm not making this up, oranges and onions and peanuts in it. You had to keep poking around your mouth to decide what you were tasting, make sure it wasn't chocolate or fish or something just as outlandish. This is how it went at dinner.

"The chicken's terrific, Natalie." This was Mike, this is the man who complains if I melt cheese over the broccoli. "Is it one of your inventions?"

Natalie grinned at him. Even her teeth looked expensive. "Oh hell no. I got it from the Sunday *Times,* and I'm sure they didn't invent it either. It's African. This is a ripping-off-the-Third-World recipe."

"Natalie's on this African kick," explained Bruce.

"I'd love to go there sometime," said Natalie. "Before it's all developed to death. The traditional culture's fascinating. Music, tribal structures, even the ways they flavor food."

"They use a lot of red pepper," said Bruce.

"I'm taking a course in Swahili now at SUNY extension," said Natalie, like, wasn't she cool.

"Swahili? Where in the world do you find the time?"

"Oh, the class is only one night a week. Very concentrated stuff. Otherwise I wouldn't have a prayer."

I forgot to mention, this Natalie is a lawyer. (So is Bruce.) And she worked on somebody's election campaign staff, somebody very big deal like the mayor or governor. And she plays racquetball. Of course they don't have any children. No women have children these days except us dummies.

Mike shook his head. "I should do an efficiency study on you, Natalie. You're probably off all my charts."

"I'm committed to my work. I don't think of it as something

I have to do, but as a series of personal challenges. That's what makes the difference, motivation. That's what your surveys don't take into account, Mike."

"Well, to a certain extent we can quantify motivation," began Mike, and Natalie leaned towards him across the table because it was all so fascinating. It made me sick, to see the two of them playing up to each other like that. Natalie wasn't even all that good-looking. Too hard-edged, too much scrawny brown neck shoved forward over the table, too much gold jewelry swinging and dangling on her. You could see she did this sort of thing all the time. Played up to men by pretending to be interested in what they did, and asking these intelligent questions, and all the while trying to fall out of her blouse. Mike was eating it up, just like he was eating her weird chicken stew. (Not only did it have peanuts in it, I decided, it had peanut *butter*.) It drives me crazy how he doesn't see through things like this. Don't get me wrong. I didn't think the two of them, Mike and Natalie, were going to sneak off to the kitchen together and neck. That wasn't what Natalie really wanted. She was just practicing on my husband for the next big-time lawyer or politician she wanted to impress. That's all it was, practice. She did it to keep in shape, like racquetball.

Bruce knew what was happening. I expect he'd seen it plenty of times before. Him I didn't mind. He was a friendly sort of guy, a little red in the face, a little chunky. You could tell he'd put on the weight just recently, for the first time in his life he was getting fat. Natalie probably made him eat all her cooking experiments. He smiled at me. A friendly guy.

"So," he asked me. "How's that big boy of yours doing?"

Whenever people don't know what else to say to me, they ask about the baby. I know that. But from Bruce I didn't mind. He was just trying to be nice, and I felt sorry for him too, having to watch his wife carry on like that, and having no one more interesting to talk to than me.

"He's just fine," I said. "At least, I hope he is. There's a sitter service, a nursery, right in the hotel. It looks okay. But you can't help worrying."

"I'm sure they're very reliable," said Bruce, not because he knew anything about it, just because he was trying to be nice.

"They have the number here. If anything goes wrong, they can call."

At the other side of the table Natalie was saying, "But the potential for abuse is there. We used polls all the time in the campaign. It was downright sinister, how accurately we could target."

Sooner or later those types always get around to talking about themselves. Mike was nodding and uh-huhing and in general acting like this was all pearls of wisdom. Just once I'd like him to even pretend to be interested in something I was saying. The shock would probably kill me.

Meanwhile Bruce and I were trying to keep up our end, though it was getting a little thin. He asked me who Robin looked like, and I said Mike. Not Mike now, but his baby pictures. And I dug up my wallet with Robin's picture in it. They didn't have any children we could talk about. They had a Doberman.

"Bruce," said Natalie. "What was that guy's name. The one we met at the Meirhoff's, who wrote the article in *Village Voice*."

"It sounded like Carrie Nation," said Bruce.

"Kronestaten. Louie Kronestaten."

"Well, I was close."

"It was an article about TV advertising. And it raised the same point. How politics and advertising have become so closely related. How politics really is advertising these days."

"A funny article," said Bruce. "Do you know how many man-hours go into making one Kool-Aid commercial?"

Natalie smiled at me then. Smile is the wrong word. She narrowed her eyes and showed me her teeth. Then she started in talking again. You see, she was telling me. We are all more interesting than you are. Watch me charm the stuffing out of both these men, your husband and mine.

This was when I said to Mike, "I think we ought to be going soon."

That stopped them. This was how they looked: Bruce a little

confused, Natalie shocked that I had the nerve to interrupt her very important and completely phony discussion. And Mike. I didn't care what he thought any more. "It's early," he said, in his I'm-too-polite-to-say-more voice. "There's no hurry to leave."

"It's a long drive. I'm worried about Robin."

After a minute Natalie said why didn't we have dessert, and she and Bruce started clearing things away. I could tell she was mad that she had to get up; she'd been having such a grand time. She'd wanted to sit there all night showing off for my husband and ignoring me and drinking too much and stubbing out cigarettes in her dinner plate.

Dessert was another weird one. She'd taken all the most peculiar fruits you can find in the grocery, kiwis and guavas and mangoes and things like that and dumped them in a bowl and poured coconut milk on top. I ask you. I didn't even touch it. I listened to the others talk about how great it was, then I excused myself and went upstairs to the bathroom.

Goddamn them all. I was crying by the time I shut the door, I hadn't meant to start crying but I felt so bad. I ran cold water and blotted my eyes. I was going to wreck my face if I kept up. The bathroom was all black and white. The sink basin was black and so were the towels. It was probably some idea Natalie got from a magazine.

I just stayed there until Mike came up after me. I knew it was him. Who else would they send.

"Elizabeth."

I didn't answer him. I felt too bad. It seemed I always ended up like this, crying bathrooms.

The door wasn't locked so he came in. I didn't look at him. I was afraid to see how angry he was.

But he didn't say anything except we were leaving. All the rest would come later. We stood by the front odoor, the four of us. Bruce said to me, "I'm sorry you aren't feeling well." I guess that's what Mike had told them and we were all going to pretend it was true for at least the next two minutes. Bruce did look worried. Probably mostly on Mike's account, like, what's the poor guy gotten himself into? And Bruce said it was crummy to get sick on vacations, didn't that always seem to happen.

Old Natalie was just standing there trying to look smooth. Later I thought of what I should have said. I should have said it must have been something I ate. But you can never come up with things like that when you need them. They were all waiting for me to say something. I said, "I'll feel better once I'm home." What I meant was, once I'm out of here.

Mike told them thank you, and how good it had been to see them, and all the things you're supposed to say. Everybody was going to pretend there was nothing really wrong, the way Natalie had to pretend she and my husband had this great intellectual bond so she could shake her boobs at him. Now she leaned over and squeezed his arm. "I'm going to send you the offprints I was talking about. Tribal structures versus modern-day institutions."

I said, "Why don't you just strip buck naked and do one of your tribal dances for him?"

I really said that. Their faces were all lopsided, staring at me.

"Stupid Africans. Who cares how they cook. They all have malnutrition anyways."

Mike was pushing me out the front door. Really pushing me. The steps were dark. I hoped I'd go ahead and fall and break my leg. Then I could sue them. But Mike kept a grip on me all the way to the car. He slammed both doors and jumped on the engine so it roared. The wheels spit gravel all the way to the street.

"Oh goody," I said. "Let's have an accident."

"Just shut up, Elizabeth." He was still driving like a lunatic. We must have been doing seventy, just on their street.

"Go on and try to scare me. Big man. You don't one bit."

"Either shut up or drive yourself." He punched the accelerator again. It was one of those little cars. Everything rattled on it.

"Oh heavens no. We might get there alive or something."

"What, you want an accident? Dandy. Why not. Stick around."

"Big man. Big talk."

"Don't push me."

"Why not. What'll you do. Big talker."

"Maybe I should just run the goddamned car off the road. How about that? Perfect end to a perfect evening."

By this time we'd reached the Parkway. I thought maybe a trooper would stop us. But no, I guess everybody around here drove like a lunatic.

"From now on," Mike was saying, "I'll just apologize for you in advance. This is my wife, please don't feed her or poke your hands through the bars of the cage."

"And I'll say, this is my husband, please don't sit on his lap."

"Oh for Christ's sake."

"Would you mind slowing down? Do you want to kill us both?"

"Sure. Rest in peace. Sort of has a nice ring to it, don't you think?"

"Stupid stupid stupid *talk*. That's all you are, you know? You think this is another stupid little dinner party kissy-face game? Go on, find a tree or something, you don't care what happens to me, you wish I was dead, don't you, go *on*."

I was screaming by then. It was a terrible sound in that little car, like one more piece of something coming loose. I really did mean it. I didn't care what happened to us anymore. The inside of the car was like a tin box with nails loose in it, everything bouncing and jolting. He looked over at me, a heavier shadow in the darkness, and though I couldn't see his face I knew he was afraid. He was afraid but I wasn't, and that meant the worst of it was over because he'd gone as far as he dared.

"Fuck you," he said, but he slowed down.

"Don't use that language to me, please."

"Oh excuse me. I forgot, you're the only one who's allowed to run your mouth. You're the only one allowed to insult people."

"That's not true. People insult me all the time and get away with it."

"Bullshit."

"It is *not* bullshit, Michael, will you listen to me?"

"Do I have a choice?"

"Just listen to me for a change, I know you think I'm too stupid to chew my own food, but just for once will you listen?"

He didn't say anything. I could hear him thinking, all right. Let her try. Let her just try. The dark air streamed over us, whistling. You couldn't see a thing outside except the instant the lights caught something, a sign or curve in the road. It was spooky, like Halloween. It was Halloween and I guess I was supposed to be the witch on the broomstick.

I said, "There's different ways to insult people. You can do it straight out or you can pretend you're just making conversation. That's what the Queen of the Jungle was doing."

He clamped his jaw tighter but he still didn't say anything.

"Her acting so frisky all night to you and pretending I don't speak English. That's an insult. And I'm not supposed to say anything about it because we're all being so polite? That's what I'm saying I hate. When people get away with things because they do it so polite. Maybe I *am* stupid, because I don't know how to be bitchy-polite back to them. I guess it shows, too. People like Natalie look at me and they figure I can't fight back, and I can't. Not like them. I'm sorry. I'm sorry for everything."

I was crying again by the end of it. I wasn't trying to. I was just so tired, and everything had turned out so wrong.

"All right," said Mike after a minute. He sounded tired too. "All right. I'm not deaf and blind. She was sort of embarrassing, if you want to know the truth. But so what. She's somebody I won't see half a dozen times in my life — " He made a move like he wanted to turn both palms up, but his hands were still on the wheel. "So it's nothing, why can't you let it stay nothing? Why couldn't you just keep quiet?"

"Because I hate women like that. I bet I know why she was making such a big deal over you. Because she's doing something really dirty with somebody else. I bet a million dollars. And this was all for old Bruce's sake, it's, you know, strategy, to throw him off. I bet if her real boyfriend comes over to dinner she doesn't say two words to him."

"You don't know any of that."

"Maybe not for a fact. But I know her type. I know what sort of woman cheats."

"Oh Elizabeth," he said. "Oh darling."

"Don't you cry too. Please. I can't stand it."

"OK. I'm OK. Just give me a minute."

Funny. How a fight like that can be over all of a sudden, how it can end up all right. You empty everything out and float to the top of it. We didn't say much the rest of the way back but it was all right. Oh darling. Love and murder, who'd imagine you could think of both in the space of half an hour. We walked up from the parking garage holding hands, listening to the concrete echoes. The baby was fine. A little warm under his blanket, but that's just sleep. The woman in the nursery said he'd been good as gold. The nursery had moons and stars on the walls, the kind that glow in the dark. The moon had a smile. We stood, breathing in the warmth and the sleep for a minute. It was peaceful, we were peaceful with each other. I could feel Mike's breath in my hair. We would be good to each other from now on. We promised. We would be good to each other because it was too terrible not to be.

And that's how it should have ended, that night. With the making up, and the two of us together in the stuffy hotel bed that had almost come to feel right to us. If only anything ever ended where it was supposed to.

I was asleep. Then I was still asleep, but hearing things, like sleep didn't end where it was supposed to either. I swam up to the edge of awake. I opened my eyes in the darkness, nothing. Stale pillow smell, body smell. Nothing there either. Something I'd heard, but what?

I turned my head and listened hard. It was a sound like rain, or water drumming, or maybe feet going too fast. A crack of light showed from the edges of the window curtains. You could see better once your eyes got used to it. Mike was on his back. Snoring a little, just in his nose. The baby, a lump under his blanket. The room was fine. Whatever it was was outside us.

Something popped, very loud but far away. Then another

pop, then a long ripping string of them. It was like hearing fireworks from a distance.

I got up then and went to the window, and pushed the heavy plastic drapes aside. But there wasn't a street below us, only another building's roof, about six stories down. The sky was dirty-milk color like a city sky always seems to be, never really dark. I heard sirens, and they seemed close, but what city doesn't have sirens. And I still couldn't see anything at all.

I stayed there for a while. I couldn't hear the rain-sound any more. If there was something wrong, the hotel people would tell you. At least that's what you always think.

Once, when I was a little girl, there was a fire near us that we all went to watch. It was just a big storage shed, but it had something in it — machinery, maybe — that made it burn hot and hard. I remember the oily orange flames growing each time the hoses hit. It was grand to watch. We all stood across the street, waiting for it to get worse, I guess. There was the shed, and a vacant lot, and then a house, and in this house an old woman was watching the fire too. She stood at the window with its sheer, fussy, old-lady curtains and African violets. She was all crouched over so she could see better. She wasn't moving a muscle, and her face wasn't moving either. She was waiting to see how far the fire would spread, if it would burn all her African violets and china dogs and embroidered pillowcases, everything she had. For a while the fire looked like it might get to her, but I don't think it did. I forget exactly what happened. But I remember two things: the living, gorgeous fire and the old woman waiting to be burned.

I went to the door and looked out into the hallway. Nothing. It was such a big place, this hotel. We were about a mile from the elevators. There was a flight of service stairs across the hall. I pulled the door of our room nearly shut, careful I didn't lock myself out. Nobody was up to see me, thank goodness, wandering around in my nightgown. I opened the stairway door.

You couldn't see smoke, but you could smell it. It didn't smell like autumn leaves or bonfires either. More like something trashy. Something that wasn't supposed to burn was burning.

I shut the door quick. I went back to our room and shut that door too. I looked around at everything, our clothes and suit-cases, like something there would tell me what to do. We had so much stuff. I took Robin out of his crib, blanket and all. He fussed a little but he didn't really wake up. He sleeps through the night mostly and wakes up early. Maybe if he'd woken up it would have been different.

It could be nothing. Somebody's rug or something caught on fire, and the fire trucks here already, everything's under con-trol. How stupid I'd look then, waking everyone up to pack, making sure we had hard shoes and wet towels like they always tell you, and then it would be nothing at all. That was how I started thinking. After all, there weren't any alarms. I should wait a little longer and see what happened.

So I put the baby down on the bed between me and Mike, and lay down again. Mike was still on his back with his arms wrapped around himself in this way he has, like he's trying to fit himself into the narrowest space he can. I'd put Robin on his stomach and he was all scooted up with his bottom in the air, like babies do sometimes. I wondered how I should lie. On one side, I guessed, facing the others with my arms around them. Now we were perfectly arranged, a family. We would be like those people in ancient someplace that got buried by a volcano, and when they were dug out you could see exactly what they were doing.

I heard another siren, a thin sound in the corner of my ear. And then a door slammed somewhere not far off. It was still hard to believe anything was really happening. After all, the hotel was so big, so busy, so splendid with its green-and-gold porters and marble floors and expensive gimcracks everywhere you looked. There were so many people in charge, surely they wouldn't let anything really bad happen.

Once you're dead, nothing more bad can ever happen. I thought that, or else I just remembered thinking it, I'm not sure which. I listened to us all breathing. Mike the loudest, his snuf-fling nose-sounds. And Robin, a funny sound, a squealing back in his throat, like he hadn't had that much practice breathing yet and was working hard to get it right. And me, making my breath light and even. We should always be like this, peaceful, at rest, making a little symphony of breath.

I thought I smelled the smoke then. Maybe I imagined it, since I'd already smelled it once. It's hard to tell. It seemed like something I'd known was there. It was really a nasty sort of smell, but I would try not to mind it.

I thought of the old woman again. I was pretty sure her house hadn't burned that day. And she would have died later, of cancer or something.

By now I was sure I smelled smoke. I reached down to the foot of the bed and spread the covers over us more evenly. I was very quiet, very careful not to wake anyone. No one had to wake up. It would just scare them. It would just start things up all over again. That seemed like a shame.

It's not something you really think through, the way you act at times like that. It's not something you plan. You're so scared. Or maybe I was watching the woman in the mirror again, the ghost-woman who wasn't afraid of anything anymore.

I stayed quiet. I put my hand on the baby's head, just lightly. It felt warm, and the skin seemed to flutter, like that was where the breath came from. Babies' heads are so fragile. I remember when I could cover his whole head with my hand and feel the blood beating through it. I used to imagine it was an egg about to hatch. Isn't that queer? He wasn't hatched, he was born, and I ought to know, I was there. But maybe their heads are like eggs in a way, because who knows what sort of ideas or feelings, what sort of *person* finally hatches out. He was still a perfect, unbroken egg, my baby.

There was an alarm at last, a sharp drill-like sound from the hallway. I turned my face into the pillow to muffle the noise. I was trying very hard to fall back to sleep.

But the noise wasn't going to stop. Mike lurched up in the bed. *"Whassat."*

I didn't move. Maybe he would lie back down. I watched him in the darkness. He got up, stumbling a little, and went to the door. When he opened it smoke and light came in together, all at once.

"Christ." He coughed and slammed the door. I heard him banging against the wall for the light switch. He found it finally. The smoke hung like fabric, big folds of it draped from the ceiling. It made your eyes sting a little.

"Christ," he said again. He bent over, still coughing. "Elizabeth." Then he saw I was already awake.

"It's all right," I said. "Come back to bed."

He stared at me. He was still naked. How strong a naked man looks, just standing. "This goddamned place is on *fire*."

"I know. Hush. You'll wake Robin."

I don't think he noticed till then that I had the baby with me. He stared for a minute more. His eyes were all bruised-looking from sleep. Doors were opening and closing, more and more people waking up. A woman started screaming, a scream with words in it.

Then he had the phone in one hand and his pants in the other. Whoever he was calling didn't answer. "Get dressed," he told me.

I just looked at him. It was like in the car, when he was scared and I wasn't. I was glad I wasn't scared anymore. And I would have explained it to him if I could, how I felt. How I'd known something like this would happen. I really had. And that maybe it wasn't so bad. It just took a little time to get used to, he wasn't used to it yet. "Come here," I said, and I held out my hand. "Just come back to bed."

He was really afraid now, of me, the fire, everything. He backed away from me, knocking into the nightstand, and his face looked all *loose*. Then he was in the bathroom, running water. He came out with wet towels and stuffed them in the crack of the door. I remember thinking, approvingly, that it was a good idea, he always knew the right sort of thing to do.

The baby was awake by then. Crying. He always wakes up crying. Mike gave me a wet washcloth and told me to breathe through it if I had to. He didn't say anything more to me. He stood by the window but I guess there still wasn't anything to see. He kept trying to phone someplace, the front desk I think, and I could hear the phone squawking, that too-fast busy signal that means something's wrong.

And that's how we stayed for I don't know how long, waiting. The alarm was still ringing. You couldn't hear anything else, couldn't tell anything at all. You couldn't even tell if the smoke was still coming in, there was so much already in the air. Fourteen floors up. I remember thinking there were a million people on all sides of us, all those people and not a one of them knew anything about us. They wouldn't even know if we died or not.

We were lucky, they said after it was all over. Someone came and knocked on all the doors and told us it was over. The fire was so far below us the smoke didn't have a chance to spread. It started in a kitchen. They got everybody out they had to except one man had a heart attack and died later. Maybe you saw the pictures in the paper of everyone out in the street in pajamas and blankets.

I was just scared, I told him later. I was just confused, and he said Of course. Very polite, like he believed me. Of course. That was really all we said.

Because how could we have said the rest of it? Even now I can't really explain how I felt that night, maybe I was a little crazy, I don't know. How it would have been a good end to things. And the next minute or the next morning of course you don't feel that way anymore. You get up, there are things to do, meals, telephones, weather, everything goes on and on, there's no time to think. Maybe I could have explained it if I'd picked the right words or the right moment. But now it was too late. Everything had begun all over again. We had another plane to catch.

CHAPTER
8

Flora was reading. She sat on her living room floor, bent over the newspaper spread between her legs.

Studies have shown that infants deprived of verbal stim-ulation in the first few months of life have significantly lowered intelligence. Now Dr. Everett Brockie of Johns Hopkins University is trying to discover if the reverse is true. Twenty-five infants in Dr. Brockie's study, ranging from newborns to three months in age, spend at least four hours a day listening to researchers read aloud a variety of materials, including Mother Goose, poetry, and magazine articles. Tapes are made of these readings, and then played to a separate group of youngsters. "We want to see if language itself makes a difference," says Dr. Brockie, "or if it needs to remain in a human, social context."

So far the program's only difficulty has been keeping the tiny subjects awake for the duration of the readings. And researchers must pause when one of their charges needs diapering or a bottle. Rhymed poetry seems to draw the most animated responses, the readers report, with the National Geographic *bringing up the rear.*

Dr. Brockie concedes that his experiment is only a pre-liminary study, and that it will be some time before its results can be measured at all. But the implications for

parents are important ones. "We may discover that any
exposure to the spoken word raises intelligence. Perhaps
parents should establish their own schedule of speech-
related activities. And of course, there are computer
possibilities."

Flora closed the newspaper, appalled. She wished there was
someone else in the house so she could denounce and thunder.
It was child abuse. Dr. Brockie was probably motivated by a life-
long resentment at being named Everett. And how had he intimidated fifty mothers into handing over their children? Your baby's intelligence can be raised, madam, unless, of course, you
want him to remain stupid. Flora had a vision of rows and rows
of babies, like an oyster bed, each tiny ear scientifically irritated
to produce some pearl of intelligence.

She got up off the floor, restless from too much reading. It
was Sunday morning and newspapers lay in blowsy heaps around
her. Flora padded into the kitchen, looking for something that
might amuse her. All the amusing things seemed to involve alcohol. She mixed a screwdriver. That at least seemed Sunday-
morningish.

The newspaper was full of appalling things. So many people
were afraid of catching venereal diseases that telephone sex services were doing a rousing business. You could call certain numbers and have people talk dirty to you. You paid by credit card.
Hygienic, but appalling. Teenagers in the Los Angeles sub-
urbs — it seemed teenagers in Los Angeles were always doing
appalling things — were making videotapes of automobile crashes,
staged surreptitiously in local parking lots. Advances in genetics
would soon make it possible to determine which genes were responsible for skin pigmentation in Negroes.

Flora lifted her glass and drank to New, Improved Life.
Choked on it a little. Down the hatch, regardless. Surely some of
these things were Progress. Dr. Brockie was a form of Progress,
even if he seemed to hate children. Telephone sex was Applied
Progress, at least, it filled a need. Why was she such a stick-in-
the-mud, such a fuddy-duddy (even her terms were outmoded),

why did she not march forward, clear-eyed and firm of purpose, to embrace the luminous Future? Why didn't she own a computer, or at least a car that talked? No wonder she made such a mess of things in general, with her lurking, messy, subversive romanticism. Her romanticism consisted of a shopworn belief in individuality. Her romanticism endowed technology with sinister qualities. In school she'd opted for all the traditional girl-things, the language arts, the humanities. That was hardly individualistic of her at all. Science, as taught in her early years, was a mixture of droning and futuristic cheerleading. We would farm the oceans. We would colonize space. Conquer hunger, solve overpopulation. Even then she hadn't believed any of it.

Well, whose fault was it that these splendid things had not happened, or had not happened yet, hadn't other equally splendid things been accomplished, heart transplants, solar heating, corn hybrids? She wouldn't want to live in a world without corn hybrids, would she? She was only a sneerer, a slacker. Wasn't it conveniently lazy of her to say that since she was bored in the fourth grade, she would be forever ignorant of technology? Of course it was. She had confessed as much Friday night to a man named Kevin. Kevin was a computer systems engineer. He had red hair and a doll's blue eyes. He listened gravely.

"You're not the only one, you know," he said when she'd finished. "I hear a lot of them in my line of work. Science inadequacy confessions, I mean. It's a little like being a priest."

"Oh dear," said Flora. "How boring. I've been boring you senseless."

"Not at all. People get anxious. They feel like they've lost control of their lives. They want reassurance. They want absolution. I like giving absolutions."

Flora smiled. He was really very nice. They were in a bar, one of those bars that offer drinks with funny names and costumed waitresses. It was a theme bar, someone told Flora. She wasn't sure what the theme was. The waitresses were dressed in red suspenders and baseball caps. She would have to peek at the menu and see if the drinks were named after sports figures or firemen or something.

"Another?" Kevin asked her, and Flora realized her glass was empty. She said yes, thank you very much, and wondered if she'd looked like she was angling to have a drink bought for her. She hadn't been; she'd only been standing there, slack-jawed, the glass in her hand. She didn't even know the man. She should have kept a weather eye on things, maybe offered to buy him a round. Oh well. She watched his neat beige-suited back, edging through the bar traffic. She didn't know him at all. At Flora's elbow, her friend-from-work was talking to Kevin's friend-from-work. The two of them were friends from somewhere other than work, and had been so animated about it for the last half hour that Flora and Kevin felt a little wan by comparison. Of course they weren't obliged to keep each other company. It was just easier than being rude. You never knew, at such times, if you ought to be buying each other drinks.

"Here you are." He handed over her wine glass, the stem carefully wrapped in a paper napkin. Flora thanked him again. His hands were small, she noticed, not much larger than her own. What was inside computers anyway, wires, she imagined, lots of wires you had to do delicate things with. A small, neat man with careful hands. Flora approved of him.

"So tell me," she said, drinking gamely. "What should I do to overcome my computer illiteracy?" The bar was noisy, but there was a little well of quiet around them, some acoustical quirk that allowed them to speak in almost normal tones.

"I don't think you should do anything at all."

"Really? Why not?"

"Why should you, if computers don't interest you?"

"But isn't it one of those things everyone ought to know about? Sort of like knowing how to change the oil in you car?"

"And do you know how to change your oil?"

"No," Flora admitted. "But I always feel guilty about not knowing."

"Save it for when you're fifty. It can be something to look forward to. When you're fifty you can learn all about computers and car repair."

"You mean, I can put it all off until then? Thank you."

"Go now, and sin no more."

So they talked, harmlessly. He had lovely skin for a redhead, neither paper-pale nor inflamed and freckled. He had skin like the inside of a good apple. They talked about politics. He said he was a Republican. Flora couldn't remember the last time she'd met anyone who owned up to being a Republican. It was nearly exotic. She kept waiting to hear other bits of exotica. Maybe he had a basement full of model trains or baked all his own bread. And did she have anything to offer up, any endearing or peculiar habits, anything she could use for self-promotion? For some reason she found herself telling him about Gordon's work with toxicity in blood products. Perhaps she could be interesting by association.

Flora became aware that her friend was tugging at her arm, saying she had to be getting home to do something. Whatever it was, it was something unconvincing, and her friend looked dejected. Kevin's counterpart was nowhere in sight. "Oh," said Flora. "Of course." She turned to Kevin. "Hey, thanks for the drink." What else did you say that was bright and zippy? Don't take any wooden nickels? See you in the funny papers?

"You're welcome. Remember. You're absolved."

"Thank you." She didn't recall, right away, just what he meant . . . Her friend was already striding away through the crowd. Flora managed a flip of the hand, a shrug, a disorganized smile. Kevin raised his glass . . .

Oh well. In the parking lot her friend said the man had gone back to his ex-wife, and wasn't that too typical, wasn't that just her luck. At least he told you, Flora reminded her, and her friend sighed and said yes, you had to give him that. She supposed you had to give him that, he'd even managed to be tactful and timely about it. Had Flora noticed that men usually had such awful timing? Like, thirty seconds before sexual intercourse, asking if you used birth control? Oh Flora, had you wanted to stay, shit, here I dragged you off bodily, now I feel like a complete jerk.

No, Flora told her. It was all right. And it was, really. She was too confused to know if she was disappointed. He was a nice man, Kevin, no doubt he had excellent potential as a human being, dinner companion, sexual partner, life's mate, what have you. But how predatory to size the poor man up that way, how alarming of her. He was only an innocent bystander. A speck in the human mosaic, a chance encounter, a grain of sand already carried away by the tides. She was romanticizing again. After all he was an adult, he was perfectly capable of tracking her down if he wanted to. If she wanted him to. She wasn't sure she did. Wasn't she already in love? Besides, even men who said they were going to call you never did. That was such a common occurence you could hardly afford to feel personally offended, she had decided after comparing notes with numerous friends. Men never called.

Wasn't she in love? Yes she was, she decided, she just was not happy. She said good-bye to her friend and drove home. It was murky autumn, a season of drips and damps, of fogs and sodden leaves underfoot. She was thinking in autumnal terms. If she and Mike were not exactly drear and forlorn, then at least the fine edge had worn off. Sometimes it surprised her to realize they'd been going on for an entire six months now, and sometimes it seemed to have lasted forever. The trees dripped and dripped. She was catching a cold, she was beginning to honk and wheeze. Yes, the edge, or the bloom, or whatever, was off, why else would she be spinning fantasies about other men?

Now, Sunday morning, she drained the watery end of her mildly indulgent, mildly decadent drink. The weather was still gloomy. Veils of fine rain blew through yellow leaves. The sky seemed to lower visibly as she watched. Her nose was clogged. The weather was sere, she decided, pleased with herself for thinking of the word and finding a use for it. Then she frowned. Didn't sere mean dry? She had it wrong, then. She thought about Kevin. Thinking about Kevin was mildly indulgent, mildly decadent. Although if her motives were just lustful, she wouldn't have felt so guilty about it. Her motives were spiteful. Another man would be a way of punishing Mike for having a wife. It was also an admission that perhaps she could no longer pretend to be consumingly, flawlessly in love; perhaps she was only behaving foolishly.

The phone rang. She considered not answering. She wondered if she would ever achieve enough indifference or temperament to leave her phone unanswered. She let it go four rings, flirting with the notion of not answering. Four seemed to be her limit.

"Hello?"

"Hello yourself. Were you sleeping?"

It was Mike. You should always answer the phone. "Hi there. No, I was drinking. Drinking and looking out the window."

"It's that kind of day."

"It's a wretched day." She thought of asking him about *sere,* but decided against it. "So what are you doing?"

"Feeling sorry for myself, mostly. I've been working all weekend. It makes me dull. Do you think I'm dull, Flora?"

She told him of course not. "Oh, but I am," he insisted. "I'm dull with everyone but you. Did you know that? No, I guess you couldn't. Don't laugh. It'll make me feel even duller."

"Why do you think you're dull, Mike."

"Because I'm basically sober and industrious and self-absorbed. Go on. Try and deny that I'm self-absorbed."

"You're self-absorbed in an interesting way."

"Nuts."

There was a pause, while Flora waited to see if he had called for any particular reason. He had. "So, would you like to get together? Do you have time today, I mean."

"Sure. What would you like to do."

"Let's mount an expedition. Let's *do* something. If I sit inside I'll grow mold."

"All right." Flora wondered at this. They did not, as a rule, mount expeditions. They usually just stayed in bed. "Where would you like to go?"

He said there was a gallery, an exhibit of photographs he wouldn't mind seeing. The exhibit was called Percussion and Repercussion. Flora said she would meet him there. He said that would be fine. He sounded nearly relieved, as if he'd expected her to kick up some sort of a fuss, whine or resist. Instead she was only curious. She was trying to imagine Mike as a gallery-goer. Perhaps he was attempting to be undull. He must get tired of stimulus-response, linear thinking, provable hypotheses, and all the other serious baggage of his trade. She would have to remember to tell him about Dr. Brockie.

Flora searched her closet for gallery-going clothes, and came up with a long full skirt, sweater, boots. She would pass for an art student, maybe. No. She would look like a woman ten years older, trying to pass for an art student. And the two of them would try and pass for a normal upper middle class couple, bored with their Sunday afternoon.

But of course that was exactly what they were. They were a perfectly normal pair of lovers, for this day and age. They went to galleries together. And if some of the fine edge, the breathlessness, had worn off by now, that was probably all right. It would be a new dimension for them, Intellectual Companionship. She would try and look the part. Flora rummaged through her jewelry box. The art student would wear silver, she decided. Dangling earrings and a chunky medallion around her neck. Artsygaudy. She was getting into it now. Her sweater was black. She looked acceptably somber. An art student having a tragic love affair. Maybe she should try another approach, wear something pink and fluffy or tight and red, see what that did for her life. After all, one did not always want to look like the kind of woman who was taken to art galleries. Flora wondered why so many of her personal crises centered around things that had to be bought.

The gallery was new and aggressively modern, with floors of cool gray tile, and cool white angled walls that divided the small space into rooms the shape of pie wedges, wings, or sometimes the letter Z. Lumps of sculpture were planted here and there. The sculpture was all of some highly polished black stuff. Flora, who had arrived first, wandered politely through the small empty lobby, trying to draw an aesthetic bead on the place. It was all done for some reason, she was sure, no doubt someone could explain the rationale to her at length. But the sculpture reminded her of her dentist's waiting room when she was young, its bulging 'modern' lamps and mysterious shiny objects which always turned out to be ashtrays. And these rooms, with their overdramatic ceilings and skewed angles, wasn't all that just trying to get a rise out of you, wasn't it just novelty and shock value? Flora thought of Michelangelo and da Vinci, of their perfect squares and circles. She seemed to be a reactionary when it came to art too. She even had a sneaking fondness for ornate gold picture frames.

Mike arrived, wrapped in an enormous dripping green poncho. His shoes squeaked, and puddles grew in his wake.

"You weren't walking, were you?"

"Just from the office. I felt like it. I felt like being elemental and robust. Serves me right. Actually, I'm perfectly dry underneath."

They found a corner out of sight and left the poncho there to drip and stream. They were surreptitious about it, since it seemed a rather nasty thing to do to the floor, but no one turned up to scold them. The gallery seemed to be empty except for themselves, though eventually they stumbled across an elderly moth-like couple. It was a little eerie, having no one in charge. Flora wondered if the attendant or keeper had dropped dead in some back room, if maybe they should look around for a pair of feet sticking out from under the curtains. No, Mike said. They were probably monitoring everything through the ceiling, like gambling casinos did. He squeezed Flora's shoulders. He smelled human and musky, as if the rain had brought out some stronger scent in him. She kissed him on the throat. She wondered if, after they finished with intellectual companionship, they might get around to bed.

The photographs were very droll, but in a nasty way, Flora decided. A great number of them were of female nudes, double and triple exposed, set against such objects as light bulbs or dinner plates. Some of the exposures were stark and high-contrast, some of them filmy, and all of them were labeled Untitled Number 2, or 16, or 40, which was no help at all. Flora examined the woman's body, very white and elongated and unnatural-looking, perhaps through some trick of the camera. You couldn't see a face, only a smudge. Flora wondered who the woman was, whether she was the photographer's girlfriend, whether she thought the pictures funny at all, what it must be like to remove your clothes for the sake of art. She was not taking a very elevated view of all this, it seemed. "Are they supposed to be funny?" she asked Mike, who was regarding them with perfect sobriety.

"I think so. But are we amused?"

"I'm not. I'm not sure why I'm not, though."

"Give it a try."

"All right. It's because he's making fun of the woman. He's putting her alongside all these stupid things —" Flora waved at the photograph in front of her, which showed the nude on her stomach with a dozen eggs balanced carefully on her spine — "eggs, doorknobs, coat hangers, the most insignificant objects he can find, and he's saying she's not any more important than they are. He's reducing her."

"Is it a he?" asked Mike, looking around for clues.

"Of course it is. Aren't all the great artists men?"

"Now Flora."

"I'm sorry. It just makes me angry."

"Maybe it's supposed to make you angry."

"I doubt it. If you asked him, the photographer, he'd probably tell you it was a study in form, or juxtaposition, or texture, and I've got it all wrong. I guess I'm out of my depth. You remember how they used to paint pictures of hams and apples on grocery store windows? That was art I could relate to."

The other photographs were less problematic, if also less interesting: street scenes, lunar landscapes, and a great many disembodied hands set against what appeared to be an ordinary tweed carpet. One picture, which did please her, showed a dozen or more hands beckoning from the surface of a pond. "Do you suppose they're asking for help, or saying come on in, the water's fine?"

Mike didn't answer. He was scrutinizing one of the street scenes. Flora wandered into the next room, if room you could call it. She sat on a bench to wait, and asked herself why she was working on such a bad mood. Was it the photographs, the rain, Mike, or some chemical combination of it all? She set herself to analyze. Rain was rain, and bad art shouldn't be enough in itself to ruin your day. Was she unhappy about Mike?

She watched him examining the photographs, stooping a little before each one. His hair was still damp, which turned it a shade darker than usual. He was wearing a forest green sweater and jeans, he looked impeccably casual, like something out of a cigarette ad. He should be doing something wholesome and normal, like the men in those ads always did. He should be building a birdhouse, or raking leaves, or stacking firewood, and there should be some equally impeccable sweater-clad woman rumpling his hair in sexy fun. And who was that woman, Flora wondered. Something within the walls ticked and rumbled, and a current of tepid air blew about her ears. It wasn't her, Flora. Was it Elizabeth? Elizabeth would photograph better. Flora watched Mike straighten and walk towards her, frowning a little. Art was serious business. Love was serious business. Maybe what she envied in the cigarette ads was some sunny and placid state, some vision of love without grief.

She stood up when he reached her, and smiled.

"Why do you suppose he called it Percussion and Repercussion?" she asked him as they strolled, idly now, through the asymmetrical rooms. She had taken his arm.

"Because he didn't want to call it Naked Lady and a Bunch of Stuff I Had Lying Around the House. Sorry if it was boring."

"Oh it wasn't boring at all. It was . . . . I'll decide later what it was. Who runs this place anyway? Isn't it awfully, uh, advanced for this town?"

"It is that. I heard it's some rich lady who got talked into being a patron of the arts."

"And here she could be spending it all on power boats or face lifts or something. Oh my. What's this?"

In a separate small white-walled cubicle were an armchair, a mirror, and a gun. The gun was enclosed in Plexiglass, except for its protruding barrel, and suspended in mid-air just to the left of the armchair. If you sat you could look in the mirror and see the gun pointing at your head. There was a placard bolted to the wall.

This gun is loaded, and the trigger has been placed under pressure. The tension on the trigger has been precisely balanced so that motion around it will not cause the gun to discharge, nor can the firing mechanism be adjusted manually.

Flora looked. There were indeed a number of fine wires attached to the trigger, held in place by a complicated arrangement of clamps, screws, and brackets.

Pressure increases gradually by a system of weights and pulleys, Inevitably, the gun will fire. No one knows or can predict how soon this will happen, only that the bullet's release is unavoidable.

Those viewers who wish to, and who fully understand their risk, are invited to sit. Their participation in this exhibit is entirely a matter of free choice. The gun may or may not fire while they are seated. The purpose of this exhibit is neither frivolous nor reckless. It is meant as a comment on human choice and human limitations, and the issues of inevitability and will. This exhibit was assembled on July 19, 1982.

Flora said, "This is the absolute limit. This is beyond decadence. It's probably illegal too. Is this thing really loaded?"

She caught sight of his face in the mirror. "What's the matter?"

He had dropped her arm and turned away from the gun and the chair. "Mike?"

He shook his head. She couldn't tell what the look on his face was. "There are people who would sit there," he said.

"Oh, sure. Drunks, exhibitionists — "

He cut her off. "*No*. I mean, people who'd want the gun to go off."

"Suicides."

"*No,*" he said again, and he was insistent now, almost he

was beginning to frighten her a little. "I mean, people who would sit there and enjoy waiting. They'd sit there all their lives if they could. It's a sickness, this caters to their sickness. Do you understand what I'm saying?"

"I'm not sure. You mean, they have some sort of death wish?"

He stared down at her. "That's the fashionable way of putting it."

He stood for a minute more, then he said, "Let's get out of here."

She followed him back to the entrance, walking quickly now. He retrieved his poncho and shook it out. It still gleamed with trapped water, beads and streams of it rolling slickly to the floor. He was angry, but it had nothing to do with her. Flora stood waiting for him to remember that it had nothing to do with her. Would he walk off again into the rain? She willed him not to. He had to stay, and remember that he was not angry with her.

And when they emerged he walked to the passenger door of her car, as if it had been agreed he was coming along. She let him in and started the car. Rain melted on the windows. They could see nothing but blur and fog. The windshield wipers squeaked and thumped against the glass, smearing a path in the solid water. She let the engine run, waiting for him to say something.

"Do you know why I love you?"

She shook her head, not daring to look at him.

"Because you wouldn't ever ever sit in that fucking chair."

She could have said, A lot of people wouldn't, but he was reaching out to hold her, awkwardly, through the flapping poncho and over the gear shift. She could feel his hands trying to reach her. They clutched at each other, with everything in the way, and wasn't it always like that. There was always so much in the way, hair, clothing, machines, other people. When they untangled themselves and drew back, they were both a little rumpled.

"Are you OK?" she asked him, and he nodded.

"Thanks," he said. "For putting up with me."

"I like putting up with you."

"I don't know if I can explain why it got me so upset. It's just morbid."

He was calmer now, reaching into his shirt pocket for cigarettes. After a moment he said, "I don't want to be an unhappy person. I really don't."

"And I don't want you to be either." He had rolled the window down a crack, and smoke was streaming thinly from his mouth. In the ads the smoke never got in the way.

"I don't think I'm very lighthearted, Flora. I probably sound like Hamlet most of the time."

"You're not Hamlet. And I'm not Ophelia."

"No, for God's sake, don't be Ophelia. Should we be going somewhere? Let's go somewhere. Let's go to your house and take a bath together or something, OK?"

"We could do that." But she made no move to go.

"What's the matter?"

"You're not in the mood. It'll sound too much like a Hamlet speech."

"Flora."

"All right then." She would try and explain, and maybe when she heard herself speak she also would understand how she felt. "I think I hate the modern world. Not because life used to be so much better. I just hate my own time because it seems to have exhausted everything natural. It scares me. That stupid gun thing. What kind of a world is it when people think like that, when it's fashionable to go against all your instincts?"

Flora paused and looked over at him being serious and attentive and uncomprehending. She started in again, slowly, waiting to see what she would say next. "Sometimes I think me and you, we're supposed to be having some sort of New, Improved Love Affair. Nobody knows what to expect any more. I'm not exactly your kept woman, am I? I wouldn't want to be, nobody'd want that now. But we're not the other thing either, the ones you read about in Ann Landers. You know, Dear Ann, he says he'll divorce his wife as soon as the kids are through college and he hasn't had sex with her in fifteen years, and blah blah

blah. There's a reason men say things like that, you know. It's because women want to hear them. But you don't tell me things like that and I don't ask, and nobody makes any promises, and we can be whatever we want, whatever that is, and it's all just too much," she finished despairingly, because he was looking into his folded hands and his face was set and dry. She wasn't sure if she was sorry because she had failed to say what she meant, or because she had, exactly.

"So what is it you want to do. Just tell me."

"Oh, we can go to my house." She unlocked the parking brake and peered behind her through the murk and gray water. "I can't see a thing back there."

"That's not what I meant. What do you want to happen, you and me?"

"Why haven't we had this conversation before?" She was out on the street now, maneuvering cautiously upstream. She felt mulish and sad, embarrassed that she'd tried to explain at all.

"Because we were afraid to. Because it's going to turn out exactly the way we imagined."

Flora said, "I don't think I'd want to be your wife anyway. Not if all that means is I'd get to use your credit cards."

"What do you want to do," he said again, patiently ignoring her bitterness, or maybe it was just that she had not really hurt him.

"I want you to tell her."

Rain melted on the windows. She had not known what she was going to say. She hadn't known what she wanted until she said it.

"You mean, leave her."

"No. Or maybe yes, I won't lie, I'd want that, I want all of you. But if it's not going to happen, then I want — some honesty."

"Come on, Flora. Telling her's the same as announcing I'm leaving."

"It wouldn't have to be. There has to be some way people arrange their lives so they make sense."

"The New, Improved Marriage? Where everyone's supposed to be perfectly free and easy and open? I don't know anyone like that. Do you?"

"But she can't be happy now. She can't think you're happy, or the way you live makes any sense . . ."

He didn't answer, and after a minute she said, "It's like that damned gun, isn't it. Sooner or later somebody's head gets blown off."

"Yeah."

They were both waiting to see what would be said next. Bang bang. Love, as subject to the laws of physics. How much do words weigh? A word traveling at velocity X has a force equal to what you want to hear.

Flora had reached her own driveway and shut the engine off. Still they didn't leave the car.

"I do love you," he said. "If that's enough. If that still counts."

"It counts for everything. I think there's something wrong with me. I ought to be unhappy but I'm not, really. Not in any way that matters. Because you're here with me."

"I'm what's wrong with you," he said. "But I'm glad. Come here. Let's practice being happy. Let's practice and practice. We may have to do it for real some day."

The rain blurred imperceptibly into twilight. Some words have the property of absorbing weight. The ear is a trigger, disguised as a crumpled rose. The greatest artists are those who can keep their balance. Across town the gallery closed its doors for the night. The bullet, unsure if it should be following the laws of physics or the demands of art, remained where it was.

In the modern world there are still many old-fashioned people.

The man named Kevin did call Flora. "I'm glad you remembered me. If you didn't I was going to have to make computer jokes."

"Spare me. How did you find my phone number?"

"I did a search. Just kidding. Your friend. I hope you don't mind." He sounded pleased with himself for being so enterprising. And why not? How often these days did a man have a chance to be enterprising around women? More often you just sparred and fenced in mutual distrust.

"No, I'm glad you called," Flora told him. "I felt bad about running off the way we did."

"You were sort of like Cinderella."

"Sort of. Very sort of."

A pause. He was going to invite her out now, and she was going to go, if for no other reason than to reward him for calling. People ought to be rewarded for taking chances, shouldn't they? They agreed to have dinner in a good restaurant. And if she was looking forward to the occasion as much as to the man, the ritual of dressing up and being squired around, that was all right, wasn't it? It was all right so far. She was not deceiving anyone. She was not obliged to feel guilty.

But she did. "You look delicious," he told her, when she met him in the bar of the restaurant. He had wanted to pick her up at home, but that had seemed somehow imprudent. He looked older than she had remembered him. His red hair was thin and tenderly combed in front. "Thank you," she said. "Like breast of chicken, or loin of veal, I guess." She was wearing white, a sweater-like dress, the best thing in her closet. She knew she looked good, but she also felt like some elaborately prepared menu item, garnished and served forth. She was a dish. Ha ha.

He helped her off with her coat and handed her into a booth. He was nothing if not attentive. Why did a man's good manners, any small deference or chivalry, seem only quaint to her? He had a doll's blue eyes. When he smiled Flora marveled at their perfect china roundness. She was not yet taking him quite seriously, she realized.

He said that he hoped she was hungry. "I feel like ordering something flaming, or stuck on a skewer. Something that's been ritually killed. You aren't a vegetarian, or allergic to things, are you?"

"No," said Flora. "I eat everything. Nothing's safe around me, I go on disgusting binges. Raw pie dough. Cold pizza."

She wondered, as she spoke, if she ought to be attempting to sound more delicate and rarefied. Maybe she was deliberately trying to sabotage the evening, out of perversity and guilt. It was a little like saying you enjoyed picking your toenails.

"I cook," he offered.

"Microwave Man."

"No no. Don't even own one. I have things like woks and cleavers. Chinese is my specialty. I even took a course in it once."

As if he was aware that he might be on the verge of sounding a little too much the contemporary eligible bachelor, of the sort written up in unbearable magazine articles, he raised his glass and drank. "Your turn," he said. "Tell me about yourself. I need data."

"That's a computer joke."

"I've got to get you to relax about computers. You seem to think I'm Dr. Frankenstein or something. The data."

"Oh. Let's see. I'm like they say in the personal ads. A DWF." He looked puzzled. "Divorced White Female. Don't you ever read those things?"

"I guess not often enough."

"I can't resist them. The sleazy ones, or even the sad ones. You know. 'Slim, attractive, 50-years-young lady seeks Christian, non-smoking gentleman for conversation, nature-walks, concert-going' . . . I forgot, you don't read them."

"Tell me why that seems sad to you."

"I don't know. Because they ask for so little, and probably won't even get that."

"It's like any advertising. A three percent positive response is considered a good return."

"Grim odds."

"No worse than the odds against meeting a nice woman in a bar."

They smiled. So far they were doing all right. But oh my it felt weird, all of it. She probably hadn't been on a date, as such, for eight years or more, the pre-Gordon days. She said, "I don't know why divorced people feel compelled to announce it first thing. Maybe it's like Truth-In-Lending or something."

"Was it recent?"

"Fairly. I guess, recent enough that I still feel I have to make apologies for it."

He had never been married. "And I always feel like I should apologize for that."

"Why?"

"Because families are important to me. I think everybody ought to be married and have children and do it up right. People who say that's not important are kidding themselves."

He thought a lot of other things like that. He thought nuclear weapons were needed as deterrents. He thought men were naturally more aggressive than women. He thought government interfered too much in people's lives. He thought earning money was a proof of either intelligence or God's grace, Flora wasn't entirely sure which. Oh, he didn't make such statements unpleasantly, or all at once. They appeared with about the same frequency as the waiter, as if the opinions were being served up along with the food. And of course he said many other things Flora didn't mind hearing, like, what a sense of humor she had, and weren't the oysters good, and yes, his boss was like that too. Still, by the time they were drinking their coffee, she was feeling cautious, her antennae were up. Computers? He might as well be a nineteenth century blacksmith. None of the things he said, she told herself, were that alarming. Herself was not convinced. Right-wing sexist imperialist lackey. Why did some people seem compelled to tell you straight away, and with perfect self-assurance, how they thought the world worked, or ought to work? Had she been doing the same thing to him? She thought back. No, she honestly didn't think she had. She wasn't any less opinionated than he; she was only more strategic. She smiled nicely at him over her coffee cup. She was disappointed with him.

She should be fair. Of course there were things that disappointed her about Mike too. Though once she tried to enumerate them, they all seemed either too large to complain about, like his marriage, or too small, like his smoking. He forgot the punchlines to jokes. He couldn't make a decent cup of coffee to save his soul. There had to be more she could hold against him than that. Flora thought of the last semi-argument they'd had. Mike had bought a new and elaborate phone for his den at home, with automatic dialing and other futuristic gewgaws. It was the very latest thing, it even had a video display screen that could show the number. In places like France, he told her, you didn't need telephone directories, you simply punched up the name you needed and the screen gave you the number. And then what happens when the thing breaks down, argued Flora, then you're shit out of luck because you don't have a phone book. It was, she said, like watching *Star Trek*. You knew it was fantasy because anything that complicated would always be broken. He said she was being silly and negative. And she was, she knew what she really resented was his extravagance and gleeful consumerism. The new phone was like all the other shiny equipment in his household, ostentatious and gimmicky. Maybe what she really resented was any addition to his already splendid domestic establishment. But meanwhile, here was Kevin again, this man she ought to be paying attention to. He was beaming at her across the table. "You're an interesting woman, you know?"

Flora considered just saying thank you, instead of "What makes you say that," as she was supposed to. He had opinions about her too, it seemed. She asked him why he said that.

"Because you're intelligent, and you don't bother trying to hide it. A lot of women do, you know."

"They do?" There was some insult in it, veiled in approval, which she had to sort out.

"You'd be surprised. It's hard to find women I can talk to, I mean, have a conversation on some other level besides how they broke a fingernail, or isn't John Travolta cute."

"Really."

"Even the bright ones. At some point in an evening they all seem to get giggle fits, or stupid fits, like some magazine's told them that's supposed to be attractive."

"You're behind the times. Now the magazines tell you to be spirited and competent."

"Then why aren't they? I'm sorry. You aren't answerable for all of womankind. It's just frustrating. I like intelligence."

"Most men," said Flora, "say things like that. What they mean is, they want an intelligent woman, but not as intelligent as they are. They want a woman's intelligence to serve as an ornament to their own. They want credit for having selected intelligence."

"And am I one of those?"

"I don't know. Probably."

His eyebrows tried to reach his hairline. He was surprised or displeased, and he was exaggerating it so it would not seem serious. He was uncertain if she was still flirting with him. And she wasn't. In spite of the good dinner and the soft leather of the booth and her own softness, or maybe because of all that. She was not trying to flirt, or please, or marvel, or coax. That was all it took to alarm him. And all it would take to put him at ease again would be for her to say something soft, or whimsical, or flirtatious. She was not really angry with him. How could she be angry at anyone so pleasant, so normal, so hopeful? She imagined him dressing for the evening with the same sense of mild festiveness and expectations as she had, imagined him combing his thin hair tenderly forward . . .

"After all," she said, "you knew I wasn't a computer expert."

He laughed. The right thing to say. How simple. She touched the softness of her dress, inside the elbow. "Would you excuse me?" she asked.

The light in the rest room made her skin and hair look coarsened. She rummaged through her purse for a comb and something pink to daub on her face. What had she expected? Nothing more than this, really, an evening of ritual flirtation. It was no one's fault. No one would blame her for being here except herself. She had betrayed not Mike, but herself. This man was nothing to her, nothing at all, and never would be, and her real and only life was with Mike. Whatever was wrongheaded, hopeless or stained about it, it was what was real. A tide of feeling pulled at her so strongly that it seemed not just wrong, but impossible that she should be here. He had made her into what she was meant to be, or wanted to be without her own knowing, a woman in love, something braver, wilder, finer. This, tonight, did not matter, this was not her life. She did not belong here, swathed in expensive fabrics, daubing her skin with scented grease for a man who meant nothing. This room, with its bad light, its watery mirror and perpetual faint sanitary dripping noise, its smells, its collection of bodily secrets discarded in Kleenex: it was not the estate of her soul, or of anyone's, what was she doing here?

She smiled when she sat down in the booth again. He had ordered brandy for them.

The restaurant was arranged in two wings off the central bar, so that from their table they could see the bartender busy with the drinks, and the backs of those sitting there. The light was a shade somewhere between pink and orange, and was so vision-confounding that Flora wondered if it had been chosen specifically for that purpose. She watched the small chips of brightness in the bartender's hands: coins, ice, glass. The row of backs, all men, was unmoving. Like many such small bars, it was a place for solitary and silent drinkers. Their shoulders seemed to be attempting to rise past the level of their ears. As she watched, one of the drinkers began to list sideways, a slow, fluid, and finally majestic collapse, a perfect demonstration of kinetics and body structure, the weight of the head pulling everything else after it. The man achieved a perfect forty-five degree angle just as the barstool upended. The wood made a squawking noise. The man, when he fell, made a noise like meat being tenderized with a mallet.

"That was impressive," said Kevin, who had also witnessed it. "Unprovoked too. Damned if he didn't just slide right off."

"Excuse me," said Flora. "I'm sorry. That's a friend of mine."

She walked to where Paul lay reclining on one elbow, peering up at a waitress. "No," he was saying. "Bent, but not broken. I am infinitely malleable. I have many plastic qualities."

There was a cocktail napkin floating from his hair. Flora plucked it off and presented it to him. "Yours?"

"Flora." He looked bad. Unfocused and flushed. Sweaty. "As usual, I fling myself at your feet." He looked very bad.

"Can you get up?"

He could. He was quite docile. He let himself be brushed and dabbed at. The waitress only looked concerned, the bartender indifferent. Apparently no one felt inclined to throw him out. "Come sit with us a minute," she told him. "If you'll promise to behave."

"Who's us?"

"Me and my date." She was relieved to see he could walk, although he was doing it with unnecessary precision.

"Who, that guy? Not your type. He looks like Jiminy Cricket."

"Shut up." The floor was tile; it clicked and echoed conspicuously. She supposed people were watching them from their own expensively padded enclaves. The hell with people.

"Permission to come aboard," said Paul when they reached the booth.

She introduced them. Kevin was polite. He was polite with an effort, as they say. The hell with Kevin. She wedged Paul into her side of the booth, with herself on the aisle. He was loose-limbed and droopy, and she wondered what she'd do if he passed out entirely. "Another coffee," she told the waiter.

"Shit. Coffee. Am I that bad off?"

"You know you are."

"Out in . . . I forget where, either California or New York, people go get coffee enemas. It's a weight loss thing. Honest. I read it in the paper so it must be true." He winked, or tried to. He had lost the technique of independent eyelid operation. Both eyes shut, then struggled open in a mildly syncopated rhythm.

The waiter brought the coffee. Paul took one sip and spilled the rest in his lap. "It's not very hot," he assured them, as they shifted about and mopped it up. "Disgrace, place like this not keeping their coffee hot."

They sat for a while longer, not that long, and things seemed to settle down. Remembering it later, she could not decide if she should have seen it coming.

"Flora," said Kevin. "Maybe we should get a cab for your friend."

"Would you like a cab, Paul?"

"No thanks. Just coffee."

"I don't think he really knows what he wants."

"Please don't keep referring to Paul in the third person."

"Oh, he doesn't mind," said Paul, rousing himself from the corner of the booth where he'd been sagging. "He knows he's been bad. Woof woof."

"He can wait outside. The air'll do him good."

"Look, he's in no condition . . ."

"Let's not cause a scene, please."

"I can't believe you're making such a big deal out of this."

"And I can't believe you dragging some drunk back here so he can paw and slobber on you." Paul was petting the sleeve of her dress, in fact, but that seemed harmless enough to her; he didn't really seem aware she was inside it. Flora stared at Kevin, suddenly relieved to have an excuse to dislike him. Prissy little man. Jiminy Cricket.

"Come on," she said, not particularly caring what he thought. "Haven't you ever made a public nuisance of yourself before? It can be a lot of fun. Pretend this is Paris at the turn of the century, and we're all drinking absinthe."

Paul said, "I am, how you say, ravished with grief to have disturbed the very pleasantness of your evening."

"Look," said Kevin. "He has to leave. It's the principle of the thing." Oh how she hated it when men did this, elevated their bad temper into principle. He was so full of principle he was nearly swollen. Pink too.

"I'll get my own table," offered Paul. "I'll open my own restaurant."

"How can you keep on talking so fast?" marveled Flora.

"I put some drugs up my nose. Shh. Don't tell the waiter."

"Look. The two of us have been having a very nice time. I'd like to keep it that way."

"I'm still having a marvelous time," said Flora. "Don't worry about me. Oh, relax. Paul's fine now."

"I wouldn't call this much of a date."

"But I'm only a rental. What do you expect?"

"Do you want me to do something, Flora?" asked Paul. "I could throw up on him or something."

But Kevin was already up and striding away from them, all

stiff shoulders and fury. Flora wondered if he would still pay the check. Of course he would; it would make him feel even more injured and righteous.

"I'm sorry, Flora."

"Don't be." Paul looked contrite, or maybe just ill. She patted his hand. "Don't be sorry at all. He must have been fixing to paw and slobber on me himself. I'd much rather you did."

Paul didn't answer. His eyes were closed and his face, though damp, appeared bloodless. For the first time she wondered if he needed help, a doctor maybe.

"Paul?"

He shook his head, his eyes still closed.

"Should we take you somewhere?"

"Home."

"Tell me when you feel you can get up and walk. No hurry."

"Now." He spoke as if he were trying to avoid using his tongue.

And they managed it, somehow. "Goodnight," the hostess said musically as they reached the entrance. Sarcastically? Flora couldn't tell. She struggled to get the heavy front door open, and to propel Paul through it.

The air did seem to help. He straightened and peered around him. "How do you feel?"

"Rotten."

"Not surprising."

"I think my hair hurts."

"That's what happens when you poison yourself." If he could keep talking, she decided, he probably didn't need the emergency room.

"Where'd you find that fellow anyway?"

"In a singles bar. No, a personal ad. I mean, a computer workshop." Flora was giggling. Suddenly it all seemed very funny. She was surprised to realize that she too was rather liquored.

"I'm glad you're getting out more. Are you through with old whatsis?"

"What?"

She stopped laughing suddenly, as if in that instant she knew everything that had happened and everything that would now happen. As if she could choose to know if she wished.

"You know. The one with the wife. Maggio."

"Who told you that, Paul?" They were standing within the parking garage, its girders black strips of shadow overhead, the cement floor blackly spotted with oil. The rumps and snouts of the parked cars reflected on light.

"Suzanne did, I guess."

"Come on," Flora said. "Just come with me now."

And he did, obediently doubling himself into her front seat. The blind leading the blind, the drunk driving the drunk. Given the choice, one does not really want to know everything that will happen. Not really.

CHAPTER
9

Paul lived in an apartment complex on the edge of town. By day it reared out of the prairie, splendidly isolated and artificial, like the alien cities in old Flash Gordon movies. At night it was a ship at sea, a mass of floating lights in darkness. Whatever you pretended it was, it looked better from a distance. Flora drove and drove. It took forever to get there. Paul jostled and drooped in the seat beside her. The place was called Something Village. Flora couldn't remember. Fog hung in great swags between the bare streetlights in the parking lots. She was beginning to regret taking charge of Paul, or at least, it was becoming one of those deeds that made you feel forbearing and Christian, because it was so inconvenient. Why did Paul have to live in a place that was both ugly and inconvenient?

Flora parked as close to the door as she could and unloaded Paul, who needed unloading. For the moment he was even beyond talking. "Come on. Left, right, left." The inside stairs were carpeted but had no risers. Somebody's idea of luxury and impracticality. Paul let her steer him from behind. It was like pushing a stack of pillows. "Come on, you aren't even trying."

"Am too."

"No you aren't."

"Am too."

She wasn't that worried. At worst she'd knock on doors and make the neighbors haul him up to the second floor. She suspected Paul was enjoying her fussing, he could manage better if he had to, and indeed when they finally got to his apartment he handled the keys perfectly well.

He rushed inside and she followed. She heard him in the bathroom. Throwing up? No, just pissing. She stood by the open front door and waited.

When he came out she began to say, Why don't we at least get your shoes off. "Why don't we — "

His head was under her chin and his arms around her hips. There was so much of him handling her so violently — squeezing, clutching, his wet mouth on her throat — and he was so stooped and unbalanced, she couldn't move without knocking them both down. *"Paul. Jesus."*

"Big kiss."

"No. Jesus — "

She was kept busy detaching various parts of him, swatting and slapping. It was a game and he'd let her go if she made enough fuss. It was another part of her evening's chores, like getting him up the stairs. "All right now," she said, aiming for a maternal tone, somewhere between threat and indulgence. "All right, let's just — "

Behind them in the hallway a door opened. Flora struggled to peer over her shoulder. From the apartment opposite, a young Japanese woman in a bathrobe regarded them critically. She was smoking a cigarette in a holder.

"Hey Lily," said Paul, emerging from Flora's midriff.

"Evening," said Lily. Her hair was cut in a severe spiky punk style. A terrible waste of Oriental hair, Flora reflected.

"This is Flora. She's going to marry me."

"Really."

"But I told her all about you and me, and she understands."

"So you wanna close your door? I got rehearsal in the morning."

"Lily's a dancer. She dances and stuff."

"Oh," said Flora. "Ballet?"

"Dance theater," said Lily. "We're doing a production of the Book of Job."

Flora said, "That sounds nice." Paul's knee was wriggling in between her legs.

Lily contemplated her cigarette. "I'm playing God."

"Pardon?"

"In the show. I'm God."

Paul said, "Now hear the word of the Lord."

"Yeah, and God has to get up early in the morning. Good night." Lily's door closed.

As if Paul had lost interest or simply forgotten what he was doing, he let Flora go and flopped backwards into a chair. In an instant his breathing turned stately and regular.

Flora went into the bathroom. She sat for a long time. She wondered if she was still a little drunk, or only weak and stupefied. She wondered how her evening with Kevin would have ended if Paul hadn't shown up. She knew exactly how it would have ended. They would have gotten all cross-eyed drunk and fond, and he would have kissed her good-night too hard, with too much tongue and teeth, and the next time she saw him she would have had to sleep with him. And so on. The perfectly presentable man whom you kept around because there was no very good reason not to. Unfairly or not, she felt she knew everything that would have happened.

And she seemed to arrange things the other way. She seemed to arrange things so she never knew what would happen to her next.

Finally she got up, flushed, and ran cold water over her face. Like all of Paul's apartment, the bathroom was bare and tidy and looked nearly uninhabited. One thin towel, a cake of damp white soap, and a cardboard box full of shaving and hygienic supplies. Paul was the sort of bachelor who owned espresso cups and brandy snifters, but no dustpan.

The living room was quiet. Was he asleep? Flora hoped so. Or if he wasn't, she hoped he would pretend to be. She said, experimentally, "I'm leaving now."

He raised his head and looked at her. He was crying. His eyes glittered behind his glasses and his mouth shook.

"Paul?" She bent over him but he turned his face away. "What is it?"

He pressed his face into the chair, away from her. His eyes were closed and tears leaked furiously from them. He looked so unlovely and humiliated that she moved a step back to spare him more embarrassment. He cried for a while longer in the same furious silent manner, and then he stopped, panting a little. He looked at her briefly, resentfully, then turned away again.

"Are you all right?" Flora asked. Oh God, what did you say. What did you ever say. She closed the apartment door, although she doubted that Lily would miss much anyway. Paul's nose was running and he was groping at his pockets. Flora gave him Kleenex from her purse.

"Thanks," he said nasally, and honked, and mopped. His eyes were red but the rest of his face looked stony dry, as if the tears had parched it. Both of them were wishing it was possible for her to simply leave.

"Do you want to talk?" she asked.

"What's to say."

"Anything you want. Anything that'll help."

"I'm a fucking drunk, Flora."

His face was stony dry. The crying seemed to have sobered him. He only looked sullen.

"Well . . ."

"You don't have to go all soft and tactful on me, Flora. In fact, don't. You're always so goddamned tactful. It makes everybody else look bad, you know? Like you're the official Sister of Mercy or something."

"I was about to say yes, you're a fucking drunk."

"I'm sorry."

"It's OK." She bundled her coat more tightly around her.

"I'm sorry. I mean, I feel sorry for myself mostly. Would you please sit down?"

She sat.

"Thank you. I don't want to stop drinking, you know. I just don't want to be a drunk."

She decided not to say anything. He didn't want her to say anything.

"You know the old *Thin Man* movies? With William Powell? Where they're always drinking martinis and making drunk jokes and even the hangovers are funny? That's me. I'm goddamned funny most of the time. I'm goddamned drunk most of the time. I stay in character."

She wouldn't say anything. The ceiling was lumpy textured plaster. The carpet was gold. Waiting room gold.

"I'm scared," he said. "I've never been scared before, about something like drinking, I mean."

He was looking at her then. She could feel it. "You don't want to be here," he said. "You don't want to hear all this messy stuff."

"I just don't know what to say."

"It's messy when people lose it, isn't it. Nobody knows what to say. Even Sister Flora. Listen, I'm sorry about that one."

"Don't be. You're right. I say polite things when I'm too scared to say anything else."

"I'm still sorry. You didn't deserve it. I'm on a roll, aren't I. Who else can I insult. What else can I screw up in one night."

"It's OK. Really."

"I know. In spite of everything, I'm a terrific human being."

He was crying again. Weakly this time, too exhausted to try and hide it. She was done with being embarrassed. She crossed the room and knelt in front of his chair and held him. His hair still smelled of cold air. His breath jerked him up and down in her arms. Flora found herself crying too, silently, without effort, as if tears came all too easily to her now, her native element. Was she crying for him? Herself? She didn't know. She felt as if she'd come unexpectedly to the end of her strength, to some crisis without a name. No, the name was sin. She was crying out of a sense of sin, no matter how ineffectual and after-the-fact. There were simple, honorable lives she could have led, she could have been someone's placid, middle-aged wife or a harmless solitary. Instead here she was. She had come too far, too dangerously, she had stretched her nature to its very breaking point with dishonesty and recklessness.

Paul's hand slid up the glossy length of her stocking. "Please," he said. "Flora."

She couldn't look at him. She nodded, ducking her head until her chin touched her chest. She could do anything but look at him. He stood and pulled her up with him. He was still foggy with the liquor but she could feel him trying to be careful with her, the way a man with bandaged hands might hold a glass. He steered her towards the bedroom, pressing close behind her.

The bed was a vast white drifting shape in the darkened room. Paul eased her onto it and she lay back, eyes open in the darkness, seeing nothing. What did it matter, which man you went to bed with. She thought it only mattered if you hadn't already gone to bed with the wrong one. Then her eyes closed and for a moment she must have slept. Something was pulling at her, at her dress. "What. *What.*" She struggled awake. Paul was leaning over her, trying to hitch her skirt above her knees.

"Here." She yawned and blinked. "That won't work." Flora sat up, loosened her belt, and shimmied the dress over her head. "There now." She felt weirdly businesslike and helpful, as if getting undressed, and doing it efficiently, was the only real issue here. Briskly she reached behind her to unhook her bra, then rolled up on her hips to peel off her panties and hose. There now. She shivered. She couldn't see Paul's face, only the slumped outline of him sitting on the edge of the bed, his shaggy hair and uneven shoulders.

"Flora."

She was afraid he was going to ask her if she really wanted to, if it was a good idea. She didn't want to talk about it. It would be more embarrassing to talk about it than to go ahead and do it. She closed her eyes. She heard him stand up and cross to the other side of the room, then the rumpled, furtive sounds of his undressing.

"Get under the sheets," he said from somewhere close beside her. Obediently, she peeled back her side of the covers. She hoped he would keep giving her directions. It would be easier that way.

She waited. His breath whistled in her ear. Then his hands sliding along her ribs. They bumped knees. "Sorry," he said. She could feel how cold her own skin was, cold and shrunken, like a fruit in winter. She reached out and hooked a leg around his. He fastened his mouth to one breast, and puffed as if he were trying to inflate it. Was it all going to be this bad? It was. She tried to think of something light and pleasant. Apple orchards. She would think about apple orchards. She couldn't move beneath him. He was hard, it was hurting her. She was so dry. He must feel it, how dry and merely obliging she was being. He pushed into her harder. His shoulders grew damp under her hands. She had the oddest thought. A Bible verse, which one she didn't know. Yea, though I give my body to be burned and have not love, it profiteth me nothing. Then something about a cymbal. She was thinking about the Bible during sex. No wonder it wasn't working. Though I give my body to be screwed and have not love, it profiteth me nothing.

He was going to come. She could tell by the way he was guiding her hips, and his roughening breath. She supposed men could do that. Come without feeling. She meant, without her feeling anything. She didn't know what she meant. He stopped moving suddenly and held himself rigid above her. She could see better in the darkness now, she could see his face working. Then he sank down into her. That part of it, at least, was over.

His chin was planted just above her shoulder, with his face averted. What came next? For some reason she felt better now, nearly cheery. She supposed because it hadn't been any worse. She tapped Paul's back. "Hey, it's OK." He shook his head. "Really, it's OK."

He turned to look at her. In the dimness his face was composed of unfamiliar planes of shadow and of half-light. For a moment Flora couldn't remember ever seeing him without his glasses before, although she must have. "I don't want it to be just OK. Shit, Flora. You're only being nice, you know."

She was silent. "Look," he said. "It won't happen again. I won't expect it to."

Almost decorously, he moved off of her so they lay side by side. He said, "I just wish. Never mind."

"Go on. You can say it."

"I just wish I'd done a better job. I wish you'd enjoyed it."

She reached out and patted his shoulder. She couldn't say anything. She couldn't lie and say she'd enjoyed it, but even less could she say what she really felt: that she was glad she hadn't enjoyed it. It was some sort of proof of fidelity not to have enjoyed it. That was probably the sort of thing that whores told themselves, but it was still true.

Paul was scrabbling around on the nightstand. "Cigarettes," he said. "Why don't you smoke, Flora? It's something you can do in truly embarrassing situations. Instead of shooting yourself."

"Oh come on. That's silly talk." She was still maintaining her bluffness and cheeriness, but with an effort. It would have been difficult enough even if he'd given her any help.

"Sex really does make you depressed, doesn't it? At least it makes me depressed when I, ah, fuck it up so thoroughly. A bad business."

"Come on now."

"Really, when you think about it, it seems like damned poor design."

"Paul. Please. You're making it worse. I mean all this 'expense of spirit in a waste of shame' stuff. You're making me feel truly rotten."

He didn't say anything. There was the thin, pleasant smell of a lit match, then harsher cigarette smoke. He put an arm around her shoulders, hitching it awkwardly to get past the pillows. "All right. We can at least do this part right. We can talk in bed."

"Sure we can."

But neither of them could think of much to talk about. After a while, just to be saying something, Flora asked him if he had a girlfriend these days.

"What a question. I never have girlfriends."

"What do you call them then."

"I don't know. Women I tote around town for a spell until they get mad at me. Women are always getting mad at me, you know?"

"Why do they get mad at you, Paul?"

"I'm not sure. I think because I won't marry them or something. Women are always wanting to get married. Even to me."

"What do you mean, even you. You're perfectly eligible."

"No. I'm just available. There's a difference."

Flora said nothing. She didn't want to get into a conversation about available or unavailable men. She didn't want to talk about Mike, or what Paul knew about it. She didn't want to think about any of it until later. She was so tired. She wanted to be home alone in her own bed. She didn't care, at the moment, if she never touched another man again.

Paul was saying, "I mean it about the drinking. I'm quitting. I'm quitting so you'll fall in love with me. Don't argue. It's going to be my motivational technique. My search for the Holy Whatchamacallit. Grail. Now I want you to say it. You'll fall in love with me once I stop drinking."

"I'll fall in love with you once you stop drinking."

"Thank you. You're a sport. I don't think I've ever had a woman go to bed with me just to be a good sport."

"Paul."

"Hush. Sleep now. Sleep and sleep."

She had never spent an entire night with Mike. It was one of those minor sadnesses, something she did not even bother feeling sorry for herself about on most occasions. But now, on the soft boundary of sleep, lying next to a man whose shape and breath were neither dear nor familiar to her, she allowed herself to imagine him in his wife's bed. She allowed herself to feel all of it. You could tell yourself that the body was merely the temple of the spirit, that it was frail, treacherous, subordinate, an obstacle to be overcome, but such talk never worked. It mattered. There was nothing else that mattered. Her life was this marvelous housing of skin and clean muscle, her life was the life of the body. How long it had taken her to learn it, and through what extremities. She could take no comfort in the man next to her, she could not even pretend he was someone else. Though I give my body to be burned, it profiteth me nothing. That was wrong somehow. You didn't give your body to be burned, at least, if anyone ever had, they didn't nowadays. Nothing so drastic. You just loaned it out. It profiteth nothing. Sleep opened wider and softer to receive her. She slept without dreams or wakefulness.

By the time Flora woke up in the morning, Paul was already dressed and rattling things around in the kitchen. She was glad for that, at least. She was remembering everything all at once. It would probably be all right, she decided, as long as they didn't talk too much about it. She stayed in bed for a few minutes longer, trying not to think about anything. The bedsheets were twisted into mounds and ropes. They looked like sheets always did the morning after: guilty by association. Shadowless autumn sun lit up flat squares on the bedroom wall. The wall was the sparsest kind of plastered board, utilitarian, indifferent stuff. The window was a square of equally indifferent sky. Flora told herself, severely, that she should not expect a vista of flowering meadows, and even had there been one, it probably wouldn't have made her feel much better.

But it didn't go too badly. After all, as Paul remarked to her, they weren't the first people to get embarrassed about landing in bed together. Flora agreed. This sporting, generous attitude was the best policy, she decided, and she was grateful that he'd adopted it. She drank coffee and watched Paul rummage through cupboards looking for things to feed her, though she kept telling him she didn't want anything. Finally he gave up, finally it would be all right if she left. Flora assembled her coat and keys and shoes and stood at the door, tugging and jingling nervously. She hoped she wouldn't run into Lily, then she hoped she would, just to see which one of them could act more blase. "Well," Flora said. Stupid thing to say. A preface to nothing. *Well,* she still didn't love him, sexually or otherwise, and she was sorry, and she couldn't say any of that.

"Well yourself."

"Are you all right? I'm worried about you."

"You're sweet to worry. Now cut it out."

He smiled. He was being — whatever it was when men decided not to discuss things. Stoic, or worse. He looked like an untidy old man this morning, with his hair sticking out in tufts and the grainy skin around his eyes. What drinking did to you. Flora wondered if he was serious about stopping. He didn't seem to want to discuss that either. He was only waiting for her to go.

She almost said *Well* again. She reached up to hug him, trying to make it jolly, concerned, asexual. He patted her on the back and released her. He said he would be talking to her. She said of course, and take it easy.

That was all. The door closed. Flora descended to the windy parking lot. Gray clouds and rags of gray newspaper scudded through the air. Flora wondered if Paul was watching her from a window. She thought he probably was, but she didn't look up to see. No, she didn't really want to see. That was the true sadness of it all, she decided, the obstinate refusal of the heart to love. She didn't want to know if he watched her.

Her little stucco house looked neglected. How long had it been since she'd spent a night away from it? Spending the night away seemed to add to the criminality of it all. Flora picked up newspapers and stray towels, trying to coax the place out of its funk, and herself out of the suspicion of a hangover that beat behind her eyes. She turned on the TV just for noise. Sunday morning preachers, mostly, but then she found an old Joan Crawford movie. Cleaning house was good for the soul, it made you feel righteous and productive. Once you had a clean house, and maybe clean laundry, you could work seriously on character flaws. She was down on her hands and knees in the kitchen, scrubbing at the spaces between the tiles with a little brush. The pleasing thing, of course, was that if you spent enough time cleaning house, you hardly had the energy to worry about your soul. She was feeling better already, and she hadn't done a thing about her soul. The phone rang and she bounded to her feet. "Hello," she said musically.

"I'm glad you're home, slut. It's about time."

The phone slipped and nestled closer against her ear.

"Filthy slut," the woman said. "I know all about it. Everything. Everything you've done."

"Who is this?"

"You know who it is. Whore."

And Flora did know, clever whore, clever slut that she was. Elizabeth cleared her throat. It was an odd prim sound in the middle of all the screaming.

"Think you're so smart. A pig. Dirt. That's you. Men know exactly what kind you are. Don't fool yourself. Every so often they have to sleep in dirt. None of your business. Don't touch me. Get away. Don't you dare touch me. Sleep with pigs."

The phone was grabbed, or dropped, or maybe submerged. It made muffled underwater noises. Then Mike's voice said "Hello? Hello, who is this?"

"Mike? My God. What's happening?"

"Hello? Who — Flora. Shit, listen, I'm going to call back in just a minute. Don't worry, it'll be me. Don't be afraid to answer the phone."

He hung up. Flora did too. All she could think was that he hadn't known who was on the other end of the line.

The phone rang while she was still standing next to it. Sweating, she picked it up.

"It's me. Relax."

"Where's Elizabeth? Isn't she listening?"

"No, it's OK. She locked herself in the bathroom. It's OK for now."

The television was still on. Flora could hear the raised volume and cheery, earnest tone of a commercial, though she couldn't tell which one. Was it on at Mike's house too? She thought she heard an echo, a current of identical noise strained through the wires. "How did she find out?" *She knew. Elizabeth knew.* In spite of her fear, she felt a sense of pure triumph. Elizabeth knew.

"She didn't. She didn't find out anything."

"What? Then what was — "

"She found a phone number. This is so stupid. I had your number on automatic dial."

"On what?"

"My new phone. You know, the fancy one, cordless, digital display — "

"Would you just tell me what happened?"

"I'm trying to. See, you can code in numbers you dial often. For convenience. So I put yours in. I know, it was stupid. And Elizabeth must have gone through them. When a woman answered, she started screaming. That's all. She doesn't know anything. She didn't even know who she was talking to."

"But she will now, won't she?" The television was on at his house too. She could hear the little surge of movie music in the earpiece, lagging a second behind her own set. Why should the sound take longer?

"No she won't. I'm taking the number off. And even if she had it on display — "

"On what?"

"The digital display. Never mind. Listen, I'm going to have to go. I'm sorry. About all of it. But it's all right. I'll come up with something to tell her. Don't worry. Love you."

"Love you too," Flora said, but the line was already dead.

There was something not right in it. There was some space between his words, something lost in the wires. *Why hadn't he known who was on the phone?*

There was some perfectly reasonable explanation. He would come up with something to tell her.

All day Flora waited for the phone to ring again, but it was silent. It seemed wrong that nothing was happening. No one calling, no one on the doorstep shrieking doom and curses. Flora thought of all the people who might conceivably show up at her door, accusing or demanding things. There seemed to be a great many of them. She'd left a trail of damage a mile wide. Now she was waiting for it all to catch up with her. Was that old-fashioned, thinking in terms of sin and retribution? She couldn't help it, that was the way she thought.

After a time she stopped even pretending to clean the house or do anything else useful, and lay in bed, treading over and over the same ground. It seemed fitting that she be betrayed by machinery, by a New, Improved Telephone. But was Elizabeth so barmy that she screamed at everyone, women who might turn out to be typists or cleaning ladies? Or had she overheard Mike on the phone? Why did she get suspicious? It was all too muddled, and Flora was too tired and sick with dread to sort any of it out.

Then Flora thought not of Elizabeth, locked away in her (no doubt) impeccable bathroom, but of a girl she'd known in college. This girl was the girlfriend of the roommate of Flora's boyfriend. The two boys shared a tiny apartment (one bed and a sleeping couch), which was the only space either couple had for sex, owing to dormitory rules and such. Flora and the other girl had hated each other like poison, in a polite, wordless way. It was because of the unspeakable intimacy of the situation, finding each other's used Tampax in the bathroom, or underpants wadded up in between the sheets. Flora couldn't recall the girl's name, but she still remembered what sort of birth control pills she had used. The kind that came with little blue and gold butterflies on the case. They hadn't even been sleeping with the same boy. They only had to witness the process from too close up.

And now she was older, more fastidious, more scrupulous, at least about things like bedsheets and towels. How hygienic and insulated it all was. She doubted if she would ever hate Elizabeth in quite the same way she had hated that nameless girl. Why was she thinking of all that now? It had been years. Maybe because it was the last time she'd really hated anyone over sex.

Finally, around ten that night, Flora got in her car and drove to Mike's house. She did things like that. Sometimes she called his house and hung up when Elizabeth answered. She did things like that often. Mike and Elizabeth's house. Elizabeth's house. Why did she never think of it that way? After all, Elizabeth was the one who scrubbed and tended it, the one who bought the crafts-fair planters and the fancy potholders and had the babies. It was all Elizabeth's, her creation, her territory, and Flora had to content herself with brooding on its borders. The house was quiet. Its great angled roof was like the lid on a box. One light burned downstairs. Kitchen. They were in bed. Flora parked where she always parked. A side street from where she could see the bed-room windows. It was terrible to have perfected so many of these furtive habits. The windows showed nothing, only layers of darkness. Why did she do things like this? What if one of them saw her from the house, what if she got caught? But she wouldn't. She could imagine herself breaking into their house or stalking them in the streets, she was not above anything outlandish or grotesque, but she could not imagine herself getting caught. When she got caught it would come some other way. Flora restarted her car and glided away, home.

Flora's doctor, a gynecologist, had furnished his office in womb-like colors of rust and scarlet. Every surface in the waiting room was thickly upholstered and carpeted, everything was plush. The lights were soft. It was expensive, tasteful, even comfortable, but it always made Flora feel as if she were bathed in blood. Sometimes she wouldn't have minded a little starkness and clinical white. She had a raw throat and a fever of 101. She had whined over the telephone to the nurses. You always had to whine to get in without an appointment. Flora's head was thick and her eyes were gummy. She looked like a hag. Whatever happened to those illnesses that made you look delicate and wasting?

The fever didn't burn; it floated. Although she was sitting well back in one of the doctor's deep padded couches, Flora felt tilting and precarious. Sounds reached her at a distance and drifted away, buzzing. She was a fish floating in blood-colored water. She hated being sick, she was no good at it. She resented everything about it. She resented having to sit here in this womb-room, leafing through coverless copies of *Parents* and *Redbook*. It didn't matter how snazzy the furniture was; they could never keep covers on the magazines. The other women waiting (there was one stray man in the corner, a glum husband pressed into service), they looked bad too. Of course they looked bad; they were sick. Or they were pregnant and didn't want to be, or not pregnant and wanted to be, their insides were full of clots, they leaked and swelled, they had displaced uteri, painful breasts, oh, women were nothing but messes. She was glad she wasn't one of them. She meant, she was glad she had no female problems. She wanted to announce to everyone in the room that she was only in for a sore throat.

She'd been waiting a long time already. Or maybe it just seemed that way. Flora kept looking at her watch and forgetting what it said. They were working her in between appointments. She watched jealously as other women's names were called and they vanished into the back rooms. There was more than one doctor in the office, maybe as many as three. She couldn't remember. There were at least fifty nurses, like a flock of efficient storks. One of them called Flora's name and she got up and stumbled through the rosy murk.

A hand touched her arm. "Oh, do you go to Dr. Chrisman too?"

"Dr. Frank." Flora couldn't see who she was talking to.

"I just started going to Dr. Chrisman," said Elizabeth. "He's real nice. Listen, I'm going to wait for you. I want to talk to you."

"Talk?" said Flora, but Elizabeth had walked on. "Mrs. Reynolds," the nurse said again. She should tell them to change the name on their records. Where was Elizabeth?

"So we've got a nasty old cold today," said the nurse, directing Flora to a chair and brandishing a thermometer. She was Flora's least favorite nurse. She had black hair and staring blue eyes and always seemed to be about to drop something. Flora was afraid she would faint. She'd never fainted before in her life. Where was Elizabeth?

"One hundred and one and a half," pronounced the nurse. "Why, you're a little furnace."

"I am not a little furnace," said Flora, but the nurse was already propelling her into an examining room. The door popped shut behind her. Flora shivered. Had Elizabeth been coming or going? She couldn't tell, or couldn't remember. She might be in the next room. Flora would be stretched on the examining slab under the paper cover that always reminded her of the table-cloths at children's parties, her legs obligingly spread (she was always very good about getting right down on the edge of the table like they told you), and Elizabeth would wander in to chat.

No, she was only here for a sore throat. She had no female problems.

The doctor came in. He looked tired. He always looked tired, as if he had really wanted to be a telephone repairman instead of a doctor. "How are you today," he asked wearily, then he looked at her chart. "Oh, I see."

He peered down her throat and listened to see if her lungs bubbled. Her heart was booming and leaping. She was sure he could hear it, she was sure he was going to get alarmed at it and clap her into a hospital. But he didn't. He was saying he would write her a prescription for some wonder pills, and she should gargle with salt water and take aspirin. Was that all? Flora felt she needed more healing than that. "You never had your tonsils out," the doctor said suddenly. No, Flora hadn't. She was sorry about it too, she'd done so many things wrong and now it was too late. She waited with her head bowed to hear what would become of her. But the doctor only handed her the prescription and hurried out. There were other people sicker than she was.

She couldn't stay here. She got her coat and emerged, blinking, into the hallway. The place was a warren of rooms and cubbyholes, all of them full of women being weighed, measured, scraped, inflated. No Elizabeth. Flora stumbled back into the waiting room. You couldn't see a thing in here, it was too bloody. Her ears were buzzing again. No one stopped her on her way to the door, or maybe she just couldn't see or hear. OK so far. She caught the faint sour odor of her own sweat. She could still smell.

Elizabeth was sitting outside on a bench in the little glassed-in entry. "That didn't take too long," Elizabeth said. She had the baby with her. Flora hadn't noticed before. He was dressed in a bright red snowsuit. He was chewing on the cuff of one sleeve, and making dog noises.

It had been two days. No, three days since Elizabeth was screaming whore at her over the phone. Elizabeth fussed with the child's mittens and extracted the soggy cuff from his mouth. "Are you a puppy dog?" she said. "Bow wow wow." Elizabeth was wearing a coat with fur around the collar. Flora hadn't seen a coat like that in years, and she couldn't tell if it was out of date or just now daringly current, if the fur itself (pale fluffy orange), was genuine something-or-other, or some very much lesser hide. Bow wow wow. She couldn't tell anything any more.

Flora didn't exactly faint. But then how would she know, she'd never fainted before. She felt a wave of heat, and she sat heavily on the bench beside Elizabeth. There was water in her eyes but she wasn't crying. Elizabeth's face bent over hers. It looked pale and enormous, like a mask waving before her on a stick. "Are you OK?"

"I just need to rest," said Flora, or at least she thought she said it. Her ears were blotting out sounds and everything echoed. She thought Elizabeth was telling her she looked delicious. No, that was wrong.

"I was really wanting to talk to you," Elizabeth was saying. "In fact, I was just thinking about you when you walked past in there, isn't that funny?"

"Excuse me," said Flora. "I didn't see you."

"I was just in for a checkup. I'm in perfect shape, the doctor says. But then I always am. Are you sure you're OK?"

Flora's vision cleared. The sweat was chilling on her. Elizabeth was wearing lipstick a shade darker than the fur on her coat, and her hair was a shade darker than the lipstick. It all made sense now. "I have to go home," said Flora. She stood up, balancing against the wall.

"Maybe you should go back in and see the doctor. Maybe you should lie down for a while."

"I'll be better off at home. Really."

"We'll come over then. Just for a little, to make sure you're all right. Are you driving? Can you handle it? I'll follow you. Come on, puppy dog. Up we go."

"No," said Flora, "I don't want you to," but they were already pushing their way into the parking lot, all of them, Elizabeth with the child bundled on her hip. Outside it was bright and bitter. Sunlight exploded in the ranks of windshields. Where was her car? Right where she left it. The wind stung her eyes. Keys in her hand. Why couldn't she at least manage to lose her keys?

A horn sounded behind her, three taps. Elizabeth was waving from the driver's seat of her car across the lot. The baby waved too. How had they managed to get there so quickly? Flora started her car and backed out. Elizabeth's car was a big maroon sedan, a real car, with lots of doors and chrome. The family car. It didn't go with her hair at all, Flora noted. Could she lose them on the streets? She didn't think so. She couldn't think of anything at all. The heater blew cold air around her ankles. Elizabeth pulled up behind her, obediently signaling as Flora did.

She managed it somehow. The streets were tricky, like solving a maze. She reached her own driveway and hauled herself out of the car. Elizabeth wasn't there. Had Flora lost her without trying? She couldn't remember. She got herself inside, took her coat off, and pitched face first into her bed. Even when there were no sounds her ears roared and roared. She wondered if she were dying. Now that was silly. People didn't die on the way back from the doctor's, at least, she never had before.

Something — the door — rattled, and Flora shot up in bed. Then there were paper bag noises, and cupboards opening. "No," Elizabeth said from the kitchen. "No, don't touch." Something landed on the floor but it didn't sound like it broke. "Naughty," said Elizabeth.

There was a tapping at her open door. Elizabeth came in with a glass of orange juice. "All I could find were these Flintstone glasses. I hope that's all right. Here, you should drink this. I got you some soup too."

Flora drank. She supposed she would have done anything anyone told her to. Elizabeth was looking around the room. "This is a funny house," she said. "What do you call it, Mexican or something?"

"I don't know what you call it," Flora said. She watched Elizabeth appraising things. She kept thinking Elizabeth could tell something just by looking, as if anyplace Mike had touched might glow under Elizabeth's gaze. Like what do you call it. Ultraviolet light. There was a thudding noise from the front of the house.

"Honestly." Elizabeth hurried out, and Flora looked wildly around the room. Wads of Kleenex, a nightgown turned inside out and slung over a chair. Yesterday's newspaper. Dustballs nesting under the dresser. It was tatty and unkempt, but it wouldn't betray her. No shirts in the closet or cigarettes in the ashtray, no love letters lying around, because Mike had never written any. There wasn't a scrap of him in the house. It struck Flora as strange that he should leave so little trace of himself.

Elizabeth returned with Robin in her arms. He was squirming and puffing to get free. Maybe it was the snowsuit. Flora thought she could remember hating snowsuits.

"He doesn't look much like either of you," Flora heard herself saying.

"Mike. He looks exactly like Mike's baby pictures."

"Really."

Elizabeth nodded. Her eyes were bright and enormous, and as incapable of expression as a cat's. Still, Flora felt Elizabeth was excited at being here, like a child admitted into play with an older child. She stood at the foot of Flora's bed, joggling the baby, her eyes still taking in the room. "It's a good thing I saw you. It's a good thing I could look after you."

"Yes," said Flora. She thought of the prescription she had forgotten to fill. "Yes, thank you." She found she could breathe again. She was sure she hadn't been. She began breathing cautiously, in and out.

Elizabeth said, "It's Mike I wanted to talk about."

Flora stopped breathing again. She heard Elizabeth say, "I'm not stupid. I'm not nearly as stupid as he'd like me to be. He's one of those men who needs to have a stupid woman around, you know? Not that he'd ever own up to it. He has a high regard for intelligence. A high regard. That's how he talks."

The baby kicked and squalled. Elizabeth set him down on the bed, but he cried to be picked up again. Elizabeth shooed him away. He turned his wet, red gaze on Flora. His cheeks were squeezed up tightly from crying. Little pig cheeks. He didn't look a bit like Mike, she refused to believe it.

"He likes women to be stupid in bed. I mean, he has to feel like Mr. Boss. That's how I think of it, 'Oh, we're playing Mr. Boss again tonight.' "

Flora said, "You don't have to tell me things like this."

"I still believe we have a good marriage. Better than a lot of people's. I think it's worth working on. We have common goals. We're raising a family."

"Of course you are," said Flora. "I mean, here he is." The baby was making fists in the bedspread and gnawing on them.

Elizabeth sat on the foot of the bed beside him and took the spread out of his mouth. "Messy," she scolded. "Bad."

"It's all right," said Flora. Dimly, she felt it was only fair that she be terrorized by Elizabeth and her child. It would only be fair if they pulled her house down around her ears. On impulse, she said, "Can I ask you something?"

"Sure. Bad. I'm sorry, go on. I'm listening."

"You know that dress I bought? This summer. You were with me." Elizabeth frowned. "A red dress. With stripes."

"Red with stripes."

"You remember. You were there." She had gotten sick then too, hadn't she? Reckless now, she persisted. What did she have to lose? "What I wanted to ask was this. Did you already have a dress like that?"

Elizabeth plucked at the bedspread, frowning. "I thought I saw you wearing it," said Flora. "In fact I'm sure I did."

Elizabeth shook her head. "It must have been someone else."

"You're lying," said Flora. "Look at you."

Elizabeth was still digging at the bedspread. Flora said, "Did you have it already, or did you go back and buy it? You can tell me."

"I went back."

"All right," said Flora. "That's all I wanted to know." It wasn't, but it was all she could ask. She felt as if the balance between them had changed, as if she had somehow made Elizabeth into the guilty party. She even felt less ill. "It's all right," she said, more kindly now. "It's not a big thing. I was just curious."

There was a silence. Elizabeth pulled the baby into her lap. She wouldn't look at Flora. A beautiful woman. She really was. She had a mouth like flower petals, and elegant ivory bones.

"I'm sorry," said Elizabeth, still without looking up. "It was stupid."

"No big deal." But, Flora thought, in Elizabeth's eyes, copying a dress might be a mortal affront, a breaking of some tribal code. Perhaps Flora had now shamed her for life, perhaps they could trade evenly: a husband for a red dress.

"It's just, I guess I've admired you. You know. But it was a stupid thing to do."

"No, it's all right," said Flora hurriedly, feeling the guilt shift back her way. She didn't want Elizabeth admiring her.

"Everyone likes you, you know? Everyone can talk to you. Mike. Mike admires you."

"He doesn't have to do that," said Flora idiotically. The baby was beginning to fuss again. Why didn't Elizabeth take him out of that stupid snowsuit? And she still had her coat on, with its pinky orange fur.

"Hush," said Elizabeth to the child. "Mommy's busy. I mean it. He respects your opinion. That's why I wanted to talk to you. I'm sure it's no surprise. I want you to help break it off. For everyone's sake."

"The last thing I expected," said Flora, "was for you to be so calm about it." She was calm herself, or maybe just too ill to be afraid.

"I'm calm now. I wasn't then."

"When you found out."

"When I walked in on them," Elizabeth corrected. "At least they weren't using the bed. Isn't that funny? As if that should make any difference to me. But it does, I guess. I shouldn't be talking like this in front of the baby. I know he's too young to understand, but doesn't it make some sort of impression on them? You know, subconscious?"

"No," said Flora. "I don't know."

"She's the worst kind of dirt. Her and her smart talk and always smiling, like there's nothing that isn't a joke. I'm sorry. I know she's your friend. But I'm entitled to my feelings. I'm entitled to something."

"Of course you are."

"Bare-assed naked in my own living room. Goddamn him. Goddamn them both."

Elizabeth began to cry. She cried without energy, and after a minute she stopped. The baby kicked to get down. Elizabeth said, "He promised it was over. We'd been through it all before. He had to sort out his commitments, he said. His emotional bonds. You should hear him. I hate the way he talks. Goddamn him. All he ever tries to do is talk his way out of things. All those words just so he can do whatever he wants. Oh, I'll take him back. I've thought it all through. But goddamn him."

Flora said, "I can't help you. I'm sorry."

"He *promised*. What does that mean to people anymore. Nothing, I guess. I guess it means you can still get together for old times' sake and screw each others' brains out. Listen to me. I don't need to put her kind of dirt in my mouth. I'll beg your pardon."

"Don't worry about it." She wanted Elizabeth to leave. Right now it was all she wanted.

"If you could just talk to her."

"No," said Flora. "I'm sick."

The phone rang. "Would you like me to get it for you?" asked Elizabeth. She was already up, walking lightly into the kitchen. "Hello." Listening. Then, "No, I don't think so. Wait a minute. Flora, do you want to go in for a color studio portrait? You know. A photograph."

"No," said Flora. "Not of me." The baby slid off the edge of the bed and landed, bump, on his seat. He sat there solemnly for a moment, debating, then began to scream.

"No thank you," Elizabeth said liltingly, and hung up.

"Hush," said Flora to the child. "You aren't hurt at all."

Oh yes I am too, said the baby. I'll show you. Waa waa waa.

"Hush," said Flora again, without conviction. Where was Elizabeth, what was she doing? "Grow up," she told the child. "Start school or something."

Elizabeth was in the doorway, but only for an instant. Flora would always believe she hurled herself through the air, but that was the sort of hallucination she seemed prone to. As a child, she clearly remembered seeing a full-size airliner cruising sedately down her street a few feet above the ground, and nothing could ever convince her otherwise. Elizabeth was leaning over her in the bed. Kneeling? Falling? Elizabeth's mouth was working as if she were trying to spit. *She knew.*

Elizabeth couldn't find words. Flora could see her sorting them over. *Slut, whore, pig.* None of them would do for her. The baby, seeing his mother, began to scream louder and more hopefully. Elizabeth half turned, and there was a moment when Flora thought anything could have happened, anything at all, if Elizabeth set her hands on something that would break or smash or die, but it was then that Elizabeth found words: "You too."

"Yes," said Flora, because she knew what had happened. Elizabeth had remembered the phone number. She must have thought it was Suzanne's all this time.

Elizabeth scooped up the baby, staggering a little. She was breathing loudly through her mouth. Flora heard her clattering through the kitchen and out the door, heard her car starting and pulling away. Then the sounds of the street and traffic and children loosed from school. Ordinary sounds. Who would have believed it, that she did not have the power to rock the world on its base? That her life was not monstrous enough to destroy even one bright afternoon?

CHAPTER
10

The phone rang. And rang. Flora pulled herself out of bed and went to stand beside it. Four rings? She could do better than that. She counted ten. Eleven, twelve. She couldn't imagine anyone wanting to talk to her twelve rings worth. It stopped after that, leaving a little shrill echo in the space around it, and Flora sneered at it.

Back in bed. The sky was still brassy bright. She had to think what to do. The fever raced in her. It hissed and whispered and boiled. She had to think what to do, she had to do something besides lie here while telephones exploded like bombs and Mike betrayed her and Elizabeth went through her closet looking for things that would fit her. She kept waiting to feel something she ought to. It was taking a long time. Oh goddamn them. Goddamn everybody. She started crying, a jerky, uncertain crying that dried up almost instantly. She supposed she wasn't sure if she deserved to cry.

The phone shrilled again and this time, as she knew she would, Flora bounded out of bed, catching it on the second ring. "Hello," she roared. Or maybe just said it. She couldn't tell.

"Hi darlin."

"Oh, hello." Hello prick. She thought of asking him if he was sure he had the right number.

"So how've you been?"

"Fine," she barked. There was a pause, and she could tell he was unsure. She imagined how she usually sounded on the phone to him. All girly-sugary. Oh goddamn.

"Well anyway." He was not so unsure as to be thrown entirely off stride. "I've been thinking about you. Miss you."

"Have you now." Sarcasm the best she could do. Why couldn't she just shriek at him like a witch? "Did you try and call me a while ago?"

"Nope. Not me."

"Oh." She drummed her fingers on the countertop, feeling impatient. She didn't want to talk to him, at least, not this way.

He tried again. "So, what have you been up to?"

"Hen parties. Girl talk."

"Oh? You mean — "

"Just yapping over the back fence. Just dishing out a little dirt. Where are you, anyway?"

"Me? At the office. How come?"

"I suggest you stay there. Move in a cot. Establish an easily defensible perimeter."

"Flora?"

"I'm just suggesting. A word to the wise."

"What in the name of wonder are you talking about?"

Oh he knew. He knew something. No playing dumb. The edge in his voice. Maybe he was only wondering which woman, which escapade to feel guilty for. Prick.

"I went to the doctor today," she said. Said sweetly. Said poisonously. Let him think — that she was pregnant? That he'd given her some disease? It occurred to her that this last was possible, and that it would be an appropriately sordid end to everything.

"Why? What's the matter with you?"

"Oh, nothing really." She was full of fury and loathing and fever-talk. "But the interesting thing — the *fascinating* and *instructive* thing — is the way chance encounters happen in places like that, the sudden confidences they inspire, the profound emotional bonding — "

"Would you give me a break?"

"Beg pardon?"

"Whatever it is, would you just tell me?"

"But of course. Natch."

"Just talk to me."

"Arf arf."

"Flora. This isn't like you. Come on. Don't you think we owe each other more than this?"

"An appeal to fairness," noted Flora. "I'm not sure, Mike. What do we owe each other? Perhaps this merits discussion."

"Just tell me," he said again, and because she had exhausted that brittle fever voice, or perhaps because she wanted him to deny it all for her, there was still a chance he could speak it away somehow, she said, "I saw Elizabeth and she told me about Suzanne."

There was enough silence to tell her that it was not going away. *Oh Mike.* He said, "Just what did she tell you?"

"Do you expect me to repeat it? Or you need to get your story straight?"

"That's a cheap shot, Flora."

"Do not, repeat, do not tell me about what's cheap." She was furious at him, not just for what he'd done, but for that note of cautious denial, a man trying to minimize his losses.

"Look, I'm not responsible for everything that comes out of Elizabeth's mouth. I refuse to be. She's not always in control of herself. You know that. She's vindictive. She's — "

"Very convenient. I think if I get married again, I'll get myself a crazy wife. You know what? I don't think she was that crazy, probably, until she took up with you."

"All right. I guess I deserve this. Go ahead. Say whatever you want."

"Bastard. Don't give me *permission* to be angry. I don't want your horseshit permission."

"What do you want me to say, then?"

"I don't want you to *say* anything. Can you understand that? Boy, does Elizabeth have you pegged. She said all you ever do is try and talk your way out of things."

Flora paused but he didn't answer. Well, she had told him not to. "You and your man of sorrows act. Throwing yourself on everyone's sympathy. You're so weak and so flawed and such a fascinating complicated psychological mess. Oh boy. It's irresistible. It probably is true by now, you are pitiful. I just wish you didn't get so much mileage out of it. Women love forgiving you, don't they?"

It was only what she had always known about him. It simply had not mattered to her before. She finished a little less right-eously than she'd begun. Because she knew she was hurting him? Because she was starting to feel sorry for him all over again? Why should she love him for his weakness, she was tired of loving weakness, from now on she would love only strength . . .

"Flora? Will you listen to me for just a minute? Please?"

"Of course," she said dully. Flora the good listener. Every-one could talk to her. Fool.

"I love you. Whatever else has happened, you know that's true."

Flora didn't say anything. How much truth could she stand? She was thinking of Paul. It struck her as monstrous that she had not thought of him before. *Ah, forgiveness, perhaps it did more harm than good, if there were no forgiveness to count on we might not transgress in the first place* . . . "Oh God," she said aloud. She hadn't even told him about Elizabeth. What was wrong with her, forgetting so much and so recklessly? "Elizabeth knows about you and me too. She was over here."

"At your house? What — "

"Look, I don't feel like explaining it, I'm not sure I could anyway. She was here. In fact she just left."

Flora heard his breath settling. "So," she said, almost jaun-tily. "The cats are all clawing their way out of the bag, aren't they?"

"All right." He sounded absent, or maybe just stupefied. "Flora, I need to see you. We need to talk."

"Yes, but not now. Not anymore. I'm hanging up now. Good-bye."

The phone rang again instantly. She could either pick it up or rip the thing out of the wall. She would get an answering ma-chine. She would get a short-wave radio. "Hello?"

"Thank God you're home," said Suzanne. "I've been call-ing and calling."

"And I was just thinking of calling you." But Suzanne was too frightened to notice shades of irony in her voice.

"Paul's in the hospital. He took a drug overdose last night, I mean, this morning. Abby called me. Do you know Abby? No, you wouldn't — "

"Paul? What — "

"Nobody knows how he is. I mean, I don't know."

"What happened. Just tell me." Flora was shaking and hollow. But how self-important of her to feel guilty, to feel that anything had happened on her account . . .

"They took him to the emergency room at St. Ann's. They wouldn't tell me anything over the phone, just that he'd been admitted. Policy. Whoopee shit. So I don't know anything, somebody'll have to go over there. I'll go over there."

"What happened?" Flora repeated, and Suzanne apologized and caught her breath and told her. Paul had been out with Abby. Flora was sure she didn't know Abby? Abby could be all right. Abby could be all right most of the time, she was really quite harmless most of the time, but when she started drinking she didn't stop, and she always had the most outlandish drugs around, rhino tranks or nitrous oxide or quaaludes, and it wasn't a very nice thing to say under the circumstances, but had she, Flora, noticed that Paul always seemed to take up with types like that? The borderline cases. The Near Misses. Anyway, he and Abby were off on a toot last night. They wound up back at Abby's and the last thing Abby remembered was Paul waking her up once, early, and asking her how to bake a cake. He said he'd never baked a cake before and it was something he'd always wanted to do. Abby told him to go back to sleep, and in the morning — noon, really — she couldn't wake him. He was still breathing but she couldn't wake him.

Flora asked what they'd been taking. Suzanne said she didn't have any idea, considering the two of them it could have been cans of Sterno, and she was going down to the hospital as soon as she got off the phone, and did Flora want to meet her there? They might not be let in to see him, but surely they could find something out.

Of course, Flora told her, and once more sent the phone rattling down into its shallow bed. She realized she was still completely dressed, although her sweater and jeans were beginning to feel like they'd been stuffed with old bread crumbs, sweat and bread crumbs and how hard she was shaking, *Oh God Paul.*

The hospital was red brick and elderly and presided over by many sweet-faced, peeling plaster saints. The nurses looked like regular nurses, although maybe they were nuns in disguise. You never knew these days. Crucifixes hung everywhere on the sad green walls. Flora wasn't used to the sight of so many crosses, manned ones at that, and it struck her as an odd place to bring a drug victim. Bad trip. Supposed to be a comfort, religion, why, for her, did it always mean guilt and punishment? Where was she supposed to meet Suzanne anyway?

Flora found her in a lounge on Paul's floor. She was sitting with a small, very young blonde girl who had to be Abby, a decision Flora made partly from the look of her hair and makeup and equally startling clothes. They looked up as Flora approached, and Suzanne stood.

"Flora." She made a move as if to embrace her, then danced a step backward and patted Flora's elbow instead. Suzanne not the touching type. Her face grimacing with worry. Peering at Flora. "You look terrible."

"Under the weather," said Flora shortly. *Paul,* she told herself. Everything else could wait, everything else had not yet happened. "How is he?"

"OK. Better. Flora, this is Abby."

Abby nodded shyly. Her eyelids were painted bright pink and her mouth a perfect Valentine red. Funny little creature. And they had Paul — in common. And Suzanne . . . She couldn't start thinking that way.

Suzanne was saying Paul had been — still was — comatose, but he seemed to be coming out of it. Whatever he'd put into himself had depressed the respiratory system, but not enough to stop his breathing, so it wasn't, you know, a brain death situation. They'd monitored him.

Suzanne looked . . . was it her makeup gone wrong too? Maybe nobody looked very well against these green walls, among the damp whiffs of holy death and boiled food. Suzanne must have come from work, she was wearing one of her outfits. She looked very smart and very wrong somehow, exaggerated, hard-edged, maybe just tired. Mike touching her. The way he liked it. She couldn't think about that now. She had to think about things like brain death, and her friend who lay dreaming of death.

Abby said it was probably just Valium he did. Said it with perfect wonderment, or maybe a bit of stubbornness. As if it might have been only a matter of a defective product. Flora and Suzanne traded glances. Flora's look said Harmless? This is not a harmless girl, and Suzanne's said Very well, but there's nothing we can do about her, is there.

Flora asked if they could see Paul, and Suzanne said no, but there really wasn't much point in it yet anyway. There was a moment of silence while they all imagined him looking some way he would not have wanted them to see. The three of them moved reluctantly toward the old-fashioned elevator that shrieked and plunged like a diving bell. They were feeling useless and maybe a little anticlimactic. Somewhere in one of these rooms was Paul, but they were not to see him, only family could see him, the hospital said. In the elevator Suzanne told them she thought Paul's parents were coming from Chicago. She supposed they would have to be told what had happened. Abby stood in the corner, her pink eyes fixed on the ceiling, refusing to look guilty, Flora thought, or at least, looking aggressively innocent. Well, wasn't she? It might have been her apartment, her drugs, and she might be the sort of girl who wore knickers and black leather and plastic earrings in the shape of rainbow trout to a hospital, but what had happened to Paul was not her fault.

"Abby," Flora asked her, as they groaned downward, "What was this business about a cake? You know. About Paul wanting to make a cake."

"Oh, he did make a cake. That's the funny part."

"He did?"

"Yellow cake with butter frosting. He made it last night. I didn't find it till later with all the commotion." She shook her head and the little fish twitched and winked. "He even went out and got stuff for it, you know, cake pans and stuff, because I didn't have any. He must have gone out while I was asleep." She seemed gently puzzled. She seemed the sort of girl who did not particularly mind being puzzled about the world in general.

The elevator landed, metal on metal, and they emerged onto the black and white tile of the main floor. "A cake," said Suzanne, and it was her turn to shake her head. It was getting dark and the plate glass windows sent back smeared, uncertain reflections of the three of them, like wavering candle flames.

"He cleaned up the whole kitchen too," informed Abby.

"But a cake?"

"Oh, he'd been talking about it all night. When we were out, I mean. You know how he gets. He says all sorts of funny things."

They waited while Abby rummaged in her handbag. For cigarettes? Fish food? No, a roll of mints, which she offered round. "He was saying stuff like he'd never been to Mexico. And he'd never baked a cake. He said they were his only goals in life. You know how he gets. He was making us all drink margaritas in honor of Mexico. Boy were we trashed. When I come back here I'm going to bring him some cake, do you think he'd like that?"

Suzanne and Flora watched her leave, a little figure oddly insignificant despite its trappings. They turned towards each other. "Well," said Suzanne. A preface to nothing.

"I need to fill a prescription at the pharmacy," said Flora, and Suzanne trailed after her. Her heart was squeezing and bursting in her chest. What was it she was waiting for, what would happen now? In the pharmacy she stood, letting her eyes travel over the bland packages on the shelves. None of them had names she recognized, they all seemed to be desperate remedies for desperate diseases. Rectal syringes and cervical collars. Cervical collars, my lord. The pharmacist handed her the paper sack, and Flora rejoined Suzanne, who was warily eyeing a white plaster saint.

"Who was St. Ann anyway? She doesn't look like one of the dire ones, you know, the ones who hacked themselves to pieces for chastity." Suzanne, like Flora, was something of a lapsed Protestant.

"She's the mother of the Virgin," said Flora, surprised at this bit of retrieved knowledge; how did she know something like that? Did she know anything else? Not really. "There must be a place for coffee or something here. I don't feel like leaving yet."

There was a cafeteria in the basement, nearly empty at this hour, stocked with petrified doughnuts and sandwiches of pink meat. Flora moved through the line, Suzanne lagging behind her. Since when did Suzanne follow her at anything. No. They were both just acting strangely because everything was so strange, poor Paul . . .

"So what do you think?" asked Suzanne, once they had found a table and sat across from each other.

"Think?"

"About Paul. You know. Did he mean to . . . do anything." Suzanne shrugged, looking embarrassed but defiant. "Come on. Don't tell me you haven't thought it."

"It was the first thing I thought of." For reasons she would not tell Suzanne: guilt, superstition, hysteria, doom, she was a monster, killing off Paul in her imagination because it would somehow free her own conscience. She couldn't tell Suzanne that. She was finding it hard to look at her too.

"Take your prescription," directed Suzanne. "What's wrong with you anyway? You do look sick. I mean, does anybody bake a cake, do the dishes, and then decide to get high?"

"He baked a cake so he could die happy? That's — "

"I know. Stupid. But you tell me what he was thinking."

"I can't." She couldn't look at Suzanne either, with her streaked eyes and parched mouth, her face worn and unclean. She was embarrassed for Suzanne's sake, because she looked so odd and false, because she did not know how she looked. And because she, Flora, saw too much, knew too much. To know the worst about someone was to have a terrible advantage over them.

Suzanne was saying, "I just hope he gets some help, once he's out of the woods. Professional help, I mean. Even if this hadn't happened, he can't go on living from bout to bout."

"Professional help," repeated Flora, and she couldn't tell if she was agreeing, or making an ironic comment. Oh Suzanne. Sitting there pretending to be her friend. Was she concealing great waves of guilt and passion and jealousy, or was there nothing in her to conceal, was it all just glibness, smoothness, her clever little voice going on and on? How could anyone be composed so entirely of surface? She didn't want to pity Suzanne. She didn't want to pity anyone she ought to hate, what was wrong with her that she could never hate as purely as she ought to?

Suzanne said, "Even if he went to a therapist, it'd have to be the right kind. He needs some kind of treatment where they beat him with a board with a nail in it — Why, Flora."

Flora was sobbing, open-mouthed, wet-faced, sobbing and sobbing, out of pure defeat.

"Flora? Flora, darling, it's OK, he's going to be OK — "

She wheezed and shivered and shook her head. "Not Paul," she managed.

"What is it? Here, tell me — "

Again she shook her head, weeping and weeping, and when Suzanne touched her arm, she threw it off with all the violence in her. "Not Paul," this time shouting it, and there was quiet now except for her own noise, and farther away, the cafeteria sounds of plates and scraping metal. No one paying any particular attention to her. A woman crying in a hospital, surely there were any number of good reasons to be crying in a hospital?

Once she'd begun she wanted to keep crying forever. How much easier it was. But she steadied herself, groped for the napkin dispenser in the center of the table and pulled out a handful of the cheap stiff paper. Her eyes were still swimming and everything she saw was prismed and multiplied. Suzanne saying nothing. Was that all she was going to do, sit there and acknowledge guilt with silence? Flora was damned if she was going to be the one to keep talking. Weak, furious, she fouled napkin after napkin. *Slut, whore, pig. Say something.*

"I'm sorry."

"Sure you are."

"I am. I'm sorry things like this happen at all, but they certainly seem to."

Flora stared. Suzanne stared back. Then she shrugged and spoke again, patiently, it seemed to Flora. At that moment she thought she could forgive Suzanne almost anything but that patience.

"What do you want me to say? I can tell you about Mike and me. If you're sure you want to hear."

"Oh my God," said Flora. "What are you anyway?"

"Maybe we should talk. I mean, you obviously think the worst — "

"That's for damn sure. Oh my God."

"Look, Flora, I'm sorry this had to come up at all, especially today. And I'm not happy about it, for any number of reasons. But don't expect me to start crawling around under some saint's statue." Not so patiently this time, no, even irritated, Flora was glad to see . . .

"Do you hate me?" Flora asked, for this was the only way she could think of to hurt Suzanne. "Were you trying to — win some sort of contest with me, is that what this is all about?"

"I could ask you the same thing. After all, who started out with him?"

"Elizabeth." Flora had the satisfaction of watching Suzanne's face tighten and turn away. For a moment they sat in silence in the weak fluorescent light that flickered and buzzed in the ceiling above them like some large dying insect.

Suzanne spoke first. "I try not to see things that way. As some sort of competition. I honestly don't. That's one of the things I want to get beyond. You know, the notion of exclusiveness and proprietorship, look, this isn't getting through to you. You think it's so much bullshit, I can tell, you think I'm just making excuses, you don't understand."

"Why not? Because I'm too stupid, or too hopelessly unsophisticated, or both?"

"Because you're in love with him. Thank God I'm not."

Flora contemplated this. "So, you can do whatever you want, as long as you're superficial about it? That's what you're saying?"

"Oh hell. Oh yes. That's exactly what I'm saying."

Suzanne shouting now. Good. Better to throw trays of food, or start some ludicrous women's slapping match, all hair-pulling and fingernails, than keep up this highly civilized conversational bitchery. Suzanne yanking herself loose from her chair, still shouting. "You *goop*. I'm trying to tell you something. Your head's so full of romantic trash, what are you, fifteen? You can get in the middle of a marriage, and that's one thing, but nobody's supposed to jump in the middle of your thing, because you're in love. *Love*."

Flora was on her feet now too. The room was large, it seemed to be tilting towards them, and there were people at the far end of it, people given leave to be curious because they were shouting, but that was all right. Flora knew somehow she could only be having this conversation at the top of her lungs, and in front of witnesses. "It must be fun to be so cynical. I mean, once you look at it that way, you can either screw nobody or everybody, and everybody's a lot more fun — "

They wanted to slug each other. Both of them were thinking, in that moment, that it was a shame they had no tradition in this sort of thing, no weapons, no expertise, no role models, that is, you could do something ineffectual like swing a purse, or something terribly effectual like break each others' noses with a crisp punch, and neither would be quite right.

And so instead they swayed a little, glaring, feeling more and more stupid, until Suzanne made her mouth into a kind of grin, all teeth at least, and snatched up her coat. She turned and marched towards the door, and Flora marched after her, determined not to allow anything as satisfying as a dramatic exit.

She caught up with her at the door to the women's rest room. "Don't bother hiding," Flora told her, not shouting now but still full of breath and spit. "We aren't through yet."

"Oh don't be vulgar. I don't care what you do, I have to go."

Suzanne pushed her way through the frosted glass door and Flora, deciding it would be even stupider to stand outside fuming, pushed in after her. The bathroom was like everything else in the hospital, elderly, nearly exhausted with cleansing. Flora sat on the backless green sofa, listening to Suzanne urinate in little controlled spurts, vulgar, oh yes it was vulgar, all of it, why not have it out in a public toilet. Suzanne flushed and banged the stall door open and strode to the sink to wash her hands. Flora caught her eye in the mirror, then Suzanne's glance flickered away. The room was empty, except for themselves. "It wasn't like you think," announced Suzanne. "It wasn't him leaving you then rushing over to ball me. If sex is what you're worried about."

"Yes, I guess I am that petty. Sorry."

"Oh stop trying to be sarcastic, Flora, it doesn't become you. That's the truth by the way. Look, do you want to talk about this or not?"

"Talk."

Suzanne grimaced in the mirror, this time at herself, and went to work with her brushes and make-up. "I look like a transvestite. Why didn't somebody tell me?"

Their voices boomed in all the tile and space. Well, where were you supposed to have conversations like this? Flora closed her eyes and Suzanne's voice bounced at her from all directions: "Mike and I were a mistake to begin with. All we ever did was fight. God did we fight. You'd think he'd be tired of fighting after Wacky Wife. Maybe it makes for good sex — can I say things like that? Is that all right? — because there's always drama, you're always resolving conflict, but even that doesn't last forever. All this is just to say, we were pretty well fed up with each other by the time you arrived on the scene."

The voice paused. "Go on," Flora said, her eyes still closed.

"I guess we were both — relieved about you. You took the pressure off. Now Flora, I don't mean to make it sound like some dark plot. It wasn't premeditated, it wasn't, aha, let's use good old Flora to get back at each other."

"But that's how it worked. He could have me, and you could show him you didn't care." Flora opened her eyes. Suzanne had her back to the sink, leaning against it. "For God's sake, you can sit down. What if somebody comes in here?"

"You're sure you don't just want me to flush myself?"

They both snorted a little. There probably was something funny about it all, in the fine old obscene sense. Suzanne sat down across from Flora in a wooden chair, and smoothed her skirt. An odd prim gesture, especially under the circumstances. It occurred to Flora that nothing really embarrassed Suzanne except physical proximity. "So anyway," Suzanne began, and stopped. Reluctant to start in again after their little spell of good humor.

"So anyway, you kept doing it with Mike after he started with me," Flora supplied. "Don't worry. I'm not going to scream or faint." And she wasn't, she didn't. Just what would it take by this time to get a scream out of her?

"Twice. We did it twice."

"Oh, well, that hardly counts then."

"And neither of us felt very good about it, so we quit. That was months ago."

"Last week," Flora reminded her.

"I'm so glad we found this little confessional nook, you know? You're really getting into it. All we need is organ music. All right. Last week I have no excuses for. It was stupid. We'd been drinking. I literally got caught with my pants down. The end."

"You're awfully good at admitting things, aren't you."

"Give me a break, Flora. What do you want, I can't make it go away no matter what I say. We'd gone out for lunch. We'd do things like that, lunch. Very innocent, until you realize it's been an extended flirtation all along. I gave him a ride home. Elizabeth walked in on us. Oh boy, I'm not trying to elicit your profound sympathy, but put yourself in my place, I'm sure you can. It was grotesque. She was throwing a bag of oranges at me while I was trying to get my pantyhose back on."

Flora giggled and hiccuped. Funny. All the wrong things were funny. Suzanne was still speaking, tiredly now: "I don't know why it happened, why does anything like that ever happen. Maybe they can invent some sort of electronic chastity belt . . ."

"Cervical collars," murmured Flora. "With leashes." She was thinking about Paul. Sorry things like this happen at all.

"You know," Suzanne began, then stopped as a woman entered, glanced at them dubiously, and made her way to a stall, "we, Mike and I, got along so much better after we stopped sleeping together. We could finally talk, we could talk about anything — "

"About me. You talked about me."

"Well of course we did once in a while." Suzanne had the annoyed look that Flora had come to recognize as guilt. "Just friend to friend, just talk, it wasn't as if we didn't both care about you — "

"Somehow that seems as bad as you sleeping with him. Worse."

"Maybe so, I don't know, Flora, I can't talk any more, I'm too exhausted . . ."

They waited until the room was empty again. Suzanne said, "Maybe that's what it comes down to. Everything's betrayal, all kinds of intimacy, unless you lock yourself to one person forever. And that's what I was trying to say before. People ought to be able to get beyond that kind of possessiveness. They really ought to."

"They ought to do lots of things," said Flora. She was tired too, she felt she ought to be paying closer attention. But the conversation had reached some hollow point. Flora felt they were drifting among large solemn statements, all of which might be true but none of which would change anything. In fact she was to remember clearly only two things more they said. They left the rest room and cranked and clanked their way back up to Paul's floor, where the nurse at the station informed them that there was no change, and Paul could have no visitors, and furthermore they were both a couple of drug-crazed harlots. She did not actually say this last, but she made it clear enough. It was on the way back down in the infernal elevator that Suzanne said, "He does as much damage to himself as anyone else. Mike I mean. He can be so *wretched*. Don't you think we were all just trying to mother him, isn't that sickening?" And Flora thought, for the second time that day, yes, weakness, we have made it into something attractive. We love faults in others because we love our own too well. For she did love her own faults, she decided, she fed and tended them and would have been reluctant to give them up. They gave her something to forgive herself for. Forgiveness, the one great virtue of the weak.

And later, in the parking lot, Suzanne crying. Not asking forgiveness, just sitting behind the steering wheel of her car, crying quietly in the darkness. Her breath came out frost. Or like puffs of smoke, thought Flora, watching, dreamy and exhausted. Suzanne asked if Flora thought this was the end of them, the two of them, she and Flora, and Flora said without rancor that she honestly didn't know yet. There was a lot she just didn't know yet. Suzanne nodded, she said that was really the best she could expect, wasn't it? Flora said nothing. She was too tired, and besides, she did not feel capable of consoling anyone about anything. Suzanne sniffed a little and muttered something about her disgusting nose. Then, "Look what happens to people when they throw out the rules."

"Everything," said Flora. "Everything happens to them." And she stood there until Suzanne drove off.

She had wanted everything to happen, she supposed. That night she lay in her own bed, unmoving beneath the weight of the covers, the weight of silence. She was going to be able to sleep, she realized, and while she was grateful she was not really surprised. Wasn't her body capable of the most amazing tricks in a crisis. Sleep. Hunger. Itch at the back of her knee. Fever-sweat. The whole program. Everything. She had wanted everything to happen to her and it had. She could not entirely say she regretted it, she wondered what it would have taken to make her regret it. Probably nothing short of disfiguring facial scars. One regretted consequences, but not necessarily the acts that led to them. Flora slept soundly in her unrepentant bed, too tired even to wish for some saving grace of hypocrisy.

It was not until some days later that she saw Mike. Everything was over by then and they both knew it. In a sense every-thing, including this meeting between them, had already hap-pened. She met him in a bar for drinks. They could think of nothing else to do with each other. The bar was small and every surface in it seemed plush, from the carpet underfoot to the wait-ress's upholstered bosom. They were in a booth whose soft tan jaws held them snugly, even pitched them a little forward, like conspirators. They sat, drinking carefully. Mike said, "I've been worried about you. Well I have been, Flora, don't scowl at me."

"Sorry. It just seems like worrying is what people do when they've used up everything else between them."

"You're angry. I don't blame you."

"I'm not angry, not right now at least," said Flora. "But any-way, there's no point in us having some sort of contest to label how the other feels, is there?"

He agreed, a little helplessly, and tried to sit back farther into the booth. Flora wondered if she was enjoying the spectacle of him being anxious and conciliatory, and decided she was not. He even looked unattractive to her, his face diminished into mere thinness, the eyebrows and nose too heavy, too much neck sticking up out of his shirt collar like a pale stem, everything out of pro-portion. She marveled that she had so quickly made him ordi-nary, she was a little sickened by her own fickleness and power. Could she make him beautiful again if she chose? And how must she appear to him? Mean, snappish, unforgiving, a harpy-woman with a tongue like a snake. It was a mistake to have come here, she saw that now. What had she thought would happen? Some-thing ceremonial and sentimental? They were no longer the peo-ple they had been with each other, and they were ashamed of these lesser selves.

But here they were, having to get through it somehow. "So tell me," Flora asked, since she really was curious, and since nothing was at stake any more, "how did you manage things with Elizabeth?"

"Manage?"

"Sorry. I didn't mean, how did you ever put this one over

on her. Or maybe I did mean it. I guess you don't have to tell me."

"I don't mind. You can ask me anything. I'll own up to anything."

"Please don't be that way."

"What way?"

"You know. So willing to pour dirt on your head."

"Yes, especially since it never really makes up for anything, does it? Like they say, being sorry doesn't keep you from being stupid."

"Don't," Flora said. "Just don't."

There was a pause, while they considered that they had never spoken this way to each other before, with so many false starts and danger zones. "Elizabeth," he said, and Flora nodded and composed herself to listen.

"She looks on me as a lifetime project, I guess. Whatever's wrong with me, she's going to cure. She's more hard headed than a lot of people give her credit for. Sometimes I think she doesn't *expect* me to behave any better than I do."

Flora contemplated this. "You give each other permission to behave badly."

"Maybe so. We're going for counseling."

"Are you," Flora said automatically. She didn't like the idea but she couldn't decide why, not right away. Because it implied that she, Flora, was something pathological that had to be disposed of in therapy? "Well, I hope it helps."

"Thanks."

"I hope everyone who's married stays happily married forever. I hope their children flourish and their real estate appreciates."

"Flora."

"I'm not kidding, Mike." She was crying and she didn't want to be, she never ever wanted to cry again. "I want life to work out the way it's supposed to for people. I want to live — in the middle of a breakfast cereal ad, I guess."

"Let's get out of here," he said. "Is that OK?" And Flora

nodded, yes, get her out of here. Get it over with. She really had not wanted to cry. She would not have thought she still had it in her to cry, but apparently she was an inexhaustible source of salt water.

They sat in Flora's car, looking and feeling much guiltier than they had any reason to. It was dusk of a November day and it had been raining but it was not now, and the remaining light was a deep green-blue, beautiful and drowned-looking. A traffic signal spread its colors in the pools of rainwater on the street. Such effortless beauty, such an easy trick, the living red green and yellow. She could have watched it forever, that trick of air, light and color, but she turned away from it and cleared her throat. "Good luck with the counseling."

"I wanted it to work, Flora. You and me."

"You mean, you wanted us to keep going along without getting caught." Harpy-woman. Snake-tongue.

"I mean I wanted a life with you. Please, Flora, I know I don't deserve credit for *doing* anything right, but I *wanted* — well, better than this."

Flora was once again watching the colors melting on the wet pavement. Slow-dripping green, flat gold, pool of red. It was still beautiful, and no anger or spite on her part could make it less so. Green and gold and red; she repeated the names over and over, a charm, until they lost all meaning, until she felt calm and distant.

She turned to face Mike. "All right," she said, patting his arm. "All right, I believe you, there's no point in fighting now . . ." Let him say whatever made him feel better. She needn't begrudge him that.

"Thank you. Thank you for letting me tell you just what a great guy I am."

"You are a great guy."

"Sometimes. Not at this particular moment."

"Hush now."

They were both wondering what else there was left for them to say. Mike pulled out his cigarettes, then shoved them back into his shirt pocket. They did not really have a cigarette's worth of conversation left in them. "Maybe," Mike said, "we could get together from time to time, just to talk."

Flora shook her head. "I don't think so. Not anytime soon, at least. I don't want to end up as one of your girlfriends without portfolio."

"One of my what? Why am I laughing, Flora, how can you make me laugh at a time like this."

"I have to get going now," she said, although that was not true, there was nothing she needed to do, nowhere she had to go. But neither of them belonged here any more.

He kissed her. Flora thought he might now tell her what she should do, what would become of her, but no, of couse not, it was only time for him to leave. She watched him walk rapidly through the damp evening air. Only a little distance before the growing darkness swallowed him as if he'd dropped into a pocket. Green and gold and red, she instructed herself, but the charm had lost its power to fill her mind, and the lights themselves had gone flat and commonplace. She was not crying now. She was not anything. She started her car and steered out into the roadway, waiting for the light to change. She wondered idly how they fixed the signals so the greens didn't all flash at once, so people didn't go smashing into each other. Ingenious. Rules for everything and a very good idea it was too. Green now? Oh yes! Oh, the harmonious carburation of gasoline and air! The orderly transfer of force from foot to accelerator to drive train to wheels! The helpful muses of hydraulics and electricity! The calm certainty, the rightness, the joy of moving forward in the proper lane, in obedience to all laws!

CHAPTER
11

This is me, Flora, driving again. It's OK. I know exactly where I'm going. I am in western New York, eastbound on Interstate 90. I have one of those nifty Triple-A maps, the kind made up of many small maps clipped together in a binder. If you've ever seen them you know what I mean. Each small map is a slice of the larger route, rotated so east-west appears to be north-south. On every map the highway is marked with a bold blue felt-tip arrow, so you can flip through the binder and watch it jump from page to page. It's a great comfort, that arrow. There's no way you can fall off the edge of the map, the edge of the earth, with it there to guide you. No excuses.

The arrow and I are headed to Boston. You should see this car. It has one of everything in it, I own one of everything, like I'm half of Noah's ark. One pole lamp, one bread knife, one box Kleenex, one Little Igloo cooler, one raincoat, one bathrobe, one soap dish, one electric skillet, you get the idea. Everything's nested together, Chinese-puzzle style, and leveled off so I can see out the back window. I'm anxious about tending to all these possessions, loading and unloading, locking and unlocking them, because if they stray or break I'm left with nothing at all. But at the same time I feel portable and free. If everything breaks, at least I'll know exactly what I've lost. Here's a story I like. In 1846 my great-great grandmother and her husband traveled much this same route, but westward, from Pennsylvania to Illinois, in a horse and buggy. She carried with her a pillowcase full of noodles. So the story's come down, and I don't have any reason to doubt it, because who'd make up something like that? That's probably the one thing I don't have in here, a pillowcase filled with noodles.

Right after Christmas I called up an old school friend who lives in Boston. How are you and do you have a spare room, I asked her, not in so many words but almost. I surprised myself, sounding so impulsive and decisive. In fact I wasn't at all. I had (still have) hideous doubts about the whole thing. I needed to hear somebody else be enthusiastic about it. Of course, my friend said, as I knew she would, come right out and stay as long as you want, we'll find you a job, a boyfriend, a life, everything you need, oh Flora, would you really come? My friend is divorced also, with a small, intelligent girl-child. My friend works in a design studio, very classy light industry, she does incredible deft things with ceramics and fabric and lengths of tubing and little plastic knuckles. I've often wished I had a talent like hers, artistic dexterity, or anything else that could be easily labeled, like singing or weight lifting. Whatever peculiar gifts I have seem to take a lot of explanation. My friend is creative, neat, pretty, serene, all in all she seems to do very well for herself but I'm sure I'll be learning more about that. Anyway we talked a long time, doping it out. I think that part will work, I'm even excited about living with somebody else, a family, excited about the idea of adaptation and change. It'll be good for me, like most things will.

So here I am, only a few weeks later, watching the thick gray tongue of the Interstate unroll before me. Doing it. Really doing it. Nobody stopped me and I didn't stop myself. I don't know what I expected to go wrong, but none of it was serious. Things like already packing the broom when you needed to sweep. Fussing with garage sales and bank accounts. Money isn't a problem, that is, I have so little of it to begin with, it hardly makes a difference if or where I work, at least for a while. And theoretically, I know all about unemployment. There's such a thing as being independently wealthy, but you can also be independently poor.

This road is boring but you wouldn't expect it to be anything else, maybe you wouldn't want it to be. There's something comforting about the boredom and the familiar trash of American highways, the signs for Stuckeys and Texaco and Days Inns, for pecan logs and clean restrooms and Breakfast Anytime. The signs are the same everywhere, it's like you've never left home. I am traveling at fifty-nine miles per hour, with an eye out for squad cars. The heater purrs. The radio (AM), mutters and fades in and out between stations. I'm enjoying all this hugely. I'm also terrified. Every so often I remind myself I am the master of my fate, the captain of my soul. I'm terrified of things like speeding tickets and accidents and strange men at the rest stops and the car breaking down. I think of all the things that can go wrong with cars. There are many many things, more things than I even know the names for, and none of them will I be able to prevent. I wonder if a lot of women feel the way I do about cars, powerless and resentful. I wonder if men do and just won't admit it.

Before I left town I had the car serviced. I spoke to the mechanic, an amiable, too-young fellow who said alarming things in a cheery tone of voice. "That carburetor won't last forever, not if she starts leaking on you again." Or, "You know, that same hose is messed up on every single one of these I see. A real Polack job." When I pressed him, did all this mean I needed a new carburetor, a new hose, a new car, before I tried to drive a thousand miles, he turned Delphic on me. Carburetors were so blamed expensive, I'd be better off waiting to see how it held up. The hose was no big deal even if it blew. It was all in the lap of the gods. He couldn't promise me nothing would go wrong, I knew that. He leaned over the bill and prodded at it with his smudged finger, explaining patiently, and I frowned at it, trying to understand. I was reluctant to let him go, I suppose the only thing that would have reassured me was if he'd agreed to ride along and repair whatever leaked or blew. The garage, with its rich smell of oil and exhaust, its blasts of pressurized air and ringing metal, seemed a temple of knowledge, a place where mysteries were guarded. Where people knew how to *fix* things. I left, one of the uninitiated, wondering why I'd never bothered to learn anything that was of any real use to me.

When I get tired of worrying about the car I worry because it's winter, storm season. Although there hasn't been any bad weather, I listen attentively to the forecasts on the crackling radio. There are all these things you're supposed to have on hand for winter driving: a coffee can, chocolate bar, shovel, candle, blanket, sand. I'm sure I have all that in here somewhere, I'm sure if I had to I could start my own civilization with the contents of this car. Sometimes I think I wouldn't mind if something drastic or awful happened, that is, if you could promise me in advance I'd live through it safely. I wouldn't mind having stories to tell afterwards if the stories were good enough. Odds are only mundane disasters will happen, things like having to replace a muffler in Rochester. Which will seem dramatic and vital enough to me at the time, but will rather strain my powers as an anecdotalist.

When I was a kid I had a number of private obsessional games, like stepping on sidewalk cracks or holding my breath while I climbed stairs. They were complicated rituals, as complicated as I could make them, with sub-rules and margin for error and places I was allowed to start over without penalty. The way I bargained with myself was this: if I did those things right, avoided all cracks (or stepped on all cracks), and negotiated every stair, nothing bad would ever happen to me. Does every child do things like that? Equip themselves with charms against the world? Now, for reasons that aren't that opaque, even to me, I've decided that if I live through this trip, everything else in my life will thrive and prosper. It will be a new start and I will make no more mistakes ever again. I have all my eggs in one basket, literally, I think I have eggs, hard-boiled ones, in the cooler. I've reduced everything to the tangible. It's refreshing, like being a figure in an old allegory. If I can keep my front wheels correctly positioned and ticking off the miles, if my carburetor will refrain from bleeding and my radiator from bubbling and erupting, if the machinery in general will just *behave,* then I feel I have a crack at surviving the world at large.

Paul survived. I went to see him in the hospital a second time. He'd been roused and tidied up by then, he wasn't even feeling all that bad. There was a vague sense that he was being kept in bed as a sort of punishment. He was embarrassed, mostly, and more than a little hostile, and I sat in a chair on a layer of day-old newspapers and wished I hadn't come. "Stop looking guilty," he instructed me. "Everybody who's been through here looks like they just robbed a bank or something." He settled back into his pillows, aggrieved. "And don't apologize. That's the next thing you'll do. Apologize when you haven't done anything."

He had me, but what could I say now? I had to ask myself why I was there to begin with, if not from guilt, plus a sprinkling of the better motives. None of this was easy and he wasn't making it easier. It was too much like the night at his apartment, when he'd seemed to want me around, but only to snarl at. Now I wasn't even sure if he wanted me here. I wondered just how many friendships I could exhaust in the course of one week.

But Paul seemed to realize some of this, at least, the next thing he said was possible to respond to: "I feel like shit. Imagine the world's biggest hangover. Now imagine having two of them."

"Sorry. I guess you have to expect some of that."

He regarded me in a way that was grumpy yet not unfriendly. They had one of those awful hospital gowns on him, the kind that remind you of printed paper towels and leave half your butt hanging out. I think they're designed not just to humble you, but to make you realize just how utilitarian and basic the body is, how very little concepts like personality and dignity matter compared with easy access to your behind. I asked Paul just what they were doing to or for him.

"They're observing me. They're making sure I'm stabilized."

"So are you?"

"Oh sure. What they really worry about is things like aspirating your own vomit while you're passed out. Sorry. That's the sort of talk you get around here."

"I'm not being squeamish. Just glad nothing like that happened."

"I'm stabilized. I don't think that's such a bad idea, actually. I think I should come in and get stabilized every week or so."

"If you want to be stable."

"Yeah. I've been thinking about all that."

"What did you decide?" It was a nervous thing to say, I thought he'd snarl at me again, but he didn't.

"I've decided to clean up my act." I didn't know exactly what he meant, but he was looking at me expectantly. I started to say something encouraging, I don't know what I would have come out with, because he raised a hand. "Don't say anything, I guess you don't have to slobber on me just because I have good intentions. But see, Flora, I never even got that far before. I had bad intentions. So I'm getting there, and you don't have to give me one of your tactful pep talks, I know exactly what I have to do. And I appreciate you coming by, I really do even if I'm acting like a total asshole and don't bother denying it."

"This is a great conversation. When I get clearance to talk, I mean."

He laughed then, an honest laugh without an edge to it. We didn't say anything for a while. We were alone in the room. There was somebody, a lump of old man, living in the next bed, but they'd borne him away a while ago to some nether region of the hospital where they did the real dirty work. It was sunny outside, nearly dazzling, in a way that seems peculiar to hospital rooms. It's light reflecting off all the sheets, maybe, or the flatness of the windows. I thought about that day last spring when I'd wrecked my car and Paul had come to retrieve me. Our own peculiar brands of inverted anger. That was another thing we could both have good intentions about.

Paul said, "That guy was worthless, you know? Bad for you."

I shrugged. There were things I didn't want him to say either. And I didn't know why he said *was*, how news of Mike had reached him even here, smothered by nuns and drugs. Maybe Suzanne had told him, or he was guessing, or maybe I had a look on my face that said I was no longer in love. It irritated me to think that people might have been discussing the whole thing all along, as if it had been perfectly obvious to everyone but me what a mess I was making. I even wanted to defend Mike, just to redeem my own judgment, but that impulse passed.

When I didn't answer Paul said, "Sorry. I just meant, I think you deserve better."

"Of course I do. We all deserve better. But I don't know if we should expect it."

"Cynicism."

"No. Not really. What I'm aiming for is realism. I want to expect exactly what I get."

He smiled at that. Things were not so bad if we could sit in a sunny room and smile at each other. We sat a while longer, talking about easy things like the hospital food (it tasted briny, Paul said, as if the cooks wept into it), and work, and by then Paul was tired and it was time for me to go. He watched me assemble my coat and all my other little scraps of wool, and I was reminded of the morning I'd marched so briskly out of his apartment. It was the same thing now, waiting to hear myself come up with something dopey or inadequate. I said, "If you tell me what I'm not allowed to say, I'll clobber you."

"Go ahead. I mean talk, don't hit me."

"You scared the shit out of everyone. Out of me."

"Yeah. Out of myself, too."

"OK. OK then." I'd meant to go on and tell him a lot of other things, all of them helpful and nosey and faintly bullying. But none of that needed to be said. I wondered if he was really going to stop drinking. I thought it took more than just declaring your good intentions, probably even more than the complicated embarrassment of waking up in a hospital. I thought Paul was the sort of person you believed most when he talked the least. And that was one thing I didn't want to say at all.

Anyway, I have my own act to clean up. I want to think I've learned something from all this. That's one of my earnest and suspect mental habits, thinking you learn from all experiences, and everything contributes towards making you a Better Person. This vague and misty optimism seems to be the closest thing I have to religious feeling. If I look at it more closely, it contains echoes of social Darwinism, and even worse, a kind of self-centered snobbery. After all, there are conceivably other things to worry about in life besides your own perfectibility. After all, you have to be one of a privileged fraction of the world's population to believe so confidently in things like progress and perfectibility, to believe you have any control over your circumstances. Suspect. But it's habit, as I say, personal baggage I've lugged around for years. Upward mobility in moral terms.

I don't hate Mike. I guess I'm entitled to, and at some point I may work my way into hating him just as a kind of exercise in mental hygiene. But right now I am merely not in love. There was a point in the delirium of it all when I did believe we would have a life together, that he would divest himself of Elizabeth and cleave to me. I think Mike believed it too. He's not a conscious villain; he's only a villain out of weakness. He and Elizabeth are perfect for each other, I should have seen that right off. As I told Mike, they give each other permission to behave badly, and the drama of their fights and reconciliations absorbs them more completely than any mere happiness would. I think I know now what he and Suzanne might have been saying on that day I saw them in the parking lot. She was telling him he would never change, he was too attached to his own theatrics, his own nearly enjoyable sense of tragedy. And of course she was right. I don't hate Suzanne either, by the way. Sexual disloyalty is not the ultimate sin I once thought it to be. That's one thing I've learned.

But you can't really learn from mistakes if you knew all along they were mistakes. With Mike I cast aside what was safe, conventional, blameless — nobody *blamed* me for divorcing Gordon — and launched into something more dangerous. I opted for all the gaudier technicolor emotions. I wanted him so badly I thought I was willing to accept the consequences. Look what happens, Suzanne said, when people break the rules. And the real answer to that is always, More than you expect.

There's a scud of snow on the highway, fine snakelike lines racing across the pavement. Not even enough snow to turn on my windshield wipers. But the air is milky now, harder to see through. It's like driving into a large white box. The ground on either side of the highway is noncommittal, with no visible history of storms. Bare earth, with snow beginning to sift into the ditches and low points. I study the racing lines of snow. I've driven enough winter roads back home, I know how these things develop. The snow-snakes, then the layer of wind-driven white on the pavement in scalloped patterns like surf. Then the snow freezing into a crust under your wheels. The air alive with snow. Whiteouts, skids, mad truckers barreling through behind you, and if you weren't killed outright you ended up off the road dying of carbon monoxide poisoning, that is, until you ran out of gas and then died of exposure.

I sure scare easy. There's still only this faint, sugary spray across the road, weirdly beautiful, even sinister, but hardly life-threatening. I have to learn to stop counting my disasters before they hatch. I ask myself what a sensible person would do, sometimes it helps, pretending to be a sensible person. The radio is playing squeaky pop songs, the same songs I've been hearing for a day and a half now, virtually indistinguishable from the commercials. I'm trying to find a weather forecast that doesn't originate five hundred miles away. You know those highway signs that say for weather information turn to AM 1600, or some such outer space setting? I can never find them. If anyone can I'd like to hear about it. Anyway, I lean over to fiddle with the radio, and just then the car gives a kind of lurch or shimmy. The closest thing I can compare it to is when your heart flutters and lags a beat. A little stall, a loss of power, an intimation of mortality. Now I'm trying to remember if maybe it happened before. Wasn't there the same little hiccup, the same palsy yesterday when I slowed for the exit ramp, and when it idles isn't there a peculiar vibration or ticking I never noticed before, have the brakes gone a little mushy, the steering sullen, and what does it all mean? Cars these days are such odd combinations of computers and aluminum foil. Everything is hooked together with electronics or rubber bands, everything's built either too complicated or too cheap, designed to self-destruct at the most cunningly inconvenient points. Stop this, I tell myself. Witless paranoia. Nothing's wrong. My car and I will live forever.

I find a radio station with a good clear signal and one of those nice boring announcers that signifies news or public radio. They're talking about drought in Africa. Drought in Africa, snow on the New York State Thruway. I listen for a while to see if I can tell just where the station's coming from, if it will do me any good at all. I'm trying to get as far as Syracuse tonight, another couple hundred miles. I've planned this trip in sensible, ladylike hops, as Triple-A recommends. No amphetamine-crazed sixteen-hour driving shifts, no white line fever for me. Last night I stopped somewhere around Cleveland (though everything within a hundred miles of Cleveland, on the highway at least, seems to be indistinguishable from Cleveland itself, afflicted with Clevelanditis), in a budget motel. There was no chain lock on the door or phone in the room. For much of the night I watched the parade of revolving shadows against the window and listened to bodies and furniture being hurled against the cardboard walls and wondered why I ever left home. Bestial voices outside the door. This block of rooms reserved for a convention of escaped convicts from the Tri-State area. Tonight I've promised myself I'll stay at a highway palace, some motel with acres of mattress and ugly expensive pictures on the wall and a heater that could cook a roast. That is, if I live that long, if I get as far as Syracuse, if I keep from stepping on the cracks.

The radio station is telling me it lives in Philadelphia. Oh, bummer. What would they know or care about any of us out here on the Interstate tundra? But in fact the snow squall's abated, and my car is droning along nicely, and I've loosed my death grip on the steering wheel. Weather not important anyway, not just now. The announcer comes back on. "Now it's time for Bill Pitt's Call-In Car Care Show, the Pitt Stop." Bill Pitt, I think, is not a real name. Like Rusty Jones or Mr. Goodwrench.

But Bill himself is real enough. "Good afternoon everybody, and welcome to the Pitt Stop," he says, and it's hard to explain just how attractive this voice is, I haven't yet heard enough to analyze my own quick-leaping response to it. Later I can say that Bill Pitt has a perfect broadcasting voice. Authoritative but personable, upbeat yet down-to-earth, reassuring, accessible. He sounds like you'd want your doctor to sound, or maybe God. You have to imagine all this and me raptly listening, praying to my engine. "If you've got a problem with your car, I want to hear from you," says Bill, already warming to his work. "Eddie's our first caller today. How you doing out there, Eddie?"

"Just fine, Bill." Eddie's voice thin, tentative, unmuscular. The kind of wimp who probably deserves to have car trouble. Bill asks Eddie what he can help him with. "Well Bill, I've got an '81 Ford Escort, and, uh, the problem I've noticed over the last couple of months is this. When I accelerate there's a knocking in my engine. It happens mostly at speeds over forty, and it happens pretty consistently, so I'm wondering if I'm looking at some kind of major repair, you know?" Poor Eddie. He finishes up a little breathlessly. I know exactly where he's coming from. He's afraid to have anybody actually *look* at the car for fear of what they'll tell him, he has visions of having to sell his house and live in his car so he can pay the garage bill. He's the kind of guy who won't go to the doctor about a sore throat until he coughs up blood. Poor chump. I ought to sympathize with him but I don't. He sounds even more pathetic than me.

"Well Eddie, it's probably not a big expense item," says Bill, and I can tell Bill is a nicer human being than I am, more generous and kindly. Eddie is his friend, he cares about Eddie's welfare. "What you're talking about is a pretty common problem. It's the result of pre-ignition or detonation caused by an extremely high cylinder temperature. And the cause could be something as simple as using a gas with a too-low octane rating. Does your gas have an octane below ninety-three?"

Eddie says he thinks it does, he's not sure. You can tell he never notices things like that. Bill tells him to try it, if that doesn't work ask his mechanic to do an engine scan with an oscilloscope. But you'd be surprised how often this sort of thing is a fuel problem. Eddie, emboldened and hopeful now, asks Bill if any particular brand of gas is better than another. "No Eddie, not really. You see, in our area of the country, three suppliers provide ninety percent of the fuel. So there may be different names on the pump, but it's still the same gas." Eddie didn't know that and neither did I, but Bill, who has pondered all the mysteries, does. Nor does he mind sharing his wisdom with us. He blesses Eddie and sends him on his way a better person. Bill enjoys this sort of thing, you can tell. He is happy to be of use. If it were within his power he would tune every balky engine in the world and soothe all our anxieties.

The next call is a little out of my league, a guy with a Porsche 911 that runs rough and no one can find the problem. Out of my league but not out of Bill's. He and the Porsche's owner discuss various symptoms and diseases. The Porsche's owner is no Eddie, he knows his shit, and Bill instantly recognizes this. His tone with Eddie had not been condescending, but now it is more professional, consultation rather than instruction. God, this guy is good. I find myself wondering just who he is, what sort of life he lives away from the microphone. I'm tempted to pull off the road and call Philadelphia. Oh Bill, I will tell him, I am afraid of driving, of living my life, of stopping and starting, forward and reverse. And Bill will say, Stay right there and I'll come and get you. Just tell me the mile marker and I'll be there in a twinkling with a tow truck and a tool box. Everything can be repaired.

In reality Bill is telling the Porsche owner that it could be fuel again, that contaminated gas may have worn the O-rings in the fuel injectors. "Now I'm not saying that's got to be it," cautions Bill. "But it sounds like you've eliminated all the obvious things, your garage has done everything I would have done myself." The Porsche owner is gratified to hear this, he had the suspicion they were just dicking him over and he's not the kind of guy who likes being taken for a ride. I imagine the Porsche owner, a belligerent jowly type who has more money than is good for him and spends most of his time loudly claiming his prerogatives. The type who'd drive me crazy in ten minutes but Bill can handle him. Bill is all things to all people, mechanic to our souls.

There's a commercial now, and a blast of static. I think I'm losing the station, I'm considering backtracking to retrieve it and spending the rest of my life on the same loop of highway listening to the Voice of Bill. But it must have been a power line or something, because here he is, back at full strength. "Ready for our next caller here in the Pitt Stop, go ahead." Brisk, cheerful, calm, the ultimate professional. Too good to be true, in fact I'm forced to consider the possibility that all this is a little less than true. At the very least it's a rebroadcast tape. After all, who hangs around on Wednesday afternoons, calling in about cars? It's probably taped. Ah, but then, when *would* we call Bill? In the watches of the night, in the small, desperate hours before dawn.

The next caller is a lady. Her name is Yvonne. She's older, you can tell, but still feisty, she's not above a drink or a good time. Bill asks her how she is today and she chuckles. Her voice has a million cigarettes in it. "Well I'm hanging in there, Bill." Bill's glad to hear it. But, Yvonne goes on, she's wondering about her car, a middle-aged Buick. "It's when I turn a corner, you know, my tires keep squealing all the way through the curve. Now I'm no hot rodder, Bill, I'm not out there laying rubber when it happens."

"You're not into stunt driving, huh, Yvonne?" cracks Bill, and they share a laugh. A ladies' man when he wants to be, watch it Bill, you devil you, Yvonne's going to be calling in every show. But Bill gets down to business soon enough. "Yvonne, it sounds like you've got an alignment problem in your steering axis inclination. Your wheels aren't turning evenly. One wheel's turning at say, twenty degrees and the other at nineteen degrees."

Yvonne marvels at this, one little degree making all that difference. I like Yvonne. When I reach her age I want to be a feisty old broad too. Bill assures her that yes, that one little degree does make a difference. Yvonne promises she'll get it taken care of. "You do that Yvonne, because you know how alignment problems can wear down your tires. Keep your car in good alignment, make sure your tires get rotated and balanced on a regular schedule."

Yvonne thanks him and Bill escorts her to the door, so to speak, with appropriate gallantry. "I'm really glad Yvonne called,"

Bill continues, "because I've been meaning to talk about tires, particularly under winter driving conditions. If you've got a car that's stuck in the snow and you're trying to push it out, please, please, never stand directly behind the drive wheel, and I'm going to tell you why. When your speedometer's reading forty m.p.h., and you're spinning your wheels, your tire speed's doubled to eighty m.p.h. You can see it's not impossible to have those tires spinning at speeds up to two hundred m.p.h., and folks — "

More static. There's a country-western station encroaching now and I'm afraid it's the real thing, good-bye to Bill. Yet he survives a few moments more, his voice still calm, magisterial, kindly, like a brave captain going down with his ship.

" — just aren't designed to take that kind of pressure. They can explode with — " Static and fizz. " — force. If you've noticed, most tires today are sold with a safety warning — "

And he's gone. Someone singing a song about beer instead. Even his last words were unselfish, full of concern for us. I'm glad I know that about the tires, I'm just the sort of person who gets cars stuck in snow. Bill has probably saved my life, or at least a piece of my face.

I turn off the radio for a while. I am thinking about tires and traveling, about learning and love. It was a real stroke of fortune, finding Bill, a revelation of sorts though of what exact sort I'm still trying to comprehend. But I know I was ripe for it, ready to reach this plateau of peace and good driving. If there had been no Bill, it would have been necessary to invent him, that calm, friendly voice assuring me that all problems have solutions. He has shown me that everything can be repaired, or if need be, replaced. If I can't fix it myself I can find someone who can. No big deal. I even have a little thrill of aspiration, a sneaking hunch that I can achieve a modest competence of my own if I half try. Tires can be balanced, batteries recharged. None of it beyond my powers.

And love? I'm thinking now it has nothing to do with the desperation and desire I once believed it did. I was afraid of being denied my rightful portion, as if love was something finite and consumable. I had become too accustomed to sizing people up, to judgment and appraisal, as if only by taking their measure would I know my own, only by gauging their threat or worth to me could I know the extent of my own fears and needs. What love can come of that? When I reach Boston, no, Syracuse, or wherever my next stop turns out to be, I'll try and approach people with the true, Bill-like benevolence, with curiosity and wonder. We are all of us worthy of love, of decency and fellowship and happy motoring. Such at least is my resolve. Taking it on the road now.